David Wellington was born in Pittsburgh, Pennsylvania, where George Romero shot his classic zombie films. He attended Syracuse University and received an MFA in creative writing from Penn State. He lives in New York City.

To find out more about David, visit his website at www.davidwellington.net

Praise for David Wellington's novels:

'These books are great, fast-paced, modern, pulp action machines, yet Dave Wellington somehow manages to preserve the weird mystery, the magic, of the old classic vampire stories'
Mike Mignola, creator of *Hellboy*

'Wellington is moving the literature of the undead into the twenty-first century'   *Los Angeles Times*

'Vampirism is the dark side of the idea of immortality, as well as a nightmare personification of parasitism, viral infection and the concept of sharing blood. Wellington uses all of these ideas and they make his novel more than just a gory story . . . a well-constructed novel with a good plot'

Sydney Morning Herald

Vampire Zero

A Vampire Tale

DAVID WELLINGTON

piatkus

PIATKUS

First published in the US in 2008 by Three Rivers Press,
An imprint of the Crown Publishing Group,
a division of Random House, Inc., New York
First published in Great Britain as a paperback original in 2011 by Piatkus

A CIP catalogue record for this book
is available from the British Library.

ISBN 978-0-7499-5436-9

Typeset in Caslon by Palimpsest Book Production Limited,
Falkirk, Stirlingshire
Printed and bound in Great Britain by Clays Ltd, St Ives plc

Piatkus
An imprint of
Little, Brown Book Group
100 Victoria Embankment
London EC4Y 0DY

An Hachette UK Company
www.hachette.co.uk

www.piatkus.co.uk

For my parents

Rexroth

Assist me! you may save me – you may do more than that – I mean not life, I heed the death of my existence as little as that of the passing day; but you may save my honour, your friend's honour.

John Polidori, *The Vampyre*

i.

A crystalline sweep of snow flashed across the road as her headlights gouged white tracks through the darkness. It wasn't far to Mechanicsburg, to the address the special subjects unit dispatcher had given her. In the middle of the night there was no traffic, just white lines in the road to follow. She arrived still partially asleep, but that changed the instant she popped the door and stepped out into the freezing winter air.

It was just past Thanksgiving. Arkeley had been under-ground for two months and she'd been chasing him night and day, but maybe this was where that trail ended. Where her guilt, and her duty, ended. Maybe.

'Support's on the way, ETA ten. In thirty we can have this place buttoned up,' Glauer debriefed her, not even bothering with hello. He was a big guy, a head taller than her and far broader, and the epitome of a Pennsylvania police officer – bad haircut, thick but not bushy mustache, pasty white except where the sun got his ears and his neck. He wore the uniform of a Pennsylvania state trooper – the same as Caxton. Once he'd been just a local cop, one who'd never even visited a murder

3

scene. He'd seen a lot of terrible things since he met Laura Caxton, but now at least he'd reached a higher pay grade. After the massacre in Gettysburg – his hometown – she had him assigned directly to her SSU. He was a good man, and a great cop, but he still had visible fear lines etched into the crinkles around his eyes. 'I figured maybe we could wait this one out.'

'That's not how it works,' she told him. She followed him as he strung up caution tape around the entrance to the self-storage facility. He had a patrol rifle on a strap over his shoulder. 'He taught me that.'

'He taught you to go running into an obvious trap?'

She tried to peer in through the glass doors of the storage center's lobby, but she couldn't see anything from the street. Glauer had already checked the place out and reported two bodies – dead, of course, very dead – but she needed to see for herself. She needed to see how far down Arkeley had fallen. 'Yes,' she said.

The lobby was a glaring space of white light in the night, all plaster and scuffed drywall. She could see a counter inside where the night watchman should have been sitting, a white countertop marred with dripping red splotches.

'I'm going to have to go in there,' she said. 'How many exits does this building have?'

Glauer cleared his throat noisily. 'Two. This one in front and a fire exit in the back. The one in the back has an alarm, but I haven't heard any bells ringing so far.'

'Of course not. He's waiting for me inside. He won't wait forever, though. If we sit tight until the reinforcements arrive, he'll come out that door so fast you'll never get a bead on him.' She tried to give him an ingratiating smile, but he wasn't buying it. Instead he turned away and spat on the frozen pavement.

She understood his reluctance. This was a bad situation, a

4

real death trap. Not that she had any choice in the matter. She slumped a little inside her heavy coat. 'Glauer, this is the best lead we've had. I can't let it go.'

'Sure.' He finished up with the caution tape, then jogged around the side of the building without waiting for further orders. He knew exactly what to do. Stand by the fire exit and keep his eyes open. Blast anything that came through.

His concern – and the careful way he let it show – meant something to her. It really did. But not enough to stop her. She pushed through the glass doors and walked into the lobby, her Beretta already in her hand but with the safety still on, one more thing Arkeley had taught her. She approached the desk as if she wanted to rent a storage locker, then leaned over it to look at the floor behind the counter.

The carpet there was slick with coagulating blood. There were two bodies behind the counter, as advertised. One wore a uniform shirt and sat slumped forward over a security monitor, his neck torn open in a wide red gash. The other wore a janitor's coveralls and his open eyes stared up at the acoustic ceiling tiles. His right arm was missing.

She backed up a step, then turned to look at the elevator bank at the left side of the lobby. One of the elevators stood partially open, the door kept from closing by something wedged in the jamb. She bent down and saw exactly what she expected. It was the janitor's missing arm that held the door, the fingers pointed inward like a sign telling her where to go next.

That kind of thing passed for a joke among vampires. She'd learned not to let their sick humor get to her. She picked up the arm – she had no worries about ruining fingerprints, since vampires lacked them – and placed it as reverently as she could to one side. Then she stepped into the elevator and let the door close behind her.

5

Someone had already pushed the button for the third floor.

Exactly twenty-seven minutes earlier, according to Caxton's watch, someone had placed a call to the SSU's tip line. That wasn't so uncommon. Ever since the massacre at Gettysburg people were seeing vampires in their back gardens and going through their Dumpsters and loitering outside of shopping malls all the time. Caxton and Glauer had run down every one of those leads and found nothing worthy of note. This call had been different, however. She'd heard a recording of the call and it had made her skin creep. The caller's voice had been inhuman, a rough growl, the words slurred as they were drooled out through a mouth full of vicious teeth. The caller hadn't wasted any time, instead just reeling off a street address in Mechanicsburg and announcing, 'Tell Laura Caxton I'm waiting for her there. I'll wait until she comes.'

A trap, an obvious trap. Arkeley had loved it when the vampires would set traps – because then you actually knew where they were. The vampires loved traps because they were predators, and often lazy, and they loved it when their victims came to them. Now Arkeley was one of them, but she had somehow expected more of him.

The arm in the elevator door wasn't his style either. But that didn't mean anything. It had been two months since he'd changed, since he'd accepted the curse. He'd done it for all the right reasons, of course. He'd believed it was the only way to save Caxton's life. He'd probably been right about that, as he was with most things.

There had been only one flaw in his reasoning. When a human being dies and returns as a vampire, he loses some of his humanity. With every night that passes he loses a little more. Arkeley had been a passionate crusader once, a killer of monsters. Now every time he crawled into his coffin a little less of him crawled out. In the end every vampire became the same creature. A junkie for blood. A sociopath with a sadistic streak. A pure and ruthless killer.

A bell chimed inside the elevator door and then the door slid open.

She stepped out onto the third floor with her handgun at the level of her shoulders, clutched in both hands. She kept her ears and her eyes open and she tried to be ready for anything. She tried to be ready to see him, to see Arkeley, and to be ready to shoot on sight.

Arkeley had never thought of himself as her mentor. She'd been useful to him in a very limited way and so he'd requisitioned her as a partner. Sometimes he'd used her to do his legwork, the way she used Glauer now. More often Arkeley had used her as bait. She'd had to learn not to take that personally – he hadn't meant it to be personal. He was driven, obsessed, and he had found her useful. By letting him use her she had learned so much. Everything she knew about vampires had come from him, either from grudging answers to her incessant questions or by way of his example. She had worried often enough when he was alive – and far more often since he'd died and come back – that there were things he'd never bothered to tell her. Secrets he'd kept for himself.

Time to find out, she guessed.

A long corridor stretched out before her, metal walls painted a glaring white, studded with countless locker doors. Some were the size of closets and some were wide enough to drive a car into. She looked at their latches. Every door she saw had a hefty padlock, some of them combination locks with purple or yellow dials, others that required keys to open. Was Arkeley inside one of these lockers? she wondered. Was it his lair? Maybe he hung from the ceiling by his feet like a giant bat.

The thought almost made her smile. Vampires and bats had

nothing in common. Bats were animals, normal, natural organisms that deserved a lot more respect than they got. Vampires were . . . monsters. Nothing else.

She studied the doors, looking for one that didn't have a lock. Even a vampire couldn't lock himself into a storage space from the inside. She looked down the row of doors, all the way to the end where another corridor crossed laterally. She counted off the locks in her head – lock, lock, lock. Lock. Another lock. Then – there. Near the far end, one narrow door had no lock on its latch.

It probably wouldn't be that easy. Still, she had to check. She moved slowly down the hall, her back to one wall, her weapon up and ready. Her shoes clicked on the unfinished cement floor, a noise anybody could have followed. When she reached the unlocked door she stood to one side and slid the latch open with her left hand. The door rattled noisily and then opened on creaky hinges. Nothing jumped out.

She pivoted on her heel until she was facing the locker. She slipped off her pistol's safety lever. She glanced inside – and saw immediately that it was empty. There had been no lock because no one had rented this particular locker, that was all.

Caxton let herself exhale. Then she froze in midbreath as raucous laughter ran up and down the hallway, echoing off the row of doors and making them all shake on their hinges. She swung around quickly, unable to tell which direction the laughter came from, and—

At the end of the hall, back by the elevators, a pale figure stood in the shadow between two light fixtures. It was tall and its head was round and hairless and flanked by long triangular ears. Its mouth was full of long and nasty teeth, row after row of them. Her heart stopped – then started up again twice as fast when she saw the vampire held a shotgun.

8

2.

Caxton's brain reeled, leaving her unable to react for a critical second. Vampires didn't carry guns. Ever. They didn't need them – at Gettysburg she had seen a single vampire mow down squads of National Guardsmen carrying assault rifles. Their claws and especially their teeth were all the weapons they ever needed.

The Beretta in her hand forgotten, Caxton could only stare at the shotgun as the vampire brought it up and pointed it in her direction. She barely managed to duck as his white finger closed around the trigger.

Somehow she recovered her wits enough to roll to the side, behind the open door of the empty storage locker. Buckshot pranged off the door and dug hundreds of long tracks through the white paint on the walls. When her hearing recovered from the noise of the shot she heard his bare feet slapping on the cement floor, running toward her, as she ducked into the locker and closed the door shut behind her.

Stupid, she thought – she'd done something very stupid. There was no way out of the locker, and no way to lock the door from inside. The door itself would be little barrier to a vampire, especially one that had already fed on the two men down in the lobby. Vampires were strong enough at any time, and close to bulletproof, but they grew exponentially tougher after they drank blood.

She backed up, feeling behind her with one hand until she found the back of the unit, and raised her pistol in front of her. When he tore the door open to get at her she might have one chance – she could fire blindly through the door and hope that somehow she hit him squarely in the heart, his only vulnerable part. If she shot him anywhere else his wounds would heal almost instantly. All the bullets in her gun wouldn't even slow him down.

She pointed the nose of the pistol at the door. She aimed for a spot at the level of her own heart, then raised her aim about six inches. Arkeley was taller than her, she remembered. Arkeley—

The image of the vampire in the hallway was seared into her mind's eye. She couldn't not see it standing there, leveling the shotgun at her. Holding the shotgun with both hands.

Vampires healed all wounds they took after their rebirth, but any old injuries left over from their human lives lasted forever. Arkeley the vampire would still be missing all the fingers from one hand. This vampire had ten fingers, all the better to hold a shotgun with. *Crap*, she thought.

It's not him.

It wasn't Arkeley. She hadn't been able to process that fact while he was shooting at her, but as she waited for him to come and kill her she couldn't deny it anymore. Whoever the vampire might have been, whatever he had become, he wasn't her former mentor.

Which made things much worse.

There was only one way for a vampire to reproduce, and it involved direct eye contact. There were only two vampires

10

at large in the world who could pass on the curse – Arkeley, and Justinia Malvern, a decrepit old corpse that Arkeley kept close to him at all times. If the two of them were creating new vampires, if Arkeley had become a Vampire Zero—

The door rattled in front of her. She steeled herself, adjusted her grip on the Beretta. She would shoot in just a second, when she thought her chances were best. She would let him start to tear the door open first.

The door rattled again. She heard a metallic click and knew instantly what had happened. The vampire wasn't going to tear open the door at all. Instead he'd closed the latch with a padlock, sealing her inside. He must have had one in his pocket, just for this eventuality.

Whoever he was, he was smart. Smarter than she, apparently. She cursed herself. You never ran into a place with only one exit – that was one more thing Arkeley had taught her. She should have remembered.

'Who are you?' she shouted. 'Don't you want to kill me?'

She didn't really expect him to respond, and he didn't. She listened closely as her voice echoed around the metal walls of the locker, listening for any sign that he might be standing directly outside the door. She heard nothing.

Then, a moment later, she heard his feet slapping on the floor. Moving away.

'Damn it,' she breathed. Was he running away? Maybe her backup had arrived and he was fleeing the scene. She couldn't let that happen – she couldn't let another vampire get away. Every one of them out there meant more sleepless nights, more searching. She had always pitied Arkeley for the way his hopeless crusade had devoured his life – he had spent more than twenty years trying to drive vampires to extinction, only to fail utterly at the last minute. She was beginning to understand what had pushed him so hard, though. She was beginning to understand that sometimes you had no choice, that events could drive you regardless of what you wanted. If she could get this guy, and Arkeley, and Malvern – all the vampires she believed to exist – if she could get them all she could stop. Until then she could only keep fighting.

There had to be something she could do. She looked at the walls around her, but they were made of reinforced sheet metal. She would never be able to kick her way through them. The door was fitted neatly into its frame. There was no way she could pry it open, no way to get her fingers around its edge and pull.

Then she looked up.

The lockers didn't go all the way up to the ceiling – there was a foot and a half of open space up there. The ceiling of the locker was nothing more than a thin sheet of chicken wire. The wire was higher up than she could reach, but maybe – maybe – she could jump up and grab it.

Shoving her Beretta in her holster – safety on, of course – she rubbed her hands together, then made a tentative leap. Her fingertips brushed the wire, but she couldn't get a grip. She tried again and missed it altogether. Third time's the charm, she promised herself, and bent deep from the knees.

The fingers of her left hand slipped through the wire. She closed her fist instantly as she fell back – and pulled the wire back down with her. The wire tore the skin of her fingers until they were slick with blood, and the noise was deafening as the wire shrieked and tore under her weight, but she was left with a hole directly above her that she could probably wriggle through. She grabbed the dangling wire with her other hand and started to pull herself up, a handful at a time. It felt like her fingers were being cut to ribbons, but she had no choice – she needed to get out.

She froze as she heard the vampire out in the hall. 'What are you doing in there?' he asked, half of a chuckle in his

12

voice. The voice confused her. It sounded different, somehow, from the voice on the recording that had lured her to the facility. Less guttural, less – inhuman.

She didn't bother to answer. She pulled herself upward, hauling herself hand over hand until she was perched on the top of the locker's side wall. She could look down the other side into the locker to her right. Cardboard boxes, a pair of skis, plastic milk crates full of old vinyl records filled the narrow space. From where she was perched she could slip down into the corridor, though the vampire was waiting for her there, alerted by all the noise she'd made. Vampires had far better reaction time and reflexes than human beings. Trying to pounce on one from above was probably suicide.

Not that she had much choice. She leaned out just a little and looked down into the corridor. She saw the white bald head of the vampire below her. He was leaning up against the door of the empty locker, one triangular ear pressed up against it, one long pawlike hand splayed against the white metal.

She drew her weapon – and leapt. With as little thought as that. She landed hard on his shoulders and must have caught him off balance, because he went sprawling down on the floor on his back with her on top. She flipped off her safety and fired in one fluid motion, not even taking the time to aim. Her bullet blew open the skin of his shoulder and sent bone chips flying, and realizing her mistake, realizing she'd missed his heart, she brought her arm back and pistol-whipped him across the mouth.

His fangs snapped and shattered and flew away from the blow. He started gagging and coughing and then he spat out the broken fangs, revealing round white normal teeth below them. She stared wildly into his blue eyes, and saw the shiny gloss of stubble on the top of his head.

'Oh, shit,' she said. She grabbed one of his triangular ears and yanked it off. It was made of foam rubber.

13

3.

Outside a SWAT team crouched in the snow, high-powered rifles leveled at the glass doors of the lobby. Blue and red lights flashed in Caxton's eyes and she blinked them away. 'Move, you idiot,' she said, and shoved the subject forward, out into the street. He whimpered as the broken bones in his shoulder rubbed against each other. The SWAT team relaxed visibly when they saw the handcuffs binding his arms together, but they didn't stand down completely until she gave the order.

'Glauer,' she called, and the big cop came running around from the back, where he'd still been watching the fire exit. *Good soldier*, she thought. 'Glauer, call an ambulance. This one's wounded.'

He stared at her in total incomprehension. The job of the SSU wasn't to arrest vampires, and it certainly wasn't to get them medical attention. It was to exterminate them.

'He's a wannabe,' she explained. She tore off the subject's other rubber ear. Revealed beneath was a round, normal, flesh-colored human ear. She had to admit the subject had done a good job of faking it. In poor light conditions even she hadn't

14

been able to tell the difference between this kid and a real vampire.

Of course, she should have been able to. Real vampires were unnatural creatures. If you got near them you felt how cold their bodies were. The hair on the backs of your arms stood up. They had a distinctive, bestial smell. There was no way for the wannabe to fake that, and if she had kept her wits about her she would have noticed. She had been so desperate to find Arkeley, to finish her job, that she had made a bad mistake. What if she had killed him? What if she had pumped three shots into his heart, just on principle?

The wannabe had killed two people and then discharged a firearm toward a police officer conducting a criminal investigation. Had she killed him, that would have been enough to keep her out of jail. It was close to the textbook definition of permissible use of force, but even if the state police's internal investigation cleared her, it couldn't shield her from a civil action if the kid's family decided she'd acted excessively.

The special subjects unit was brand new. It couldn't survive lawsuits – or dumb mistakes like this – and without the SSU the people of Pennsylvania would be at risk. People everywhere would be at risk. She couldn't afford to screw up that way.

Glauer brought his car around, a marked patrol unit with the SSU acronym painted on its hood. It was their only official car. Caxton helped shove the wannabe into the back, pushing his head down so he didn't smack it on the doorjamb. He could sit there until the ambulance arrived.

She'd already got a field dressing on his wounded shoulder. A bad bruise had lifted on his lower lip where she'd pistol-whipped him, but she couldn't do much for that. 'Take these,' she told Glauer. She handed him the wannabe's shotgun and the bloody hunting knife she'd taken off his belt. She was willing to guess he'd used the knife on the two bodies in the

15

lobby. It had a nasty serrated edge he could have used to saw off the janitor's arm. She shook her head in disgust and stared down at her hands. They were covered in blood and white greasepaint. She didn't want to wipe them on her pants – her best pair of work pants – so she grabbed up handfuls of snow off the ground and scrubbed them together.

'What's your name?' Glauer asked. He was squatting next to the subject, talking through the open door of the cruiser. 'You don't have to tell me if you don't want to. Is there anybody you want us to call?'

Caxton stared at her officer as if he was crazy. Then she realized that he was just trying to calm the subject down. One reason Caxton needed Glauer on her team was for just this – for talking to people who were scared and in pain. Caxton had never been much of a people person herself.

'Rexroth,' the wannabe said.

'You have a first name? Or is that it?' Glauer asked.

Caxton leaned against the side of the cruiser and closed her eyes. It would be a long wait until the ambulance arrived, and even then she wouldn't be done with this guy. What a waste of time.

'Make sure he's aware of his rights,' she said, just by reflex.

Glauer stayed focused on the subject, though. 'What were you hoping would happen tonight?'

Rexroth – almost certainly an alias, she decided – started crying. He couldn't wipe the tears and snot off his face with his hands cuffed behind him, so they gathered in oily beads on his painted face. 'I was supposed to die. She was supposed to kill me.'

Caxton's body stiffened. The guy had wanted to commit suicide – suicide by cop, they called it in the papers. He'd wanted to go out in a blaze of glory, and maybe take the famous vampire hunter Laura Caxton with him. Maybe he thought that would be enough to turn him into a real vampire. You had to commit suicide to join that club, one way or another. Of course, you also had to be exposed to the curse – which meant a face-to-face meeting with an actual vampire.

The closest this kid had probably ever got to a real vampire was seeing some bad movie on a Sunday afternoon. She stared into the darkness, willing the ambulance to hurry up. The sooner it could arrive the sooner she could get back home, and back into bed. She doubted she would sleep at all, but at least she could lie down and close her eyes and pretend.

Something in her chest loosened up and she sagged against the side of the car. Suddenly she cared very little about this idiot Rexroth, or anything else keeping her away from her bed. How long had it been since she'd had a true night's sleep? Even a fitful six hours she could call her own? She couldn't even remember. There was too much in her head these days to let her ever truly relax.

'Trooper?' Glauer asked.

Her eyes snapped open. How long had they been closed? She didn't know.

'What do you want me to do?' the police officer asked.

'His rights,' she told Glauer. 'Read him his rights now. Then take him to the hospital. When they discharge him, take him to a holding cell somewhere. Process him and book him with the two homicides. With – Christ, whatever. With endangering a police officer. With whatever else you can think of.'

'A holding cell where?' he asked.

It was actually a good question. The SSU didn't have any dedicated lockup facilities. She hadn't considered they might ever need a cell of their own. 'The local jail is fine. Coordinate with the locals – this can be their case, it's outside our brief.'

He nodded, but he didn't look satisfied.

'What?' she demanded.

'Don't you want to interrogate him yourself?' he asked.

'Not right now.' She looked for her car, found it where she'd parked it when she arrived. Back when she thought she might be driving to her final showdown with Arkeley. What a joke. She started walking away.

'Hey,' he called, 'aren't you going to stick around?'

'No,' she said. 'In four hours I need to get up and get dressed again. I've got a funeral to go to.'

4.

The sun had turned the kitchen windows a shade of pale blue by the time she'd finished her breakfast and started getting dressed. Out back it touched the dark shape of the empty outbuildings behind the house. It lit up one wall of the shed where Deanna's artwork used to hang, before she'd taken it down and folded it carefully and put it in a trunk in the crawl space, with the rest of Deanna's things she hadn't had the heart to throw out. It lit up the kennels, too – also empty. The last three dogs she'd boarded there, a trio of rescue greyhounds, had all moved on to better homes. She hadn't had a chance to pick up any more dogs since, though there were plenty who needed her help.

The house felt cold and dark, even as the sun grew stronger. Laura knotted her tie on top of her white dress shirt and then pulled on her one pair of dress pants. She looked around for her black blazer and realized she'd left it in the bedroom closet.

She was about to go and get it when Clara came out of the bedroom already dressed in a modest black dress. Her silky black hair, cut just below the ears, was clean and shiny. Laura had worked hard at being quiet so she wouldn't wake Clara up, but she must have been getting ready the whole time.

'Here,' Clara said, handing her the blazer. 'We need to get moving. It's at least an hour-and-a-half drive. Longer if we're picking up the Polders.'

Laura took a deep breath. 'I said you didn't have to come. You always hated him.'

Clara smiled warmly. Far more warmly than Laura deserved. 'I did, and still do. But funerals are one of the few times I actually get to spend time with you, these days.'

Laura stepped closer to take the blazer, then pulled Clara into a deep hug. She didn't know what to say. That she would try to change that, to spend more nights at home? She couldn't make that promise.

Clara was the one spark of light left to her. The only thing that felt good. She was losing her, and she knew it.

'Okay. Do you want anything to eat?'

'I'm fine for now,' Clara told her. 'Do you want me to drive?'

Laura did.

The two of them had gone to a lot of funerals together in the previous two months. Gettysburg had been a success from one point of view – from the point of view of the local tourism board. The civilian population of the town had survived, because Caxton had them evacuated the day before the fighting began. From a law enforcement perspective it had been a fiasco. Local cops, SWAT officers from Harrisburg, even kids from the National Guard, had died by the dozens. They had laid down their lives to keep the vampires from getting out into the general population. More than one family had sent Caxton hate mail after that, but she had made a point of going to every funeral she could.

This one was a little different. No, it was a lot different.

They didn't talk much on the way to Centre County. Laura found herself nodding off and then jerking back to wakefulness every time she got near to real sleep. It was a familiar feeling, if not a welcome one. Before they reached State College Clara pulled off of the highway and took them deep into a zone of high ridges and dead fields, brown and golden and slathered with snow. They passed weathered farmhouses and barns that looked like they'd been hit by bunker-busting bombs, some of them slumped over on their sides. They passed a herd of unhappy-looking cows, and then Clara turned off once again, onto a dirt path that was easy to miss if you didn't know where to find it.

They pulled up in front of a farmhouse that looked in better shape than most, with a well-kept barn and a silo hung with hex signs. The Polders were waiting outside for them. Urie Polder, still wearing his Caterpillar baseball cap, had put a black parka over his stained white T-shirt. It hid most of his wooden arm, but not the three twiglike fingers that stuck out the end of the sleeve. He used them to scratch at his freshly shaven cheek and Laura saw them move, as prehensile as human fingers. That weird hand was actually stronger and more deft than his normal one. Vesta Polder was dressed in the same dress she always wore, a long-skirted black sheath that buttoned all the way up her neck and down her wrists. Her wild blond hair was pinned back, though, and she wore a black veil that completely obscured her face.

They were the strangest people Laura had ever met, but they had also proved themselves good friends.

When the car stopped, Urie gestured back at the house with his wooden hand and the door opened. A little girl, maybe twelve years old, came racing out. She wore a smaller version of Vesta's dress but her blond hair was covered by a white lace bonnet. Her eyes were very wide.

21

Laura was a little shocked. She'd known for some time the Polders had a daughter, but she'd never actually been introduced to her. As the couple settled into the backseat of the car, the girl perching on her mother's lap, Urie cleared his throat noisily and then said, 'This here's Patience, she's a good girl, ahum.'

'It's very nice to meet you, Patience,' Clara said, leaning over the back of the driver's seat. 'I'm Clara and this is Laura.'

'Yes'm, I know ye both,' the girl said. 'The cards showed ye. You're the lover, and she's the killer.'

Laura's lip curled back in a sneer. It wasn't how she'd expected this meeting to go. She looked at Vesta, but the older woman didn't correct or even *tsk* her daughter.

'I suppose that's accurate,' Clara said, refusing to be taken aback. She looked at Urie. 'Maybe this isn't my place, but I'm not sure this is going to be appropriate for a little girl. Couldn't you get a sitter?'

Urie Polder grinned broadly. 'Little Patience ain't been under the care of no one else, not since she was born. We don't look to break that streak now.'

'Oh,' Clara replied. Without another word she put the car in gear and got them back in the road.

The funeral was to take place in a cemetery outside of Bellefonte – not much farther away. They passed the main campus of Penn State, then rolled into the quaint little Victorian town. The road took them along the shore of a frozen pond ringed with gazebos and houses decorated with ginger-bread-like carvings. Laura always thought the town looked like the kind of place where a parade might spontaneously break out, with a full brass section and prom queens in the backseats of open cars. It was a glimpse of Pennsylvania the way it had been decades earlier, back before the coal mines all dried up and the steel mills closed down, unable to compete

22

with foreign production. The Pennsylvania her grandparents had grown up in.

Arkeley had once had a house in Bellefonte. It had been his base of operations for nearly twenty years. Now he was going to be memorialized in the same town.

The cemetery, just outside town, was a vast expanse of rolling yellow hills, the dead grass sparkling with frost even so late in the morning. Most of the snow had melted or been removed from the plots. Clara had downloaded driving instructions from the cemetery's website, and she steered them confidently through endless lanes lined with obelisks and family crypts. Smaller, more modest gravestones stuck up in neat rows. She drove them deeper into a less populated region. A freshly washed pickup truck with an extended cab stood parked in the road and Clara took her spot behind it. Then the five of them clambered out and walked over the crunching grass to where three other people already waited for them. An older man, dressed in an outfit very similar to Urie Polder's, but more threadworn around the knees of his jeans – and two young people, the age of college students. Arkeley's children.

5.

'I still think this is a lousy idea. Is this supposed to give comfort to the family, or to mock them?' Laura asked Vesta Polder.

It was Urie who answered, though. 'This is for you, ahum.'

'What?'

'So's you can get used to the idea he ain't human anymore. So you won't think, when you meet him again, that he's the same man.'

Laura shook her head in bewilderment. She didn't have the mental energy left to work that one out for herself. She would have asked more questions, but suddenly they were within earshot of the trio at the headstone.

She took off her sunglasses, as calmly as she could, and studied the marker. It was a simple stone with no complicated inscription:

JAMESON ARKELEY
MAY 12 1941–OCTOBER 3 2004

She was pleased, she thought, to see it didn't read 'Rest in Peace' or give some description of how he had lived or died or been reborn. Just the name and dates had some kind of dignity, and as desperate as she was to find Arkeley and put him down, she couldn't begrudge him that. The stone's cold shape, its solid physicality, calmed her a little. Enough that she could look up and study the people who were patiently watching her. The oldest of the three – Arkeley's brother, Angus – had the same wrinkled face she knew so well, though there was a merriness behind his eyes that Arkeley had never possessed. He shook her hand and mumbled a pleasantry she didn't catch. The two children were dressed more conservatively than their uncle, but their faces shared a certain family resemblance to the man memorialized at their feet.

'Raleigh, right?' she asked, and held out a hand. Arkeley's daughter nodded but kept her own hands at her sides. She wore a formless black dress and a heavy winter coat that hung on her like a tent. She wore no makeup and her eyebrows and lashes were nearly as colorless as her dress. 'We spoke on the phone.'

'Yes, Trooper. Hi. It's nice to meet you.'

'Likewise.' Laura turned to look at Arkeley's son. 'And you must be Simon. I'm so very sorry for your loss.'

'My father isn't dead,' he told her. 'Can we get on with this sham? I have to get back to school tonight and it's a long train ride.'

Simon Arkeley had sharp pale features, a long thin nose and eyes that were just narrow slits. His black hair was badly combed. He wore a powder blue suit that didn't look thick enough for the weather.

She asked, 'You're a student at Syracuse, right? What's your major?'

He stared hard into her eyes. 'Biology.'

'We're all here,' Urie Polder announced. Laura realized she was standing right in front of the stone. She would have been standing on top of the grave, if there had been one. Everyone else had formed a rough circle around her. She stepped back and stood between Clara and Patience. The little girl reached up to take hold of her hand.

Vesta Polder took a step inward and lifted her hands, her fingers decorated with dozens of identical rings. Slowly she reached up to take hold of her veil. Laura realized the woman hadn't spoken a word since they'd picked her up. Everyone watched, even Simon, as she slowly lifted the veil up and away from her face. She smoothed it down on her shoulders, releasing her bushy blond hair so it bounced. Her eyes were closed.

When she opened them they looked wild – red and swollen, as if she'd been crying, but glinting with a feverish light. Her lips were pursed tight together. She turned to look at each of them, one at a time. She held their gazes until they looked away, even Urie and Patience. Then she began to speak.

'In the old days,' she said, in a loud, clear voice, 'there were no winter funerals. When a man died in the winter his body was wrapped in a winding sheet and then put in the back of the larder where it was coldest, and left until the first buds appeared on the trees.'

Raleigh frowned. 'Why was that? Was winter an unlucky time?'

Vesta Polder didn't seem to mind the interruption. 'No. The ground was just too hard to dig. Back then every grave was dug by a shovel. A man's back could give out if he tried to upturn frozen soil. Now, of course, we have backhoes. Graves are dug all year round. There is no grave here, however. Just a stone – not even a gravestone, but a cenotaph.'

'What's a cenotaph?' Patience asked.

Vesta did not smile at her daughter or even look at her. 'It is a monument to a man whose bones lie elsewhere. This stone reminds us of a man who has died. A man well worth remembering. Jameson Arkeley devoted his life to our protection. To the protection of all mankind. We can memorialize his sacrifice here.'

His sacrifice. Laura bit her lip to keep from speaking. Arkeley had been crippled in life, unable to drive a car or tie his own tie. He'd received those wounds fighting vampires. He had made himself whole again, and strong, when he took the curse. At the time maybe he'd thought of that as a sacrifice, too. By now he was probably thinking of it as a gift. He'd had a chance to prove that his death had meaning. After he saved her life, he could have returned to her. He could have let her put a bullet through his heart. That would have been a real sacrifice.

Instead he'd run away, into hiding. Maybe he'd thought he could beat the curse, somehow. Maybe he'd thought he could stay human. The man she'd worked with would have known better, but the curse could be very persuasive. His sacrifice had been lost to greed, greed for blood.

'Further, we may read this stone as a warning. A warning that he is still at large.' Vesta turned to face Caxton. She held out her ringed hands and Caxton took them both. Vesta looked right into her eyes. 'It is a warning, and an admonition to you, Trooper. We've made a place for him to rest. We've made a very nice grave for this man. Now it's up to you to fill it.'

Caxton's heart sank in her chest. She opened her mouth to reply, but what could she say? There was nothing, no words— 'I'm working on it' would have been grossly inappropriate. 'I'll do my best' sounded inadequate.

'No!' Simon said, and grabbed Vesta's arm, pulling her away from Caxton. The older woman reeled as if she'd been

27

smacked across the mouth. Caxton felt light-headed for a second, then came back to herself. She jumped between Simon and Vesta and dragged the boy away from the grave, away from the circle of mourners.

'What was that?' she hissed, marching him down a hill and out of earshot.

'How could you let that woman talk about my father like that?'

'She's a friend of mine. And she was right.'

'I don't want you to kill my father,' he said, as simple as that.

Caxton shook her head. 'He's not your father anymore. He's a vampire. I don't know if you understand what that really means—'

Simon let out a curt laugh that had no humor in it at all.

'— but it's my job to hunt him down. And I'm going to do it. He's a danger to the community. To everyone!'

Simon brooded for a moment before replying. 'Tell me something. No opinions, just facts, alright? Do you have any evidence that my father has harmed a single human being? Have you found any bodies?'

'Well, no, but—'

'Then leave him the hell alone.' He turned to head back to the grave. She grabbed at his arm but he broke free easily. She half expected him to assault Vesta Polder on the spot, but instead he walked right past her, headed to the cars. 'I have to go now,' he shouted, and folded his arms. It was all he had to say.

6.

The mourners were already breaking their circle and heading for the cars – it seemed no one wanted to go on with the dubious service. Caxton hurried on to where Angus and Raleigh were climbing into the cab of the pickup. 'I'd like to talk to all of you,' she said. 'You might know something that could really help me find him.'

'Now, I doubt that highly,' Angus said. 'Seeing as I hain't visited with my brother in twenty years. Still,' he said, and stopped in midthought. He looked Caxton up and down, from her legs to her chest, failing to look as far up as her eyes. 'I was gonna go wash up and take myself a nap. You want to have a drink with me tonight, that I can accommodate. I'm staying at a motel near Hershey. Figured if I came all the way up here I might as well take in the theme park. What about you, honey? You want to talk to the policewoman?'

Raleigh looked down at her feet and blushed. 'Please, Trooper. Don't be offended. My uncle's a good man, he just grew up poor. He's not really as . . .' she scrunched up her shoulders and looked up at the sky, searching for the

29

proper word and eventually coming up with 'ignorant as he seems.'

'I grew up pretty poor myself,' Caxton said. 'The daughter of the sheriff of a dead-end coal patch just north of here. It left me more than capable of handling a good old boy or two.'

Angus chuckled at that.

'But you didn't answer the question. Do you mind speaking with me? I know it might be difficult to talk about your father right now.'

The girl pulled in her shoulders and rubbed her hands together. 'No. No, it'll be okay. Just maybe not here. Cemeteries kind of creep me out.'

'That's fine,' Caxton said. 'We can set up an appointment for later – you live in Emmaus, right?'

'Near there.'

With that Caxton was ready to go. It didn't seem likely that Simon would consent to an interview, so she figured she would just leave him alone. He wasn't done causing her grief, however. He spent a long time talking quietly but animatedly with Clara, who eventually sighed in exasperation and came over to Caxton with her arms folded across her chest. 'He wants to be taken right to the train station,' she said.

'I'm sure we can do that,' Caxton said, looking at Angus. The older man lifted his arms and let them drop again.

'He wants me to take him. Because he doesn't know me and that means he doesn't hate me yet. He says he doesn't want to ride with his family anymore. He says they've betrayed Arkeley. I mean Jameson Arkeley,' she said, glancing at Angus and Raleigh. 'He says, just by agreeing to talk to you they've betrayed him. He also doesn't want to ride with you, because you want to kill his dad.'

Caxton narrowed her eyes. She failed to see how any of this was her problem. She thought of Officer Glauer, though.

30

He was constantly telling her she needed to be more sensitive to the public's needs, and to the feelings of civilians.

'Okay. We can work this out. Does he have a problem with Vesta?'

'Yeah,' Clara said, 'but not as much as with you. Or his family. He says.'

Caxton looked across at Angus. 'Can you give me a ride as far as Harrisburg? If you can, Clara here can take your nephew to the station and drop off the Polders on her way.'

'You mind riding in the backseat, honey?' Angus asked Raleigh, who shook her head.

This was tedious, Caxton thought, just a waste of time. She had work to do – a meeting of the SSU that afternoon – and it would take her time to get ready. Simon's temper tantrum was cutting into her work time. But this was what everyday life was made of for most people, these little negotiations and obligations and impositions. All the things Jameson Arkeley had brushed aside in his pursuit of the vampires. It had made him look like a jerk to everyone who met him – including Caxton. Maybe she should try to be a little more understanding.

She said her good-byes to the Polders. Urie and Vesta gave her warm smiles, but their little girl, Patience, grabbed at her hand and wouldn't let go until she made serious eye contact.

'Trooper, I would like to thank ye most sincerely for allowing me to come to thy service,' the girl said, rattling off the words as if she'd memorized them. ''Twas a great pleasure.'

'You're – welcome,' Caxton said.

The girl offered her hand and Caxton shook it.

'It is my most avid hope,' Patience said, 'that ye should slay the fiend, afore he slays ye. Even if the odds look bleak.' Then she went and climbed into the car.

Little girls shouldn't be that honest, Caxton thought.

Clara leaned out of the driver's window and blew her a kiss,

31

and then they were off, Simon sitting in the front passenger seat and failing to look over his shoulder at her once.

She sighed and turned back to the two Arkeleys waiting for her. Angus already had a foot up on the running board of his pickup, while Raleigh waited patiently to climb in behind Caxton's seat. As Caxton jumped up into the shotgun seat and pulled down her seat belt she tried to clear her mind of everything that had happened. It was time to get into interrogation mode, where she just asked questions and listened closely to the answers and tried not to make any judgments at all. She honestly doubted that the Arkeley family had anything serious to tell her, but you never knew – that was the first rule of police investigations. The last person you expected was the one who always had the best clue.

She got her first surprise when she settled down and looked around her. The pickup's cab was immaculately clean – even the floor mats looked freshly shampooed, though the vehicle must have had upward of a hundred thousand miles on it. Angus was the kind of man who would show up to a funeral wearing a white T-shirt and jeans fraying at the knees – yet he clearly took immense pride in his truck. The only thing that marred the interior was an open package of beef jerky shoved down into the area where the windshield met the dashboard.

'Hain't finished that one yet,' he said, seeing her stare at it. He turned to look at her and smiled wide, showing off a pair of gums wholly devoid of teeth. 'Nice thing about jerky is, it starts hard but if you keep it in your mouth long enough it loosens up. I bought about three packs for the ride up here and I hain't had to eat one other thing the whole way.'

Caxton's mouth opened, but she couldn't seem to get any words to come out.

'I did try to warn you,' Raleigh said from the backseat.

7.

For the rest of the ride to Harrisburg they made little more than small talk. Caxton was anxious to start interviewing the Arkeleys, but she needed to get them alone in controlled environments where she could record what they said and where she could think clearly enough to work out the questions that were worth asking. The pickup wasn't built for a smooth ride – she felt every bump in the road and especially every pothole – and it was all she could do to ask the one question that bothered her the most.

'Raleigh,' she said, 'your mother. She wasn't at the funeral.'

The girl sighed deeply. 'No. I begged and begged with her, but she wasn't interested. She said she didn't care to share any memories of Dad, not with strangers. Especially if Vesta Polder was there.'

Caxton frowned. 'They know each other?'

'From way back. Mom introduced Dad to the Polders a very, very long time ago. That was back when we lived in State College. Then maybe ten years ago Mom and Vesta had some kind of falling-out. At least, they haven't been in the same place together since and neither of them seems to want to change that. I don't really know the details. Sorry.'

Caxton had always been possessed of a certain morbid curiosity concerning Arkeley's wife, Astarte. She had never met the woman, nor seen so much as a picture of her. Arkeley had rarely mentioned her and never provided even cursory information about her background. Caxton believed she still resided in Bellefonte but didn't know for sure.

'I'd really like to talk to her. Can you call her for me?'

Raleigh gave her a polite but negating smile. 'I can . . . try.'

'Okay,' Caxton said, feeling a headache come on. 'Can you give me her number, so I can call her?'

The girl nodded and recited the digits from memory. Caxton fed them into her cell phone and then pushed the call button. The phone on the other end rang again and again without going to voice mail or even an answering machine. Eventually Caxton ended the call.

It wasn't very much farther to Harrisburg, to the state police headquarters. Caxton made an appointment to speak with Raleigh, then got out of the truck and headed into the building.

Her destination was a room in the basement. It had at one time been a classroom where rookie troopers had studied the finer points of interrogation and collar processing. There were no windows in the underground room, but it did have a pair of wall-length whiteboards and a couple dozen adult-sized desks, which Caxton had found useful. It also held a bookshelf that Caxton had bought for herself and installed near the door. The bookshelf held mostly three-ring binders full of photocopied documents – every police report on vampire activity, every news account they could find, and the very few scientific papers written on vampires. On top of the bookshelf sat a laptop that got spotty Wi-Fi reception down in the basement. They were still waiting for funding to get everything digitized and put into a searchable database. Most of the SSU's funding went to keeping the tip line open and paying Caxton's and Glauer's meager salaries. Next to the bookshelf stood three enormous metal filing cabinets that were still mostly empty but were meant to hold transcripts from the tip line and Caxton's own detailed reports. At the far end of the room Glauer was there already, writing on the whiteboards.

He had bought a coffee box at Dunkin' Donuts and had a sleeve of cups ready to go. He offered a cup to Caxton, but the trooper got her caffeine mostly from diet soda. There was a machine upstairs that sold it, but she didn't have time to run up and get one. The meeting was just about to start.

She sat on the edge of a desk near the whiteboards and greeted each member of the SSU as they came in. Glauer was the only other full-time member of the unit, but there were a dozen or so other cops who attended the briefings and were always on call if she needed them. The SSU was a joint task force operation, encompassing multiple jurisdictions. Some of its members were state troopers like herself, members of the area response team (the PSP's equivalent of a SWAT squad) or troopers from the Bureau of Investigation. They came in first – most likely they were in the headquarters building already, just killing time before lunch. Later came some local cops from various boroughs, a lot of them from Gettysburg. Some were survivors from the vampire massacre there. Other local cops came from as far afield as Pittsburgh, Philly, and even Erie. These were regular cops who were looking to log a little overtime and they served as her eyes and ears in those distant cities. They looked half distracted, as if they had better things to do elsewhere, but they came, and that was what mattered. The last person to enter the room was a man in a black suit with a red tie. He had a small badge affixed to his lapel – a star inside a circle. The first time she'd ever seen one of those had been the first night she met Arkeley. 'Deputy Marshal Fetlock,' he said, introducing himself to Glauer. He was maybe fifty years old, but he still had raven black hair swept back from a high forehead. His sideburns had gone gray, but they were cut so short that you could barely tell. 'Just here for a backgrounder,' he said.

Caxton was not surprised to see him there, though she had not invited him. The man was a U.S. Marshal, just like Arkeley had once been. Long before he had become a vampire Arkeley had retired from that service, but she knew that Fetlock and his superiors were taking an active interest in her investigation. If Arkeley started tearing people up it would look bad for the Marshals, so they had good reason to help her if they could.

She got started once Fetlock sat down, a cup of lukewarm coffee untouched on the floor next to him. She introduced herself to the new faces and thanked everyone for coming while they took out their PDAs and their spiral notebooks. Then she got right to business.

On the whiteboard Glauer had taped up a number of photographs and drawn lines connecting various actors in the investigation. 'Those of you who have been here before will notice something new,' she said, using a dry erase marker to indicate a section of whiteboard labeled VAMPIRE PATTERN #2. Underneath was a picture of Kenneth Rexroth. It looked like a mug shot. Next to his name Glauer had written IN CUSTODY. Below the picture were two crosses with names next to them that she didn't recognize. She knew who they must be, though – the night watchman and the janitor that Rexroth had killed. She thought about the janitor's severed arm for a second, then got control of herself and went on.

'Last night I investigated a report of vampire activity in a self-storage facility in Mechanicsburg. It turned out to be a waste of time. The subject, one Kenneth Rexroth, address unknown, other aliases unknown, turned out to be a normal human being made up to look like a vampire. A copycat. He'd had no exposure to vampires before except through the media. I took him in without much of a fight and I'm considering this pattern closed for now, but we wanted to make sure people were aware this sort of thing is happening. Dumb kids. Bored kids, who think vampires are cool. We've had reports of this before, but this one ended in two fatalities. I don't want to see this anymore – frankly, I don't have time for it. Officer Glauer has suggested we get a task force together to hit the schools and try to educate these kids about what a dangerous game they're playing. Not my department. I'll let him talk on that idea later.'

She moved down the whiteboard to VAMPIRE PATTERN #1. The Arkeley investigation. 'This is why we're really here. It hasn't gone away. For the benefit of the new faces in the crowd,' she said, looking specifically at Fetlock, 'let me go over some of the details.'

8.

Three photographs had been taped to the whiteboard. The first showed the face of what should have been a corpse. The skin was rotting away from the skull and one of the eyes was missing, leaving an empty socket. The mouth hung open, showing row after row of once-vicious teeth, some of which were missing, others of which had rotted down to black stumps. 'This is Justinia Malvern,' Caxton said. 'The oldest living vampire, though *living* is a relative term. Vampires do live forever, if they aren't killed, but contrary to what you've heard they do age, and not very gracefully.' That got a few chuckles from the audience. At least they were awake. 'With every night that passes they need more blood to stay strong and active than they did the night before. After three hundred years Malvern can't even sit up in her coffin. That doesn't mean she's harmless. A year ago she made four new vampires and good people died putting them down. She was also responsible for the army of vampires we fought back in October, at Gettysburg – and you all know how badly that could have gone. The last vampire she made was this guy.'

She pointed out the second photograph on the white-board, and then the third. They showed Jameson Arkeley – as he had been in life, and as he had become, in death. The before photo showed an aging man with eyes so piercing she had trouble looking at them still. The after photo just showed one more vampire, as far as she was concerned. It was not an actual photograph but a computer-generated extrapolation of what Arkeley would look like as a vampire. She'd seen the real thing and knew the picture didn't do him justice. It just wasn't scary enough. 'In the aftermath of Gettysburg, Arkeley here voluntarily accepted the curse. He did it to save lives, and I don't know what would have happened without him being there.' She shook her head. 'He promised me, at that time, that as soon as the last vampire was dead he would turn himself in. So I could kill him, and put an end to this. It's been two months since then and so far he hasn't shown himself.' Next to his vampire photo Glauer had written *POI* on the board. It stood for 'person of interest,' meaning he was wanted for questioning but had so far not been named in direct connection with any crime. 'We haven't found any bodies we can link to him. We haven't turned up any half-deads he's made—'

At the back of the room Deputy Marshal Fetlock raised his hand.

She didn't bother calling on him. 'A half-dead is a vampire's slave. Once a vampire drinks your blood, once they kill you, they have the ability to bring your corpse back to life. Your body doesn't like it and your soul can't stand it. You rot away at an accelerated rate, so most half-deads only last about a week before they just collapse in pieces. But while it lasts you do everything the vampire demands. Everything, including killing your best friend.'

Fetlock lowered his hand and nodded. She had answered his question.

'Jameson Arkeley was my partner,' she said, which was mostly true. That was how she'd thought of him, anyway, regardless of how he'd seen her. 'He was a good friend. He asked me to kill him because he knew what happens to people who become vampires with the best of intentions. The first couple of nights they're almost human. They can be noble, and good, and wise. But then they get thirsty. They start thinking about blood. They think about how it would taste, and how strong it could make them. How there are so many people out there just full of the stuff and how one or two of them could disappear and nobody would much mind. I've seen it again and again. No matter how strong their willpower might be – and Arkeley was one of the strongest men I've ever known – they always succumb. With each kill it becomes easier for them. It becomes more exciting. Their bodies start demanding more blood, always more . . . '

She turned and looked at the photos. At Arkeley's eyes. She wondered, as she always did, about that last moment at Gettysburg, when he'd promised her he would come back. That he would let her shoot him right through the heart. He had believed, truly believed, that he could do that, that he could surrender to her like that. She'd believed it, too.

Yet somewhere between that moment and the dawn he'd changed his mind. He had run off into the shadows, to some place she couldn't find him. What had he been thinking? Had he just been scared of dying? That wasn't the man she'd known and respected. Had he thought he could control the bloodlust? Yet he'd been the one who'd taught her that was impossible.

Off to one side of the room Glauer cleared his throat. She blinked rapidly and turned to face her audience again. 'Arkeley is dangerous. He needs to be destroyed on sight,' she stressed. 'The amount of damage he can do on his own is enormous.

40

He's much, much stronger than a human being and infinitely faster. He also knows every trick any human has ever used to kill a vampire. Worst of all, though, is that he could become a Vampire Zero at any time.'

She took a dry erase marker and drew a simple diagram on the whiteboard. Below Arkeley's picture she drew two circles, each connected back to his picture with a short line. Below the two circles she drew four, then eight. She connected them all up. 'That's a term we invented for the SSU. We borrowed it, kind of, from epidemiology. When you're tracing the progression of a killer virus you want to get as far back as you can, all the way back to the first person who was infected. That person is your Patient Zero. You need to find that guy and get him out of the way as soon as possible, before he infects other people.

'It's the same thing here.' She tapped Arkeley's picture. 'Vampires can make other vampires. They do it because they get lonely, or to have someone to feed them when they become too old and decrepit to look after themselves. If they think they're in danger, they make more vampires because there's safety in numbers. This is the biggest danger they represent, their ability to cooperate and to increase their numbers. With enough motivation one vampire can make a couple of others every night. Each of those others can make more. The number gets very large, very fast. We're talking about a pathological organism that can reproduce a new generation every twenty-four hours. And each new vampire is just as deadly as the last, and just as hard to kill.

'The only way to make sure that doesn't happen is to find Arkeley and Malvern now. Find them and destroy them, without hesitation, without compunction.'

She stopped, then, and looked around the room. A lot of people had heard this speech before. The new people, though, had the expression she expected from them. Their mouths hung open. Their eyes were very wide.

They were scared.

Good. They needed to be.

Fetlock's hand went up again. She pointed at him. 'You say we need to find Malvern as well. I thought she was in custody.'

Caxton shook her head. 'She was in Arkeley's custody at the time he changed. I went looking for her afterward, but she was gone. Clearly he took her with him when he disappeared. He may have wanted a mentor, someone to teach him about his new existence. He may also have just wanted to protect her. That's something else we know about vampires. They stick together and look after their own. Now she's out there, too, and in some ways she's as dangerous as he is.'

'Wasn't there a court order protecting her from execution?' Fetlock asked.

'Yes,' Caxton said. 'After Gettysburg it was rescinded. The judicial system finally came through and figured out she's a real threat. If I find her, I'm within my rights to kill her on the spot. That's exactly what I intend to do.'

She pulled the cap off her dry erase marker, then shoved it back on with a popping noise.

'We have a plan on how to get them both. I'm interviewing subjects and following up on leads, with Trooper Glauer's assistance. What I need from all of you is help with finding their lair. We're hoping it's somewhere in Pennsylvania, where we have jurisdiction. It could be just about anywhere, though vampires have very specific needs when it comes to their places of residence. It'll be somewhere isolated, where nosy people don't tend to go snooping during the daylight hours. It may be underground, or partially buried. In the past we've seen them use abandoned steel mills, hunting lodges, and disused electrical substations. Each of you probably knows a

42

place like that in your community. I need you to check it out, but carefully. Only approach the place in the morning, when you have plenty of daylight. Be very careful even then – half-deads are active during the day, and they'll lay traps for anyone who threatens their masters. If you find anything, any sign of recent occupation, anything out of place, just leave, immediately. Call me, and I'll come and check it out myself. This is how we'll get them, people. This is how we're going to make vampires extinct. Any questions?'

There were no questions. The cops and troopers got up and filed out of the room, some of them pausing to speak with her for a moment, most of them leaving without a word. Fetlock was one of the latter. She had expected him to stick around, but when she looked for him he was already gone.

9.

Work filled up most of the rest of the day – paperwork, the kind she hated the most. She had to fill out a full report on what had happened the night before in Mechanicsburg. Then she had to sit through an interminable conference call with the district attorney and the Mechanicsburg police chief, going over evidence, presenting a clear case why Rexroth should be prosecuted. It should have been obvious, she thought. He had murdered and mutilated two people. The wheels of justice grind slowly, though, and by the time she signed out and got back on the road it was already four o'clock and the sun was setting. She needed to interview Angus and try to make contact with Arkeley's wife again before she could call it a day.

The latter errand was easier said than done. She called the number Raleigh had given her and let the phone ring ten times before she hung up. She hadn't actually expected an answer. She was going to have to meet the woman, and the sooner the better – most likely, Astarte was the last member of Arkeley's family to see him before he accepted the curse. For the time being, however, she would have to settle for

Angus, who had already told her he hadn't seen his brother in twenty years.

Angus was staying at a very seedy motel on the road to Hershey, a single-story building with rooms that let out onto a shared porch, the whole construction stuck haphazardly in the middle of a black asphalt parking lot. The vacancy sign buzzed furiously out at Route 322 – only two of the rooms had lights on. Across the street lay an undeveloped field of dry, dead weeds streaked with snow that glowed eerily in the last purple-and-orange light. Caxton pulled into a parking space near the motel's office and stepped out into the chill. The temperature had fallen considerably since the morning's memorial service and she reached into the backseat of her car for her jacket. As she leaned over, out of the corner of her eye she saw an orange light glow and sputter in the shadows out front of one of the rooms. Just the ember at the tip of a cigar. Angus smiled at her out of the darkness and waved her over. He had dragged two chairs from his room and put them in front of his door. He had a bottle of Malibu rum and a two-liter bottle of Coke to mix it with. He handed her a motel glass as she sat down. 'Figgered we could talk out here, if you're amenable, and if you ain't, that's too bad,' he told her with a smile. 'They won't let me smoke in the room here.'

'That's fine,' she said, drawing a digital audio recorder out of one pocket. 'Do you mind if I record our conversation?'

'Naw,' he said.

She started the recorder and tried to clear her head. Tried to think of what to ask first. Glauer had always told her she should start with a joke, to ease the tension inherent in a police interview, but she didn't know any jokes. She knew a little bit about small talk. 'Angus and Jameson,' she said, to break the ice. 'Are those old family names?'

Angus chuckled. 'You want to know about our family? Well,

the only fancy thing we ever could afford was those names. I suppose when you're poorer than dirt, you take the best you can get, and names are for free. Our father named us both. Now, he was a character. Longlegs Arkeley, they used to call my pop, 'cause he always ran away the police got too close. He was what you call a man who enjoyed life to the full. Which means he was a man who enjoyed his whiskey, fine cigars, and young women. Had us when he was in his seventies, and lived to be a hundred and one, and his last girlfriend came to the funeral. Now, our mother, Fae, she was from old North Carolina hill women for seven generations, what they call down there a witchbilly. She could curdle milk in the pan, if she wanted, and she had an evil eye that could take paint off the side of a Cadillac, but she died young. Most like from trying to keep up with Longlegs Arkeley's two sons.'

'Your father didn't like the police. Interesting. Was he a bootlegger?' Caxton asked. She thought Jameson might have mentioned that once.

Angus nodded. 'Yes'm. For a while it looked like young Jameson was goin' that way too, toward a life on the wrong side of the law. He and I were real hellions in our prime. Got up to some pretty creative mischief 'cause there was a solid lack of aught else to do where we were brought up.'

'Where was that?'

Angus shook his head. 'Didn't have a proper name. A length of North Carolina that didn't get electricity till the sixties, if that tells you something. We called it Bald Hill, but you won't find that on any map.'

Caxton smiled. 'It's funny. I never thought of him as a country boy.'

Angus scratched his chin. 'That's understandable, since he weren't. He got out quick as he could. Tried learning his daddy's trade, but then one time when the law did catch old Longlegs

46

– it weren't the first time, or the last – Jameson came to his ma and told her he wanted to move away. Said he had saw the light and he wanted to go be a copper himself, 'cause they always won in the end. Old Fae she just grinned ear to ear, and gave him forty dollars she kept in an old pomade tin, and sent him off to police school in Raleigh-Durham. Far as I know he never went back to Bald Hill again. He was a patrol cop in town for a while, but that didn't suit him either, so he studied up for some big examination and got himself a job with the federales.'

'The U.S. Marshals,' Caxton said.

Angus nodded. 'Longlegs didn't care for that, not one bit. Disowned him and everything. Best thing Jameson could have done for himself, though, I always thought. I always wished I had the same idea. Instead I spent another forty years knocking around the hills, working one angle or another. Old Fae taught me a mite of what she knew about magic, though not enough to get me in real trouble. I told fortunes for a while, telling people what they wanted to hear. In the eighties I had a good thing going selling voodoo supplies and the like to farmworkers, but that all fell through with the scare about Satanists stealing babies left and right. Turned out that was all a hoax, but I was ruined. After that I switched to religious articles – statues of Saint Joseph to bury in your front yard when you want to sell your house, scented prayer candles for getting money or love. You know.'

Caxton frowned. 'After he joined the Marshals – after he came to Pennsylvania – did you see much of Jameson?'

'Like I told you, there ain't much to tell. Jameson and I had a visit in 1984, when I saw him married. Before that it must have been sometime in the seventies, 'cause I remember my hair was still black.'

Caxton's heart slumped in her chest. This whole trip had been a waste of time, she thought. 'That was the last time you saw him? Did you ever talk to him on the phone, or via email, or anything since then?'

'At Christmas, most years.'

'I see.'

'Of course, often as not he'd ask how I was doing, and I'd say fine, and I'd ask how he was doing, and he'd say he was busy, and then he'd pass the telephone over to Astarte or one of the kids.'

'Okay.'

Angus stubbed out his cigar on the plastic arm of his chair until it bubbled and hissed. 'You're clutching at straws, aren't you, girl? You got no better lead to follow up than something he might have said to me at his wedding.' He was looking right at her, searching her face. 'That must mean you don't even know where to start looking for him.'

Caxton's face burned, even in the cold. 'I'm on his trail. I'll find him. But if you must know, no, I don't have a lot of leads.'

Angus shrugged expansively and drank from his frosty glass. 'Well, if you don't mind a little advice, especially since it's free, I'll tell you you're barking up the wrong tree. Don't go talking to his family.'

'I need to interview everyone who knew him, just in case.'

Angus shook his head. 'You do what you need to. All I'm saying is this is one man who cared less about his loved ones than he did about what he was going to have for breakfast. You seen those kids of his? They barely know him, and what they do know is hate. They hate him for not being there most of their lives because he was too busy off chasing vampires, and when he was there they hated him for not loving them enough. They're rotten little brats, both of them, but maybe they got a reason to be. Jameson was my brother once, my little brother, and still I looked up to him. But since he worked that first vampire case, just before his wedding, he's not been the same man I knew. He's not been any kind of man at all.'

Caxton's immediate reaction to Angus' words shocked her. She felt her heart grow cold and heavy in her chest. She almost stood up out of her chair. She was, she realized, offended.

He was a great man, she thought. *He was a hero.*

But she guessed that was behind him, too.

'Ah, hell,' Angus said, suddenly. 'What the hell's he doing here? He ain't supposed to arrive yet, not for hours.'

Caxton was still too busy being angry to get what he meant. Then she turned and saw that a late-model maroon sedan had pulled into the motel's asphalt lot. Its headlights dazzled her eyes for a second and then cut out as it rolled to an uneasy stop. Maybe it had stalled out, or maybe the driver was drunk, she thought. Immediately her eyes went to the license plate and memorized the number, just in case.

'You're meeting someone?' Caxton asked. 'I have some more questions, but they can wait.' She turned back to face Angus, but he was still staring at the car.

Grumbling, swearing a couple of times, he levered himself up out of his chair. She could only stare in disbelief as he pulled a massive buck knife out of his pocket and snapped open the blade.

She turned around again then, and looked as the car's door popped open and something sagged out onto the dark pavement. It was a body, a man's body, and at first she thought the driver must be so drunk he couldn't even stand up properly. Then she saw it was just a boy, a teenager in a hooded sweatshirt. He turned to face the two of them and she saw his face was torn and bloody, with pale strips of skin hanging from his cheeks and chin.

'Half-dead,' she breathed, and grabbed for her weapon. Angus was already halfway to the car, his knife out and low by his side.

49

10.

'Angus, get back,' Caxton called, grabbing for her Beretta and jumping out of her chair. The old man was well ahead of her, closing quickly with the half-dead.

'Don't you worry, young lady. I can handle this sort.' The half-dead knelt on the asphalt, down on all fours as if it was too weak to stand. Angus grabbed at the creature's arm and yanked it painfully up until it was standing on its feet. 'You said you'd call on me at midnight. It ain't time yet!'

Caxton moved quickly, her weapon down and pointed at the ground next to her feet. The half-dead wasn't armed and it seemed barely capable of standing – in fact, it was tottering back and forth as if it would fall as soon as Angus let it go. That didn't mean it wasn't dangerous. Half-deads were the victims of vampires, drained of their blood and then raised from the dead. They were nasty little creatures, spiteful and cruel and lacking all the human qualities they'd had in life. The curse that animated them corrupted their flesh as much as it did their souls; a half-dead's body started to rot and fall apart almost instantly, and it was rare that one of them could last more than ten days before disintegrating completely. This one looked at least a week old and smelled terrible, even in the cold night air. Weak as it might be, however, it could bite Angus and give him a nasty infection, if nothing worse.

'Let him go and stand back,' Caxton ordered, but Angus acted as if he hadn't heard her.

'Twenty-four hours, you said,' he told the thing. 'You're early!'

She had another interest in the half-dead, beyond protecting Angus. It took a vampire to raise a half-dead – which meant Jameson Arkeley had done it. That meant all kinds of things, some of which were more pleasant to think of than others. It meant Arkeley had killed a human being, proof positive that he had gone over to the darkness. If Caxton could keep the half-dead from falling apart for a little while, though, it could also mean a real break in the case. The half-dead might know the location of Jameson's lair.

She could interrogate it. She could intimidate it into telling her everything it knew. As long as Angus didn't finish it off first. She started to raise her weapon, planning to point it at Angus if he didn't start complying with her orders.

The half-dead spoke, though, and Caxton froze in her tracks.

'My master grows impatient,' it creaked. Its voice was high and unnatural, like the sound a nail makes when pulled out of a rotten piece of wood. 'He has offered you a gift, and you have failed to accept. You know what the alternative is. What say you, Angus Arkeley?'

'How about this?' the old man replied, and slashed the half-dead across the face with his hunting knife. The half-dead screamed and dropped to the pavement. Angus kicked it viciously. 'You like the sound of that? My answer is no, you son of a bitch. He can ask a million times and it'll always be no.'

'Get back,' Caxton commanded. 'Leave it alone!'

Already drawing his foot back for another vicious kick, Angus turned to glare at her, his eyes traveling down her arms to the pistol in her hands. 'Shee-yit,' he said. White foaming spittle flecked his lips and chin. 'I can take care of this. You weren't supposed to get involved.'

'That thing is a vampire's servant. That makes it my responsibility. Now get back,' she said, as calmly as she could. Her heart was thudding in her chest.

Angus raised his hands, holding up the knife. No blood marked the shiny blade, just some scaly bits of gray flesh. 'You got me outgunned, I guess,' he said. 'But this is my trouble.' His foot came down and slammed into the half-dead's side, making it choke and sputter.

'Step back. You've been lying to me, haven't you? You had some kind of contact with Jameson. Is that right?'

Angus grinned at her as he took a step backward. 'I said I hain't seen or talked to Jameson in twenty years, and that's the truth. Still haven't. I seen this fellow last night, said he was sent by my brother. Said he had a message for me, a kind of a deal, and I had twenty-four hours to think it over. He also knew you'd be around asking questions. Said if I told you anything it would be the death of me.'

'I can protect you. If I'd known – I could have taken you somewhere safe,' Caxton said, shaking her head. She glanced down at the half-dead and saw it wasn't moving.

'A man takes care of his own. I didn't expect you to understand. Jameson's my brother, and that makes it my job to kill him – to—'

Angus' eyes moved to stare at the half-dead's car. Caxton thought it might be a trick – a ruse to break her concentration and let him get another kick in. Stepping backward slowly, she turned to glance at what he was looking at.

Inside the car a massive dark shape stirred. A pair of red eyes glared out of the darkened backseat. Caxton started to swing her weapon around, to train it on the car, but she was just too slow. The far side rear door exploded outwards and a black-and-white blur bounced across the black pavement toward Angus. It slowed down enough to grab him around the waist, and in that moment she saw exactly what she expected to see.

It was Jameson Arkeley, the vampire. He wore a black shirt and pants, but his feet were bare. His skin had lost all pigmentation and all its hair, even his eyelashes. His triangular ears, his red eyes, and his mouth full of ugly teeth couldn't hide the resemblance he still bore to his brother. Yet where Angus' face showed the lines of age and care, Jameson's features were smooth and unblemished. Only his left hand was less than perfect. It was missing all its fingers. He'd been maimed when he was still alive, and even his curse couldn't grow them back.

His red eyes stared right at her. She felt like a cold breeze blew right through the chambers of her skull and she heard his voice – his very human voice – calling her name, though his mouth didn't move. Her arms fell slack at her sides and her eyelids started to droop. Caxton knew exactly what was happening. She'd felt like this before, far too many times for comfort. He was hypnotizing her. Freezing her in place.

She had a charm on a thong around her neck, a spiral of silver metal, a talisman Vesta Polder had given her to allow her to break that kind of spell. She tried to reach for it even as she felt it growing warm against her clavicle, but her hand felt resistance as if it were moving through gelatin. Jameson had plenty of time to kill her before she could grab the charm and regain control of her own body.

Yet that didn't seem to be what he wanted. His eyes broke with hers and suddenly he was gone from her head.

53

She reached up and grabbed the charm through her shirt, felt its heat scorch her fingers, but she was already free. Her other hand, her gun hand, came up and she aimed automatically at his heart.

Too slow, still too slow. He was moving again, moving faster than she could track. She dropped to one knee to improve her aim and tried to get a bead on his back, even knowing that the chances of shooting him through the heart like that were slim to none. Worse, he had Angus dangling over his shoulder and she couldn't risk shooting the living brother, for many reasons.

'Freeze,' she shouted, but she could hear him laughing in her mind, a drawn-out evil chuckle that faded as his hypnotic hold on her dissipated altogether.

She jumped back up to her feet and gave chase but didn't get very far. Jameson had run right into the motel, kicking open the door to Angus' room. He ducked inside with his brother still in tow. The door swung shut behind him and cut him off from view.

Caxton raced to the door and threw herself against the wall just to the left of it. If Jameson came exploding back out the way he'd gone in she didn't want to get in his way. She raised her weapon to shoulder height and tried to breathe, tried to work out what to do next.

Jameson Arkeley, vampire hunter, would have known without thinking. Did you rush in and hope for the best? Did you wait outside for the vampire to come back out? He wouldn't have even had to ask himself the question. Yet Caxton couldn't decide that quickly. If she rushed the door she could be running right into a trap. Vampires *loved* setting traps. Jameson could be waiting inside ready to grab her and tear her to pieces before she even saw him. Yet if she waited him out – who knew what he would do to Angus?

Her duty, she decided, was to the living brother. If she had any chance of saving him she needed to move fast. Already she'd wasted valuable seconds. Weapon at the ready, she launched herself at the door, then rolled into the room with her head down and scrambled behind the bed. Raising just her eyes and hands over the jungle print bedspread, she swung her Beretta back and forth, covering the room.

It was empty – but the door to the bathroom was open. No light burned inside and she could see nothing but shadows. She rolled across the bed and rushed, shoulder first, through the open doorway. She pivoted on her heel, covering the toilet, the plastic sink, the pebbled-glass shower door. When nothing tried to kill her instantly she reached out with her left hand and switched on the lights.

The shower door was painted with blood.

11.

'Oh, God, no – not your own brother,' Caxton sighed. She hesitated a second, not really wanting to know, but then she slid back the shower door. It slid back all too easily, its track slick with wet blood. More blood half-filled the tub, almost but not quite submerging the body of Angus Arkeley. The old man sprawled in an ungainly mess across the porcelain, one arm folded under his body, the other reaching up toward the soap dish. His eyes were very wide and blood still bubbled from a massive wound at his throat.

Protocol demanded she call 911, and she did – though she knew Angus would die before help could arrive. 'I have a man down in room four,' she told the dispatcher, once she'd provided her credentials and her location. 'I'm looking at massive blood loss from deep lacerations to the neck. I need an ambulance right away and every officer you can send.' Clicking her phone shut, she grabbed up a stiff white towel. She shoved it into the wound, but the blood surged out from under it, coming in thick gouts so fresh they hadn't begun to clot.

Angus' eyes rolled slowly down, trying to fasten on Caxton's face. There was no emotion there. The old man lacked the strength to even beg for help. Caxton thought of questioning him but knew he couldn't reply. He had told her enough already, she thought, even though he'd lied to her.

As bad as Angus' condition might be, she had another Arkeley to worry about.

She looked up, around the bathroom. There was no sign of Jameson. She had read old folktales about vampires who could slip through the crack between a door and its frame, but she knew better. Jameson was a big guy and there was nowhere he could hide in the small room. She looked up and saw a window above the toilet. It was open, letting cold night air blast inside. It looked too small for Jameson to have wriggled out of – yet she knew he had. The metal frame of the window was buckled outward. With enough strength and determination and a complete disinterest in physical pain (all of which any vampire possessed), she figured he could have just made it through. She was tempted to jump up and follow him the same way, yet first she spared another glance down at Angus in the bathtub.

Protocol also required her to stay by the man until the paramedics showed up. Simple human decency required as much as well. Yet if she waited she would just be giving Jameson a chance to get away – and Angus was going to die regardless.

'I'll get him,' she swore, looking down into his dimming eyes. It was as much comfort as she had to offer. She hoped he could understand her and know that he wasn't going to die unavenged. Ignoring his eyes, she leaned over the toilet and peered out through the window.

She couldn't see a damned thing. The lights of the motel and the highway out front didn't reach to the back. She thought there was a field back there, maybe some farm acreage left fallow for the winter. She could just about make out a thick growth of weeds directly below the window. Jameson could be out there, close enough to reach out and touch, but she knew she would never see him. His black clothes would hide most of his body and shadows would do the rest.

Protocol had it she should go back, out through the front door, and circle round the back. Protocol also suggested she have a partner with her at all times, someone who could cover her movements. *Screw protocol*, she decided, and shoved her weapon in its holster. She climbed up onto the toilet tank and pushed herself head and shoulders first through the window. Getting her hands down to brace herself, she let her legs slither through the window and dropped to a tense crouch.

This was the moment, she knew. This was when Jameson would attack, if he planned to. When her handgun was still in its holster and she couldn't fight back. She braced herself, expecting him to slam into her like a freight train before she could even get her bearings.

Nothing happened. Nothing moved. Her eyes slowly adjusted to the dark as she brought her weapon up again. She saw that the gray weeds around her ended about twenty feet away at the sharply defined edge of a field. A thin layer of white snow lay atop the furrowed earth, glowing slightly in the starlight. The flat plane of white screwed with her depth perception and made her eyes buzz. The hair on the backs of her arms started to stand up after a moment and she—

Wait, she thought. She knew that feeling. It was the barely perceptible sensation of wrongness, of something unnatural quite close by. It was the feeling she always got when vampires were near. Jameson. He hadn't just run off. He was sticking around, waiting for her. Toying with her.

The thinnest crinkling sound came from her left and she

spun, nearly falling over on her hip. A shadow cleaved off from the dark back of the motel building and she fired without hesitation. The gunshot shattered the darkness all around her, made her ears ring. The shadow darted out toward the snowy field and she squeezed her trigger again. The shot hit home, knocking Jameson sideways. For a second she saw him, his white face lost amid the snowy field but his black shirt sharply defined against the light. She saw him raise his hands to his chest as if he were clutching at a wound.

It was a chance – a break, an opening. She didn't waste it. Rushing forward, toward the shadow, she fired a third round, but she knew it went wide of the mark. She had a lot of trouble telling just how far away he was, but she pressed on, watching his silhouette grow larger and larger before her until he was looming up over her, until she was so close she could feel the cold of his body, feel him colder than the night around him. He raised his good hand to stop her, but she kept coming, her head down so as not to make eye contact, so as not to give him another chance to hypnotize her.

'Trooper,' he said, and his voice was a low growl. 'Laura. Let's talk—'

Jameson Arkeley, in his vampire hunting days, would have known exactly what to do then. So did she. Caxton closed to point-blank range, the barrel of her weapon only inches from his chest, pointed just left of his sternum. She fired before he could get another word out.

The bullet left the barrel of her weapon at well over the speed of sound. It struck him dead on and knocked him backward as if he'd been kicked by a horse. Sprawling on his back, his legs and arms pinwheeling, he landed in a heap.

It could have been enough. The bullet had plenty of energy – over 450 foot-pounds – to cut right through his skin, his pectoral muscles, his bony ribs. It would have had plenty of force left over to cut right through his heart. Caxton knew what a bullet could do to a body at that range, even a vampire's body.

It had to be enough. She had killed vampires before. She knew they were tough, that sometimes they seemed bulletproof, but she also knew they weren't invulnerable. Do enough damage to a vampire's heart and he'll stay down, permanently.

She had killed him. That was what it looked like. That was what it felt like.

So why couldn't she believe it?

In life Arkeley had been a tough bastard. In undeath he would be ten times as difficult to kill. She had killed vampires before, sure, but this one – this one was different. She had to be certain.

Stepping forward, she kept her feet apart. Steadied her weapon with both hands. He lay at her feet, unmoving, apparently immobile. She couldn't see the wound on his chest, not in the near-utter darkness, but it had to be bad. She thought about firing into his heart again, just on principle. The idea sickened her. It felt like desecrating a dead body, she thought.

Jameson Arkeley, vampire hunter, would have done it anyway. She lined up her shot carefully, took her time, fired again. The body didn't jump or twitch. If he hadn't been dead already, she thought, that would do it. That was enough.

The second she lowered her weapon he was up on his feet, grabbing her up in a bear hug with one arm, slapping the pistol out of her hand with the other. Her wrist bones shrieked as her hand flew away from the blow. She didn't see where the pistol went. She didn't see anything but his teeth. They were huge, and jagged, and stained with clotted blood. They were inches from her eyes.

His breath stank. His breath stank of his own brother's blood.

'Kill me,' she said. She couldn't breathe, couldn't think – couldn't even be afraid, her brain wouldn't let her. She knew that small mercy wouldn't last. 'Just do it quickly. You owe me.'

He chuckled, the fetor of his breath filling her nose and throat and making her twist her head around, making her wriggle in his grasp. 'I owe you a lot more than that,' he said. 'And I intend to repay you in full.'

He yanked her head up, the fingers of his good hand digging into the flesh under her chin. He was so strong that she couldn't resist. Their eyes met and every thought went flying from her head like bats from a cave at dusk.

Time stopped – and when it started again she was lying on her back in the snow, staring up at dark blue sky and silver stars. So many stars—

She sat up, clutching at her head, forcing herself to focus. Looked around, looked everywhere. There was no sign of him, not even footprints in the snow.

But – she had hit him! She had put a bullet right through his heart. How was it possible he had gotten up again and run away?

12.

Hours later. In the east, a pale smudge of red stained the horizon. Just a few minutes before the dawn. She started to feel safe again, a little. Yet when Deputy Marshal Fetlock came up behind her and tapped her on the shoulder she still jumped.

'I'm sorry, Trooper, I didn't mean to—'

She held up one hand and looked at her shoes until her heart had stopped thudding in her chest. 'It's alright. They told me you were coming in. I should have been ready to greet you.' Slowly she uncoiled her arms. They had been wrapped tightly around her stomach. She held out one hand and the Fed shook it. 'It's just – it's just been a very long night.'

'I appreciate your taking the time to talk to me,' he said, smiling patiently for her. 'I'm sure you're busy.'

She shrugged. She'd been busy an hour before, coordinating the police response, securing the motel, and leading a team of troopers who dragged the field looking for any sign of Jameson. When nothing turned up she'd eventually decided she could go home, that there was nothing more for her to do at the scene.

Then Fetlock had called and asked for access to the crime scene. The timing was lousy – it was six in the morning; she hadn't slept all night and she just wanted to get home. She'd thought about making him wait until she'd had some rest, but he assured her it was important, that he really needed to see the crime scene while it was fresh. Caxton had been a cop long enough to know how the hierarchy worked. Nothing good could ever come from saying no to a Fed. So she had been stuck at the motel while she waited for him to arrive. She had no idea what he wanted. He'd come to her briefing of the SSU but then left without saying anything, and now he was muscling in on her investigation. None of it made sense. 'It's not that I'm not glad to see you,' she said, 'but maybe you could explain your imperative interest in this scene. Especially at this time in the morning.'

He smiled broadly. 'I guess I'm just a morning person. As for my interest, it's purely informal, I assure you. If you'd prefer not to meet with me now, I'll be happy to get out of your way.'

She shook her head. She'd worked with Feds before and she knew that was likely all the explanation she would get – at least until he wanted something from her.

'No, no,' she said. 'I'm just not sure how I can help you.'

'Why don't you tell me what happened here?'

'It started with a routine interview. I'd made an appointment with Angus Arkeley, who was Jameson's brother, and we were chatting. Then the situation deteriorated.' She filled him in briefly on the night's events, omitting only her mental state – the doubts she'd felt, the moments of panicked fear, the blank spots when Jameson had hypnotized her.

When he'd heard her narrative – he declined to comment on any of it – she started showing him what remained behind.

When Jameson had left her, when she'd recovered enough

to stand, she had made her way back to the front of the motel. The ambulance she'd called for arrived first, but the paramedics hadn't known where to start, and she had to explain that the corpse in the parking lot wasn't their patient. It should have been clear, she thought. The remains of the half-dead stank like they'd been moldering in the ground for months and there was so little left of its musculature and internal organs that she could have easily picked it up in one hand. The paramedics had eventually put up caution tape around the body and then just thrown a blanket over him. Now, as yellow light crept across the parking lot, she twitched the blanket back so Fetlock could see what he looked like.

The Fed winced visibly. Maybe at the smell, maybe at what the half-dead looked like. 'It's going to be hard to make a positive ID on that,' he said.

'You're not kidding. The skin's too degraded to get prints and his teeth are all broken up, so matching dental records is out. There's no wallet or any kind of identification on him or in the car. I already checked.' That had not been a lot of fun.

'So Angus kicked him to death?' Fetlock asked. 'That wouldn't explain the decomposition.'

Caxton shook her head. 'Angus was pretty hard on him, but I think he would look like this anyway. No, he died of old age.' Fetlock frowned at that, but she just shrugged and went on. 'Jameson must have raised him from the dead more than a week ago and he's been rotting away ever since. This guy wasn't a threat to anyone. He couldn't even stand up, much less hold a weapon. I think that was intentional.'

'What do you mean?' Fetlock asked.

'Jameson must have known how little life his servant had left in him. He could have sent a fresher corpse to bring his message, but if he had, if the half-dead had lived just a few hours more, I could have interrogated him and learned where Jameson's lair is. This guy won't be telling me anything.'

She pulled the blanket back over the half-dead's face. Supposedly a hair and fiber unit was coming from Harrisburg to take a look at him, but she doubted they would find anything. The body was still decaying at an accelerated rate, and by the time they arrived he would probably be nothing more than stinking goo and splintered bones.

'That might explain why Jameson came here so early. The half-dead was supposed to arrive at midnight to get Angus' answer, but it was closer to six p.m. when they arrived. I think Jameson didn't expect his servant to last until twelve.'

'You mentioned that before. That Jameson had approached his brother with some kind of offer and that Angus refused it. You didn't say what the offer was.'

'Well, nobody got around to telling me, either.' Caxton led the Fed toward the motel room. A pair of state troopers stood outside the door, guarding it, while a team of photographers worked inside, documenting the place of Angus Arkeley's last moments. 'Angus intentionally lied to me and didn't tell me anything about the deal. It sounded like Angus felt this was family business. That he thought he could take Jameson down himself. Come on in, I'll show you what that got him.'

They squeezed into the small bathroom, ejecting a photographer and a corporal who was in charge of maintaining order on the scene. Caxton pulled back the shower door and let Fetlock look into the tub.

It was empty, or at least there was no body in it. The paramedics had taken Angus away, pumping him full of plasma and trying to keep his heart going until he could reach a hospital. It had been no use – he'd been pronounced dead en route, inside the ambulance. The body was in the hospital's morgue now under careful supervision. Jameson had the power to bring his brother back from the dead – in the form of a half-dead like the one out in the parking lot. Caxton had no reason to think Jameson would do that – it would only give her a chance to question Angus again – but she wasn't taking any chances.

'Jameson dragged him in here, mostly to get him away from me. He had about five seconds alone with his brother before I broke in and started shooting. What do you see here?' she asked.

Fetlock turned his head to one side. 'I see strawberry jam. About a gallon of it.'

Caxton let herself smile a little. She was starting to dislike the Fed. He kept his cards too close to his vest when they were supposed to be helping each other out. 'That's coagulated blood, of course. Angus' blood. What I see when I look at this is a vampire who had already fed last night.'

'That's an interesting conclusion.'

She nodded. 'A hungry vampire would have found a way to drink more of the blood. He would have seen every drop as precious. This is just thoughtless waste. Jameson didn't bring his brother in here to feed off of him, he brought him in here to murder him. Plain and simple.'

'His own brother. Why?'

'Because he said no. You asked me what Jameson offered Angus and I told you I don't know for sure, but I think I can guess. A vampire only has one thing he can give you, which is his curse. I think Jameson Arkeley offered to make his brother a vampire. He gave him twenty-four hours to think it over, and maybe Angus was even tempted – eternal life must sound pretty good to an old man, even if he knows what price he's going to have to pay. When Angus said no, Jameson killed him before he could say one more word to me.'

For the first time Fetlock showed a little surprise. His face paled a shade and his eyes opened a little wider. 'He wanted to make his brother like he was. If he couldn't do that he wanted to keep him from talking to you. And he intentionally used a moldering servant so he couldn't tell you anything.'

'Yeah, that theory looks good,' Caxton said.

'Then he's afraid of you.'

She actually laughed at that. 'Yeah. I'm his biggest threat.' She led Fetlock over to the toilet and showed him the window that both she and Jameson had crawled through. 'Out there,' she said, 'I put two nine-millimeter rounds in his heart at point-blank range. Then he stood up again, incapacitated me, and fled the scene completely unscathed. Sure, I'm a real threat.' Fear surged through her again and she couldn't help but shiver. Fetlock must be able to see how terrified she was, she thought. She couldn't hide it anymore.

Fetlock shrugged. 'Of all the people in the world, you're the one he has the most to fear from. You're the one who knows him best. You know his strengths, that's something. And you know more about killing vampires than anyone else alive.'

But not necessarily, she thought, *anyone undead*. Jameson had taught her everything she knew. Now he was proving he had some secrets he hadn't shared. 'Thanks,' she sneered. 'It's nice to hear that.' And yet she realized she sort of meant what she'd said. It did help to know someone believed in her. 'Now. How about you tell me why you're actually here?'

'Alright,' he said, sitting down on the toilet. 'I'm here to offer you a star.'

13.

'A star,' Caxton said, scowling. 'You want to give me a star. What, like a teacher gives a good student a gold star?'

'This one's silver, actually.' He reached inside his jacket pocket and brought out a lapel pin in the shape of a star inside a circle. She recognized it instantly, of course. Fetlock was wearing one himself. Jameson Arkeley used to wear one, too. Special Deputy Jameson Arkeley of the U.S. Marshals Service. 'I'm authorized to temporarily deputize any law enforcement officer I choose into the Service, for as long as I see fit.'

'What, like a sheriff rounding up a posse of cowboys?'

'That's about exactly right,' he said. 'The Service is the oldest branch of the Justice Department. We were originally organized to clean up the frontier. A lot of cowboys were Marshals – Wyatt Earp, Bat Masterson, Bill Hickock.'

She shook her head. 'I'm not a big fan of Westerns,' she told him.

'Frederick Douglass was one of us, too. Later on President Kennedy had us on the front lines of the civil rights movement and desegregation. We're the white hats,' he said, his eyes twinkling.

She stared at the pin in his hand but said nothing. What the hell was this about? she wondered.

When she didn't take the pin immediately, he closed his hand around it but didn't put it away. 'You've asked why I came down here. You probably wondered what I was doing at your SSU briefing. I was sent by the director of the Service. He's very concerned about your investigation and he wants us to help you any way we can. Maybe I should start by giving you some background information, tell you our side of this. Where I come in. At our headquarters in Arlington, Virginia, on 21 November, I was asked to gather all of Jameson Arkeley's old files from our archives. I was supposed to make photocopies of everything we had and send the originals on to you. The online catalog showed there wasn't much – a few notebooks, a couple of case jackets and his personal dossier. None of it was digital, which meant I had to go down to the stacks in person and find the paper documents by hand. When I attempted to do so I made an unnerving discovery. Every single folder I was looking for was missing.'

He studied her face, but she refused to give anything away. She wouldn't even shrug, not until she'd heard more.

'My next step, of course, was to find the Service's librarian and check the circulation records. The files I wanted had all been checked out at the same time and then never returned. They'd been signed for. I bet you can guess whose signature was on the sheet. Jameson Arkeley's.'

Caxton let herself blink, maybe too rapidly.

'Sounds absurd, doesn't it? This was all well after he became a vampire. More than a year after he retired from the Service. He would have needed a photo ID to check out those materials. He would have needed ID just to get into the building. I checked with the unit that issues those ID cards and they told me that they're supposed to destroy the cards once a deputy leaves the Service, but that sometimes people don't turn in the cards when they clean out their desks. Sometimes they want to keep them as souvenirs of their old jobs, and sometimes they just forget. The ID unit never bothers to check if a given card has been turned in and destroyed or not. Well, they will now, I am told. Somebody down there is probably going to get fired over this.'

'Videotapes,' Caxton said.

Fetlock watched her as if waiting for her to say more, but she figured he knew exactly what she meant. 'You mean, is the entrance to the archive under electronic surveillance? Of course. I watched the footage myself – it's not actually on videotape, you understand. It's all in compressed files on our servers. I watched the six hours before and after Arkeley supposedly signed out those files. If you're wondering if I saw a tall albino with pointed ears and no facial hair, no. Nothing of the sort. He might have sent a half-dead in his place, of course, but the librarian would probably have noticed someone coming in with no skin on his face.'

'A human associate, then.'

Fetlock nodded. 'Has to be. That person's identity remains unknown at this time. When I presented the director with the story I just told you, he made a decision very quickly. We couldn't take that kind of security failure lightly. Maybe you're thinking that the theft of a few library materials is no big deal, but it demonstrates something much more frightening. It shows that he knows all our tricks – and how to get around them. Jameson Arkeley conspired to trespass on Service property, in addition to any other crimes he might have committed. He is now considered a rogue deputy of the U.S. Marshals Service. That means he goes to the top of our

Major Cases list – our version of the FBI's most wanted, I suppose you could say.'

She wondered why the Service really wanted Jameson so badly. Maybe Fetlock was just gunning for promotion and wanted to take credit for closing up some unfinished business. Maybe it was just bad PR. After all, an ex-deputy turned mass murderer would look very bad for the Service. Or maybe the director was just truly concerned about public safety. Based on her experience with federal cops she kind of doubted that.

Fetlock raised his closed fist and rattled the pin around the way a gambler rattles his dice before he throws them. 'While he still hadn't hurt anybody we kept his name off the website and out of the media, but after what happened here last night I doubt that remains an option. We're committed to catching him. We're going to put every resource we have behind that. We want you to be one of those resources.'

She shook her head. 'I already have a job.'

'And you would keep it,' he said. 'This is strictly a temporary deputization. It'll last just until you catch him. Then you'll go right back to what you were doing before you started fighting vampires.'

She wasn't even sure what that meant anymore, if she was honest. She'd been putting her life at stake for so long she'd never really considered what she would do if the vampires were driven to extinction. Maybe she would retire and work as a dog trainer. That would be nice.

Not yet, though. For now, she was a cop.

'What's in it for me?' she asked. She couldn't see it. Did he expect her to just jump at the chance?

He leaned back and seemed to think about it before answering. 'It would open a lot of doors for you. It would allow you to track a fugitive across state lines, for one thing.

Right now if Jameson runs to West Virginia you can't legally follow him.'

She would anyway, of course, legally or otherwise. But it could be useful to have police powers anywhere in the country. She had often considered what might happen if the vampire moved outside the Commonwealth of Pennsylvania. If she were him, she would have done it months ago.

'You'd also have access to the resources of our Major Case Fugitive Program.' He sighed and stood up. 'Let me show you something you've probably already seen.' He took a pen from his pocket and pointed at the warped frame of the bathroom window. 'Here.' He indicated a tiny scrap of black cloth stuck in a corner. 'Fiber evidence. Maybe something useful, maybe something that could take you to Jameson Arkeley.'

'Maybe,' she said. 'I went through there, too. It could have come from my pants. Anyway, I already have our Forensic Services on the way. They do hair and fiber and DNA matches all the time. I've yet to see anything useful out of that kind of evidence.'

'And why would you? Your unit operates in a strictly prosecutorial role. They make the case after the subject is in custody. How long does it take them to do a thorough search? Six weeks?'

'About that,' she admitted.

'A lot of bodies could pile up in six weeks. My guys can take those fibers and run them against every national database and have something for you in twenty-four hours. All it takes is a phone call and I can have them here by lunchtime.'

'Vampires don't have any hair and they don't wear a lot of clothes. If they even have DNA, nobody's ever found it.'

Fetlock sighed. 'Alright, then what about manpower? You have two full-time people in your SSU, including yourself. You can't afford to hire anyone else, so you rely on part-time volunteers. With federal money you could hire anyone you want for as long as your investigation lasts.'

She had to admit it was tempting. 'What's the catch?'

He shrugged good-naturedly. 'You'll have to follow Justice Department guidelines. The paperwork is a bear. But you can hire somebody to fill out forms for you.' He turned slightly away from her and looked down into the bathtub again. 'Also, you'd be working for me.'

'But I'd still be lead on the investigation,' she said, needing to make it clear.

He smiled. 'Of course. Like I said before – you're the one who's going to bring him down. I'll just be there in the background to provide help when you need it. I'm not even a field agent, just a desk jockey. This is not my kind of thing, to be honest.'

'Yeah,' she said.

'I'm sorry?'

She reached into his cupped hand and took the pin. 'Yeah, I'm in. Anything that helps me get him. What do I have to do? Swear an oath on a Bible?'

He beamed at her. 'I think we can skip the formalities. I think this is going to be a very profitable relationship, for both of us.' He shook her hand and the two of them walked out of the bathroom and back out to the parking lot. The sun was an orange disk on the horizon, carved into pieces by the black branches of dead trees.

Caxton scratched at her head – her hair felt greasy and thick – and started walking toward her car. 'Alright, Fetlock. Get your fiber people down here as soon as possible,' she said, while pinning the star to the lapel of her jacket. 'Who knows? Maybe they'll turn something up. I'm going back to headquarters to tell my Commissioner about this. He ought to know.'

73

'Special Deputy,' Fetlock called as she yanked open her door.

At first she didn't recognize her new title. 'What?' she asked.

'Maybe – since I am your boss now – you could refer to me not as "Fetlock" but as "Deputy Marshal."'

Caxton bit her tongue before she could say what she thought of that. She had no great love for the Marshals Service. She'd been a state cop too long to ever really trust the Feds. If all he wanted was a little respect, though, she figured she could give him that much. 'Of course,' she said. 'Please get your fiber people here as soon as you can, Deputy Marshal. Is that better?'

'It's good enough for now,' he said.

She was already climbing in her car and driving away.

14.

The silver star felt weird on her jacket. She'd never worn a badge before – Pennsylvania state troopers never did. It was part of their oath that their good conduct was all the badge they needed. Well, she supposed she would get used to it.

There were a million things to do. The first order of business was to go take a nap. Her house was too far away, so instead she headed to the state police barracks on Cocoa Avenue in Hershey, the closest place she could think of. The academy was there – the place where she'd taken countless training classes – and she knew the place well enough to feel safe there. The trooper on early-morning desk duty showed her to a ward room with a narrow little cot and a buzzing Coke machine. It wasn't uncommon for troopers to show up and use the spare bed. Troop T, the turnpike patrol, worked weird hours and very long shifts and were encouraged to keep themselves sharp by taking occasional naps. The desk trooper asked no questions as he sorted out a blanket and foam pillow for her, though he stared openly at her new star. When she refused to follow his gaze he eventually just told her to sleep tight and left her alone.

She switched off the lights, but the Coke machine filled the room with a baleful red glow. She ignored it, lay down on the cot with the pillow still in her arms, and was asleep before she could even think of covering herself with the sheet.

Four hours later her eyelids popped open and she was awake. Her body creaked and moaned when she sat up, protesting that it needed more sleep, but her brain knew better. She glanced down at her watch and saw it was just after noon. Half the day gone and she had accomplished nothing. Well, she'd been upgraded to an honorary Fed, but that didn't feel real yet, not at all.

She turned in her pillow and her neatly folded sheet and headed back to her car.

There were a lot of people she needed to notify of her new employment status – including the Commissioner of State Police and, more important, Clara. As she drove toward Harrisburg, fighting with herself to stop yawning so much, she reached for her cell phone, only to find that its battery had died sometime during the night. Worrying that she might have missed some important call, she plugged it into her car charger. Instantly the phone chimed at her. She had new messages – a text message and at least one new voice mail message. Exactly as she'd feared.

Caxton looked at the text message first – and dropped the phone. When she picked it up again and stared at the words on the screen, she felt her blood run cold.

> *'Twas a nice service, Laura.*
> *He was brought to tears.*

Caxton bit through a hangnail on the side of her thumb. There was no signature on the message. The phone said it came from an unknown number. She knew exactly who had sent it, though, based just on the archaic phrasing. Justinia Malvern. The ancient vampire couldn't speak, at least not the last time Caxton had seen her. She was too decrepit to even sit up in her coffin. She had been able to communicate only by tapping out cryptic messages on a computer keyboard. It looked like she had learned how to text as well.

It also looked like she had been watching the ceremony over Jameson's empty grave. No, Caxton thought, that was impossible. The ceremony had taken place during the day, when Malvern would be dead to the world inside her coffin. Which meant that she must have sent a half-dead to observe it. The whole time she was arguing with Jameson's kids, some undead freak must have been standing close by, keeping an eye on her.

She wondered how long Jameson and Malvern had been watching her. The idea made her skin crawl. If only to clear her head, she decided to listen to her voice mail. She held down the one key until it automatically dialed her voice mail, then put it on speaker mode. 'You have six new messages,' the phone told her. 'First new message.'

'Trooper, it's Glauer. Just checking in. I took Raleigh home, just like you said. Except it's not exactly what I would call a typical residence. Some kind of weird hospital or halfway house or something. A big old mansion, red brick with ivy all over the front. Really big lawn, and the whole place is surrounded by a ten-foot wall. She said I couldn't go inside, that it's for women only. I figured that was okay, so I just dropped her at the gate and confirmed your appointment to come talk to her. I'm headed back to HQ now. I'm probably going to go home in an hour or two, but I'm on my cell if you need me.'

'Next new message,' the phone said.

'Hey, cutie! It's me, the much-neglected but still wonderful

77

Clara. I'm at work right now and I can't really talk. The sheriff and his boys have knocked over another drug lab. No shots fired, thank God, everybody went quietly. I'm taking pictures of all these bags of heroin and stacks of money. I'll bring you home something nice. Just kidding! Actually I'm calling because I miss you, like, a lot, and I'm going to be done here by one or two and I thought we could have lunch. That way at least I'll know you're eating. I miss you. Did I mention that? I really do. Call me.'

'Next new message.'

'Trooper, this is Glauer. I just got into work and I heard – well, I heard what happened last night. It's all anyone wants to talk about here at HQ. I was glad to hear you're alright, and sorry to hear about Angus Arkeley. This is – I guess this is what we've been bracing ourselves for the last two months. It's funny, I don't know how I'm supposed to feel. Between you and me I'm kind of relieved. Listen, I'm sitting here with no direct orders, so unless you need me for something I'm going to get to work. Kenneth Rexroth has been talking to the local police in Mechanicsburg. They left me a message last night saying he had all but confessed to the two homicides – they said he was gloating about those kills. I want to get out there and talk to him myself. I know what you said, that he's just a wannabe and that he's not worth our time. But, Trooper, this is a real bad guy. You did a real good thing putting him away. I'll talk to you later – I'm on my cell phone if you need me.'

'Next new message.'

'It's Clara. Again. Call me. Please, call me as soon as you can. I love you.'

'Next new message.'

'Trooper, it's Glauer again. Things have gone from weird to worse. I arrived in Mechanicsburg about an hour ago. I met

78

with the cops there and asked to talk to Rexroth. They said he was sleeping – he sleeps all day, because he's supposed to be a vampire. They asked me if I wanted them to wake him up, but I decided I'd get more information out of him if I waited. I thought maybe I'd made the trip for nothing, but the locals had some information for me themselves. It turns out that Kenneth Rexroth is an alias, that the kid's name is actually Dylan Carboy. He's nineteen years old and lives with his parents up in Northumberland County, in Mount Carmel. Lives – lived, I guess. The Mount Carmel cops sent a car out there to try to contact the Carboy family and got no response at the door. They popped the lock and went inside and found three dead bodies, all in states of advanced decomposition. The victims were, let's see, Mark Carboy, father, forty-three years old, Ellen Carboy, mother, thirty-nine, and Jenny Carboy, sister, seventeen. The two parents were killed with shotgun blasts, the same gauge as the shotgun you took off Dylan at the storage facility. The sister was strangled in her bed, and had . . . Jesus. She had bite marks on her neck. Made by human teeth, not vampire. I don't think he woke her up first. I really don't think he did. I don't want to think he did. They recovered a bunch of stuff from Dylan's room. Notebooks full of handwritten journal entries and newspaper clippings. They sent them on to Mechanicsburg, where I got to take a look at them. I asked if I could borrow the notebooks to show you and the locals said that would be fine, as long as I left a receipt in case they need them for the trial. The kid had plenty to live for, Trooper. He had one prior, for possession of marijuana, but the judge threw it out as long as he promised to go back to school. He was in community college studying to be a chef. You need to see these notebooks, Trooper. I think you should see them. They have your name all over them. I'm going back to Harrisburg now. I have my cell phone if you need me.'

79

'Next new message.'

'Laura, it's Clara. I heard about – I heard – the guys here are talking about it, they're talking about you, just call me. I'm scared. I'm scared for you, so just call me, alright? Call me, damn it.'

'End of new messages. You have forty-five saved messages.'

Caxton flipped the phone shut. Thought about whom to call first. Glauer shouldn't be working the Rexroth angle. It wasn't even an angle! Finding and killing Jameson Arkeley was the only thing that mattered. She called his number, but it went straight to voice mail. Typical. For two months while they'd had nothing real to do he was always at her heels, always waiting for his next order. Now that she actually had an order to give him he was out of cell phone range.

'Officer Glauer, this is Caxton. I want you to stop playing around. You've heard what happened last night. Well, you're right, this is it. This is what we've been waiting for. This is what we've been studying for and working toward, and it's happening now. I have no doubt that Arkeley will want to kill again, and we need to get him before that happens. So when you get this, start putting together an action item list we can send around to everyone in the SSU.' She glanced down at the star on her lapel. 'There are going to be some changes to how we work, but I'll tell you about them when I see you next. Stay focused, Glauer. Stay with me.'

She snapped the phone shut. Centered herself. The next call required her to be calm and collected. She scrolled down to Clara's cell number, then pressed SEND.

She got Clara's voice mail. The phone didn't even ring once.

'Hi, baby. I got your messages,' she said. 'Listen, I'm okay. I'm going to be okay.' *He didn't even want to hurt me*, she started to say, then stopped herself. Clara was no idiot. She knew that if a vampire didn't kill you one night it only meant he was saving you for the next time he got hungry. 'Let's do lunch, okay? Get to Harrisburg, to the HQ, whenever you can and we'll eat and talk and I'll tell you everything. I miss you too.'

She ended the call – and then immediately wanted to call back, to say that she loved Clara, that she wanted nothing more than to go home and be with her alone and quiet and not talk or think about anything, just be in each other's arms for a while with nothing to do, nowhere she had to be.

She should just call back, she told herself. She really should. She even started reaching for the phone again.

Then it rang on its own. Thinking it might be Glauer or Clara calling her back, she responded immediately. 'Trooper Caxton,' she said.

'Good afternoon, Officer,' a woman's voice said. She didn't recognize the caller.

'I'm not an officer. I'm a state trooper.' She thought of her new star. 'As of today I'm also a special deputy of the U.S. Marshals Service.'

'Really? How very wonderful for you. Why, that's the same title Jameson had.'

Caxton's blood went cold hearing the name of the vampire. 'Who is this?' she demanded, then regained control of herself. 'I'm sorry. May I ask who's calling?'

'Of course. This is Astarte Arkeley. The widow. I believe you've been trying to get my attention.'

15.

'Yes! Yes, I have,' Caxton said. 'Thank you so much for calling me. Can I ask who gave you my number?' It seemed like everyone had it these days – even Malvern.

'You may,' Astarte told her. 'It was my son, Simon. He was quite intent on my contacting you. He seemed to think I could appeal to your mercy and convince you to stop your desperate pursuit of the vampire. I told him I would do no such thing.'

Caxton pulled over on the side of the road. This was important – she needed to focus on the call. 'I'm kind of glad to hear that. I need to tell you something, Mrs Arkeley. It's sort of upsetting.'

'Then I'm very glad that I am sitting down. Please proceed.'

Caxton rubbed at her forehead. 'Last night Jameson killed his own brother. He killed Angus. I was there.'

'How sad. I suppose the vampire attempted to kill you as well. That's what they do, of course.'

'Actually—' Caxton stopped herself. She knew almost nothing about Astarte. She had no idea how far she could trust

82

her. Deciding to err on the side of full disclosure, she said, 'Actually he didn't. I tried to kill him.'

'Which is what you're supposed to do.'

'Yeah. Yeah, it is. I tried to kill him, but I couldn't. He was stronger than I expected. Stronger than any vampire I've ever seen. He could have killed me easily, with just his bad hand, but he didn't. He said he owed me something. You don't have any idea what that might be, do you?'

'I couldn't begin to imagine.'

'Okay. Alright. Listen. I'd really like to come meet you. Today if possible. I'd like to sit down and ask you some questions about Jameson and the last time you saw him. Is that something we can do?'

'I think not,' Astarte told her.

'This is very important, ma'am. A man has already been killed and others are sure to follow. I wouldn't ask, not in your time of grief, if I didn't think it would help keep people safe.'

'Of course you wouldn't. Yet I find I don't have any compelling interest in speaking with you further. I only called today out of a sense of courtesy.'

'Your husband is killing people,' Caxton said, trying not to shout.

'Allow me to correct you on that misapprehension. I doubt very much that you are initiated into the secret doctrine of theosophy, so I will attempt to explain what I mean. The murderous creature you are attempting to apprehend is not my husband. When he took his own life, my husband ceased to exist in this plane. His soul was lost. As a result he's certain to regress in his path and be reincarnated as an insect or, if he is lucky, some variety of plant. It's a shame, as I was hoping the two of us could evolve together, but that's impossible now. His body may continue to move and to operate after a manner, but it is not Jameson, nor any part of the true being once called Jameson. Do you understand this?'

Caxton slapped the steering wheel. 'No!'

'I was afraid you would not. In time perhaps you will learn to look within. Now I'm afraid I must go. As we will not be talking again, I wish to thank you.'

'Thank me? For what?'

'For making the last year of Jameson's life more comfortable. The physical pleasure you gave him must have been some kind of solace. I'm sure you received something from your couplings as well, of course. He was an experienced and passionate lover, as I remember.'

Caxton put a hand over her mouth to stifle an abrupt laugh. 'You think I was sleeping with him? Oh, come on.'

'It's an age-old story, Officer. When you put a man and a woman together in a perilous situation they will be drawn together, as irresistibly as magnets. There's really no need to pretend that it was otherwise, dear. Honestly, I forgive you both. Good day.'

The phone rattled, an old-fashioned sound as if an antique handset were being placed on its receiver.

'Magnets! Yeah, maybe, except this magnet is a fucking lesbian,' Caxton howled, as if Astarte could still hear her. She slammed the steering wheel with the palm of her hand again and then, when she was finished fuming, got the car back on the road.

Astarte wouldn't talk to her. Wouldn't help her. Well, she thought, at least she and Clara would have something to laugh about over lunch. She couldn't remember the last time the two of them had shared a real laugh.

She hurried back to Harrisburg, to the PSP headquarters, and parked in the lot behind the building. A couple of troopers were having lunch at a picnic table by the rear door – men with close-shaved heads wearing fleece-collared standard-issue jackets, their Smokey Bear hats sitting next to them on the benches. They were eating big hoagies full of ham and provolone cheese, and Caxton's mouth started watering when she saw them. She hadn't eaten anything all day, and though her morning nap had thrown off her sense of time it couldn't convince her stomach she wasn't hungry.

'Trooper,' one of the men said when they caught sight of her. He stood up, though he didn't salute. 'We heard about last night, and we just wanted to—'

'I'm okay, thanks,' Caxton said, barely slowing down. She pushed open the swinging doors and went inside, into a wave of furnace-heated air. She hadn't realized how cold it was outside until she came in. Her hands suddenly felt like icy, bony claws, so she rubbed them together until they started to hurt.

Down in the basement she saw Glauer organizing the library in the briefing room – he was probably desperate for something to do. She waved at him, then headed into her own office at the end of the hall. It was a cramped little space, its cinder-block walls painted glaring white, but the paint had chipped, revealing a sickly beige underneath. They had the same color and texture as rice crackers. Heavily insulated pipes ran across the ceiling and down one wall. Ever since autumn had turned to winter sometimes they dripped on her desk and even, alarmingly, on the monitor of her computer. The only thing on the walls was the certificate she'd received when she graduated from the academy, making her an official state trooper. Maybe the Feds would give her one for her ascension to special deputy, she thought.

She had just sat down at her desk and started paging through her email when a knock came on the door. She stared at the screen, at a very long email from the U.S. Marshals Service describing what kind of health insurance she was now eligible for, and called out, 'Come in, Glauer.'

The hands that grasped her shoulders from behind were female, though, with small, thin fingers. They dug into the muscles there, gouging away at the tight knots of her neck.

Caxton let her head fall forward and tried to enjoy the massage. 'You're fantastic,' she said. 'Nothing has ever felt this good.'

Clara laughed, then grabbed her chin and lifted her head for a deep, soulful kiss. 'Invite me to lunch more often and maybe you'll feel something even better.' The smaller woman's face clouded then. 'If you called me every day at a specific time, just to let me know you were alright—'

'— then you would just worry more than you do now if I was late making the call,' Laura replied, pulling her partner down onto her lap. She frowned. 'It was pretty bad. I'm sure you heard all the gory details. But I know what I'm doing.'

'What's this?' Clara asked.

Laura looked down and saw her running one thumb over the badge on her lapel.

'I'm a special deputy now,' she said. 'I'm working for the Marshals Service. Apparently that makes me an honorary cowgirl.'

'A special deputy. Just like he was.'

Laura shook her head. 'It's just a formality, really. It gives me federal jurisdiction and apparently I can spend taxpayer money on the investigation. It's a tool. Something to help me do this job.'

'First he put you in danger. He made you his vampire bait. Then he made you a badass, a real vampire killer. Now you're turning into him for real. Maybe you'll end up just like he did. Willing to do anything to keep fighting. Willing to do horrible things.'

86

'No, no, no,' Laura said, pulling Clara into a tight hug, burying her face in her girlfriend's neck. 'It's not like that.' But it was, of course. She had to become more like Jameson every day. She had to – the alternative was getting killed in some stupid way or, worse, far worse, letting the vampires get away.

'Let's just go to lunch. It's already two o'clock.' Clara pulled away and stood up. She leaned against the door of the office, not even looking at Laura. 'Is there someplace you want to go to? What about that Greek place?'

Laura bit her lower lip. She got the message that Clara was sending – the conversation was over. They would talk about nothing but gossip and trivia at lunch and not address any of their real problems. She could play that game, too. 'That place is so expensive, though.'

'Considering how often you take me to lunch, we can afford it.'

Laura stood up and started putting her more lethal gear away in a cupboard by her desk – her handgun, her pepper spray, her collapsible ASP baton. All she needed for lunch was her wallet and her cell phone. 'Actually,' she said, 'I've been thinking about that. About a way we could have lunch together almost every day.'

She followed Clara out into the hallway. Clara turned to look at her with mistrusting eyes but half a smile. 'Really?'

'Yeah,' Laura began, but just then Glauer came running up the hall. 'You need to see these,' he insisted, and shoved a heavy plastic bag into her arms, so forcefully that he nearly shoved her backwards. She looked down at the bag and saw it contained three spiral-bound notebooks, the top one stained with a bloom of dried blood.

16.

'Jesus, Glauer. I thought I told you to drop this.' Caxton had humored him enough to take the bag into the briefing room and spread its contents over some of the desks. One of the notebooks literally came apart in her hands and turned into a pile of random sheets of paper. The bloodstained one proved hard to open – the blood had soaked right through the pages, and each time she turned to a new leaf the notebook would creak and rip and spill shiny maroon powder down her pantleg. She quickly put that notebook down and took up the one that was in the best shape. Rexroth – or Carboy, that was his real name – had decorated its cover with a crude picture showing a jack-o'-lantern with vicious fangs, much like a vampire's. 'I guess this was the Halloween issue,' Caxton said, flipping open the cover.

The next page contained only six words, but they were inscribed in giant jagged letters, outlined and embellished liberally. They'd been written in ballpoint pen, and Carboy had pressed down so hard that he'd torn the paper in places. The message was simple enough:

LAURA CAXTON WILL DIE
ON HALLOWEEN!!!!!

Caxton grunted. She didn't know how to react to that. So she turned to the next page. This proved to be some kind of journal entry, written in a cramped, sloping hand she could barely make out. The corners of the page were decorated with crude line drawings of vampires. One of them had baby-sized legs sticking out of its mouth. She studied the text and quickly found her name, repeated several times, usually in the middle of an elaborate threat. 'Laura Caxton is going to, to,' she read. 'What's this? Oh, I'm going to *pay*. I'm also, apparently, going to bleed – it's repeated three times – and then he's going to dance in my blood wearing his favorite pair of boots. He's going to chop me into tiny bits, and when the kids come by on Halloween he's going to give pieces of me away as treats. Apparently I deserve this because of what I did to Kevin Scapegrace. Interesting.'

'You remember that name?' Glauer asked. 'Scapegrace?'

'Yeah. Of course I do. Teenaged vampire.' She shrugged. 'He went down as quick as the rest of them.' Her bravado couldn't quite keep her from drawing her shoulders in closer to her body and wrapping her arms around her chest. Scapegrace had captured her and tortured her before he died. She didn't like to think about it.

'I think you should read the rest,' Glauer insisted. 'I haven't had a chance to go through it all myself, but—'

'No,' she said.

'What do you mean? This doesn't worry you?' he asked, turning the page to show her a picture of a state trooper hanging from a noose, her Smokey Bear hat still perched on her head even though her face had turned blue and her tongue hung out of her mouth. 'This doesn't bother you?'

'It would bother me a lot more if Carboy wasn't already in

89

custody,' she admitted. 'But he is. So – so what? According to this I was supposed to die by Halloween, and that was over a month ago. He was late even by his own schedule.' She grabbed the cop's arm. 'Listen. I appreciate your concern. But Dylan Carboy was just a lonely kid with nothing better to do than scribble threats in a journal and fantasize about being a vampire. He probably got my name out of the newspaper and just fixated on it. It's truly sad that nobody stopped him before he got as far as he did, but now he's going to jail, probably for the rest of his life, and I'm safe.' She dropped the notebook on one of the desks. 'Now put this all back together and take it back to Mechanicsburg.'

Glauer shook his head. 'I think that would be a mistake. There's something here. I can feel it. Just let me take one more look,' he pleaded.

Caxton rolled her eyes. 'Fine. But you don't have a lot of time to waste here. After last night things are going to get very busy, very fast. In fact, you'd better come to lunch with us – we have a lot to talk about.'

Clara had been waiting outside the briefing room the whole time. She looked slightly confused when she heard that Glauer was going to join them, but she said she didn't mind at all. She and the giant cop had always gotten along, though they rarely saw each other.

Caxton and Glauer took her Mazda – Clara had come in her own car – and drove out to the Greek place, which was only a few minutes away. Over dolmades and feta she told the two of them about Fetlock and her battlefield promotion.

'They can just do that? Wave a wand and, poof, you're a Fed?' Glauer asked. 'I thought you had to take all kinds of tests and then go through their academy and everything.' Back when Caxton had formed the SSU she had tried to get Glauer made into an instant state trooper and been told the process was much more complicated. Technically he was still on the payroll of the Gettysburg Borough Police Department, though the PSP reimbursed Gettysburg for his salary and he hadn't checked in with his chief in weeks.

'Apparently the Marshals do it differently. It's just like a sheriff riding into town and deputizing the local gunslingers to take down the black hats. It's just as temporary, too. For now, though, it makes me the national go-to person for all vampire cases, and it gives me some police powers I never thought I'd have.'

'Okay,' Glauer said, 'but what does it mean for us?'

'Well, first things first. We're both getting a big raise.' The three of them smiled at that. 'It also means I can finally, officially hire you on.' She reached across the table and shook his hand. 'Welcome aboard. Fetlock tells me I can hire anyone I want, including somebody to do all our paperwork.'

'That'll be a relief,' Glauer laughed. He picked up his large Diet Coke and sipped thirstily at it. 'You're probably going to want to bring in some other people, too, right? I can recommend some guys we should have with us. Johnson, from Erie – he used to be a linebacker in high school, he's one tough son of a gun.' Glauer shifted his own massive bulk around on the chair – he barely fit in it. 'Then there's Eddie Davis, from Troop K. I've never seen anybody who could drive like that guy, he could be your automobile specialist, and—'

'Actually,' Caxton said, 'I kind of like having most of our people just be on call. I want to build a core team of just a few people. I was thinking three of us. You, me, and her,' she said, grabbing Clara's wrist.

Clara had been tearing her paper napkin into a pile of tiny pieces. 'Bullshit,' she said.

Caxton frowned. 'What do you mean?'

91

Clara looked to Glauer for support. 'You're spouting bullshit. What do you mean, me? I'm not part of your team.'

'I'd like you to be, though,' Caxton said.

'To do what? Every time I see a vampire I can scream, so you know it's nearby? Or maybe I can startle them with the flashbulb of my camera. That's what I do, Laura. I take pictures of crime scenes and dead bodies and gross stuff. I'm very good at it, but I don't think you need a photographer in your core team.'

'You could be my forensics guy. Like on *CSI: Miami*,' Caxton said. 'You could do all my hair and fiber and DNA research.' The idea had come to her when Fetlock had mentioned his own forensics team.

Clara just laughed. 'Huh? You do realize those guys go to school for that. They're scientists. They train for years and years and read scientific journals and go to conferences to talk to other eggheads about just how many legs a certain species of cockroach has. I went to Slippery Rock for art photography, and I don't even use anything I learned.'

Caxton shook her head. 'I don't expect you to just pick it all up by reading a couple of websites about forensics. But you can coordinate with the people the Marshals Service uses. You can manage them – you know a lot more about vampires than they do, by now, so you can tell them what to look for, or how to interpret what they find.'

'There are so many people better qualified than me,' Clara protested. 'Why on earth would you pick me for this?'

'You said we weren't spending enough time together,' Caxton admitted. 'You said I spent all my time at work and never got to see you at home. Well, this way we'd both be at work all the time. We could see each other a lot.'

Clara shook her head in disbelief.

'Well?' Caxton asked. 'Are you going to give me an answer?'

'No!' Clara said. 'At least – not right away.'

92

17.

They polished off a good-sized moussaka without saying much more. Clara excused herself before the baklava arrived, saying she had to get back to work. 'That goes for us, too,' Caxton told Glauer. 'Come on. We can take dessert to go.'

The two of them headed back to HQ together, Caxton enumerating the things they had to get done as she drove. 'We have to try to make some kind of ID on the half-dead from the motel. There's not a lot to work with, but maybe we can get some idea of what he looked like and run it against the missing persons list. Who knows, maybe we'll turn up a match. Then there's the field out behind the motel – I had it searched once, but maybe we missed something in the dark. Get some people over there to have a look around. When you get a chance we need to contact the Feds and see if they have a file on Angus Arkeley – he said he had some trouble with the law a while back. He wasn't clear on whether he'd actually been processed or convicted, but there might be something there. Oh, and I put a guard on his body, but they need to be relieved, so find somebody who can go over to the morgue and take care of that. I'm going to try to get in touch with his family and get permission to have him cremated as soon as he's been autopsied.' It was standard practice to cremate the remains of vampire victims. Otherwise the vampire could call them up as half-deads whenever he chose.

By the time they got back to the HQ building it was already four o'clock. The sun was starting to set and pink clouds streaked the sky. Stepping out of her car, Caxton studied the horizon as if there were some clue there. Night was falling, which meant Jameson Arkeley would be active again. He had killed at least twice so far. Would he kill again tonight? she wondered.

All vampires started as people with individual personalities, with moral codes all their own. Eventually they ended up all the same. How long had Jameson lasted before he killed his first victim? Probably longer than most. He had fought it, she was sure, with every fiber of his being. He must have spent night after night curled around himself in his lair, desperate to go outside, to hunt, but knowing what it would make him.

Then again – maybe he had given in early. Maybe he had known it was inevitable, and decided it wasn't worth torturing himself just so a few humans could live another day. Vampires saw death – human death – through a very different lens than she did. For vampires, human beings were simply prey. Game animals to be culled as needed. Angus had been given the option of becoming one of the predators. When he refused that gift, Jameson must have seen death as the next best thing for his brother.

She shivered uncontrollably.

'You okay, Caxton?' Glauer asked.

She blinked her eyes and looked away from the sunset. Phosphor afterimages glared behind her eyelids. 'I'm fine. Let's get inside.'

Down in the basement she booted up her computer and started composing her report of the previous night's events. When she'd worked with Arkeley, when they took down Malvern's brood, and later when she'd defended Gettysburg during the massacre, she had never worried so much about paperwork. Maybe Jameson had filed reports every night, but she'd been mostly concerned with staying alive. Now that she was head of the SSU she wasn't able to avoid it anymore. The Commissioner of State Police demanded constant updates on her investigation and forms filled out every time she discharged her weapon. Every time she discovered a body she had to fill out a Non-Traffic Death Investigation Report, a much more complicated form than the traffic fatality reports she'd filled out as a highway patrol officer. It took her hours every day to type up all the necessary official files, and hours more to create files for the SSU database. She'd actually taken a touch-typing course at the academy in Hershey just to speed things up, but still much of her day was filled up with bureaucratic nonsense.

At five o'clock, when people with normal jobs finished their days (or so she believed, having never held a normal job herself), she sat back in her chair and rubbed the bridge of her nose. She was just getting started.

When Fetlock came up behind her and cleared his throat she jumped and banged her knees against the underside of her desk.

'Deputy Marshal,' she said, remembering how she was supposed to greet him. 'I was just writing up a report.'

He nodded and came to lean against the edge of her desk. 'I'll want a copy, of course. Send it to my email.' He stuck a business card between two rows of keys on her keyboard. 'In fact, send me every document you create from now on. Just so the Marshals Service has a record.'

'Yeah, of course,' she said. 'So I have Officer Glauer – I

95

think you met him at the SSU briefing – Officer Glauer is organizing the mopping up at the motel crime scene. He'll head over there tomorrow and see what we missed in the dark. I haven't heard yet from your forensics people—'

'They've come and gone already, Special Deputy,' Fetlock said. 'They'll have something for you tomorrow.'

Caxton nodded. 'In the meantime I have a guard on Angus' body and—'

'Fine,' he said.

She frowned, not understanding. 'You don't want to hear this?'

'Not particularly. Like we said, it's your investigation. I didn't come by to check up on you, if that's what you think.' He smiled warmly down at her. 'I may do things a little differently than other people you've worked for. A little more hands-off. Actually, I just came down to give you this.'

He handed her a manila envelope with her name on it. She opened it, hoping he might have brought her something useful – a description, perhaps, of the man who had stolen all of Jameson's files from the USMS archives. Instead she found a thick brochure, printed cheaply on newsprint. It was a federal government employee manual, laying out among other things the nature of her employment as an independent contractor and information on civil servant pay grades.

'Oh. Thanks,' she said.

'You need to sign the last page and fax it to me as soon as you get a chance.'

She nodded. Then she started to laugh. She couldn't help herself. He smiled at her as if he didn't understand. 'I'm sorry,' she said, clutching her lips. 'It's just that . . .' She shook her head, unable to go on. 'Less than twenty-four hours ago I was fighting for my life. Now I'm supposed to be thinking about pension plans.'

He stood up from the desk and shot the cuffs of his suit. He looked mildly annoyed.

'I am sorry,' she said, getting control of herself. 'I'll make this a priority. Now, was there anything else—' She stopped as her cell phone started ringing. She looked up at him and he shrugged.

She took the phone out of her pocket and saw the incoming call was from Astarte Arkeley. *This ought to be good*, she thought. Maybe the old bat wanted to accuse her of adultery again.

She flipped the phone open. 'Hello, ma'am.'

Astarte's voice on the other end was very tinny and distorted by heavy static. She caught very little of what the woman said. ' – Deputy, I – assistance – most serious—'

Caxton swore under her breath. She'd forgotten what lousy reception she got down in the basement. 'Hold on, ma'am. I can't really hear you. Give me a second and I'll try to move to a better location.'

Mouthing *I'm sorry* at Fetlock, she stepped out of her office and headed for the stairs. Astarte kept talking. Maybe she hadn't heard what Caxton said.

' – really quite – wouldn't have, if not—'

In the stairwell she lost another bar of the signal, so she rushed up the stairs two at a time. At the top she pushed open the door and stepped into the main lobby of the headquarters building. Troopers in various states of uniform were congregating there around the duty sergeant's desk, probably receiving their orders for the night.

Caxton pushed through them and out the front door into a flurry of snow and darkness. Four bars. Good. 'Ma'am, can you repeat all that?' Caxton said. 'I'm very sorry about the bad connection.'

'There's no time,' Astarte said. Her voice sounded strained, but it wasn't the phone. 'I told you already – he's here!'

18.

'Mrs Arkeley, please, stay on the line,' Caxton said, then took the phone away from her face. She rushed back inside the HQ building and pointed at the first trooper she saw. 'You – get Officer Glauer up here. He's in the basement.' She pointed at another and said, 'You, call the local cop shop in Bellefonte and tell them there's an emergency.' She checked her phone and gave them Astarte's number so they could do a reverse look-up and get the address. She hated to send local cops into a vampire scene – they wouldn't be ready for what they found – but she had no choice. It would take her more than an hour to get there herself, even if she sped recklessly the whole way. Astarte's life might hang on a balance of minutes.

'Ma'am, Astarte, are you still there?' she asked, lifting the phone to her face again.

'Yes, dear. Momentarily. He's outside the house right now.' Caxton heard a distant chiming sound. 'Ah! He just broke a window in the kitchen, I believe. You're not going to make it in time, are you?'

'I have people on the way. If he sees the police coming he'll probably scare off out of there,' Caxton said, trying to make herself sound as if she believed it. 'I'm coming as fast as I can. Lock yourself in somewhere, if you can – anything to slow him down.'

'Then you think he was serious, when he said my only other option was death? Yes, Laura, I can hear it in your voice. It's odd. I'd always assumed that when my time came I would greet the Reaper with arms wide open.'

'Get somewhere safe, as safe as you can,' Caxton said. 'I'm coming!'

Glauer came thumping up the stairs and rushed out into the lobby. He didn't need to be told what was going on – when Caxton beckoned him and ran out into the parking lot he just followed.

A thin layer of powdery snow had covered her Mazda when she reached it. She didn't have time to brush it off. Climbing inside, she grabbed the blue flasher she kept for emergencies and clamped it on the roof of the car, then plugged it into the cigarette lighter. She didn't have a siren built into the car, but the light would at least keep them from getting pulled over on the way. She waited for Glauer to cram himself into the small passenger seat, then slammed on the accelerator and tore out of the parking lot and shot out toward the highway. The windshield wipers made short work of the snow in front of her, but new drifts kept piling up on the hood. At the on ramp she fought her way through the midst of the rush-hour traffic – for once people actually got out of the way when they saw the flasher – and raced up the fast lane, heading northeast.

'It's Jameson's wife. His widow. His whatever,' Caxton explained. Glauer hadn't asked, but she figured he must be wondering where they were going in such an all-fired hurry.

'She's under attack.' She risked a glance over at him. He sat patiently looking straight ahead, his hands on the dashboard to brace himself every time she stepped on the brake. 'From what I heard she hasn't got a lot of time.'

Glauer took a look at the speedometer. 'We'll make it,' he promised, though he must know as well as she did that he was just being optimistic.

She tossed her cell phone to him. 'Coordinate with the locals. Bellefonte can't have much of a police force; it's a tiny little place. Isn't there a state police barracks out there, though?'

He flipped open the phone. 'Yeah. At Rockview Station. That's just a couple miles from town.' He made the calls, got people moving. Before she was halfway to Bellefonte he had three patrol cars headed for the scene, and two more cars with a pair of local cops each already parked out front. 'There's no answer at the door. They want authorization to force entry. Do I send them in?' he asked.

They'll probably get killed if they do, she thought. Astarte would definitely get killed if they didn't. 'Yeah,' she said. 'But tell them – tell them to be careful. Tell them to treat this like they're breaching a survivalist compound full of gun nuts. Tell them not to get themselves killed if they can help it.'

Confirmation came back shortly that the troopers were leading an assault on the house, with the locals covering their backs. It would be long tense minutes before they heard anything more, but Caxton grabbed the phone out of Glauer's hand and held it against the steering wheel, ready to answer the moment anyone called.

She tried to focus on her driving. The road conditions weren't great – lots of thin crystalline snow blowing across the road, patches of black ice every time she crossed a bridge or a sketchy piece of highway. The Mazda wasn't built for that

100

kind of driving to begin with, and at her speed – eighty or better – it would slip and slide the second she let up a little on her grip on the wheel. She had to cut her speed drastically as she tore through State College. The road went right through the university town and she couldn't risk hitting any students. Once she was past the Nittany Mall, though, she pushed the car back up to its limit.

The phone rang in her hand and she nearly lost control. No time for the hands-free unit, she decided, and pushed it up against her ear, holding it there with her shoulder. 'Go ahead,' she nearly screamed.

'Trooper?' the voice on the other end asked, sounding slightly surprised. 'Is that you?' The voice was deep and rasping and she didn't recognize it at first.

'Special Deputy, actually. What's going on over there?'

'They made you a Special Deputy. That's fascinating. I spent my adult life thinking I was unique, that no one else could fulfill my special purpose. Yet practically the moment I was gone, destiny just plugged someone else into the empty socket. Have we come full circle?'

'Oh, fuck,' Caxton said. Her foot eased off the accelerator. She was suddenly too scared to drive as fast as she'd been going. 'Jameson. It's you, isn't it?'

'That's a question for the philosophers. My wife seemed to think not.'

Caxton swallowed thickly. If it was Jameson on the phone, if he had somehow acquired the phone belonging to the lead of the state trooper team, that meant a lot of very bad things were also true. 'You came for Astarte. You offered her the same choice you gave Angus, didn't you? Become like you, or die. And she also refused.'

'It's probably best if you stay away from my family for a while, Special Deputy. You're on your way here right now, I presume.

101

It would be better if you just turned around and went home. Of course, we both know you won't.'

'When I get there will you be waiting for me?' she asked. She wasn't sure if she wanted him to be there or not. The last time they'd met she'd put two nine-millimeter slugs in his heart and it hadn't done the trick. Would three work? Would the whole clip of fifteen in her Beretta be enough?

'I'm going to do my level best not to kill you yet, Special Deputy. I have a reason to want to keep you alive. But if you put yourself in harm's way I can't be held responsible anymore for your safety.'

'Stay there. I'm very close now,' she said, her pulse pounding in her temples. 'Stay there and we can finish what we started. You didn't want to become this monster, Jameson. Do you remember that? You accepted the curse to do one last good deed. To be a hero one more time. You've undone all that now, but it doesn't have to go any further. We can still salvage something of your reputation.'

She was talking to dead air. The phone beeped at her twice, telling her the connection had been terminated.

She dropped the phone and screamed, pounding against the steering wheel with her hands. Glauer reached over to take the wheel away from her, but she shook herself violently and said, 'Don't. I'm alright.'

She wasn't, of course. Not in the slightest. But she could still drive.

19.

The roads were nearly empty as they tore into Bellefonte, racing up Water Street where it followed Spring Creek. By moonlight, sprinkled with snow, the town was eerily beautiful. Caxton had driven past the built-up section of riverbank at the western end of town a thousand times and admired the gazebo and the parks there, but never before had it looked so spectral, so haunting.

Stop that, she told herself. She was letting the night's events get to her. She yanked out the cord of the blue flasher as she turned down a side road, cutting her speed to a bare crawl. 'There's a shotgun in the trunk,' she told Glauer.

'I thought this was your personal car,' he said.

She shrugged. 'The last two months have been all business. It's loaded and there's a box of shells there too. You grab those the second I stop the car, then follow my lead. This is not going to be fun.'

'Got it,' he said.

She took them down a street lined with massive trees that sheltered Victorian houses topped with mansard roofs and elaborate gables. Astarte's house wasn't hard to find. She just looked for the one with all the police cars parked out front.

Caxton stopped the Mazda well back, parking in the middle of the street in case she needed to make a quick getaway – or in case anyone else tried the same thing. Her car would block the main route back to the highway. It was a trick she'd learned in a course on tactical parking at the academy. She killed her lights and wrestled her Beretta out of its holster before she set a foot on the pavement. She didn't watch Glauer get out of the car – her eyes were fixed on the street before the house – but she could hear him moving to the trunk. She could count on him, she knew. It was why they worked so well together. He always did exactly what she wanted.

Keeping her weapon low but ready, she moved quickly to the nearest cop car – one of the local units. Its flashers cycled wildly on its roof and its radio crackled with occasional calls from the Bellefonte dispatcher, but the seats were all empty, front and back. She moved to the next car, the other local patrol cruiser, and heard that its engine was still running. It was as empty as the first one, but there was blood on the windshield. The inside of the windshield.

The Bellefonte cops hadn't even had a chance to get out of their car before Jameson was on them like a cat on a flock of pigeons. She bit her lip and tried not to think about the fact that she had authorized their approach. She was directly responsible for whatever had happened to them, but she could worry about that later.

Farther up the street the three state police cars made a roadblock across the eastern end of the street. Their flashers and engines were off, but she could see right away they were empty too. She didn't see any bodies anywhere, nor any pieces of bodies. There was some more blood on the snow that covered Astarte's lawn, but not enough of it to account for all

104

the cops. There had been three state troopers and four local cops on the assault – seven men and no sign of any of them.

It wasn't like a vampire to clean up his own mess. She considered the fact that some of them might still be alive. If so she had to move fast. Beckoning to Glauer with a hand signal, she rushed up the steps of Astarte's porch and threw herself against the green clapboard wall just to the left side of the door. There was a plaque there of polished brass, showing the outline of a hand crisscrossed with curving lines. Underneath was written:

MADAME ASTARTE
READINGS AND ADVICE
BY APPOINTMENT ONLY

Glauer came thundering up the steps to take up position on the right side of the door. He had the shotgun cradled in his arms, his pockets stuffed full of extra shells.

'There's probably a back door. We do this just like in Mechanicsburg, okay?' she whispered. His shotgun would be little use against Jameson, but she doubted the vampire would rush right into its firing cone either. 'You take the back, and don't let anybody out. If I give the signal you come inside fast, loaded for bear.'

'What's the signal?' he asked.

'If I start screaming, that's the signal,' she told him.

He nodded and ducked around the side of the porch, his boots clomping on the boards. When she couldn't hear his footfalls anymore she kicked open the door.

It was unlocked – the state troopers had already breached it for her – and she was inside in less time than it took for her heart to beat twice.

A single lamp at the far end of the room bathed the front

hall in an orange light. It dazzled her eyes for a moment and she turned away to let her pupils adjust. It was warm inside, warm enough to make her uncomfortable in her winter coat. When she could see clearly again she looked around and saw a Persian carpet on the floor and overstuffed armchairs around a round wooden table. It looked like the perfect setup for a séance. To her left a grand staircase curled up toward a second-floor gallery. On the wall before her hung a huge tapestry, black with gold embroidery showing a snake swallowing its own tail. Inscribed in the circle the snake made were the words WE SHALL ALL RETURN.

Caxton looked up the stairs. She could almost imagine Astarte making a stately entrance down the wooden steps, wearing a dowdy old dress, her hair up in a loose bun. It was how she had imagined the woman when they spoke on the phone, though honestly, she had no idea what Jameson's widow actually looked like.

Doors led off the foyer in three directions, but they were all closed. Jameson could be hiding behind any of them, she knew. Forcing herself to breathe calmly, she tried to pay attention to the hairs on the back of her arms, to the sensitive skin behind her ears. If he was close she would feel him, feel the aura of wrongness that vampires exuded. She made herself wait for five seconds before she decided she couldn't feel a thing.

Then she heard something and nearly jumped out of her skin. It was a very soft sound, a faint pattering, reminding her of the sound snow made when it fell. It came from the base of the stairs. Caxton moved closer, but the shadows cast by the single lamp made it impossible for her to see anything there. She reached into her pocket and took out her Mag-Lite. Switching it on, she played its beam across the bottom three steps.

106

The sound came again. She twitched her light to the left and saw where it was coming from. A thin trickle of blood was dripping down the steps, dropping gently on each riser. She lifted the light higher and followed the trail of blood all the way up to the landing above.

Trying to move quietly, trying not to breathe too raggedly, she started up the stairs, keeping her feet on the woven runner that lined each step. Keeping her flashlight handy, she brought her gun up to the level of her shoulders, ready to shoot anything that popped its head over the banister. When she reached the landing she turned left, then right, covering both ends of the gallery, but nothing showed itself.

The blood trail started under a doorway directly ahead of her. It gleamed in electric light that shone around the edge of the door, which stood slightly ajar. Caxton tapped the door gently with the back end of her Mag-Lite and it swung easily back and away from her, revealing the room beyond.

The light inside wasn't much brighter than the single lamp down in the foyer. It showed her enough, though: A narrow room almost filled by a large four-poster bed and a chest of drawers. A tall stand that looked like a perch for a parrot or some other kind of bird, currently unoccupied. Framed black-and-white photographs hung on the walls, but Caxton didn't bother to examine their subjects.

Lying on the bed was a woman about forty-five years old. She was dressed smartly in a maroon mid-length skirt and a black silk blouse. Her chin-length hair was almost pure silver, save for a single streak of coal black that curled around her very pale cheek. Her eyes stared at the ceiling, but they didn't see anything. The blood that pooled on the floor and ran out onto the landing came from her right arm, which hung down from the side of the bed so the curled fingers almost brushed the rug.

107

Her wrist had been torn open right to the artery. As bad as the wound was, considering what vampiric teeth were capable of the wound looked almost gentle, as if Jameson had retained enough humanity to want to make his wife's passing as painless as he could. Caxton checked the woman for a pulse and found none, as she had expected. He had always been thorough. There was no doubt in Caxton's mind that this was Astarte, and that her husband had been her murderer.

Caxton closed her eyes and lowered her weapon. 'I'm sorry,' she said. 'I tried to make it here in time.' Foolish, she knew, talking to a corpse. Yet the feeling that she had failed here, that the woman's death was her fault, could not be shaken.

She turned to go. There were plenty of other rooms to be searched, and maybe some actual evidence to be turned up. She took a step out of the room and then another toward the stairs.

Below her, in the foyer, the single burning lamp was smashed just then and darkness closed on the first floor like a curtain being drawn. Caxton heard someone moving down there, clumsily bouncing off the furniture, and someone else hiss in disgust. Two people, at least – and she didn't think either of them was Glauer.

20.

Caxton stepped backward into the room where she'd found Astarte's body. She thought about closing the door behind her, but the only light in the house was coming from the doorway. If she closed it, anyone downstairs would know she was there when the light was cut off. Instead she crouched on the far side of the bed, where anyone passing by the open door wouldn't be able to see her.

There was one problem with that, of course. There was no other way out of the room. She had got herself stuck in a corner with nowhere to go. Assuming the people downstairs intended her harm – a safe assumption, if there ever was one – they could come for her any time they liked and she would be hard-pressed to defend herself with her back up against the wall.

Jameson had taught her better than that. He'd taught her more than once not to get herself into exactly that situation. She needed to move. She needed to think straight. Fear was clogging up her brain. She needed to shake it out, to start being smart again.

What did she know? There were multiple persons inside the house with her. She was pretty sure none of them were vampires. The hair on her arms was lying flat and she had no sense at all of vampiric corruption nearby. That meant the intruders were probably half-deads. She could handle a couple of them without too much trouble. She'd learned a lot from Jameson about how to fight dirty and keep her opponents guessing. This wasn't going to be an easy fight, though. The intruders had darkened the house and presumably they were lying in wait for her, ready to ambush her as soon as she showed herself. She had no idea how many of them there were, either. A lone half-dead was weak and slow, but in groups the murderous bastards could be dangerous.

She thought about her options. She could rush down the stairs, make a break for the front door. Once through she could get to her car and escape. That was assuming they weren't waiting by the door, and that they hadn't left any traps for her along the way. It would be very stupid to make that assumption.

A far better plan would be to signal Glauer and have him come rushing in with a shotgun blast to scare the hell out of the intruders. Jameson had always maintained that half-deads were cowards at heart. If Glauer surprised them enough they might just scatter, allowing her to escape without actually having to fight them at all.

Caxton reached into her pocket for her cell phone, so she could call Glauer and set up a surprise attack. Her hand found the bottom of her pocket but didn't find the phone. She cursed silently when she realized she'd left it back in the car. She could still signal him by shouting for his help (screaming seemed undignified, even if that was the signal they'd agreed upon). Doing so would of course alert every half-dead in the area to her presence and give them a bead on her location.

110

They could be on her like a plague of locusts before Glauer could get through the door.

If the room she was in had possessed a window she could have opened it and looked down at the back of the house. From there she could have signaled Glauer somehow. The room did not possess a window. But maybe one of the other rooms on the second floor did.

It was worth a try, she decided. Moving slowly, keeping very low, she crept around the bed and past Astarte's dangling arm. She crouch-walked through the pool of blood on the floor – it made her a little queasy to think that she was walking through someone's spilt-out life, but she'd been through worse before – and out through the door.

She could hear the half-deads moving about below her on the ground floor. She heard drawers yanked open and what sounded like someone rummaging through a pile of cutlery. The half-deads were arming themselves, she thought, divvying up the steak knives in the kitchen. Their beady little eyes were probably shining with glee. Half-deads never used guns, because their decaying bodies lacked the coordination necessary for aiming a firearm. They loved knives, though. Passionately.

Keeping her back against the wall, Caxton slid to her right, toward the nearest door on the gallery. She passed across its width, then reached back to turn the cut-glass knob. The door opened with the barest of creaking noises, but she stopped and stood perfectly still, listening. The half-deads were still about their business in the kitchen – they must not have heard her. She pulled the door open further and peered inside.

Neat stacks of folded white blankets and tablecloths sat on shelves inside, smelling of old, clean cotton. She had found the linen closet.

No time to curse her luck, she thought. She glanced over

the gallery railing into the darkness below, looking for any sign of movement. The only light came from the flashers on the cruisers inside, which occasionally stabbed a blue or red beam through the first-floor windows. Anything could have been down there and she wouldn't have seen them, even if they were moving around; the strobelike effect of the flashers ruined her dark-adapted vision every time they cycled through.

Moving as silently as she could, she pushed onward to the next door down. Neither the light of the flashers nor the softer light from Astarte's room reached up that far. She had her Mag-Lite still, but she didn't dare use it. In the deep gloom she ran a hand over the door's polished surface, then found a brass plate with a keyhole in it. She lifted her hand a few inches and found a cracked porcelain knob that turned with a barely audible squeal. Slowly she opened the door, an inch or two at a time, ready to stop the instant the hinges creaked. Just a little more. Once she had it open wide enough she would slip in and close it just as carefully behind her.

A high-pitched scream tore through her consciousness and a once-human body slammed into her, knocking her down. She could only register that its breath was horrible as he pushed her down to the carpet. She saw a long weapon glint as it was raised high – a meat fork, it looked like, a foot long and with four wicked barbed tines – and then it was all she could do to throw her head to one side as the fork came down right where her left eye had been. The half-dead on top of her screamed again and she saw the tattered skin of its face jiggle, felt spittle fleck her cheeks and upper lip. It tried raising its fork for another attack but couldn't. The tines had gotten stuck in the wooden floor.

Caxton had been trained in some very basic martial arts, so she knew what to do next. She got one knee between her attacker's legs and pushed up with all her strength. Whether

112

half-deads had sensitive testicles or not was a moot point; the maneuver was intended to roll the thing off of her body, and it worked. She could have followed up by rolling on top of it and pinning its arms down, but she didn't bother taking the move that far. Instead she yanked her Beretta out of its holster and shoved the barrel up under the half-dead's chin. Its eyes went wide just before she squeezed the trigger, but afterward what was left of its face went slack.

She took a second to study the dead thing, trying to figure out who it had been and what it was doing in the house. One look at its clothes told her the whole story.

It was dressed in the gray shirt and navy blue pants of a Pennsylvania state trooper. One of her own. Jameson must have been waiting in the house when the troopers broke in. He would have made short work of them. Though she had tried to warn them what dangers awaited inside, she had known when she sent the troopers in that they weren't prepared or trained in how to fight a bloodthirsty monster. Once he killed them they had become his to play with, and he must have raised them from the dead even before Caxton arrived on the scene. That was why there had been no bodies in the cars out front – because the bodies had already been inside the house.

There could be as many as six more half-deads inside the house, then. She didn't have time to feel guilty.

As fast as she could, she rolled over and jumped to her feet. She peered through the door her attacker had come through and saw the room beyond, a kind of butler's pantry lined with cupboards. The room also contained a simple table, a few chairs, and at the far end a very narrow staircase leading down. She figured it had to go down to the kitchen. She could already hear more half-deads clattering up those steps.

She thought fast. A brass key stood in the keyhole on the

inside of the door. She yanked it out, slammed the door shut, and locked it from the outside. When the mechanism clicked she hit the key with the butt of her weapon, breaking it off inside the lock.

Her next move was easy to figure out. There was no more point in subterfuge. 'Glauer!' she shouted, as loud as she could, just in case he hadn't heard the gunshot. 'Glauer! Now!'

21.

The half-deads inside the butler's pantry hammered on the door and it shook wildly in its frame. It was constructed of thick oak, though, and Caxton thought it would hold awhile.

She rushed to the head of the stairs, still shouting for Glauer. She hoped he could hear her, through the walls of the house. If he couldn't she was in real trouble. She could hear more half-deads moving around on the ground floor, but she couldn't see anything. Sweeping her Mag-Lite around the base of the steps revealed nothing but faded carpet and motes of dust that twirled in the light's beam.

She was going to have to run down there and hope for the best. She had her Beretta, and plenty of ammunition, but she knew better than to think she could shoot accurately in the dark house. Holding her light high and her handgun low, she started down the stairs. She took them carefully, one at a time.

She was halfway down when a knife sailed past her cheek to clatter against the steps behind her. It passed so close to her skin that she could see the brass rivets in its wooden handle and the serrations on the blade – close enough that it made her weave over to one side and lose her balance. She stumbled down three stairs, her left hand lashing out for the banister. She caught it, but in the process her flashlight tumbled free and bounced down the steps. Its jumping, falling light caught the torn face of a half-dead for just a moment, showing the gray, twitching muscles beneath the raveled skin. The creature was smiling broadly – but then the light bounced away again and rolled to the bottom of the stairs, where a pale hand grabbed it up and switched it off.

Caxton crouched low in case another knife came flying up at her and fired two rounds wildly down at the monsters who lay in wait for her. One of them screamed, a high-pitched wail that made her nerves twist, a sound like a cat being thrown into an ice-cold bathtub. It wasn't a mortal scream, though. She must have just winged her target.

The flare of the gunshots was enough to dazzle her eyes and she was blind. Things had gone from bad to worse, and then they grew worse still. From above she heard the locked door splinter and crack and finally burst out of its frame. Hurried footsteps came rushing down the gallery toward her.

Unable to see, surrounded on every side, she did the only thing she could think of. Caxton's hand was still on the banister. She holstered her pistol, grabbed the banister with her other hand, and then vaulted over the side of the staircase into empty, lightless space.

Almost instantly her feet struck the top of the round séance table. Unable to see where she was going to land, she had braced herself to drop all the way to the carpet, maybe eight feet down. She hadn't been prepared for the table to be in the way, and her feet went out from under her. Painfully she struck the table with her side and then half rolled, half dropped to the carpeted floor.

'Where'd she go?' one of the half-deads demanded.

'I can't see her!' another replied.

Caxton knew from past experience that the half-deads could not see in the dark any better than she could. Unlike their vampiric masters, they were at as much of a disadvantage as she. Yet they benefited from the darkness anyway. Her only advantage had been the range of her Beretta, which would have allowed her to pick them off before they could reach her with their knives. In the blackness that advantage was lost – if she couldn't see, she couldn't aim. If she couldn't aim, she might be better served just swinging the butt of her handgun back and forth and hope she pistol-whipped them all to death.

She could try to find a light switch – but in the process she would probably knock over an ottoman or a candelabra or something and give away her position.

Where the hell was Glauer? She had gotten out of one ambush but only ended up in a spot nearly as bad. The little flashes of red and blue light coming in the windows showed her nothing at all where she lay behind the table. She could hear the half-deads moving through the foyer, spreading out to find her.

Time for another silent profanity to climb across her lips. When a victim was raised as a half-dead its soul died first, its personality wiped away and replaced with nothing but hatred and gleeful bloodlust. Yet it retained some part of his memory. These half-deads had been cops once. They'd been trained in how to search a room and how to keep a subject from escaping. She had no doubt they would cover the three doors that led off from the foyer. She had moments – mere seconds before she was surrounded.

Both ankles ached as she pushed herself up against the rear wall of the room and got her feet under her again. She didn't think any of her bones were broken, but even if they were she

117

needed to move fast. Thinking her best bet was to move toward the back of the house, she pushed her way along the wall, feeling for the tapestry she'd seen on her way in. There – her hand touched the cloth, grabbed a corner of it. The door was just on the far side. She reached forward for its knob – and then yanked her hand back when the door jumped and thudded as if someone behind it was hammering to get out.

'Over there!' a half-dead squeaked. She heard them come toward her, running through the dark. One hit a chair and went sprawling to the ground with a pathetic yelp, but the others kept coming on. Caxton didn't even know which way to run.

Then the door burst open and a powerful beam of light speared through into the foyer, lighting up two half-deads with steak knives raised high. The barrel of a shotgun came through the door next and it discharged with a roar, blasting Caxton's ears with its report and filling her nose and throat with the stink of gunpowder so that she coughed and gagged.

The two half-deads fell out of the beam of light and thunked to the floor, not even having a chance to scream their last.

Glauer burst through the open door, pumping his weapon for a second shot. Evidently he didn't see the third half-dead, the one that had tripped over the chair, coming straight at him with a fireplace poker.

Caxton reached out as fast as she could and grabbed the half-dead's arm. She twisted it back hard and the poker fell to clunk on the floor. She saw Glauer raise his shotgun and had time to shout for him to stop, but it was too late. The heavy wooden stock came down right between the half-dead's eyes and crushed in its skull.

'What do you mean, stop?' he asked when the creature dropped to the floor. He shone his heavy-duty flashlight in her face.

'I wanted to keep it alive for questioning,' she answered. She pushed the flashlight away. It was hurting her eyes. 'What took you so long?'

He shrugged amiably. 'There's about fifty doors in this place and they were all locked.'

It didn't matter. He was here now. Caxton did a quick calculation in her head. 'There were seven of them originally, assuming Jameson raised them all.'

'Seven? There were seven cops called to this scene—'

Apparently he was just figuring out whom he'd been fighting. She raised a hand for silence. 'I got one upstairs.' She grabbed the light out of his hands and pointed it at the two on the floor, their bodies twisted around by the shotgun blast and completely lifeless. She pointed it again at the one with the knocked-in skull. 'That's four.'

'Two more of them tried to get me back in the kitchen,' Glauer said. 'Check this out.' He tried to show her a bad cut on his arm. 'Went right through my jacket and my shirt. Just a little paring knife, but that guy wanted me bad.'

'Six, then, all dead – and one left,' Caxton counted, too busy to worry about his arm. She spun around with a sudden intuition and pointed the light at the front door. It hung open to the night. 'Come on, hurry,' she said, and sprinted out across the porch and down into the street.

At first she saw nothing, just the cars piled up in the road. She had expected the last half-dead to steal one and make a break for it, and had just hoped it wouldn't be the Mazda the monster chose. All the cars were in their proper places, though.

'There,' Glauer said, and pointed at the road. A thin layer of new powdery snow had coated the street since they'd arrived. A trail of boot prints curved away from the house and off to the west, toward the highway. Glauer started for the passenger side of her car, but she shook her head. 'No time for that. We can catch him on foot.'

She raced down the street, her eyes bleary with the light from the streetlamps and the glare off the snow after the darkness in the house. She had no trouble following the trail, however – the footprints were dark against the snowy street and they headed due west, never weaving back and forth, never turning as if the half-dead had looked over his shoulder to see if he were being pursued.

She had a bad feeling she knew what that meant. Half-deads for all their wicked humor and spite were bound to the whims of vampires. They could no more resist the commands of their masters than they could make themselves alive and whole again. This one wasn't just escaping a hopeless fight – no, it would have stayed until the bitter end if Jameson had so desired. It was carrying out some other order.

She ran as fast as she could, her work shoes slipping constantly in the wet slush. She hadn't had a chance to put on proper boots. Glauer came chugging along behind her, more sure-footed but not as quick. Yet it was he who first caught sight of the half-dead ahead of them.

He shouted and pointed and Caxton followed his finger. There, a block ahead, the half-dead was moving fast. It was limping badly and one of its pant legs had been torn away. It had a nasty bloodless wound in its calf, where part of the muscle had been blown away. It must, she realized, be the one she had wounded with her wild shots on the stairs. Yet as crippled as it was, it forced itself along, forced itself to keep moving.

She had closed the distance to half a block when she realized they were about to run out of road. The street ahead curved southward to follow the creek, but the half-dead wasn't turning with it. It hurried on forward in a straight line.

She tried to sprint after it and nearly fell on her face. 'Glauer – grab it, quick,' she called, and the big cop shot past her, puffing mightily. She raced after them both and arrived at the built-up edge of the creek just in time to watch the half-dead jump awkwardly over the edge and split the dark water like a falling stone. It disappeared with a gurgling whine and was immediately lost from view.

Glauer started to pull off his jacket as if he would jump in after it, but she grabbed his arm and yanked him back. 'Don't be an idiot,' she said, breath surging in and out of her chest. 'You'd freeze to death in minutes.'

'But it's getting away!' Glauer cried back.

'No it isn't,' Caxton knew. She understood right away what Jameson had demanded of his creature.

She didn't know if the icy water would have hurt it, but she knew half-deads didn't breathe. She imagined they weren't very buoyant. It must have sunk like a stone. Under the water its brain would freeze and that would be the end of its short un-life. 'Back when we were working together – I mean, Jameson and me – it was standard practice to try to capture half-deads. That was our best source of information. He knew I would want to talk to this one, and he made damned sure I didn't get the chance.'

Raleigh

I have been long waiting for you. At last you have come.
Tonight I shall feast; before long we will feast together.
E. F. Benson, *The Room in the Tower*

22.

Caxton and Glauer trudged back toward the house through the snow. It had grown significantly colder since they'd arrived in Bellefonte, and the sky had turned heavy and the color of lead. The snow flurry that had come just after dark had stopped, but it looked as if the clouds weren't done for the night.

'What's our next step?' Glauer asked, his voice nearly lost under the noise of their shoes crunching the powdery snow. It sounded like teeth grinding together to Caxton, teeth gnashing and tearing.

She shook her head. It was only seven o'clock, but it felt much later. 'We secure the scene. Call in the necessary people and wait for them to arrive.'

'I meant—' Glauer began, but then he just shook his head.

They walked the rest of the way in silence. Astarte's house remained just as they'd left it. The cars out front had gained a thin skin of snow that diffused the light of the red and blue flashers so that instead of stabbing out at the night they just glowed fitfully, first one color, then the other. Glauer wanted

125

to switch off the engines of the cars, but Caxton said no – it was important to maintain the integrity of the scene, down to the last detail.

She made the required phone calls. A lone officer of the local police department came quickly, but he did little beyond stringing up some yellow caution tape. He didn't go inside the house at all. Ambulances arrived on scene next, but the paramedics had to wait for the local coroner's office to officially pronounce everyone dead. A technician from the morgue arrived half an hour later, an annoyed-looking doctor in a fur-lined parka with the hood up. He went inside the house and came back out five minutes later. He just nodded to the paramedics and they went inside. Not that there was much for them to do.

Lights came on in other houses up and down the street. Anxious-looking people peered out of their windows, but none of them came down to have a look for themselves. Glauer offered to canvass the neighborhood, knocking on doors and asking if anyone had seen anything. 'I doubt anybody did,' he said, 'but it'll calm them down if they have somebody to actually talk to.' Caxton cared very little what Astarte's neighbors thought, but it was something for the big cop to do, and she let him go with a sigh of relief. He'd been pacing up and down the sidewalk, looking like he had something to say but never actually coming out and saying it.

Her own tension kept mounting, and she just wanted to get away. It was nighttime – it was going to be nighttime for another twelve hours – and she knew she wouldn't relax until dawn came. There was work to be done, but she couldn't leave, not until she could hand the scene over to someone officially capable of taking charge. Before she knew it she herself was pacing. The exercise kept her joints from freezing up if nothing else.

An unmarked late-model car drove up and she squinted through the headlights, trying to see who was inside. There were two occupants, a man and a woman. She was very surprised when she saw them get out of the car – it was Fetlock and Vesta Polder.

The deputy marshal nodded at her, then walked over to talk to the local cop, who was standing guard at the front of the house. Vesta came straight over to Caxton and took her hands.

The older woman looked over her shoulder, scanned the trees lining the street as if she expected to see ghosts there. 'Astarte has passed,' she said, and it wasn't a question. 'Ordinarily I wouldn't have come, especially not at this time of day. I don't like to be away from my home at night, as you know. But I must see her.'

Caxton wasn't sure what to make of that. It was against every protocol she knew to let a civilian into a crime scene that was still under investigation. Exceptions were made sometimes for direct family members, but Vesta Polder was no kin of the Arkeleys. Vesta wouldn't explain why it was so important she see the body, either. She just stared into Caxton's eyes as if trying to hypnotize her.

'Come on,' Caxton said, finally. It was still her scene, until a detective from the local PD showed up, so she was still in charge of who went into the house. She led Vesta inside, warning her not to touch anything, then took her up to the room where Astarte's life had ended.

The widow lay exactly as Caxton had first seen her. The blood on the floor had started to dry in the warmth of the house, but Vesta walked around it with mincing little steps, careful not to get any on her black boots. Caxton knew Polder enough to understand she wasn't just being squeamish.

Vesta moved to the foot of the bed and closed her eyes.

Her lips moved, but Caxton couldn't hear what she might be saying. A prayer, she supposed. When she had finished she remained there, eyes closed, hands held out slightly at her sides.

Caxton wondered how long this was going to take. After a minute or two she cleared her throat and Vesta opened her eyes.

'Judging from the size of that wound I'd say he didn't hurt her much,' Caxton said, gesturing at Astarte's arm. 'When he killed Angus he was in a real hurry, but here he took his time.'

Vesta nodded in agreement.

'First his brother. Now his wife.'

'Do you know why he killed them?' Vesta asked, sounding as if she already knew but she just wanted to hear Caxton say it out loud.

That was pretty typical for Vesta Polder. She saw all, knew all – or so she wanted people to think. Caxton was pretty sure it was mostly an act, a practiced technique to draw people out and make them give away what they knew. It still creeped her out.

'He made them both the same offer, I think. They could join him and become vampires or they could die on the spot. As to why, I don't really get it yet.'

'He loved them,' Polder replied. 'He loved them but they were human, and to a vampire human life is contemptible. He could not reconcile those two feelings. To resolve that tension he had to either make them like himself, to bring them up to his level, or extinguish them altogether.'

'I got that,' Caxton shrugged. 'But vampires see us as prey. As livestock. He didn't feed on either of them, just tore them up and let them bleed out.'

'Perhaps,' Vesta said, 'to Jameson, now, that is affection. He put them to sleep, as one would a beloved pet, instead of making a meal of them like a cow or a pig.' She moved around the side of the bed and leaned over Astarte's face, close enough that Caxton started to raise a hand in warning. Vesta passed one hand over Astarte's mouth and then swept her ring-bedecked fingers together as if she were catching a fly. 'She has moved on. Jameson will not be able to raise her as a half-dead. That's what I came for. May I close her eyes?'

Again, that was something you just didn't do at a homicide scene, but Caxton just bit her lip and nodded.

Vesta lowered the dead woman's eyelids gently, with two fingers of her left hand. Then she drew back. She was clearly finished. Before she could go, however, Caxton had a few more questions for her.

'The night's just begun. I'm worried he'll strike again.'

'Not tonight,' Vesta said, shaking her head so her blond ringlets bounced on the shoulders of her severe black dress. 'This moved him. It affected him, that portion of his heart that remains capable of love. He'll return to his lair and sulk.'

Caxton couldn't really imagine Jameson sulking, but she accepted what Polder said. She knew things, somehow, that other people didn't. It was best not to question *how* she knew them. 'You don't happen to know where his lair is, do you?'

Polder shook her head again. 'That is hidden from me, and from all human eyes. Good night, Astarte,' she said.

She started to come around the side of the bed as if to leave the room, but Caxton stopped her. 'You went out of your way to come here tonight.'

'Astarte was a friend. Someone needed to be here, to do what I have done.'

Caxton had thought otherwise. 'Raleigh – back at the fake funeral – Raleigh told me about you and her. She said you and Astarte had a falling-out or something. Care to tell me what that was about? She said you hadn't spoken to each other in years.'

'You haven't guessed already?' Polder asked. She looked away. 'I had an affair with Jameson, of course.'

Caxton dropped her hand. If she couldn't imagine Jameson sulking in his lair, she was completely incapable of seeing that in her mind's eye.

Polder lifted her chin and stared at the ceiling. 'It was in 1987. Jameson and Astarte had been married only a few years, but already they were drifting apart. It had been a sort of arranged marriage, of course. Jameson was the dashing hero who had slain the great darkness – the man who had single-handedly driven vampires from the face of the earth. Or so we thought. He didn't tell anyone that Justinia Malvern had survived, not at first. Astarte came from a very respectable, extremely old family. She could trace her lineage all the way back to the foundations of this country.'

'To Plymouth Rock, you mean?'

Vesta smiled. 'To Salem. Still, it wasn't a very good match. He was twenty years her senior, for one thing. They were never happy. He spent far too much time at his work and left her to keep house here, all but abandoned. He only seemed to drop by to impregnate her – that autumn, and then in the winter of the following year. She struggled with raising the children alone, virtually a single mother. I helped her as much as I could – back then I was less limited in my move-ments. She was my best friend, you see. That's how I met Jameson. I didn't like him at all back then. He never beat her, of course, and every word from his mouth was loving, yet I thought he was a monster for the way he neglected her.'

'And yet,' Caxton said, 'you somehow got involved with him.'

'There are those among us who find monsters quite attractive,' Vesta said. She had a knowing smirk on her face that made Caxton cringe. 'Such a powerful man. Passionate, and

130

driven. That kind of focus is very hard to resist when it is turned in your direction.'

Caxton scratched one of her eyebrows. 'When I spoke with Astarte, um, recently, she – suggested that he and I might have been romantically connected.'

'That's rather foolish. Anyone with eyes in their head can see that you're a girl-lover.'

The conversation had taken a turn that wasn't going to help her investigation, Caxton decided. She led Vesta out of the room and back down to the street. Fetlock waited there to talk to her. He looked impatient.

'You do know this woman, then,' he said, when Vesta Polder climbed back into the passenger seat of his car. 'She came into the state police HQ a little after you left, demanding to be taken to you at once. I tried to get some ID out of her, but she said there was no time.'

'She probably doesn't have any ID. She lives pretty far off the grid. But she's one of the good guys.'

Fetlock nodded as if he was satisfied with her vouching for Polder. 'We could use more of those. Especially since we just lost seven of them.' He nodded his head in the direction of the house. 'You know this doesn't look good, right? You know this was kind of a disaster.'

Caxton admitted she could see how he might think that. 'When people fight vampires, some of them die,' she muttered. It was the kind of thing Jameson might have said.

'Tell me at least one good thing came out of this,' Fetlock insisted.

Caxton looked him right in the eye. 'I know where he's going to strike next.'

23.

'Alright,' Fetlock said. 'Tell me what you know. And how you know it.'

Caxton sat down on the hood of his car. Warmth from the engine seeped up through her clothes. 'He approached Angus, his brother, with an offer – join him or die. Tonight he made the same offer to his wife. He's going after his own family. He thinks he's doing them a big favor, making them as immortal and as powerful as he is. They don't see it that way, and the only other option as far as he's concerned is to kill them painlessly. He can't just let them lie in peace.'

'But why?' Fetlock asked. 'What's in it for him?'

'Reinforcements. He knows he isn't invulnerable. He killed too many vampires himself to think that. No matter how tough he may be, there's going to come a time when he just won't be strong enough. When somebody is going to get him. I don't think he's all that worried about me. I'm just one person and he knows all my best tricks – because he taught them to me. Individually, nobody is tough enough to be a serious threat. But he's smart, and he knows he's outnumbered. If I can't stop him, eventually he'll be up against more than just me. If he wants to keep drinking blood – and he can't stop now – he knows we'll fight him over every drop. If he creates new vampires they can fight by his side.'

'So he's a Vampire Zero now. Just like you warned about.'

She nodded. 'At least he's trying to become one. Angus and Astarte both turned him down.'

'You think he'll try the same offer with someone else,' Fetlock offered.

'Yeah. I think he's going to approach everybody he supposedly loved when he was alive. Jameson Arkeley was a lot of things, but a good family man was not one of them. He got as far as he could from his brother and then never looked back – they hadn't seen each other in twenty years. He cheated on and nearly deserted his wife. His kids barely knew him. His kids—'

'—are next on the list,' Fetlock finished. 'Jesus.' He pressed his fingers against his temples and then ran them down his cheeks. 'There are two of them, right? Raleigh, and Sam?'

'Simon,' Caxton corrected. 'He's twenty, she's nineteen. Way too young to die. I don't know which of them he'll approach first, but I already have an appointment to talk to Raleigh tomorrow. She lives outside of Allentown. That's up in coal country, near where I grew up, actually. It's an area I know well, so it's a good place to make a stand. If I can be there when Jameson arrives, I can set up an ambush and maybe that's all it takes. As for Simon, I don't know. I tried to talk to him recently, but he was adversarial to say the least. He won't want to cooperate. He's farther away, too. He's a student up at Syracuse.'

'You're not limited by state jurisdiction, now that you're a Fed,' Fetlock said. 'I can send some deputies up there to scoop him up. Put him in protective custody. The Marshals

Service has all kinds of safe houses we can use. We administer the Witness Protection Program – we can definitely put the kid up for a couple of days.'

'But not against his will. Like I said, he's not going to cooperate. Not happily.'

'No. But if we can convince him his life is really in danger, why would he refuse? How sure are you about this, about him going after his kids?'

'Ninety percent. On the phone he told me to stay away from his family. I think that's a pretty clear indication of—'

'Excuse me?' Fetlock took a step toward her and leaned in close, as if he wanted to hear her better. 'Did you just say you spoke with Jameson Arkeley on the phone?'

There was no point in denying it. 'Yeah. Earlier, he procured a cell phone from the lead unit in the assault here. I called that number hoping to speak with the trooper in charge, but that man was already dead. Jameson answered in his place, and tried to warn me off. It'll all go in my report, I swear.'

Fetlock straightened up and scratched under his nose. 'That's – that's interesting.'

She bit her lip. 'I've . . . heard from Malvern, too. Via text message.'

Fetlock went a little pale.

'Listen,' he said. 'I'm going to get you a new phone. We'll just switch out the SIM card, so you can keep the same number. But the phone I give you will let you record incoming calls. It'll also allow me to listen in. If he calls you again, we'll at least have a copy of anything he says.'

Caxton frowned. 'I'm not sure I'm all that comfortable with you listening to my calls. That's kind of intrusive, don't you think?'

'Part of the job. Besides, it's not like you're using your phone for personal calls. It's just a work phone, right? The government pays for those minutes, so they belong to the taxpayers, not you.'

Caxton forced herself to smile. 'Alright, Deputy Marshal.'

'Looks like you have your work cut out for you. Tomorrow you can start securing the kids. What about tonight, though? Is Arkeley going to strike again, somewhere else?'

Caxton shrugged. She thought about what Vesta Polder had said – about Jameson sulking in his lair. There was a better reason to believe he was done for the night, however. 'Probably not. He's fed enough to keep him full for a while, and he hasn't reached the point yet where he's killing for fun. Thank God.'

Fetlock nodded in agreement. 'I want to know everything that happened here tonight. But I can see you're exhausted. Get out of here and get some sleep. You can write up everything in your incident report and get it to me tomorrow.' With that he took his leave, taking Vesta Polder with him.

The chief of the Bellefonte Police Department showed up shortly thereafter. She shook his hand and gave him a very quick idea of what had happened. She didn't want to go into the gory details – his own people could tell him about those. Having officially turned the scene over to him, she found herself more than ready to leave.

She found Glauer still going from door to door, telling Astarte's neighbors there was nothing to worry about. She called him back down to the street and told him it was time to go home. 'I'll drive you back to HQ. We should both be in bed before midnight – there's going to be a lot to do tomorrow.'

He didn't say a word. She led him back to her car, but he just stood there, staring up at Astarte's house. A number of lights had been turned on inside and the front door stood wide open. Caxton could see local cops inside bent over the bodies of the three half-deads in the foyer. Flashes of light told her

135

they'd brought a photographer to document the scene, which made her think of Clara. Clara, who would be waiting for her at home. Maybe there would even be hot food there for her.

'Come on, Glauer, I'm tired,' she said.

The big cop turned and looked at her with haunted eyes. He made no move to get into the car.

She knew what was under his skin. 'It was us or them,' she said.

'They were police officers.'

'They were half-deads,' she said. 'They weren't themselves anymore.'

'They were police officers before they were half-deads,' he replied. 'You sent them here. You sent them here knowing he was going to kill them.'

'No, you're wrong,' she insisted. 'I sent them here knowing there was a chance they could get killed. Also knowing that was part of their job. Policemen put themselves in the line of danger all the time. It's what they sign up for. It's what we signed up for.'

He shook his head. 'Sure,' he said, 'cops go up against bad guys all the time and sometimes, occasionally, one of them gets shot. Sometimes one even gets killed. This was something more, something worse. I'm not necessarily blaming you for their deaths. But the bodies are starting to pile up real high.'

'That's why we're doing this, to keep Jameson from killing any more.'

'Really?' Glauer asked.

'Yeah, damn it!' Caxton scowled at the big cop. 'Yeah. Everything I do. Every day of my life since October has been devoted to that. I put my own life at risk every night, and I never ask anyone to do something I wouldn't do myself. I have to make hard decisions sometimes. I have to make them fast. Sometimes I make the wrong choice.'

136

'Tonight was one of those times. I'm just saying—'

'I've said all I'm going to. Get in the car before I freeze my ass off.'

'You need to be more careful with the people around you. Maybe you don't care if you live or die, but the families of those men are—'

'Get in the damned car!'

'Yes, Deputy,' he growled, and yanked the passenger door open.

'It's Special Deputy,' she shot back, and climbed in her own side.

She drove him back to Harrisburg without saying another word. When they arrived he jumped out and ran inside the building without even looking at her.

24.

In the morning Caxton woke to pure white light streaming in through her window. It had snowed so much during the night that it had piled up against the windowpane. She couldn't even see the backyard.

She could smell bacon and eggs cooking in the kitchen. Reluctantly she kicked off the electric blanket and went to the table in her pajamas. Clara beamed at her from the stove. 'The way you looked when you came in last night, I figured you could use a hot meal.'

Caxton tried to smile back, but her face didn't quite feel up to it. When Clara put a cup of coffee in front of her she sipped at it, grateful but unable to say so. She wanted to tell Clara everything that had happened. She wanted to just grab her around the legs and hug her. She couldn't do that either.

'I've been thinking,' Clara said, when she had finished making her omelets and had placed them on the table. 'About what you said yesterday. Obviously I can't be your forensics specialist. But maybe I could do what you said. You know, coordinate with those guys. I could come work with you. If that would be helpful.'

Laura's eyes went wide. 'It would.'

Clara nodded and started to eat. 'You can buy me lunch every day, too. If you want.'

'I do,' Laura replied.

'Where should we go today, then?'

'Ah.'

'Ah?'

'There's only one problem,' Caxton said. 'Today I'm going out to Allentown. To talk to Jameson's daughter, Raleigh. And I'll probably have to spend the night there, too.'

'Of course,' Clara said, and turned back to the stove.

'Hey,' Laura said, as soothingly as she could, 'you've been great about this so far. I know I have no right to ask for more understanding, but I need it.'

'Yeah,' Clara said. 'Yeah, of course it's okay. I suppose she's in mortal danger, this girl.'

'Her own father is going to try to kill her.'

Clara turned around with a sad smile on her face. 'I can't compete with that. Go. Do what you do best. I'll be here when you get home.'

Laura kissed her. She ate her eggs and bacon, though she was too distracted to taste anything, and then she went to get dressed. In half an hour she was on the road, headed for her office. There were errands to complete there. She had to write her report on the previous night's disaster, for one thing. She found her new phone waiting on her desk, still in its box – Fetlock must have delivered it during the night. *The Fed travels fast*, she thought. It was bigger and clunkier than her old one, with a tiny black-and-white screen. Sighing with pointless misgivings, she slipped the SIM card out of her old phone and into the new beast and then shoved it in her pocket. It started to ring almost instantly. It was Fetlock calling.

'You're going to watch Raleigh?' Fetlock asked, once she'd said hello. 'Good. Don't let me stop you. I saw that you had activated the new phone, so I thought I'd test it out for you.'

'It seems to work fine,' she said.

'Yes, on this end too. Listen, I've just sent you an email – take a look now. I'll wait.' While Caxton booted up her computer he explained, 'I've had my best people working on the video-tapes from our archives facility. I thought we might catch our intruder in the act. It looks like we might have something.'

Caxton opened her email and saw a picture start to load. 'This is the guy who broke in and stole all of Jameson's files?'

'I believe so, yes,' Fetlock confirmed. 'We only caught him for a split second, but my digital analysis people cleaned up the image quite a bit. I thought you should see this.'

The picture on the screen showed a man in a light blue suit walking through a metal detector. The shot was blurry at best, and the face couldn't be seen at all – just the back of the man's head. His hair could have been brown or black – the image was too poorly lit to be sure. 'He was using Jameson's ID, right? It's not him, though.'

'You don't think it could have been the vampire in disguise?' Fetlock asked.

Caxton frowned. 'I suppose it's possible. Vampires do alter their appearance sometimes. They put on wigs, throw on some makeup. I knew one, once, who tore off the tips of his own ears so they'd look more human.' She tapped at the screen of her computer. 'This is different, though. Those vampires wouldn't fool anybody except from at an extreme distance. It would take Hollywood-level makeup artists to make one look this human. No, I still think this is a human being pretending to be Jameson. He found someone human and sent him in his place. Besides. He's got all his fingers. Jameson is missing all the fingers from one hand.'

'He could be wearing a prosthesis,' Fetlock suggested.

Caxton frowned at her screen. 'A guy walks into your offices, wearing powder on his face, an obvious wig, and a fake hand. Even if the makeup job was good, don't you think somebody would notice something?'

'So it definitely wasn't Jameson. Which only begs more questions,' Fetlock said.

'Yeah. Now, if it's alright, I have to get going – time's wasting,' Caxton said. She didn't particularly care about the archives theft. She was far more worried about losing another one of Jameson's family members.

She wasn't quite done, though. Before she left she stuck her head into the briefing room. She hoped to find Glauer there. She planned to apologize to him. It had been a bad night for everybody, but he hadn't deserved the crap she'd given him. She found him just where she'd expected, and he'd been busy.

He had taken the liberty of updating the whiteboards. For VAMPIRE PATTERN #2 he had pasted up pictures of the Carboy family underneath the pictures of Rexroth/Carboy's other victims. For VAMPIRE PATTERN #1 he had found pictures of the state troopers and Bellefonte police they'd fought at Astarte's house, as well as the anonymous half-dead from the motel where Angus died. Jameson's brother and his widow both had their own memorials there, circled in red marker. The boards were getting crowded; there wasn't much room left for future victims.

It was fine that he'd done all that – but when she saw what else he'd done she nearly lost it. He had taken one of Dylan Carboy's notebooks – the one that had been gummed together with dried blood – and separated all the pages. They lay spread out on the desks like an enormous tarot card reading.

She had given him specific instructions to stop reading the notebooks. Clearly he'd decided he didn't have to obey her orders. Before she could blow up at him, though, he held up his hands. 'I can explain,' he said. 'I know you think this is all garbage. And the vast majority of it definitely is. There are whole sections where he just copied down the lyrics of his favorite songs, and there are pages where he pasted in printouts of websites, some of them pretty random. It looks like he was obsessed with the Columbine school shooting for a while. I think maybe he was planning something similar at his college – that might have been when he bought the shotgun.'

He tapped one of the desks. 'But starting here things change. None of his journal entries are dated, but he talks about a TV show he watched and I looked it up. The episode he mentions ran the first week in October.'

'Right after Jameson accepted the curse,' Caxton suggested.

'Yeah.' Glauer picked up one of the sheets. 'The show's not important except that it gives us a time frame for the transition. Before that date most of his entries are long, rambling passages about how he feels like no one understands him and how he feels alienated even from his family. Then we have this one. It stuck out at first only because it was so short: "I saw him outside my window tonight. He's close now, and coming closer."'

Caxton raised an eyebrow.

Glauer pushed his way between the desks, knocking them sideways in his excitement so their feet squeaked across the linoleum. 'There's more! Here, maybe a couple days later: "He told me the strong will always prey on the weak. That's the laws of nature. He said if you were weak you had a duty to make yourself stronger, or to get out of the way. Nobody is as strong as him."'

'Does he ever mention Jameson by name?' Caxton asked.

142

Glauer dropped his head. 'No. At least not in the journal entries. There are newspaper articles about vampires all over this notebook. A lot of them about what happened at Gettysburg.'

Caxton leaned against the bookcase. 'But you think this "he" is Jameson. You think he was in contact with Carboy somehow. Presumably not through their MySpace pages.'

'We know they can communicate telepathically,' Glauer tried.

Caxton couldn't deny it – she'd had her mind invaded by more vampires than she liked to remember.

'And after the second week in October he starts talking about a "she" as well. Here: "She was beautiful once, and can be again. It would be an honor to feed her, to make her whole. It would be an act of love."'

'So he was talking to Malvern, too. Okay. And this kid sounds about the right type to get a vampire's interest. He was fucked up already, spiraling toward violence, ready to obliterate himself as long as he could take some other people with him. That would make him a perfect candidate to accept the curse.'

'Yeah,' Glauer said.

'But in the end they didn't give it to him. He had to pretend he was a vampire. We know Jameson is recruiting. We know Malvern has recruited in the past, and I have no doubt she wants more vampires to come worship her. Neither of them gave Carboy what he wanted. That suggests to me he never met either of them face-to-face. Maybe he just imagined these conversations. Maybe he was just crazy.'

'Maybe, but there's something here. Something . . . I need to read more.'

Caxton threw up her arms. 'Alright. I don't need you right now, actually. I'm going out to Allentown, to Raleigh's place, but they don't let men in there, you said. So spend the day on this if you need to. One day.'

He nodded gravely. 'Thanks. This one is haunting me. If I can figure out what made him do it . . . I don't know. I don't know what that will achieve, in concrete terms, but it means something to me.'

'One day,' she repeated. 'Wish me luck.' She left the basement and headed up to her car, finally ready to go to Allentown. She had her key in the ignition before she realized she hadn't actually apologized to Glauer. Well, maybe, she thought, letting him dig through Carboy's diseased brain was apology enough.

She hoped so.

It was a long ride to Allentown, and she needed her sunglasses the whole way. Snow lay deep and thick on the fields she passed through, but the sun was out. In the towns, as she drove through the quiet residential streets, the eaves and gutters glittered with ice melt and the streets were filled with dark slush. The radio told her it was going up to fifty degrees by afternoon but that more snow was on the way. If there were blizzards coming, she thought, she would have to get Fetlock to give her a four-wheel-drive vehicle. The little Mazda wasn't made for slippery conditions.

Eventually she started to recognize landmarks, old family restaurants that had been in business for decades, the main squares of little towns she'd visited a million times. Caxton had grown up in small towns all around the area, the old coal mining part of Pennsylvania, sometimes in the cities and sometimes in places that were nothing more than rows of cheap company housing built for coal miners in the previous century – places that didn't even deserve the title of 'town,' so instead they were called patches. She got to see one or two of them as she drove past, though very few of them lay near the main road. Almost all the old patches had been forgotten by time once the coal dried up or the mines were just shut down.

The directions she'd downloaded from MapQuest took her

south of Allentown proper, through the borough of Emmaus. Emmaus was famous as the original home of the Moravian Church in Pennsylvania – an offshoot of Protestantism with its own unique customs, though not as severe as the Amish or the Mennonites. The one thing she remembered about the Moravians was that they had a special kind of cemetery called a God's Acre. Instead of burying their dead in family groups, the Moravians filed them by age, gender, and marital status. She couldn't remember why – maybe they wanted them filed appropriately for God when he came to get them again on Judgment Day.

There were a lot of religious groups living their own way in the area. There were monasteries and retreats tucked away in the hills she drove through, and plenty of churches. When she finally found the side road she wanted, she headed down through a long copse of dead trees that ended in a stone wall surrounding what she took for either a museum or a rest home. The building stood four stories high and as wide as a city block. It was made of redbrick dressed with carved stone and studded everywhere with windows, some of them with Gothic arches. Ivy covered most of the face of the building, brown and dead now, but she could imagine it bright green in summertime. The building sat on a broad lawn of yellow grass that peeked up sporadically from under the snow. A number of stone monuments, a fountain, and a rustic gazebo stuck out of the snow here and there. Behind and to one side a stripe of water cut through the lawn, a creek full of pale stones.

There was no parking lot. A few very old and very nondescript cars sat on the lawn near the main gate in the wall, and she pulled in beside them. She got out and went to the gate, a huge wrought-iron contraption surmounted by a simple cross. She started looking for a bell to ring, but before she found one someone came to let her in: a teenaged girl wearing a baggy dress and a parka two sizes too big for her.

'Hi, I'm Special Deputy Caxton,' she said to the girl.

The girl smiled broadly and nodded her head.

'I have an appointment. I mean, I'm supposed to speak with Raleigh Arkeley. She lives here, right?'

The girl smiled and nodded again. Apparently she didn't speak much. Caxton looked up at the cross over the gate and wondered if she'd come to a convent or a nunnery and if everyone inside had taken a vow of silence. It would make it damned hard to interview Raleigh about her father.

'Can you take me to her?' Caxton asked.

The girl nodded again and then turned around and started trudging across the lawn. The hem of her dress dragged through the snow, but she didn't seem to notice or mind. Caxton followed close behind.

25.

Caxton was brought into the main hall of the huge building, an echoing cavern with marble floors and high columns. A spiral staircase in wrought iron rose from the rear of the hall while massive fireplaces on either side roared with heat and light. The only other illumination in the room came from standing candelabras. There didn't seem to be any electric lights in the hall. Caxton wondered if the place was even on the power grid.

Her silent guide led her toward a door set in one side of the hall. The girl knocked once, hesitantly as if afraid of making too much noise, then stepped back quickly. She turned and smiled at Caxton again, with lots of teeth.

Someone beyond the door called, 'Enter.' Caxton shrugged and pushed the door open, then walked into a small but pleasant little office. The walls were lined with crowded bookshelves, except where they were pierced by a broad window that looked out on the lawn and another, if much smaller, fireplace that crackled merrily. Behind a massive oak desk a young woman was seated, dressed in a severe black dress and with a white cloth over her hair.

'You'll be Trooper Caxton, then,' the woman said, rising from where she sat to hold out one gloved hand. Caxton shook it. 'Welcome to our little sanctuary. Raleigh has told us about you. I'm Sister Margot.'

'Sister?' Caxton asked. 'I didn't realize this was a convent. I guess I should have guessed from the – the clothes.'

'This place was a nunnery once, but it's moved on with the times. The staff remain under holy orders but we're purely nondenominational. As for this outfit I'm wearing . . . it's commonly called a habit,' the woman said. 'We like to say it's the last habit we ever want to take up. Please, please sit down. Can I offer you something to drink?' She turned to where a plastic cooler sat next to the window. It looked distinctly wrong in the room, which otherwise might have been furnished in the previous century and never renovated.

'I'd love a Diet Coke,' Caxton said. It had been a long, thirsty ride.

'Sorry. We don't take stimulants. How about apple juice?'

'Sure.' Caxton took the proffered bottle and twisted off its cap.

'It's vital to stay hydrated.' She offered a bottle of water to the silent girl standing in the doorway. 'You've already met Violet, but of course she didn't introduce herself.'

'Pleased to meet you both. I guess you know why I'm here.'

'Of course,' Sister Margot said. 'Sister Raleigh will be down in a while. She's currently engaged in a group therapy session that can't be interrupted. In the meantime I'll be happy to answer any questions you have. We may look as if we've turned away from the world, and we have,' she giggled – behind Caxton Violet bubbled with mirth as well – 'but we believe in hospitality as well, which includes cooperating with the authorities whenever we must. We also pay our taxes, quite regularly.'

148

'Good to hear it, though that's not my department. Nice place you have here, by the way. All women, from what I hear. Must be very peaceful. So are you a Moravian? I never heard of Moravian nuns before.'

'Oh, no,' Sister Margot exclaimed. 'There is no religion within these walls. When I want to pray, I actually step outside. We're very careful not to exclude anyone.'

'Except men,' Caxton suggested.

Sister Margot shrugged. 'They can be a distraction to the work we do here.'

'I see,' Caxton said, although honestly she was pretty confused. 'What kind of work would that be? I'm afraid I don't know as much about Raleigh as I thought I did.'

'This is a place of refuge. The girls who come here have all met the dark side of life, one way or the other. They need a place they can go far away from the temptations and stresses of modern life. We provide counseling and therapy, but mostly our work is to provide a different way of life. A simpler way.'

'So this is a halfway house?'

Sister Margot's smile dimmed, but only by a fraction of a watt. 'More like a retreat. A shelter from the storm. Trooper, we try to provide an oasis from all distractions, that's all.'

'It's, uh, Special Deputy. Not Trooper. So religion is one of those distractions. But you're a believer yourself, aren't you? I mean, you're a Christian or something.'

Margot's smile faded a few degrees. 'I have taken certain vows, yes. I am required by those vows to wear this habit. The building we're in was once consecrated to a holy order, as well. In the past it was a home for wayward girls – unwed mothers, to be exact. In recent years we've broadened our scope and also our outlook. The work we do here is vital and it must be completed in an atmosphere free of judgment and prejudice. The girls who come here have all made bad

149

mistakes in their lives. The last thing they need is authority figures – like God – to remind them how they've failed.'

'Mistakes?' Caxton asked.

'Some became addicted to drugs or to less material pursuits. Some are just lost. What you would call mentally ill. I started out here myself, years ago. I suffered from schizophrenia and delusions of grandeur. This place helped me immeasurably.'

'Oh,' Caxton said. She turned in her seat to look at the girl behind her. 'What's Violet in for?'

The mute girl grabbed her throat and simulated strangulation.

Sister Margot explained. 'She attempted to commit suicide by drinking drain cleaner. It was only through an act of great blessing that she survived, though as a result she'll never speak again or eat solid food.'

Violet shrugged, her smile returning as bright as before.

'I take it some people stay here longer than others,' Caxton suggested.

'As long as they need to. Some of our patients never leave.'

What on earth, Caxton wondered, had Raleigh done to get herself sent to a place like this? 'It's important I see Raleigh as soon as possible. Before dark, at the very least. How much longer is her session going to last?'

'Another fifteen minutes or so. She'll be brought to you the second she's done. I want you to know, Trooper, that you are perfectly welcome here, for as long as you must join us. I'd be less than honest, however, if I said that your prolonged presence here was desirable. I worry that you'll make some of the girls uneasy. A number of them have histories with law enforcement that were less than . . . convivial.'

'I promise, I'll be as quick as I can. Where can I talk with Raleigh?' she asked.

Sister Margot looked to Violet. 'Please find a room where they may talk and prepare it with candles and fire.' The mute girl bowed her head and ran off without looking back. 'In the meantime, can I offer you a quiet place to wait?'

Caxton checked her cell phone. She got lousy reception in the office, and she hadn't checked in with Glauer in a long time. 'Maybe some place with a phone?'

Sister Margot's smile dropped for a moment. 'There's only one telephone in the building, and that's here, in my office. If you'd like to use it, I'll just go wait out in the hall.'

Caxton started to protest, but the nun didn't give her a chance. She headed out the door and left Caxton all alone. Whatever, Caxton thought, and reached for the woman's phone. She called in to HQ and got Glauer, who had some information for her.

'You asked the members of the SSU to start looking for potential lairs,' he said, and she got excited for a second. 'They've turned up sixty-one possibles, from Erie all the way to Reading.'

'That's good,' she said, though the number was surprisingly large. The cops who worked part time for the SSU must have tagged every abandoned farmhouse and disused factory in the state. There was no way she could investigate all those leads on her own, though. 'Get Fetlock in on this. Tell him – scratch that, ask him politely, he's a little sensitive – to get his people to run all these down. Get as many of them as possible checked out before nightfall. You know what we're looking for. Places that haven't been used for years, but have signs of recent activity. They can rule out the places the local teens go to drink, and anywhere clearly visible from a main road. That should narrow the search.'

How awesome would it be, she thought, if they turned up the lair in the next hour? Knowing Jameson, his lair would be well guarded and probably booby-trapped. There were ways to deal with that sort of thing, however. If she could get to the lair by daylight, if she could find Jameson and Malvern inside, still in their coffins – it would be the work of a few minutes to remove their hearts from their bodies. To destroy the hearts. To end this.

Then she could go home. Go to bed for a week.

Then she could be alone with Clara, for a long time. She could fix everything. Everything that was wrong with her life.

She knew with a depressing certainty it wasn't going to happen that way.

'Jameson's smart,' she said. She said it so often it had become a mantra. 'He's not going to be anyplace I think to look for him, is he?'

'We might get lucky,' Glauer said.

She snorted a response and ended the call.

In the silence that followed – she could hear nothing but the crackling of the fireplace – she sat back in her chair and sipped at her apple juice. She thought about what could have made Raleigh come to such a place, to cut herself off from the world altogether like this. It was not, she had to admit, without a certain attraction. Tell everyone to go to hell. Run and hide from all her problems. She'd love to.

But no.

The only reason a place like this repurposed convent could exist was that there were people out there in the real world, people who fought and bled to protect Sister Margot's right to be safe and immune from danger and harm. Caxton knew a lot of old cops – her father had been one, and so had all his friends – and she remembered back in the seventies they'd had a certain way of thinking, a metaphor for what they did. The modern world with all its crime and drugs and violence and crazies was a trash can, a big, bulging trash can too small

152

to hold everything inside of it, always threatening to burst, to run over and spill out onto the streets. As cops, they were paid to do nothing more than sit on the lid.

Now that was her job.

There was a knock on the door. It was Sister Margot. 'Raleigh's ready for you now,' she said.

26.

Sister Margot led Caxton to a windowless square room on the second floor with a table and a few less-than-comfortable chairs. It was freezing cold inside, but a brazier had been set up in one corner to warm the place and tall candelabras flanked the table, giving some light. Raleigh already waited inside, sitting at the far side of the table. She greeted Caxton warmly, then sat back down and smiled.

Caxton pulled a digital audio recorder out of her pocket. 'Is it alright if I use this? I noticed you don't have electricity here.'

'Sister Margot says we don't need it. That if we had it we'd be tempted to get radios, or even a television set, which would be a mistake. Sometimes I think she must have been Amish before she became a nun. I don't think that little thing will be a problem, though.'

Caxton nodded her thanks and set up the recorder, putting a small microphone on the table where it could catch both their voices. She decided to get right to business. 'I wanted to ask you a few questions about your father. Have you been in touch with him recently? I mean before he changed.'

The girl shook her head. 'Not for about six months. The whole family is sort of estranged. Until two days ago I hadn't seen Uncle Angus since I was a child. Mom I saw just a few weeks ago, but we didn't speak for very long, we were—'

Caxton stopped her, not wanting to talk about Astarte. That would probably bring up a lot of emotional stuff she didn't need. She needed to keep this interview on track. 'When was the last time you spoke with your father?'

'I was in . . . Belgium,' Raleigh said. Her face clouded as if the memory was painful.

'You were in college at the time. Your father told me that. You were doing a semester abroad.'

Raleigh shrugged. 'That was how it started. I wanted to study great art. They have a lot of amazing museums in Belgium. Have you ever been?'

Caxton smiled. 'No.' She'd never been out of the country, except one quick visit to Canada when she was a kid. She'd rarely left her home state. 'So you saw the museums,' she prompted.

'Yes. And they were wonderful. But you can't just look at paintings all day, and write papers about them all night. I went with a friend of mine, Jane. She—'

Caxton took a notepad out of her pocket. 'Last name?'

The girl frowned. 'That's not important to the story I'm telling.'

Caxton smiled through gritted teeth. 'You never know what's important. It's often the little details that matter.'

'I suddenly feel like I'm being interrogated,' Raleigh said.

I don't have time for this, Caxton thought. 'I'm just trying to learn everything I can. This isn't even an official conversation, just a backgrounder.'

'It's just I don't want to get Jane in any trouble. She's – well. She's living a certain lifestyle. Some people don't approve of that lifestyle. It involves breaking some very silly laws.'

155

'You mean she's a drug user,' Caxton said.

Raleigh looked startled. 'Yes! How did you know that?'

'It's not magic. Just experience.' She'd heard that kind of evasion before. 'Is Jane currently within the borders of the United States?'

Raleigh shook her head.

'She's still over in Europe?' That got a nod. 'Then I couldn't arrest her even if I wanted to. I don't have any jurisdiction over there. But let's forget about her last name. Just tell me what happened.'

Raleigh looked up at the ceiling. She exhaled a long and noisy breath and then launched into it. 'I was young and very foolish at the time. I was also very bored. Jane and I were roommates in this tiny little place in Brussels. The rent was nothing, but we were always broke anyway. We ate a lot of French fries because they were cheap – they actually invented French fries in Belgium, did you know that? They aren't really French at all. Living so cheaply was in some ways a very spiritual experience. There's a liberation that comes with owning next to nothing. We would sit around talking about art, like, all night long. We didn't get a lot of sleep, but we didn't ever feel all that bad the next day. You know how it is when you're young.'

Caxton smiled and nodded, though she didn't know at all. Her own experience had been quite different.

'Jane really liked to party. You know what I mean? It was just drinking, at first. We had this really cheap wine that came in a blue bottle and it tasted awful, but you could buy cases of it for nothing. We would have people come over, other students, sometimes even Belgian kids, and we would just have so much fun. Laughing and singing until the people who lived downstairs would bang on their ceiling with a broom handle, which always just made us laugh more. Sometimes people would bring other things.'

156

'You mean drugs.'

Raleigh nodded and looked away. 'That wasn't my thing. I always said no. I mean at first. They would pass around a joint and it just looked nasty, with everybody's spit on the end. Sometimes they had pills and then they wouldn't sleep for days. Jane liked that. She loved doing her classwork at like four in the morning when it was quiet, she said. The guy who had the pills started coming around a lot more often. His name was Piet and he had really beautiful eyes. One time we were in the kitchen and he kissed me. Then he just stood there looking at me for so long, until I got embarrassed and ran out of the room. That same night he hooked up with Jane, and before long he moved in. He started bringing his own friends around and some of them weren't so, well, nice.' Raleigh started to scratch at her arms as she spoke, digging her fingernails into the crooks of her elbows, through the sleeves of her shapeless dress. 'They did heroin. Over there, it's not like here. People don't call you a junkie just because you tried something once. Jane started shooting up with Piet and then there were no more all-nighters. Then they would just collapse on the couch and they wouldn't get up. She stopped going to classes.'

Caxton sighed. 'When did you start taking heroin?' she asked.

That same startled look as before, as if Caxton had read the girl's mind. 'I didn't say I did. I never said that.'

'You did try it, though,' Caxton said. 'Didn't you?'

Raleigh nodded in acceptance. 'Yes. They said it was the best feeling in the world. They said you could do it a couple of times safely before you got addicted. That if you just did it a couple of times you would be okay. I figured – I mean, this was near the end of the semester. I thought I'd try it once. Maybe twice, if I liked it. Then I would have to fly home, since I already had booked my flight back, and I wouldn't be tempted again.'

157

'What happened then?'

'I liked it. I liked it a lot.' Raleigh looked down at her hands. Under the table her feet were swinging back and forth. 'I did it more than a couple of times. We didn't have any money, I said that before. We couldn't afford to buy drugs and pay the rent, so something had to happen. Jane convinced me we should cash in our plane tickets. We would explain to our parents that we needed the money for rent, and then they would send us new tickets. Except we didn't want to go home anymore. The college called and said that if we didn't come home we could get expelled. There was this funny thing that happened, it was like I knew that things were going bad. I knew it, but I couldn't do anything about it. When I was high it didn't matter, and when I came down I just felt like I couldn't concentrate enough to do what I needed to do. We got kicked out of the apartment because we never did pay the rent, and we went to live with Piet. And his friends.'

'What did you do for money then?'

Raleigh looked up across the table and stared directly at Caxton. 'I don't want to say. Not when I'm being recorded.'

'Okay,' Caxton said. She didn't think she wanted the sordid details anyway.

'You asked me about the last time I saw my dad. I'm sorry. I've been rambling. The answer is I saw him about six months ago. He knew something was up when I didn't come home. He went to Vesta Polder and asked her to take a look, to see where I was. She can do that sort of thing. Anyway, she came back to him and said she'd found where my body was, but that she couldn't see my soul anywhere.' The girl's voice rose in pitch as she finished her story. 'Daddy came for me. He showed up and he hurt some people. Some of Piet's friends. I called him so many bad names, I said such mean things, but he didn't even listen to me. He dragged me out of there and got me on

158

a plane. We sat next to each other the whole way back. I got sick, really sick. I threw up a lot. He held my hair back but he wouldn't talk to me. Not while I was like that. He told everybody I was just airsick. When we got home he brought me right here. He couldn't come in through the gate, but Sister Margot took one look at me and just brought me inside. They locked me up for a couple of days, and when I finally came out of my room they were just waiting with this ugly set of clothes. They said if I wanted to stay here I had to dress like everybody else. I put the clothes on, because I needed something. I needed something to replace the heroin. I had no idea what I was getting into. I can't tell you how scared I was. Now everything's different.'

'How did your father know to bring you here?'

'Vesta recommended it as a place where I could get clean again. It's really special here. You should spend some time with us.'

'I'd like that,' Caxton lied. 'So this all happened six months ago.' The summer of 2004, then. Just a few months before the massacre at Gettysburg. He'd never told Caxton about what had happened, not even a hint. That wasn't surprising, though, if you knew Jameson Arkeley at all.

'He saved me,' Raleigh said, sitting back in her chair. She looked spent, as if the effort of telling the story had taken something out of her. 'He saved my life. And my soul.' She shook her head. 'I heard what he did to Uncle Angus. So horrible. I'm doing a three-week fast in his honor.'

'That's . . . nice of you,' Caxton said.

'He's not my father anymore. He's not the same person anymore, is he?'

'Your poor mother didn't think so,' Caxton agreed.

'My poor mother? What do you mean?'

Caxton's heart jumped in her chest. Raleigh didn't know.

159

'I'm so sorry. I assumed the Bellefonte police would have contacted you. I guess maybe they didn't know where you were.' She wondered if she should reach a hand across the table, to comfort the girl, but she didn't. 'Last night your father killed her. Exactly the same way he did your uncle. I'm – I'm sorry.'

Raleigh started to scream.

27.

Sister Margot threw the door open and grabbed Caxton's arm and pulled her bodily out of her chair. Caxton didn't fight back but let the nun drag her out into the hallway. She didn't want to find out what Margot was capable of when excited.

Margot's face was wracked with pure anger, her delicate features twisted around and darkened by congested blood. Her eyes were narrow slits pulsing with rage, and spit flecked her lips. She looked as if she was about to invoke some dread curse. Then she looked toward the open door, looked in at where Raleigh was crying with her head in her hands. Visibly struggling to regain her composure, Margot closed her eyes and then said, in a sweet, soft voice, 'Is everything alright?'

Caxton frowned. 'I had to give her some bad news. Her mother died last night.'

A vein in Margot's left temple throbbed alarmingly. 'Yes,' she said. 'I know.'

'You do?' Caxton was confused.

'The police called me last night, and when I said they

couldn't talk to her, they told me what it was about. I decided, after long contemplation, that it would be best for Raleigh to not be exposed to such negative outside influences.'

'Do you think that's fair to her?' Caxton asked.

Sister Margot lowered her eyes. 'She's undergoing extensive therapy for drug addiction, and that takes a great deal of time, rest, and peace. The first time, when they came to tell her about her uncle, I allowed her to go to the gate and hear the news herself. She came back quite disturbed. I would have told her about her mother eventually, of course, but I decided that two such shocks in such a short space of time would completely unhinge her.'

'I see,' Caxton said.

'I wasn't sure whether to let you talk to her at all, but in the end I decided I did not wish to create trouble with the police. I'm beginning to wonder if that was a mistake. Is your business with us done now?'

'No,' Caxton said. 'Believe me. I'd love to leave the whole bunch of you in peace. I'm afraid I'm going to have to spend the night, though.' She could see Margot's face darkening again, so she added, 'This is an emergency situation. Do you know about Raleigh's father?'

'The vampire?'

'Yeah,' Caxton said. 'I have reason to believe he'll come here and try to harm her. It looks like he's intent on destroying his own family. If I had any choice in the matter I'd take Raleigh out of here right now and get her somewhere safe.'

Margot didn't seem impressed. 'I can assure you there's nowhere safer than here, especially from that sort. No such creature would ever dare cross the threshold of this place. It's still holy ground. And as he is a man there is no chance of any of the sisters inviting him inside.'

'You mean, because a vampire can only enter a place where

162

he's been invited first? That's a myth,' Caxton said. 'They don't have to be invited into a place. They can go anywhere they want. Even on holy ground. Sorry.'

'Perhaps we'll see,' Margot said, with a wry smile. 'Very well, I'll find a place for you to sleep—'

'I'll need to sleep in the same room as Raleigh,' Caxton interrupted.

'You might find it a tad crowded. She shares a very small room with Violet,' Margot warned.

'I'll make do.'

'So be it. Is there anything else you require, Special Deputy? If not, dinner will be served at five o'clock. If you would be good enough to leave Raleigh alone until then, I would appreciate it. And please, would you do something for me? Don't tell her you think her father wants to kill her. That would just be too much for her mental constitution to take.'

That sounded like a terrible idea – Caxton had always lived by the notion that forewarned was forearmed – but she just nodded her head.

When Sister Margot was gone she considered going back into the small room to comfort Raleigh, but then decided she wasn't the one for that job. Instead Caxton found her way out of the dark building and into the fading light of afternoon. It was three-thirty and already the sun was low in the sky, casting long sharp shadows across the snow-crusted lawn. She spent a while just walking around, checking out the wall, looking for any place a vampire could sneak through. Of course, a determined enough intruder could climb over the wall anywhere, but she thought Jameson might try for a stealthy approach. The biggest weakness she found in the wall was a brick-lined arch at either end of the property where the creek flowed through. Neither arch was more than three feet high, but Jameson could easily crawl in through them.

163

It would be next to impossible to guard both arches unless she had some help. She had to make some phone calls.

Caxton took out her cell phone – she didn't want to antagonize Sister Margot again by using her office phone – and was not surprised to find that she got terrible reception even outside the ex-convent, just a single bar that flickered in and out. She tramped around the grounds until her shoes were soaked through, hunting a clearer signal. She only found it as she approached the iron gate where she'd left her car. Immediately the phone chirped, telling her she had a message waiting.

It was from Clara. 'Hey, honey, I hope you're having a good day. I dropped by your HQ earlier so I could meet with your forensics guys. I missed them, but they left a report for me to read. There were two things in it that sounded important. One was that they couldn't get a positive ID on the half-dead, but that they were trying to rebuild its skull so they could build up a computer-enhanced facial reconstruction. I wouldn't hold your breath, though – they said it could take a couple days to do the rendering. The other thing was that they were able to match the fibers taken from the motel bathroom window. They found three different kinds of thread: cotton, nylon, and an aromatic polyamide, um, which they said also goes by the trade name of Twaron. I hope that helps.'

Caxton bit her lip. It didn't help at all, of course. It was just like she'd told Fetlock. Fiber analysis was no use on this case. She called Clara, intending to thank her for her help anyway, but the number went straight to voice mail. She left a short message and hung up, then dialed Fetlock.

'I've got the location secured, as much as possible,' Caxton told him when he asked how she was going about protecting Raleigh. 'I've got some ideas on how to handle him if she shows up here. Though I have to say I'm not looking forward to it.'

'Understandable,' he told her.

'The big thing worrying me right now is that I know he's going to go after Raleigh and Simon, but I don't know which one he'll try to hit first. I could be in the wrong place right now, just spinning my wheels.'

'You'll find out soon enough.'

'Yeah.' Caxton rubbed at her eyes. She needed sleep. Well, she'd needed sleep since Arkeley took the curse. Since Gettysburg. She was learning to live on just a couple hours a night. 'Did Glauer call you about checking some possible lairs?'

'Yes. I have people on it.'

Caxton closed her eyes. 'How many people? Do they know how dangerous this could be? How many places can they check out before dark?'

'Let me worry about that. You have enough on your hands.'

Caxton held the phone away from her face and tried not to scream. Of course she was going to worry about it. This was her case. She wanted to say a number of things in response. Then she rethought them and instead just said, 'Okay, good. Did you send a deputy up to Syracuse to collect Simon?'

'I . . . did,' Fetlock acknowledged.

From his tone Caxton could guess what had happened. 'He refused protective custody, I take it.' *Shit*, she thought. She had called that one.

'I'm told he refused to leave his current residence. Said he had an experiment going on he couldn't let out of his sight. Is Simon some kind of scientist?'

'He's a college student. Probably worried about getting a B in geology or something. Not the most levelheaded guy I've ever met.'

Fetlock tried to sound encouraging. 'I've detailed three units to watch his place, in shifts. We've got round-the-clock coverage. If Jameson shows up there we're ready for him.'

She thought of the cops she'd sent to protect Astarte. 'No. We're probably not. If he comes for Simon tonight I don't know what's going to happen.'

'So what do you want to do, Special Deputy?'

'I can't be in two places at once,' Caxton said. 'And I'm already here. I'll keep in touch, Deputy Marshal.'

'Please do,' Fetlock said, and hung up.

She made a couple more phone calls, preparing for the night to come, and then headed back to the convent building – it was time for dinner.

28.

Dinner at the convent proved simple enough, a salad of mixed greens, vegetable barley soup, and some grainy bread that Caxton chewed and chewed until it was soft enough to swallow. She was seated at a long table with twenty girls, all dressed in over-sized clothes that covered them from neck to ankle. Apparently attractive clothing was a distraction, and therefore to be avoided in the retreat. None of the girls spoke a word as they ate, but they all kept looking up at Caxton with wide eyes, clearly wondering what she was doing there. Raleigh sat on the other side of the table but didn't make eye contact during the meal.

Tall arched windows lined one long wall. Nothing showed beyond them but blackness. If Jameson came crashing through one of them, if he chose that moment to attack his daughter, there would be little Caxton could do to stop him. In the dark she would be at a distinct disadvantage. To Caxton the dining hall was a swaying cavern of guttering light. To a vampire it would be lit up like Christmas – they could see human blood glowing with its own light even in the thickest gloom. To make matters worse, if Jameson attacked the room would be full of panicked girls running every which way. Caxton couldn't shoot through that crowd, not if she didn't want to hit Raleigh or one of the other inmates by mistake.

She was relieved, then, as the sisters rose one by one from the long tables and left the dining hall without a word. They stacked their soup bowls and their plates in a tall metal rack by the door and filed out individually, presumably headed for their rooms. When only a few remained, struggling with their hard bread, Caxton bused her own bowl and plate and then made her way toward where Raleigh still sat.

The girl sat alone, her arms wrapped around her chest, staring down at the rough surface of the table. No food sat before her, just a glass half full of warm water. Caxton remembered that she was fasting in honor of her uncle Angus, and maybe in honor of her mother now as well. She supposed she had to respect that kind of reverence, though she doubted a doctor would agree – Raleigh couldn't weigh much more than a hundred pounds, a fact even her baggy clothes couldn't hide. Caxton touched the girl on the shoulder and she looked up and nodded, then stood and started walking toward the door. Caxton followed close behind, only turning around once when she noticed Violet following them at a discreet distance.

After dinner most of the girls headed for a common room, where they could read or talk quietly among themselves. There wasn't a lot else they were allowed to do. They weren't even allowed to play board games or cards; when Caxton asked why not, Raleigh pointed out a girl named Kelli, who sat alone on the opposite side of the room, just staring into space. 'She's here because she was addicted to Internet gambling. She went through a whole trust fund in six months and then she started borrowing money with no way to pay it back. If we had so much as a game of Go Fish in here, she'd be looking for somebody to bet with on who would win.'

168

One by one, or in small groups, the girls wandered off to bed. It was no later than eight o'clock when Raleigh announced she was tired enough to sleep, herself.

It was understood that Caxton would be sleeping in Raleigh's room that night. Caxton had expected the girl to be suspicious when she'd heard about the arrangements – surely she must have guessed something was up. Yet Raleigh had asked no questions nor even given Caxton a quizzical look. She had simply accepted Caxton's continued presence as a fact of life and moved on.

In the hallway Violet sat waiting for them in a massive carved wooden chair bigger than she was. The mute girl jumped up when she saw them and came racing to catch up.

'What's her deal?' Caxton whispered to Raleigh, nodding in Violet's direction.

'She drank drain cleaner and—'

'No, I heard that from Sister Margot. I mean, is she supposed to keep an eye on us or something? She creeps me out a little.'

Raleigh shrugged. 'Sister Margot would never spy on us. She's not like that.'

'Yeah, okay,' Caxton said, not convinced.

'Besides, Violet is harmless. She's a little nutty, I suppose you could say.'

That Caxton could believe.

'I asked her once,' Raleigh went on, 'why she tried to hurt herself. She can't talk, of course, but she's very good at mime. She rolled up her eyes and sighed dramatically, which I think means she did it just because she was bored. One of the other girls told me that Violet was the daughter of one of the wealthiest families in Ohio. They sent her here to get the rest she needed.'

'Psychotherapy wouldn't have been a better option?'

Raleigh shook her head. 'She was seeing a therapist four times a week when she – when she self-harmed. But look how happy she is here.'

Behind them Violet stopped in midstep and beamed at Caxton, showing lots of big white round teeth.

'This place works miracles,' Raleigh said, her eyes slightly moist.

If I have to spend more than one night here, Caxton thought to herself, *I am going to start praying for a vampire attack. Just to break the boredom.*

They had reached the room that Raleigh and Violet shared, its door identical to dozens of others in the hallway. Inside it proved to be little bigger than a closet. There were two wooden pallets with thin mattresses and thinner sheets, one built into either side wall, and a tiny iron coal-burning stove bolted to the far wall. There were no windows, and definitely no room for a table or chairs or a third cot. Caxton frowned, realizing she would have to sleep either on the floor or outside in the hall. It was freezing cold in the hall – at least the stove would keep her warm during the night.

'I don't see a private bathroom,' Caxton said, trying to smile at Raleigh. 'Is there someplace I can wash up before we turn in? And do you have a spare toothbrush?' It had been a while, and she imagined her breath was getting pretty rank.

Raleigh gave her what she needed, including a washcloth and a bar of organic, cruelty-free soap. It all went in a cute little plastic bucket. Then she pointed her toward a communal bathroom, where half a dozen girls in various states of undress were getting ready for sleep. There was a single bathtub, which was in steady use. Not wanting to wait for hours for her turn, Caxton gave herself a disco bath – a good solid face wash and a scrub or two under the armpits with the washcloth – then headed back to the room. Raleigh and Violet were already lying on their pallets, curled up with their eyes closed. They had taken off their ugly clothes but wore flannel nightgowns instead.

170

'Good night,' Caxton said, but Raleigh didn't answer – maybe she was already asleep. Violet opened one eye to look at her, winked mischievously, then closed her eyes again and started to snore.

Caxton closed the door, pitching the room into near-total darkness. Only a little orange light came around the edge of the iron stove's door. She sat down on the floor between the two pallets and placed her Beretta between her knees. She had no intention of sleeping, at least not until she was sure Jameson wouldn't attack that night. She leaned up against the far wall, careful not to touch the stove, and waited.

And then nothing happened.

Nothing at all. And then, more nothing.

At some point she noted that her chin was touching her chest. Her mouth was hanging slackly open and drool was rolling down the front of her shirt. She sat up suddenly, knocking her head against the wall behind her. Had she dozed off? If so, for how long?

She stared around the little room, desperately hoping Jameson hadn't caught her napping. But no, both sisters were still lying on their pallets, fast asleep.

Wiping down her shirt with one hand, she forced herself upward until she was standing. Her head rang like a bell with interrupted sleep and she could feel the blood rushing down into her body, into her legs. One of these nights, she told herself, she was going to have to actually get eight hours of uninterrupted sleep. Thinking she would splash some water on her face, she gently opened the door and stepped out into the hall. A single candle inside a hurricane lamp stood at the end of the hallway, providing just enough light for her to find her way to the bathroom.

Halfway there she heard someone cry out in the dark.

29.

Caxton rushed forward with her weapon drawn, barely able to see in the dark corridor. The sound had come from far off, perhaps from a completely different part of the building. She had made a note, earlier, of the plan of each floor and she knew there were dormitory wings at both ends of the structure. Getting from one side to the other in the dark was going to be difficult, she thought, and unless the cry came again she might never know which room it had come from.

She stopped herself, tried not to breathe too hard, and listened.

There – she heard it again. Was it a cry of pain, or just terror? She couldn't be sure. It seemed to come from a room closer by, this time. She tensed herself, closed her eyes, and – yes, there.

Sprinting down the hall, she turned a corner and found herself in another almost lightless hallway, this one, like the other, lined with the narrow doorways that led to the girls' rooms.

What would she do if she found Jameson inside one of the

rooms, tearing somebody to pieces? She would shoot, of course, but would it do any good? She had fired into his heart at point-blank range and achieved nothing. What made her think it would be different this time? Yet she had no idea what else to do.

It was no time to think of such things, she told herself. She forced herself to concentrate, to listen again for the cry. She had no choice. This was what she was pledged to do, to protect people from the vampires. Clamping her eyes shut, she put every ounce of her attention into her ears.

'Oh my God,' she heard – a sound of desperation.

She rushed forward, into the dark. Her rubber-soled shoes slapped on the flagstone floor and she wondered if Jameson could hear her coming. The cry was louder now, and it came repeatedly – 'Oh my God'; this time it was nearly a sigh, and then she heard it again, much louder – 'No way!'

She stood outside the door she was certain was the source of the cries. Her weapon up and ready, she reached forward to touch the doorknob, to throw back the door and confront whatever was inside. Something bugged her about the sound, though. It wasn't a fearful shriek at all. It was more like—

'You're so dead,' someone said from behind the door.

Caxton knocked the door in with her shoulder. It wasn't locked.

Inside sat six girls with their knees up on the two pallets, looking terrified. One of them held a cheap flashlight that gave off less light than the coal stove.

On the floor between the pallets lay a pile of very old, very tattered magazines. They'd been glossy once, and were folded open to pictures of various movie stars. Brad Pitt. Angelina Jolie. Tom Cruise.

One of the girls was holding a lit cigarette as if it were a joint.

173

'Please, no,' one of the girls whispered. She had a lipstick on her mouth and she hurriedly smeared the back of her hand across her lips, trying to rub it off. 'Please don't say anything. Oh, please. We'll get in so much trouble—'

Caxton stepped back out into the hallway and pulled the door shut again. From inside she could hear desperate whispers shooting back and forth.

Shaking her head, taking her time, Caxton worked her way back toward Raleigh's room. It had not been what she'd thought at all. She'd been so primed and ready for a vampire attack that any sound would have alerted her. Now she wondered if Jameson was nearby at all. He could be miles away. He could be up at Syracuse.

That thought gave her a shiver. Or maybe it was just the frigid air in the convent. She rubbed at her own arms, and then swung them back and forth rapidly, trying to get her circulation going. She headed around the corner and tried to remember which room belonged to Raleigh. They all looked alike.

Violet solved the problem for her by opening the door then and peeking her head out. Her eyes were very wide.

Caxton hurried toward the mute girl and asked her what was the matter. Violet's answer was to open the door up all the way and step aside, letting Caxton look into the little room. The stove was glowing merrily and its light clearly showed that both pallets were empty.

'Where's Raleigh?' Caxton asked. Maybe she had just gotten up to go to the bathroom, she thought. Maybe she'd been unable to sleep and had gone for a little walk to clear her head. She wouldn't let herself think of the other possibility, the more dreadful one.

Violet's face clouded with anxiety for the first time since Caxton had met her. She shook her head from side to side, then

174

raised her hands in a gesture of submission. Caxton frowned, which just made the girl more upset. She held up one hand with the index and ring fingers pointing down. Moving them deftly, she simulated someone sneaking away, walking carefully and softly so as not to be heard.

'Okay, thanks,' Caxton said. She started to run off, but then stopped herself. She had no reason to believe Raleigh was in danger, not really. She had no indication that Jameson was anywhere near the building. Yet she had an obligation to the inmates to keep them safe. That was far more important than her desire not to disturb their sleep. 'Go wake up Sister Margot,' she said, staring into Violet's eyes until the silent girl nodded in understanding. 'Tell her – tell her we may have some trouble tonight.' Then she was off like a shot.

Raleigh could be anywhere. Caxton would search the entire building if she had to. Back around the corner. Down the hallway that led to the other dormitory wing – maybe Raleigh was just headed to a midnight magazine session in some other room, Caxton told herself.

Maybe she had gone to meet her father, to tell him that yes, please, she'd like to become a vampire.

No. That wasn't possible. Caxton had seen enough of the girl to know she wasn't capable of making that kind of choice for herself. Simon, on the other hand – but Simon was in another state, under police guard.

No time to worry about Simon.

Caxton grabbed a candle from where it burned at the top of the main stairway, studied it for a moment, then shook her head and put it back. She had a mini Mag-Lite in her pocket and wasn't afraid to use it. Hurrying up the stairs, she switched it on and played it across the long white plaster walls.

The third floor was empty, and silent, as it should be – it was all therapy rooms. All cold and deserted.

Caxton moved on. The second floor, which consisted of dormitories (which she'd already checked), a big unused library, and a couple of yoga studios, was deserted as well, though the central hallway resonated with the breath of all the sleeping girls, their snoring making Caxton's candle flicker. She peered through the gloom, looking for half-open doors or stealthily broken windows, but there was nothing to be found.

Main floor next. The central foyer was empty. So were the offices – Sister Margot's office door was wide open and Caxton glanced inside, found nothing. She hurried to the other wing and the big dining hall. The long wooden tables had been cleared off and the rolling carts full of bused bowls and table-ware long since trundled away. Caxton studied the long, sharp shadows of the big room with her mini flashlight but found nothing, not so much as a mouse.

She turned to go, not sure where to check next, when a noise made her shoulders jump up around her ears. It was a sound that would have made her jump at any time, but at that particular moment it nearly made her squeal in terror.

It was the sound of a dropped spoon bouncing on a flagstone floor. A jangling, pealing sound, as loud as cannon fire in the still dining hall.

Caxton dashed across the big room and knocked open the door at the far end with her shoulder. Beyond lay the kitchen – a room full of big prep tables and wide sinks, with iron pots and skillets dangling from the ceiling on hooks. Caxton's flash-light beam shattered as it passed through the hanging pans and griddles and showed her odd-shaped patches of the wall beyond. She moved quickly to the side of the room and hurried toward its back, where the food was stored in massive walk-in pantries.

Caxton licked her lips. They had suddenly gone very dry.

She moved slowly, quietly, toward the open door – then threw it back all at once.

Her flashlight shone down like an accusing finger on Raleigh, who kneeled on the floor, her face upturned and wracked with terror. She held an open jar of honey in one hand. It was her spoon that had fallen to the floor.

'I thought you were fasting in your uncle's memory,' Caxton said, suddenly very angry. She fought to control herself.

'Do you know how hard it is to eat nothing for three whole weeks?' Raleigh asked, in a very small voice.

'Come on,' Caxton said. She'd had enough of the girls' after-hours hijinks. 'We're going back to your room. You're going to sleep there all night if I have to sit on you.' She grabbed Raleigh's arm, not too roughly, and dragged her up to her feet.

The girl didn't pull away from her as Caxton marched the two of them through the dining hall and back toward the main stairwell. Just outside the entrance hall, however, Raleigh grabbed Caxton's arm very tightly and shook her head.

'Did you hear something?' Caxton asked. When she shut up and listened for a second, she heard it, too. 'What is that?' The sound changed to a kind of pathetic gagging and hissing that didn't sound like an animal at all.

Caxton pushed open the door to the main hall and pointed her flashlight beam through, a narrow cone of light spearing through the darkness. It lit up Violet, who was slumped across the bottom steps of the stairway, her arms up in the air as if she were fending off a brutal attack. Caxton swiveled her light to the side a little – and saw Jameson Arkeley's red eyes burn brighter than the room's candles as he crouched over the silent girl.

177

30.

Caxton raised her weapon and fired right at Jameson's heart.
The shot tore open his black shirt, just a few inches off. The
vampire spun around and glared at her, but with her free hand
she was already reaching for the amulet around her neck. It
felt warm in her hand, which meant it was working.

On the stairs Violet writhed and pushed herself up a step.
Her face was contorted by fear and her hands were clutching
at nothing.

Caxton fired again, and this time hit her target. The bullet
clanged off his chest and spun away into the darkness. How
was it possible? Jameson's body curled up like a caterpillar in
a fire, but only for an instant. He straightened up quickly –
and then he was on her. It was that fast. She felt a cold wind
blowing toward her and then she was on the floor with the
vampire on top of her, pinning down her gun hand, his teeth
pressing against her cheek. He felt cold and wrong and he
stank of death.

His weight pressed down on her wrist and the tendons there
bent and twisted. Her fingers spasmed and then flew outward

and her weapon fell away. He snatched it up and threw it into the darkness.

He held her there silently while she struggled. He outweighed her by a considerable margin, but it was his strength that truly held her – she might as well have fought off a stone statue. Clamping her eyes shut, she turned her face to the floor and tried to get her free arm up to protect her eyes, but he just grabbed her wrist and smashed it painfully against the flagstones. Her flashlight rolled away across the floor.

She could hear Violet gasping and choking on the stairs. She could hear her own breath pushing in and out of her chest. She could hear her heart beating in her throat. Jameson was as silent as a tomb.

Then he pulled back a fraction of an inch. Enough to let her roll over on her side. Not enough to get her legs underneath her. 'I warned you off,' he said, 'but you wouldn't listen. There's part of me that still doesn't want to kill you. Do you believe that?'

She didn't answer – couldn't. But then he shook her violently.

'Yes,' she managed to exhale.

'That part,' he went on, 'gets smaller every night. The other part of me, the curse, gets stronger. Right now it's telling me to tear open your carotid artery. To lap at your blood. I can imagine how good that would feel. How good it would taste. It would solve some problems, too. It would make my task easier.'

He was trying to convince himself to kill her, she realized. He was psyching himself up. She had to think of something fast.

'You did this to save me,' she tried. 'You took the curse to save my life. If you kill me now that sacrifice means nothing.'

179

'I spared your life once, at the motel. Maybe that makes us even.'

She shook her head from side to side. 'And what about at your wife's house? You left seven half-deads to kill me.'

'I knew you could handle those. They were only there to cover my escape. Now. Shh,' he whispered, and drew a finger down her cheek. He found her pulse point and tapped her skin in time with her heartbeat. His fingernail, she knew, was sharper than a wolf's claw. He could cut her open right there and let the blood come rushing out. If he even scratched her, if even a drop of her blood was spilled, then nothing would hold him back. He would smell her blood fresh and warm on her skin and it would drive him into a frenzy. No moral compunction he'd ever had would be able to stop him then.

He knew it, too. He lifted his finger away from her throat and then brought the nail down to touch her skin. It felt cold and hard. He started to press, gently at first, but she knew in a moment he would cut right into her.

'Daddy,' Raleigh said then. Caxton's eyes were still shut. She couldn't see the girl. 'Daddy, please, no. I'll do whatever you want. Just don't hurt her.'

She wanted to scream *No*, wanted to tell Raleigh to run, to get away. She couldn't seem to get the words out of her throat.

'Please, Daddy.'

Jameson's finger lifted away from her neck. The mangled palm of his left hand still held her wrist against the floor. She could feel his body moving above her, moving away from her, but still he held her fast.

'Raleigh, I want to give you something,' he said. 'Something wonderful. I was never a very good father.'

'No, Daddy, don't say that.'

Caxton could feel his body shaking. 'I was lousy. But I can make it up to you now. Come here. Come closer.'

'No,' Caxton managed to shriek, at the same time as she heard something hard and metallic smash into Jameson's skull. Her eyes shot open and she saw Violet standing over them both, a massive wrought-iron candelabra in her hands. One of the candles remained in its socket, guttering wildly.

Jameson leapt up off of Caxton and backward, away from the girl's follow-up attack. He laughed as she swept the candelabra across his face like a rake, laughed again as she swung it over her head and down into his ear.

'Raleigh,' Caxton called, rolling over onto her stomach, 'get the fuck out of here right now.'

Jameson's daughter nodded and disappeared through the doorway again. Caxton got her feet underneath her and half-crawled, half-ran toward where she thought her handgun had landed when Jameson threw it. In the dark hall she couldn't see it. She had to find it. She had only seconds, she knew, before Jameson stopped laughing at Violet's attacks and decided to do something about them.

Where was the pistol? Where? She saw a shadow ahead of her on the floor and dove forward, her hands stretched out to grab it. Cool metal met her fingertips and she grabbed it up, ran her thumb across the safety, making sure it wasn't on. She rolled over on her back and sat up, sighting on where she expected Jameson to be.

She was off by yards. The gun barrel pointed at nothing but darkness. She spat out a profanity and swept the gun left – just in time to see Jameson lift Violet off her feet and into the air. His mouth sank into her chest and red blood rushed down her baggy shirt. Her candelabra lay on the floor beneath her, forgotten.

'No,' Caxton moaned, and fired into Jameson's back. The vampire cringed and then spun around, and she thought he might come at her again, might grab her again, and this time she knew he would kill her. Instead he tossed Violet's body away like a doll and raced for the front door and out into the night.

She followed as fast as she could, her body twitching with adrenaline. Outside the stars burned in a deep blue sky and lit up the snow with an unearthly pale radiance. She couldn't see Jameson at first, and she worried he might have tricked her, that maybe he had just run out the door and stopped, put his back up against the ivy-covered wall to wait for her to run past him. That he would reach out of the dark and grab her and kill her easily.

Then she saw him running ahead of her, his dark clothes a pillar of black against the snow, his legs and arms pumping. She dashed forward, her weapon raised, knowing it was pointless to shoot while they were both running. Worried it was pointless to shoot at all. How many times had she hit him? She'd barely slowed him down.

He was running for the front gate, the iron gate with the cross on top. She could never catch him, of course – he was far too fast, his new body capable of converting stolen blood into incredible speed. On foot she was no match for him, and he must have known that.

Luckily, she'd had time to prepare.

She grabbed up her cell phone out of her pocket. Running as fast as she was, she couldn't check the screen to see if she had any bars or not. She flipped it open anyway and hit the send key. Hours earlier she'd typed in the appropriate number and now the phone dialed automatically.

Pressing it against her ear, she heard a single thready ring, the atmosphere tearing at her signal with invisible fingers. A second ring and then someone picked up on the other end.

'Now,' she said, and light blasted through the gateway, dozens of headlights on high beam coming on all at once. If everything had gone according to plan there would be as many as ten patrol cruisers sitting out there, all of them loaded with local cops. After the disaster at Bellefonte she'd been leery of actually bringing them into the convent, but they could serve her just fine out there beyond the gate.

The light hit Jameson like an artillery barrage. He threw his arms up across his face and dropped to his knees in the snow, hurt far worse by car headlights than by all the bullets she'd wasted on him. He was a nocturnal creature and his eyes were meant for night vision. They couldn't handle all that light.

Slowly he rose to his feet again, turning away from the gate, his face clutched in his hands.

'There's no escape that way,' Caxton shouted. 'And I have guys waiting at the creek if you try to go that way.' She lined up a shot on his back. 'I'm willing to give you a chance to surrender.'

Jameson rose to his full height, still rubbing at his eyes with his hands. Behind him she could see cops milling about, poking rifle barrels through the gate, lining up shots. She didn't know if they would have any more luck than she had, but there was one way to find out.

He started to laugh then. Maybe it was the laughter of a man who knows there's no way out, but she didn't think so. She lifted the phone to her lips and said, 'Fire at will.'

31.

The rifles cracked and spat fire and filled the air with whizzing bullets, but Jameson was already on the move. He leapt out of the light and landed on all fours like a cat on the shadowy snow, then swiveled around and jumped again as the rifles tracked him. Caxton ran out of the field of fire, terrified that she might be hit by a stray shot from one of the police guns.

She could still hear the vampire laughing, a cold chuckle that rattled around inside her head like a dried pea in a cup. She jammed her fingers in her ears, which helped with the noise from the rifles but didn't quiet the laughter at all.

Moving faster than she'd ever seen a vampire move before, Jameson crouched low and dashed behind a statue of the Virgin Mary. A rifle shot took off part of her wimple in a puff of obliterated masonry, but already Jameson was moving on. A row of weathered headstones was his next cover, and she could just see his dark clothes in reverse silhouette against the faintly glowing snow as he pressed his back against one of the stones. For a moment he didn't move at all, or no – his good hand was moving, working at his belt. Had he brought some weapon, a firearm, with which to fight back? She'd never seen a real vampire with a gun before. They didn't need them. Maybe that was just hubris on their part, however. Maybe Jameson had decided to buck the trend.

It wasn't a gun he pulled out, though, as she watched. It was the belt of his pants. He whirled it around for a moment, then flung it into the air. The rifles tracked it and one or two of the cops took a shot – but already Jameson was moving in the other direction.

'Keep it together,' she shouted into her phone. 'Don't get distracted.'

It was hard for her to follow her own advice, however. Ducking behind a massive boulder, Jameson nearly got away from her as he threw one of his shoes to the left and the other to the right. She tried to keep her weapon pointed at him, but the double feint dragged her attention away for a split second. In that time Jameson managed to duckwalk all the way to a massive fountain in the middle of the lawn.

She could just make out the curve of his back behind the fountain. His body writhed like a snake and she wondered if maybe he'd been hit. That was probably too much to hope for, and anyway if he'd been hit anywhere but directly in the heart it would only take him seconds to regenerate. With Violet's blood flowing through his veins he would be nearly impervious to harm.

'Come on,' she said, urging him to move again, to expose himself for just a second. Instead he seemed to relax, his body sagging to the snow. 'Come on. You can't stay there forever.'

He didn't move at all. The rifles had fallen silent, as no target presented itself. She thought about telling the cops to move in, but she knew that would just put them at risk. Assaulting the fountain was up to her.

'Hold your fire,' she said into her phone. Then she shoved

it in her pocket, the call still connected in case she needed to issue another order. Keeping low, trying not to expose herself too much, Caxton moved step by step closer to the fountain.

Jameson – what she could see of him – didn't stir.

He could be lying in wait for her. He could be just waiting for her to get close enough, just inside a crucial range where he could jump out and attack her. She kept her weapon up and held on to it with both hands. Another step closer and she could see his shirt, the sleeves stretched out as if he were hugging the round lip of the fountain. When he did launch himself at her she would have only a fraction of a second to respond. Another step, and she could see his pants, his knees bent like coiled springs. Without his shoes his feet would be nearly invisible against the snow, she thought. His skin was as white as the ground cover, and—

His feet weren't there. They weren't just difficult to see. They were missing, as if they'd been cut off just at the level of his pant cuffs. She raised her weapon a fraction of an inch and saw that his hands were missing as well. *What the hell*, she had time to think, before she understood exactly what had happened.

It was just his clothes, laid out to look as if he was still in them. A decoy.

She spun around, grabbing her phone out of her pocket even as she searched the snow. 'He's moving,' she shouted. 'He's naked and moving! There, nine o'clock, somebody shoot him!'

She could barely see him, wriggling along the ground, already twenty yards away. Completely naked, and therefore almost perfectly camouflaged. She ran after him, no longer caring if she was running right into a free-fire zone, and discharged her weapon every time she thought she had a clear shot.

It was no use. Even down on all fours, scuttling like a crab,

186

he was far faster than she was running at her top speed. In seconds he was up against the convent wall, a snowman glowing by starlight. Then he was up, his powerful legs carrying him over the wall in one spastic hop.

'No,' she howled, racing back toward the gate. There was no way she could get over that wall herself, not without wasting a lot of time. At the gate a line of cops stared at her with shock and disbelief, but she didn't have time to explain. Dashing around the side of the wall, she headed down a narrow decline, dodging tree trunks. She came around the corner of the wall and pushed on, intent on reaching the place where he had come over the top. In the dark, with pine needles overhead soaking up all the starlight, she could barely see anything. A tree root snagged at her foot and she bounced sideways, intent on not twisting her ankle, not now, not when he was so close. She struck a tree trunk with her hand, scraping half the skin off her palm, and kept running. She could not let him get away – not again.

And yet that was exactly what happened. A rock shifted under her foot and she went sprawling, her hands down to collide with a frozen carpet of brown pine needles. She got slowly, painfully to her feet, knowing he'd already evaded her.

She found the wall, and pushed her back up against it. Closed her eyes, tried to listen for any sound of running feet. There was nothing. She heard snow sliding down through branches fifty feet over her head. From far off, from inside the convent, she heard someone shouting. She heard the cops behind her climbing into their cars, slamming their doors. She heard the phone in her pocket chime. But no sound of a vampire anywhere.

She let her pulse rate wind down. Caught her breath.

Heading back toward the gate, she checked the phone and found she had a new text message:

You almost had him tonight, didn't you?
Mayhaps the FOURTH time's the charm.

Malvern again. Malvern – who had some way of knowing that Caxton had failed. Caxton considered throwing the phone away into the trees, getting it as far away from herself as possible. It was government property, though, and she knew Fetlock would disapprove. So she just switched it off and shoved it deep into the bottom of her pocket.

32.

As usual, Jameson had left her quite a mess to clean up.

Her first concern was for Raleigh. Sister Margot and several of the girls were waiting in the front hall and they demanded answers to their questions. She just pushed past them and into the hallway where she'd last seen Jameson's daughter. The girl was there, curled up in a massive wooden chair. Her face was white with fear and her hands were clenched. She said she could not release them.

'Just breathe,' Caxton said, kneeling in front of her. 'Breathe.'

The girl shook her head wildly. Caxton fought down the urge to slap her. She had work to do, but first she needed to make sure Raleigh was alright. She tried to imagine what Glauer would do in this situation. Glauer was much better at dealing with hysterical people. 'Look,' she said. 'It's going to be alright. Yeah. Your father wants to turn you into a vampire, but—'

'He wants what?' Raleigh gasped. She started breathing heavily. She was at risk of hyperventilating.

'You're safe right now. He won't come back tonight. I promise. That's his MO so far, one attack per night.'

'Then what about tomorrow night?' the girl asked.

'I'll protect you then, too,' Caxton said.

It wasn't working. Raleigh's fear level was ramping up and nothing Caxton said seemed to help. She headed back into the foyer, intending to ask Sister Margot for help. 'Did Raleigh have any friends here she was especially close with?' Caxton asked. 'I mean,' she said, after glancing at the corpse on the floor, 'anyone other than Violet. Someone needs to sit with her. I don't think she's going to sleep tonight. Also, I need some Styrofoam cups, or whatever you have.' There were shell casings all over the floor, bullet holes in the walls, and worse, probably dozens of bullets out on the lawn. She needed to start identifying their locations. Normally she could have left that to someone else, but with the girls milling about in the foyer it was going to be hard to secure the scene. She scanned the floor with her eyes, finding her brasses, until she realized Sister Margot wasn't answering her. 'Is something wrong?' she asked.

'You,' Sister Margot said, 'have brought death into this sacred place. You will leave at once!'

Caxton bit her lip.

Sister Margot stamped her foot on the flagstones. 'At once!'

Caxton watched the young woman carefully. Sized her up. 'I'm afraid that's not going to happen,' she said.

'This is a place of healing. Of peace! I've worked all my life to make it a quiet refuge and in one night you've ruined everything!'

Not shrugging was the best Caxton could do to mollify the girl. 'I'm going to need to bring in some forensics people, get this crime scene cleared, that's going to take most of the night, then I'll need to bring in some people to question

190

everyone who was out in the halls before, so we can establish when the vampire came in and what route he used. Lastly I'm going to—'

'Violet is lying there, dead!' Margot shrieked.

'Yeah. I need to contact her parents immediately.'

'I should hope you would. When they hear what happened I imagine—'

'I'll need to convince them into an emergency cremation. Whenever he wants, the vampire can bring her back from the dead. Meanwhile, I'll get an armed guard in here to watch her for signs of reanimation.' It would be much easier, of course, to just cut off the dead girl's head. Decapitated corpses didn't come back as half-deads. But she supposed the family had a right to make that kind of decision. 'Meanwhile, why don't you get everyone back to bed, alright? My people will come and go and hopefully be done by the time you get up in the morning. Thanks, Margot.'

The nun's face was bright red. Caxton turned away to head back toward the gate, where she could make some phone calls.

First things first – she called in an APB on a naked vampire, to be considered extremely dangerous. She called the local police chief and reported Violet's homicide so he could get a file going. Not that it was going to require much in the way of investigation, but you had to keep the paperwork straight. Finally she called Fetlock – or rather, she started dialing his number. Before she had half the digits into the phone he called her instead.

'Um, hello,' she said, answering his call.

'Is she dead?' Fetlock asked.

Caxton rubbed the bridge of her nose. 'No. Raleigh – Raleigh's alright. A little shaken up. How did you—?'

'But Jameson got away. I just saw your APB.'

Everybody knew about the mess she'd made. Malvern,

Fetlock – when would Vesta Polder chime in? she wondered. 'Yeah. Yeah, he got away. I'll explain how later. Listen, Deputy Marshal, how do you know all this? It only just happened.'

'I've been monitoring your phone,' he told her. 'You made it sound as if you expected Jameson to attack tonight, so I've been up waiting to hear what happened. I hope you don't mind me listening in to your phone calls.'

'No . . . of course not,' Caxton said.

'It's crucial we stay together on this case. You should have called me earlier, when you were setting up your ambush. I could have had a SWAT team mobilized or something. Why didn't you call me?'

'I figured I could handle it myself,' Caxton replied. To be honest, she hadn't thought of Fetlock at all.

'Alright, next time. Now tell me what you need right now. I can be there in less than an hour.'

Caxton thought about it for a moment. She thought about Margot – and the girls. Violet's murder would upset them more than she wanted to accept. She should try to be more sensitive, she decided. That was what Glauer would have told her. 'There are no men allowed down here. Maybe you should stay clear – though I do need some officers to guard the scene, and the body. Female officers. Also,' she said, looking around the snowy lawn, 'I have some material evidence here. Jameson left his clothes behind.'

'His clothes?'

So she had to explain how he'd gotten away after all. Fetlock said he would see what he could do about getting some female officers down to the convent and Caxton hung up. Then she went to send home the cops who had made up her ambush. She thanked them profusely and was glad to see them leave unscathed – but then one turned back. He was an earnest-looking young cop from the local borough's PD. His uniform

192

was spotless and his eyes were bright, even though the hour was growing late. He waited patiently for her to wave at the departing cars, then stepped closer, coughed discreetly into his hand, and then stood at attention until she met his eye.

'Excuse me, ma'am,' he said.

'At ease,' she replied. 'You have something to say?'

He nodded and relaxed a little. 'I hit him,' he said.

Caxton shrugged. 'So did I. Several times.'

The cop frowned. 'Ma'am, begging your pardon – you didn't so much as slow him down. We were all talking before, wondering if maybe he was bulletproof. Maybe through some magical means. But I've been hunting since I was a boy, and I know when I've hit an animal or a paper target. I saw his blood. I just wanted you to know that. He isn't impervious to bullets, at least not totally.'

She stared at him with wide eyes. 'You saw his blood?'

'I saw him turn to his left, and his arm went up, like so,' he demonstrated. 'Then blood came out of the wound. Not much. But I know when I hit somebody.'

'Thank you very much, Officer. That's actually good to hear.' And it was. She sent him home. He'd given her a lot to think about. So far she'd been unable to scratch his skin with her best shots. If the young officer had actually drawn blood – then maybe there was hope.

She secured the scene in the foyer as best she could, then went to sit in her own car and wait for Fetlock's fiber unit to arrive. The sun was just starting to color the tops of the trees when the unit showed up – or rather, when the forensics expert arrived, since it was just one woman. She was about fifty, with frosted blond hair and bags under her eyes. She was not happy about being dragged out of bed to look at some cast-off clothes. 'There's a body inside?' she asked, pulling on some latex gloves. 'Can I have that as well?'

193

'No word yet from the local coroner, so we can't remove her yet. I'm waiting on word from her family so I can cremate her.'

The forensics expert grunted. 'Tough to get anything useful from ashes. Though cremation's not as complete as some people think. Your typical flame job leaves small material, some of it recognizable. You can get teeth out of ashes, and sometimes the fillings don't melt, so you can match dental records. Titanium surgical pins, Teflon knee replacements, those survive.'

'We already have a positive ID on the body.'

The older woman shrugged.

'You want to take a look?' Caxton asked. She led the woman inside the foyer to where Violet still lay as she'd fallen.

'Vampire attack,' the expert said, after studying the body for a while. 'More violent than the previous ones we've seen. This wasn't premeditated.'

'No,' Caxton said. 'Listen, I was here. I know all this already. Do you think you could tell me something I could use?'

The expert grunted again. 'Maybe. This is not an exact science, Trooper.'

'Special Deputy. Let's go look at the clothes.' She led the expert back out to the lawn and the shirt and pair of pants Arkeley had left behind. 'Nobody has touched them. I made sure of it.'

'Good. Honestly, fiber's my specialty,' the expert said.

Caxton sighed in relief. Fetlock had sent the right person for the job, then. There would be no fingerprints on the scene, or any DNA evidence. Vampires didn't leave those behind, ever. Fibers were another matter. Anybody who wore clothes left fibers behind, somewhere.

The expert took one quick look at the clothes, then examined a few loose threads with a jeweler's loupe. 'I think

I can confirm this is a match with what we saw at the hotel. Three kinds of fibers. We left a report for your liaison.'

'I got it,' Caxton agreed.

'Yeah. She wasn't there at your HQ when we arrived. We had to leave the report with a desk sergeant. She never even followed up to let me know she got it. That's just not professional. You want some free advice? Fire this twit. You've got real forensic pathologists in Harrisburg. Any of them would do a better job.'

The woman was talking about Clara. Caxton held her tongue.

'Anyway, I'll do an actual comparison, but for now, I'll provisionally say we're looking at the same three fibers. Cotton, nylon, Twaron.'

'What the hell is Twaron?' Caxton asked. She'd been wondering all day.

The expert picked at the shirt and unbuttoned it. Beneath was another layer of cloth, some kind of vest. She picked up the vest and threw it at Caxton, who caught it – but it was much heavier than she'd expected and she nearly dropped it. Squishing it in her hand, she knew what it was instantly.

'Twaron,' the expert explained, 'is a competing product with Kevlar. It's used in the construction of police body armor, mostly. Your vampire was wearing a ballistic vest.'

33.

Caxton slapped the vest down on one of the desks in the briefing room a few hours later. Glauer stared at it as if there was some hidden message written on it, something he could read if he just looked hard enough.

'It's a type IIIA ballistic vest,' Caxton said. 'Standard police issue. Twaron fibers woven just right to reduce the impact of a bullet.' She rapped her knuckles on a spot just above where the wearer's heart would be. 'Then there's a steel trauma plate here, just in case something gets through the fibers. It'll stop pretty much any handgun bullet – .38 special, .44 Magnum, and just about any 9-millimeter round you can name, including the Parabellum rounds I load.'

Glauer tilted his head to one side. 'So when you shot him, even at point-blank range—'

'He probably felt it, but it probably didn't hurt.' She shook her head. 'If you add this to how tough a vampire is anyway – I'm not exactly sure what would kill him.'

'Jesus,' Glauer swore. The man rarely ever swore. 'But I'm confused. In the middle of a firefight he just threw it away. Why?'

'We weren't shooting at him with handgun bullets anymore. This time we were using rifles. A rifle bullet would go through this like tissue paper,' she said, poking her index finger through a hole low on the left side, about where the wearer's kidney might be. The cop who had spoken with her after the ambush had been right – he had hit Jameson, just not in his one vital spot.

'Jameson's smart. We knew that already. He's smart enough to understand his limitations. Most vampires don't. They're tougher than us, a hell of a lot faster, but they're arrogant. They think they're invincible, and that makes them cocky. Jameson is the least vain vampire I've ever seen.'

'Maybe, but then again he did leave this behind, right? So now he's unprotected. You can't just buy these off the Internet. You need to be in law enforcement to get one, and nobody is going to sell a vest to a vampire.'

Caxton punched the vest, and not lightly. 'That would be great, wouldn't it? Fetlock's forensics expert said pretty much the same thing. For about an hour I was happy. Then I got a call. A peace officer out of Lenhartsville had radioed in saying he had a subject that matched the description on my APB. Tall, vampire, naked, running along the side of I-78. He said he was going to investigate. Then he never radioed back.'

'Oh, no.'

Caxton nodded. 'A second unit was dispatched to the scene. The peace officer was found drained of blood. The engine of his cruiser was still running, but the trunk had been torn open, as if with a pry bar. You want to guess what was missing from the trunk?'

'A type IIIA ballistic vest?' Glauer asked.

Caxton touched the tip of her nose. 'He doesn't mind running around without any pants on, but Jameson feels

197

naked without a trauma plate over his heart. He didn't waste any time getting another one.'

Glauer stood back and rubbed at his mouth with his hands. 'Another cop.'

'Another funeral,' Caxton agreed.

For a while they were both silent. The Glauer said, in a very soft voice: 'At least it wasn't magic.'

Caxton sat down at one of the other desks. 'Yeah. I was beginning to think he had some kind of spell to protect him against bullets. Now I know better. Fat lot of good it does me. I can't carry a rifle around with me every time I go out. Against what I'm carrying, he's fucking bulletproof!'

'Hey,' Glauer said, stepping toward her. For a second she flinched backward, thinking he was going to give her a supportive hug. 'Let's not lose focus here. You did accomplish something last night.'

Caxton frowned. 'What? I managed to not get myself killed? I scared a bunch of girls who seriously did not need more trauma?'

'You saved her life.'

They both turned and looked then at Raleigh, who sat in a far corner of the room, on the floor, with her arms around her knees. She had been offered a chair but refused it. She hadn't said a word since Caxton led her out of the convent, except 'yes' and 'no' when she'd been asked if she was willing to come to Harrisburg, and then when she was asked if she was okay, respectively.

She was scared. Terrified. Caxton could understand that. She should be scared, frankly. It was only a matter of time before her father came after her again.

Caxton turned back to Glauer. 'Yeah,' she said. 'I saved her. She isn't going to be safe, though, until I take Jameson down.'

'Okay. How do you want to proceed?'

Caxton scratched her chin. 'Well, as I see it, there are two things I need to do. I need to go up to Syracuse and stop Jameson from killing Simon. Then I have to find Jameson's lair. Shooting him doesn't seem to work. So I have to catch him when he's defenseless. If I can get to him during the daytime, if I can find his coffin, I can pluck his heart right out of his chest.'

'How's the search for the lair coming?' Glauer asked.

She nodded appreciatively. She might be uncomfortable working with Fetlock, but he got results. 'We had a list of sixty-odd places to check yesterday. The Feds were able to eliminate twenty of them yesterday, by actually going there and checking them in person. No sign of a vampire in any of them. They'll probably finish off the list today. I'd love to be able to go and check them out myself, but this'll have to do – I'm going up to Syracuse as soon as I can, to secure Simon personally. We know Jameson is headed there next. It's his last stop. If we don't get him there – I have no idea where he'll strike next, and everything gets a lot harder.'

'How far away is Syracuse?' Glauer asked.

'A little over four hours, if you're driving. I don't know how he travels.'

Glauer nodded. 'That's a long drive. Are you sure you're up to it? You look like you need sleep.'

Caxton shrugged. 'I used to work highway patrol. I would do twelve-hour shifts in a car back then. This I can handle. I have a couple of errands to run before I go, but I should be on the road before noon – which means I can arrive before nightfall. I might even have time to talk to Simon before his father tries to kill him.'

'Okay. I assume, from the way you're talking, that I'm not going with you up there. I'll keep working on the Carboy notebooks.'

'You haven't turned up anything more from them, have you?' she asked.

Glauer's face lit up, just a little. He gestured at the whiteboards and she saw, under Jameson's portrait, a new picture. A picture of a slightly pudgy teenaged girl with spiky black hair (bright blue at the temples) and soft, very kindly-looking brown eyes.

'Who's that? I've never seen her before.'

'Yes, you have,' Glauer told her. 'Fetlock's people came through with a partial facial reconstruction while you were gone. She was the half-dead that approached Angus.'

'Seriously?' Caxton looked closer at the picture. 'I thought that one was male. She didn't look anything like that.' Of course, if she'd been dead for a week, and she'd scratched off her own face – maybe.

'I took the partial face sketch they gave me and had some troopers run it by the missing persons database. She came up pretty fast. Cady Rourke, aged eighteen. Former resident of Mount Carmel.'

Caxton squinted. 'That's Carboy's hometown.'

'Yes. And Cady Rourke was his first girlfriend. At least, that's what he writes in the notebooks. I called her family and they said she and Dylan were just friends. Either way, what was Jameson doing with her? Besides drinking her blood?'

'It's a connection,' Caxton had to admit. 'Tenuous, but it's something.'

'I'd like to keep working on this lead. Unless you have something better for me to do.'

'Actually, I do. I need you to watch her.' Caxton didn't so much as glance at Raleigh, but they both knew whom she was talking about.

'Oh. Okay,' Glauer said, nodding.

'Don't just accept it like that. This is a pretty serious

assignment. Jameson isn't done with her, not yet. He'll try again to give her the curse. Normally when we work vampire sightings, I send you around to the back door. I put you on guard duty. This time you'll be in the line of fire. You're allowed to say no if you want to.'

'I can handle it,' the big cop said.

'You should keep her somewhere with lots of cops. Like right here. It's possible that he's tough enough to take on an entire barracks of troopers, but he's too smart to try to find out. You should be okay as long as you don't make any stupid mistakes.'

'I said I could handle it,' he grunted. 'There's nothing magic about you, either.'

Caxton watched his face. Had she hurt his feelings? 'What's that supposed to mean?' she asked.

'It means you aren't the only person in the world who can fight vampires. I know we've watched a lot of cops get killed trying. But that was because they weren't trained for this kind of work. I've been learning from you for two months now.'

She tried to stare him down, with her best cop look. He didn't break eye contact with her. After a minute or so, she blinked.

She had learned how to fight vampires by watching Jameson. He'd never thought she was ready to do it on her own. She'd been about to say the same thing about Glauer – but then, Jameson had been wrong about her. Maybe she was wrong about Glauer. 'Fair enough.' Then she turned to look at Raleigh. 'Officer Glauer's going to see to your needs,' she said. The girl looked up with wide eyes. 'He'll protect you. Just do everything he says and you'll be alright.'

Raleigh's mouth fell open. 'What about you? Aren't you going to stay with me? You said you would keep me safe. You said that!'

'I have to go collect your brother,' Caxton said, going over to kneel next to the frightened girl. 'I'll bring him back here and you'll both be safe.'

'You're worried my father will attack Simon?'

What I'm worried most about, Caxton thought, *is that Jameson will make his offer to Simon, and that Simon will accept it.* 'Nobody else is going to die,' she said. 'Not if I can help it.'

34.

The state police armorer broke into a very wide grin when she told him what she needed. He disappeared into a Quonset hut at the side of the target range and when he came back his arms were full of cardboard boxes. Some contained ammunition – bullets fatter and heavier than any Caxton had seen before. Others held a variety of pistols.

'So you don't want to carry around a high-powered rifle,' he said, twirling the ends of his mustache. 'That's the best way to defeat body armor.'

She shook her head. 'I do a lot of close-quarters fighting inside of buildings. I'll keep a rifle in the trunk of my car, but for most situations I need a handgun.'

'Now, if this were some normal bad guy,' he told her, 'I'd say don't bother with toys. I'd tell you to put more time in on the range until you could reliably take him down with a head shot.'

Caxton shook her head. 'A vampire's only vulnerable point is his heart. He's got a IIIA ballistic vest and over that a steel trauma plate.'

The armorer rubbed his chin. 'Vests aren't perfect. They don't do anything against knives or, say, wooden stakes.' Before she could even react the man waved one hand in the air. 'Just a little joke. And anyway, you don't want to go into this with a knife. By the time you got close enough to stab him you'd already be dead. Okay. Next thought. The ballistic fabric loses its effectiveness when it gets wet.'

'So you're saying I should only shoot him if it's raining? I don't have that option.' She shook her head. 'I need firepower.'

'And I am most happy to oblige. I don't get to bring these out near as often as I'd like.' The armorer's small eyes burned with glee as he opened the first box. Inside lay a revolver with a ten-and-a-half-inch barrel – twice as long as the barrel on her Beretta. It was made of stainless steel and had a thick rubberized grip designed to help cut down on recoil. She lifted it with both hands and almost gasped. It must have weighed five pounds. It felt like she was holding some massive machine part, and she wondered if she would be able to even draw it comfortably.

'What's this one?' she asked.

'Smith & Wesson Model 500. 500H, to be precise. It loads .500 Smith & Wesson Magnum rounds, some of the most powerful in the world. The gun-control lobby calls that round the vest-buster.'

'What do other people call it?'

The armorer shrugged. 'The NRA claims it can't actually penetrate a trauma plate. They say they have ballistic tests to prove it. You can choose who you believe. What I do know is that this round is recommended for stopping a charging grizzly bear before it can gets its claws in you.'

Caxton's eyes went wide. She reached for a pair of earplugs. The armorer handed her a pair of cup-style ear protectors as well. 'You'll want both,' he told her.

She lined up a shot on a paper target at twenty yards, adjusted her stance, leaned into the shot. Squeezed the trigger. A jet of flame burst from the gun as it squirmed and pushed – her arm leaped up and the gun nearly hit her in the face. It felt like someone had kicked her in the shoulder. 'Jesus,' she squeaked. Her ears were still ringing when she put the weapon down and removed her ear protectors.

'You didn't flinch,' the armorer said, admiringly. 'Most women when they take their first shot with that kind of power, they close their eyes and turn away from the blast.'

She picked up the handgun again and studied it. 'Double action, at least. But this looks wrong.' Most revolvers carried six shots in a cylinder behind the barrel. 'There are only five chambers.'

'The bullets were too big to fit six,' the armorer explained. He pressed a button to bring in the target. The round she'd fired had made a sizable hole near the shoulder of the silhouette on the target, and she hated to think what that bullet could have done to a human body. Still – it hadn't even come close to the target's heart, and Caxton was a good shot. She practiced religiously and she had been trained by her father, who had been a sheriff up in coal country and who had been an excellent shot. That meant she knew her limits. She knew that the first round she fired from a new gun was never going to be a bull's-eye. She also knew she'd had a lot of trouble controlling the weapon.

'I'm not strong enough for that,' she said. 'I think maybe if I was Arnold Schwarzenegger. But I'm not.'

'With enough time and practice you'd be fine,' the armorer said.

'Time is something I'm short on.'

The armorer frowned sympathetically and put it back in its box. He had another gun for her to try, one she recognized right

205

away. She'd seen it in plenty of movies and TV shows – a Mark XIX Desert Eagle, an Israeli-made gun that she'd always thought was perfect for men with especially small penises. It had a thick triangular barrel and a massive grip she could barely get her hand around. Its barrel was almost comically long – fourteen inches, even longer than the Model 500, and when she held it she felt like she had picked up some kind of movie prop. It made her Beretta look like a cap gun.

She checked the safety, then ejected the magazine. It held seven rounds. Better than the five in the revolver, but her Beretta held fifteen.

The armorer fingered one of the bullets. 'That's your .50AE round. Pretty nasty. Very powerful.'

'Okay.'

He took the weapon from her and reloaded it. 'Usually, with ammo this big you'd use a revolver. The Desert Eagle's a little different. It's built more like a rifle than a handgun, especially with this barrel. Gas operated. Polygonal rifling. The rotating bolt is pretty close to what you'd find on an M16.'

'Cool.' Caxton replaced her ear protection, called to clear the range, then sighted and fired. The recoil wasn't as bad as with the Model 500, but still she nearly lost control of the gun after it discharged. When the target fluttered up to her she saw she'd gotten a little closer to the heart, but not much. 'Not so cool.' She sighed and put the weapon down. 'Bigger bullets isn't going to do the trick. What about a different kind of bullet – hollow-points or something.'

'Hollow-point bullets actually decrease penetration,' the armorer told her. 'They're designed for maximum tissue damage inside your target, but they'll never get through a trauma plate. If you're looking for a magic bullet what you'd really want is depleted uranium rounds.'

'Really?' Caxton asked, raising her eyebrows.

'Sure. Much denser than lead, so they hit harder. DU rounds are just about perfect for armor piercing. Plus they're pyrophoric, so when they deform on impact they tend to catch on fire and explode. They're also a little bit radioactive, so if you don't blow up your target you still give him cancer. Just one problem, though.'

'What's that?'

'You'd have to be in the Army even to see a DU round, and even the Army doesn't make small-arms ammunition out of the stuff anymore. They did back in the nineties, but then somebody realized that we were shooting radioactive slugs into every bunker, hut, and hospital in the Middle East. The political blowback on that could have been enormous, so they stopped producing them. The UN is trying to get people to stop using DU of any kind.'

'So you don't have a box of it lying around,' Caxton inferred.

'No.' He ran his fingers along his mustache for a while and then opened an unmarked cardboard box and set it before her. 'I do have these. Highly illegal, of course. We took them in evidence during a big drug raid a couple years back.'

Caxton drew one of the bullets out of the box. It was the same size and shape as the rounds she loaded in her Beretta 92. The only apparent difference was that it had a smooth green coating on the tip. She ran her finger over it and wondered why it felt so familiar. Then she looked up at the armorer. 'What are they?'

He wasn't meeting her gaze. Instead he was looking at the box of bullets. He was looking at it as if the box were full of poisonous snakes. Eventually he shifted his weight to a different foot and told her what she was looking at. 'Cop-killers.'

'No shit?' she asked. She examined the bullet again. It was lighter than a normal bullet, strangely enough. 'These are Teflon bullets?'

He shrugged. 'That name's misleading. The Teflon coating is just to protect your gun. It doesn't make them any more deadly. The real improvement comes from using a brass slug instead of a lead one. Brass is a lot harder than lead, so when it hits the target – say, your trauma plate – it doesn't squish or melt. It keeps going in one piece, with all of its energy intact. Theoretically that bullet can punch through any police vest.'

'Does it work?'

The armorer shrugged again. 'Depends on who you ask. Again, I've seen ballistics reports from both sides. No one has ever been shot with one of these – they were made illegal about ten minutes after they were invented – so we just don't know. Even I've never seen any, other than what's in that box. Theoretically law enforcement can buy them, but you should see the paperwork the ATF requires. Personally I've only fired a couple of rounds of that stuff. I can tell you those will penetrate a steel car door without any trouble. One thing I do know, which is that once that box is gone, I won't be able to get any more for a long time. So use them carefully.'

Caxton nodded. She scooped the box up and put it in her pocket. 'Thanks,' she said.

He nodded, still not looking at her. 'I've got something else for you, too. You carry a Beretta 92, right? There's an upgrade for that model.'

'Yeah?' She drew her sidearm and laid it on the bench in front of her. 'This one's been pretty good to me.'

'Here, try this,' he said, and opened another of his boxes. Inside was a gun almost identical to hers – except it might have come out of the future. The grips were more ergonomic, the entire pistol was slightly lighter, and it had a small flashlight slung under the barrel. 'This is the Beretta 90-Two.' He spelled it out for her, and showed her the name embossed on the receiver. 'It's improved in a whole bunch of ways, but let me show you my favorite parts. Here,' he said, indicating three pale green dots, 'are your glow-in-the-dark sights. So you can shoot at night. There's a red tab here that pops up when there's a round in the chamber, so you never have to retract the slide to find out. Then there's this attachment, which might come in handy, considering the places you end up.' He flicked two switches on the flashlight. The beam was bright enough to see even in winter daylight. That would be useful when she was hunting vampires on moonless nights. Even better, just below the flashlight lens was a tiny red lens that projected a sighting laser. 'With the flashlight and laser on at the same time, you've got about an hour of battery time. Keep that in mind. Also, you'll need to sight the laser in manually. With the flashlight it won't fit in your current holster, but I have a new one you can have that'll work.' He watched her point the gun downrange, then lower it and whip it up again. 'Best part: the magazine holds seventeen rounds. Two more than you're used to. Do you like it?'

It felt just about perfect in her hand. 'I'll take it,' Caxton said. 'Wrap it up.'

35.

Caxton had two more stops to make before she could leave for Syracuse. The first was going to be the hardest: she had to go home.

It wasn't a long commute to the house she shared with Clara. When she arrived she pulled into the drive and switched off the Mazda and just sat there for a while, staring at her own kitchen window. When she'd decided she'd put it off long enough, she got out of the car and walked up to the door. It was unlocked, which meant Clara was there. Caxton was not surprised to find her lover sitting at the kitchen table reading a book.

'Hey,' Clara said, barely looking up. 'Long time no see.'

Caxton stiffened. Then she forced herself to relax and pull up a chair opposite Clara so they could talk.

Eventually Clara looked up again. She put her finger in her book to hold her place and closed the cover. 'So,' she said. 'Did you ever find out what a Twaron fiber was good for?'

'Yes,' Caxton said. She placed both hands on the table and started picking at the laminate on the edge. 'It's used in ballistic vests. Arkeley was wearing one.'

Clara's eyes went wide. 'That would protect his heart and—'

'Make it next to impossible for me to kill him. That's . . . that's something it would really have helped me to know, before he came after Raleigh last night.' Clara started to react, but Caxton held up one hand. 'Raleigh's fine. Another girl didn't make it, though. If I'd known what I was facing maybe it could have been – different.'

Clara's mouth trembled. 'I'd never heard of Twaron before. I've only ever heard of Kevlar. If the report had said it was Kevlar, I could have made that connection. Hey! Come on, you can't blame me for some girl's death just because I didn't know what Twaron was. Come on!'

'I don't blame you. I blame myself. You told me you weren't trained for forensics work. I should have listened to you.'

Clara jumped up and wrapped her arms around her chest. Her face was a neutral mask. Caxton had been with her long enough to know what that meant – she felt like she was being attacked.

'All I'm saying, Clara, is that you could have Googled it. What I needed from you, when I put you in charge of this stuff, was information. Fetlock's experts are smart people and they do a certain job very well, but all they can give you is raw data. They were going to send me their report anyway, but I needed somebody to actually read it and give me the key points. You could have gone that extra distance. Next time—'

'Next time? So you're not firing me? Oh, thank you so much.' Clara stomped over to the window and stared out at the snow. 'I can't believe this, Laura. You really got me this time, didn't you? It used to just be guilt you held over my head. Now you need to make me feel stupid, too.'

'What are you talking about? Guilt?'

'Jesus! Don't pretend you don't know what I'm talking about.

Our relationship is falling apart. I should have dumped you a long time ago. But how could I? I keep asking for more time together, for more intimacy. But no, you're too busy saving the world. I can't exactly compete with that, and I feel guilty about wanting to. So I hang in there, I keep being patient and loving and making your fucking breakfast every morning. Then you come along with this job offer and I think hey, maybe you actually do care. Maybe you understand. So I jump into something I have no training for, something I'd never even considered. Now you're laying some girl's death on me, too? Jesus!'

'It's not like that,' Caxton said, but Clara was already storming out of the room. She hurried to the bedroom and slammed the door behind her.

For a time Caxton just sat at the table, hoping her girlfriend would come back. She didn't. There was too much to do, too many lives at stake to wait for very much longer, she decided. She would try to patch things up later. Before she left, though, she picked up the book Clara had been reading. It was a thick hardcover with the title on the cover in big block letters: **FUNDAMENTALS OF CRIMINAL INVESTIGATION, SEVENTH EDITION**.

She laid it gently back on the table and returned to her car.

Her next stop was Mechanicsburg, and the local jail there. The cops and corrections officers that ran the place were surprised to see her, but when she flashed her silver star they fell into line. One grabbed up a heavy key ring and led her down into the basement, to the secure cells.

'He screamed every time we tried to put him in a cell with a window,' the CO explained, sorting through his keys. 'These are our solitary confinement units, which we save for the worst kind. Padded walls, no furniture but a suicide-proof toilet. Electric lights we keep on twenty-four/seven so we can see what they're up to.'

212

'What has he been doing?' Caxton asked.

The CO shrugged. 'At night he sits staring into space, or sometimes he'll pace back and forth. The cell's only three paces wide, but he'll do that for hours. During the day – from dawn until sundown, every time – he just sleeps. It's funny.'

'What is?' Caxton asked.

'Down here,' the CO said, 'there's really no way for him to see whether the sun is up or down. But somehow, he knows. He'll be sleeping now, of course, but I can wake him up if you want.'

'I do,' Caxton said.

The CO unlocked a heavy reinforced door and opened it wide. Inside Dylan Carboy lay stretched out on the floor, his head turned to one side, looking like nothing so much as a lifeless corpse. His hands were secured behind his back with nylon restraints and his feet were bare.

'Come on, kid. Come on. You got a visitor.'

The boy didn't move.

'This might take a while,' the CO said, then grabbed Carboy under the arms and grunted and strained to get him sitting upright. 'You're a U.S. Marshal, huh? You come to transfer him?'

She understood why he would think that – prisoner transport across state lines was one of the primary functions of the USMS. 'No,' she said. 'I just want to talk to him. It's pertinent to an open investigation.'

The CO shrugged. 'Hell, I was hoping we were going to get rid of him. Little bastard creeps me out. You want to talk, feel free. I don't know if he'll answer.'

Caxton squatted down next to Carboy and studied his face. He was just a kid, even younger-looking than she remembered from when she'd hauled him in. At the time, of course, he'd been made up like a vampire. He was still pale, but not deathly pale, and his ears were round and normal. A thin fuzz of stubble coated the top of his head where his hair had started to grow back in. His eyes were open, but they didn't track, just stared vacantly forward.

'I can get him on his feet, if you want,' the CO said. 'We can drag him down to an interrogation room.'

'No need,' Caxton said. 'Tell me – has he asked for a lawyer?'

The CO shook his head. 'We offered, a bunch of times. After dark, when he was talking, even. He wants vengeance, he says. He wants blood. He says that a lot. But lawyers he can do without.'

'Okay, then. I'll speak with him awhile and then get out of your hair,' she said. The CO nodded and moved to stand by the door, hands held behind him, waiting for her to do what she needed to do. Caxton knew better than to ask to be left alone with the prisoner. That would never be allowed, not with someone as violent and unstable as Carboy.

'Do you remember me?' she asked. The boy's face didn't change. He was supposed to be a vampire, and of course vampires didn't talk during daylight hours. It seemed he was going to prolong the ruse even when no one else believed in it. 'I'm Laura Caxton. You wanted to kill me. Remember?' Caxton frowned. 'It was all over your notebooks.'

The corner of Carboy's upper lip twitched. Just a tic, but enough that Caxton caught it. Maybe that was what she needed: an in. The secret to police interrogations wasn't knowing when someone was lying to you. You had to assume everything a subject said was a lie. No, the secret was finding the button you could push, the one thing that bothered the subject so much it threw him off his game enough to get his carefully prepared facts tangled up. In this case it was finding something that would get Carboy to talk at all.

214

'We found your notebooks in your house. You remember, the house where you strangled your sister.' The tic came again when she mentioned finding the notebooks but didn't recur when she mentioned his sister. Yeah, she had him. Those notebooks were important to him. 'I didn't bother reading them all,' she said. 'They were kind of repetitive, and not very well written. So I gave them to one of my officers. He had to pull one of them apart because blood had stuck all the pages together. Completely ruined them.'

The boy's lip had curled up so far that she could see his teeth.

'What I did read was kind of funny. "Laura Caxton will die by Halloween." But look, it's almost Christmas, and here we are. I'm running around perfectly healthy, and you're stuck in here, where you can't even write bad poetry to entertain yourself.'

His mouth opened and she thought words might spill out. Instead he carefully brought his teeth together and closed his lips. They were white with the strain.

'I think,' she said, 'that I'm going to make photocopies of some of the funnier pages, and share them with all my cop friends.'

'I'd like to see those,' the CO behind her said, playing along. *Good man*, she thought. 'I think all of us here would enjoy that.'

Caxton nodded eagerly. 'Sure. I'll get your address before I leave so I can send them along. There's one part that's just hilarious. He talks about Jameson Arkeley – you know, the *real* vampire? Dylan here claims he actually spoke with him. Please!'

The boy lunged forward, his teeth clacking together on the lapel of her coat. The CO rushed forward, but Caxton waved him back. Carboy growled and his feet kicked at the floor, but she easily held him down, pinning him by pressing his shoulders against the floor. The boy was as weak as a starved dog, and she wondered if he'd been eating in the jail – if he wanted everyone to think he was a vampire, he couldn't very well eat solid food.

Down on the floor Carboy writhed and moaned. 'He came to me. He came to *me!* He knew I was worthy. He knew I could do whatever he asked, that I wouldn't fail! I proved it to him. I proved I could kill anyone, anyone I loved. Just like him.'

'And Malvern?' Caxton asked. 'Did she come to you, too?'

'Only in dreams,' the boy said.

'Where are they, Rexroth?' Caxton asked. She thought appealing to his adopted vampire persona might get a better result. 'Tell me where they are.'

Carboy shook himself violently, trying to get free. The CO coughed, his way of telling her she was on the verge of being abusive. She didn't ease up.

'Tell me. If you know so much. If they really came to you, then tell me. Or I'll never believe you. Where is their lair?'

'I am still worthy! He'll come for me again! He will free me!' the boy shrieked.

'You're lying. You're a worthless lying sack of shit,' Caxton barked. 'He never came for you. Why would he? You're nothing. You're nobody.'

'I will never betray him! He warned me you would come. He told me to say nothing. Nothing! I am still worthy, Jameson! I am still worthy!'

The CO coughed again, much louder this time. Caxton forced herself to let the boy go. She jumped up and back so he couldn't bite her again, considered kicking him in the ribs, but finally she just walked out the door of the cell and into the corridor. The CO came out a few moments later and asked her if there was anything else she needed, but she didn't even look at him. She was already heading for her car – and for Syracuse.

SIMON

'Escape – escape for your life,' cried the tempter; 'break forth into life, liberty, and sanity. Your social happiness, your intellectual powers, your immortal interests, perhaps, depend on the choice of this moment.'

Charles Maturin, *Melmoth the Wanderer*

36.

Caxton was well onto the highway – I-81, which would take her all the way to Syracuse – when she realized her face was wet with sweat. She wiped at it with one hand and steered with the other. *That could have gone better,* she thought.

She had wanted to hurt the boy. She had wanted to grind him into the floor of his cell until he told her what she wanted to know. Only the presence of the CO had stopped her. And yet she doubted that he even knew anything useful – Jameson was too careful, too good at covering his tracks, to let some crazy kid in on his biggest secret, the location of his lair. For all she knew, despite any evidence suggesting the contrary, Carboy had never even met Jameson. Glauer had her half convinced otherwise, but there was still part of her that thought Carboy had made it all up, that his stories of talking to vampires had been some deluded fantasy. The boy was, without a doubt, mentally ill. Sane people didn't murder their families, then dress up like vampires and go gunning for state troopers. But was he lying, or not?

She had gone to see him because she couldn't afford to

leave any stone unturned. Because she was running out of ideas. That made her scared – and her fear had made her violent. She had to get control of her fear.

She tried to focus on her driving. She let the lines on the road occupy her full attention so she didn't have to think about anything else. Two hours into her drive it started to work – mostly because the driving became a lot harder the farther north she went. The road turned white with snow, first as broad fan-shaped sweeps of powder that rolled across the asphalt, then as a thin sheet of slush embossed with the chevron-shaped tire marks of a snow plow that had gone before her. North of Binghamton, just across the state line into New York, the snow turned into a thick carpet of pure white and she started losing traction. She had to stop and put chains on her tires at a rest stop. She worked quickly, both because she didn't want to lose any more time and because it was cold out, colder than she'd expected, and her hands stung every time she touched the metal chains. She cursed herself, wishing she'd bothered to check the weather report. Her Mazda wasn't suited to extreme-weather driving – if she'd thought this through better she could have requisitioned a patrol cruiser or even something with four-wheel drive.

She had to keep her speed down when she got back on the highway. The chains gave her a better grip on the road, but it was still slick enough to be dangerous. Up past Cortland she caught up with the storm and suddenly the sky was as white as the road, full of big puffy flakes that splattered on her windshield. Headlights speared through the falling snow, dazzling her, while the brake lights of the cars ahead made pink roses bloom across her windshield. A flashing warning light like a strobe made her blink and nearly go off the side of the road. Up ahead a snow plow was thundering north, a fountain of wet snow blasting out from either side of its blade.

222

It couldn't be going more than thirty miles per hour, but she had to fight her instinct to pass. As bad as the snow was behind the plow, it would be impassable in front. She kept both hands on the wheel and tried to stay in the plow's tracks, two dark gullies full of slush. The tracks were the only way she had of knowing where the road curved – in the torrent of snow she couldn't even see the guardrails.

It took another three hours before she reached Syracuse, and even longer to weave her way through the maze of the city's surface streets. Some of them had been plowed, leaving one narrow lane open and mounds of snow on either side six feet high, with here and there a car buried so deeply in the drifts that she wondered how they would ever be dug out. The Victorian houses she passed were half snowed-in, their roofs weighted down with thick layers of snow like frosting on a cake. Even the street signs were often obscured by clumps of snow that clung to them, and more than once she had to stop in the middle of a street and study her map. It was four forty-five when she reached the university campus, already after dark, though it was hard to tell. The sky had taken on an uncanny blue-gray color, a haze of light from the city's buildings trapped under the heavily laden clouds. The street-lights looked like showerheads gushing down diamond-bright snowflakes, and trails of mist wandered the streets like freezing ghosts looking for some warm place to haunt.

The main campus of the university loomed up out of the storm as she rumbled past. She saw brick dormitories with fogged-up windows, libraries and classroom buildings made of big flat slabs of concrete stained dark by melting snow. She saw a massive gray building with a black mansard roof, just dripping with gables and dormer windows. It reminded her of the Addams family house from TV. Following the directions Fetlock had given her, she took a left turn and drove

223

past a massive park, the rolling hills of which looked like an ocean of heaving white waves, then another left on Westscott Street, where little shops and businesses spilled yellow light across the submerged road. She passed a big New Age book-store and finally arrived at her destination, the corner of Westscott and Hawthorne. On every side of her, two-story houses from the turn of the century hunkered down in the snow. They were painted in bright colors turned pastel by the snow, and all of them, for some reason, had balconies on their second level. She wondered what this place would look like in summer, but couldn't really paint the picture in her mind. It was so encrusted with snow that she couldn't imagine winter ever ending.

She pulled up behind an unmarked white van, a Ford E-150 with tinted windows. It was buried in snow up to its wheel wells, but the windshield had been scraped clear, and recently. It was so obviously a police surveillance van that she winced when she saw it. Apparently the local Feds had never heard of discretion. Maybe, she thought, Simon would have been so busy with his studies that he wouldn't have noticed it was parked outside his house for two days in a row. Of course, she'd never been that lucky before.

Fetlock had tasked his own men, U.S. Marshals, with this stakeout, thinking they might do better than local cops. It wasn't Caxton's job to second-guess that decision.

When she killed her engine and switched off her lights the van's rear doors popped open and a gloved hand waved her over. Popping her own door, she jumped out and hurried up into the back of the van, yanking the door closed behind her as a wraith of snow whirled and howled in through the gap.

Inside, three men with silver stars on their lapels just like her own sat in swiveling captain's chairs, passing around a thermos of coffee. They all wore parkas, gloves, and hats, and massive boots. One of them half rose from his place to shake her hand. 'Deputy Marshal Fetlock told us you'd be coming. Caxton, right? I'm Young, this is Miller, and that fellow over there is Benicio.'

'Call me Lu,' Benicio said, waving at her. 'Short for Luis, but nobody can pronounce that right. Even though it's a common name where I come from.'

'Where's that?' she asked.

He smiled. 'Utica.'

Her feet squelched on the carpeted floor, which was flooded by half an inch of murky water. Plastic water bottles floated in the muck, each filled with a yellow liquid she did not care to identify. They competed for space with the soggy wrappers of microwave burritos and fast-food cartons. It was cold enough inside the van to see her breath, though not so bad as it had been outside. She plopped down in a fourth chair and nodded at the introductions. 'You guys have been here awhile, huh? You picked a great day for it.'

Young laughed. 'What, you mean the weather? This is nothing. We're all from the local Syracuse office of the USMS, so we're used to it. Syracuse is the snowiest city in the contiguous forty-eight. We get what, a hundred and fifteen inches a year?' Miller nodded animatedly. 'Lake effect snow, mostly. It hits pretty hard, then melts after a couple of days. Wait till January, if you want to see some snow. When it gets so deep you can't open your front door, that's when we start to worry.'

Caxton shook her head. Pennsylvania was like the Tropics compared to that. 'How's our person of interest?' she asked, leaning forward to look through the windshield. The van had a good view of the house across the street that was Simon Arkeley's last known address. It was a two-level Victorian just like all the rest, painted white, so it blended in with the sky and its yellow-lit windows seemed to hang in the air. She could see into its porch, which was crammed with patio furniture and unrecognizable junk, and also into its balcony, which was mostly clear.

Lu came to squat next to her and hand her a pair of field glasses. Only two of the windows were lit. 'He's got the one up there on the second floor. He's been in there reading a book all afternoon.'

She looked where he pointed and saw someone sitting in the window, though she could only make out a rough silhouette in the bad light. It had to be Simon Arkeley. As advertised, he had a book in his hands and his head was bent over it. She watched him turn a couple of pages, then sank back in her chair.

'Who's on the ground floor?' she asked. She couldn't see anybody through that window, just the occasional blue flicker of a television set.

'Building manager,' Lu said. 'Old guy, drunk most of the time. He hasn't been out all day, except once to get beer down at the liquor store.'

Caxton sighed and looked out the van windows. She doubted Simon would be going out that night, not with the heavy snowfall. It looked like she was going to be sitting in the cold van for a long time.

'What's your plan?' Lu asked. 'I'm guessing you didn't come all the way up here to make a fourth for bridge.'

She smiled, remembering the casual camaraderie of stakeouts. She'd done her share of them on the highway patrol. 'Well,' she said, trying to think of her next move by talking it out, 'I'm going to—'

She didn't get any further, though. Her phone rang. It was Fetlock.

'We found a lair,' he told her.

37.

'Is he there? Is Malvern there?' Caxton demanded.

'No, neither of them,' Fetlock said, sounding almost apologetic. 'And it looks like they haven't been for a while. Let me just give you the details, alright?'

Caxton closed her eyes and sank back into her chair. 'Alright,' she said, holding the phone against her shoulder. She reached into her pocket and took out a small notebook, then snapped her fingers at the three Feds in the van and mimed writing something down. Lu handed her a pen.

'We eliminated all the other possible lairs from your list,' Fetlock told her, 'by about two o'clock this afternoon. Some of my men out of Reading were about to eliminate the last one, but they knew it was getting late and they didn't want to be there after sundown.'

'Good,' Caxton said, 'smart.'

'Well, you did warn us. They approached the site and made a quick reconnaissance. The site was an abandoned grain elevator just outside Mount Carmel. They saw definite signs of recent occupation – someone had forced their way into an

227

outbuilding, tearing the chains off the door and not bothering to replace them. They assumed it was probably some petty criminal looking for anything they could steal. After making sure there were no half-deads lying in wait, a three-man team entered the building and found some empty plastic bags. IV bags, like from a hospital. The kind of bags that whole blood is stored in.'

'What about human remains? Furniture made out of bones, bodies wired into lifelike postures, that sort of thing?' That was what you expected to find in a vampire lair. It was the kind of thing she'd seen in vampire lairs before.

'Nothing of the sort, but if the blood bags were enough to pique their interest, there was also a coffin in there. A very old, very cheap coffin that had fallen to pieces. They did what they'd been told to do and called in reinforcements. Lots of them. When no vampires showed up they sent in heavily armed units to secure the site and retrieve all the evidence. They did so, then immediately departed the scene, at approximately four-thirty, just as the sun was going down.'

Caxton sighed almost happily. Fetlock seemed to get how this worked, if nobody else did. You didn't stick around a vampire's lair at twilight, no matter how abandoned it might look. That was asking for trouble.

'The evidence was taken back to your HQ building in Harrisburg. I brought in my forensics people and also your team lead – Clara Hsu – to supervise.'

'Clara was part of this investigation?' Caxton asked, a little surprised. 'How was she at – I mean, did she prove useful?'

'Yes,' Fetlock said, and Caxton's eyes opened wide as he added, 'She's clearly not trained for forensics work, but she asked a lot of interesting questions and she even cleared up one mystery for us. There were some skin samples in the coffin. Just a few flakes, like dandruff, but when we tried to run a DNA test nothing whatsoever came up.'

'There was no match in the database?'

'No,' Fetlock said, 'I mean there was no DNA. Which confused the hell out of my forensics team. Then Clara pointed out that vampires don't have human DNA.'

Wow, Caxton thought. Clara had been paying attention. She'd made the connection. Caxton would have felt gushingly proud of her girlfriend if she didn't feel so guilty for not believing in Clara before.

'They were able to carbon-date the skin samples,' Fetlock went on. 'They look to be a couple hundred years old, at least.'

'So they came from Malvern,' Caxton said. 'Malvern was in this lair. She can't go anywhere without Jameson's help, so they must both have been there.'

'Not just them. We also found some fingerprints on the blood bags. When we ran *those* through the database a match came up right away. The prints belong to Dylan Carboy, aka Kenneth Rexroth.'

'Seriously?' Caxton asked. She wanted to slap herself on the forehead.

So Glauer had been right. Carboy did have some tangible connection with Jameson. It seemed she was going to have to make some apologies.

'That's all we have so far, all the hard evidence,' Fetlock went on. 'My people were willing to make one more conjecture, though. Judging by the amount of dust on the coffin and the blood bags, they say nobody had been in that lair for weeks. They won't testify to that in court, but they sounded pretty sure.'

'That's great,' Caxton said. 'That's a lot of information we didn't have before. That really helps flesh out the narrative. Blood bags – it sounds like Jameson used this lair before he went rogue, before he killed anybody. He would have been hungry, though. Desperate for blood. He must have had Carboy steal blood from a local hospital or blood bank – but that wouldn't work. Vampires can't drink cold blood. It has to be fresh or warm for them to get any benefit from it.'

'Okay,' Fetlock said. 'Not my area. I've got the site under constant surveillance – from a distance. If anyone tries to go in or out during the night, I'll let you know.'

'Thanks,' Caxton said, and ended the call. She was almost certain the old lair was abandoned, that Jameson had moved on to somewhere else, but it was good that Fetlock didn't take chances.

For a while she was buzzing with excitement, putting together jigsaw pieces in her head, adding the new stuff to what she already knew. Eventually, though, as the night wore on, that excitement faded.

The new information was useful. But it didn't change anything. Jameson was still at large. The evidence might help her catch him, eventually, but for now she still needed to focus on Simon. On keeping Simon alive.

The adrenaline rush she'd gotten from the phone call turned to nervous tension all too quickly.

She tried to relax, tried to listen to the conversation of the three Feds in the van. They were talking about the Orangemen, Syracuse's basketball team. Apparently one of the star players had been caught smoking crack cocaine in the locker room. There was some discussion as to whether he would be allowed to finish out the season before he was prosecuted. 'It's not like he was dealing,' Miller asserted. 'Just holding.'

'With or without intent to distribute?' Young asked. He opened a fresh bag of corn chips and pushed a bunch of them into his mouth.

Caxton looked out the side windows at the street, at the cross streets on either side. Something felt wrong. Maybe she was just too keyed up, too paranoid. That was probably it. Still. She hadn't survived as long as she had by assuming things were okay. 'You guys know this neighborhood?' she asked. 'What's behind this house?'

Miller grunted. 'Bunch of backyards, divided up by fences.'

'Could someone have gone out a back door of the house and slipped away without you noticing? Hopped over the fence and got away by a side street?'

Young sat up very straight in his chair. 'Sure. If there was anybody unaccounted for. We thought of that, too, and we made damned sure to keep track of where Simon and the building manager were at all times. If your POI had left that window, one of us would have gone to cover the back of the house. But he hasn't moved, not since lunchtime.'

'Not even to go to the bathroom?' she asked.

Miller shrugged. 'Maybe once a couple hours ago, but he was back in a couple of seconds. Not long enough to do anything.'

Caxton lifted the glasses to look at Simon again. The figure there was hard to make out, just a rough silhouette of a young man reading a book. A young man—

'Shit!' she said, and slapped the armrest of her chair hard enough to make the men around her jump. 'He made you. Goddamn it, he must have made you hours ago. Lu, you're with me. Miller, Young, you stay here and cover us.'

'What the hell?' Young asked. 'What are you talking about? He hasn't moved—'

Caxton snarled her reply at him. 'Look at his fingers. *His* fingers. Simon Arkeley doesn't wear nail polish.'

Lu already had the van's back door open. He jumped down into the snow and she followed close on his heels. They slogged through the drifts that covered the sidewalk and up to the porch of the house, Caxton surging forward to pound on the door.

'Open up,' she shouted. 'Open up! Federal agents!'

It seemed to take forever for the building manager to come thumping through the house to answer the door. When he cracked it open Caxton lifted her lapel to show him her star.

'Jeez, what do you want?' the man asked. He was in his late fifties, about average height. Grizzly stubble coated the bottom half of his face, and his eyes were wet and red. Maybe he'd been sleeping. His breath was yeasty with beer. He looked from Caxton to Lu and back again.

'Federal agents,' Caxton repeated. 'We need to come inside. Can you step back, sir?'

He was in his rights to demand to see a search warrant. Caxton wasn't sure what she would do if he asked. After a moment, though, he lifted his shoulders and moved back so she and Lu could push inside the house. It was warm inside, almost stiflingly hot. The front hall was full of very old furniture – a sideboard, a cheval mirror, a sofa that might have been an antique if the upholstery wasn't split and oozing stuffing.

'It's that kid upstairs, right? Arkeley? He do something bad? I always kind of figured he would get in trouble,' the building manager whispered. 'He's the only one here, anyway. Comes in all hours of the night, never seems to sleep, and I seen some of the books he brings in here, scandalous stuff—'

'Which room is his?' Caxton asked, cutting him off.

'Top of the stairs, on the left.' The building manager raised his shoulders again, a kind of lazy shrug. 'I'll be down here, you need me.' He shambled back toward his own room, where the television was blaring something about lingerie models competing to see who could eat the most bloodworms.

Caxton was already hurrying up the stairwell. The banister

232

was slick under her hand but marred by countless deep scratches and places where the varnish had been scuffed down to bare wood, probably from countless generations of students moving in and out. At the top of the stairs she turned left and found the door she wanted. She rapped twice on it with her knuckles, then drew her weapon.

Behind her Lu's eyes were wide, but he took out his own handgun.

Caxton rapped again. It sounded like a hollow-core door, the kind you could just kick your way through. When no answer came, she started to do just that.

'Whoa, whoa,' Lu said, grabbing her arm. She stared wildly into his face. 'You can't do that. It's not kosher.'

She knew perfectly well what he meant. Unless she had a search warrant or evidence of a crime being committed inside, she couldn't just bust the door down, not legally.

She didn't have time to be legal. 'The vampire is coming. Maybe tonight, maybe tomorrow, but soon. You want this kid to get killed by his own father? Have his throat torn out and his blood splattered everywhere?'

'No,' Lu confessed.

She lifted her foot again, but once more he grabbed her arm.

'I also don't want to get put up against administrative review,' he told her. 'Listen, I've only been on this job about a month. I was walking a beat in Tipp Hill before that, and I don't want to go back. Young can be a real hard case when it comes to protocol.'

'Then maybe he doesn't need to know,' Caxton said. 'Maybe the door was open when we got here and we have no idea how the lock got broken. Or maybe we thought we heard someone shouting for help from inside, but in the end it turned out just to be the old man's TV.'

233

Lu stared at her, goggle-eyed.

'There's nobody here to say whether it happened like that or not,' she said, 'except you and me.' Then she kicked open the door. It flew open effortlessly, the lock's bolt clacking in its receptacle.

'Aw, hell,' Lu breathed. 'You're nuts, lady!'

'I'm desperate,' Caxton said, and stepped inside the room.

38.

The room beyond seemed filled with books. They were heaped on the floor in enormous tottering stacks, they covered one of the room's two tables, and more than a few had been laid out, evidently with some care, on the bed. There were hardcovers and leather-bound tomes and dog-eared paperbacks, quite a lot of pamphlets, some photocopied facsimiles of books, spiral bound and with clear acetate covers. There were textbooks so new they were still inside their shrink-wrap, and some books so old their spines were curling off and spilling red dust across the covers of other books. Caxton picked up a few at random. She found a paperback called *Secret Societies*, by Arkon Daraul, and a battered old text in Latin with a picture of a demon in its frontispiece, called the *Lemegeton Clavicula Salmonis*. She somehow doubted it had anything to do with the collarbones of fish.

Caxton swung her weapon around, covering all the corners. She saw no kitchen at all, just a hot plate, which of course was covered in two neat stacks of books. She saw the bed was little more than a cot, the sheets made and unslept-in, and ducked to see dusty books shoved beneath the bed frame. The closet was full of books, but also clothes – though there was no winter jacket inside. By the window she saw a chair, unoccupied, with a book resting open-faced on its seat.

At the far end of the room stood another door, open, which revealed a bathroom also filled with books – they stood like makeshift walls on either side of the toilet and on top of its tank, and some even had been piled under the sink, where a dripping pipe had left them spotted with mold.

A very frightened-looking girl with short dark hair wearing a tattered sweater sat on the edge of the tub, her hands up to protect her face. Her fingernails were painted black, just like the nails Caxton had seen through her binoculars.

'Who the hell are you?' Caxton said, raising her pistol to point at the ceiling.

'Linda,' the girl squeaked. 'I'm a friend of Simon's. He asked me to come up here and sit in the window.'

'Why?'

Linda shrugged. 'He said the cops were watching him. He said he wasn't in any trouble, though. He said he didn't do anything. Is he okay?'

Lu started to ask the girl a lot of questions, but Caxton didn't bother to listen to them. Rushing back into the hall, she found what she expected to see – a broad window, propped open with a short piece of dowel. Beyond in the flurry of snow she saw a wooden scaffolding with steps leading down to the backyard of the house. A fire escape, a way for the inhabitants of the second floor to get out in case they couldn't use the front stairs.

On the steps of the fire escape she could just make out the round shapes of footprints sunk through the deep snow, mostly filled in again by the storm. She grabbed for the windowsill, intending to yank it upward and climb out, to follow Simon's

236

trail, but then realized that would be pointless. The boy would have made as quickly as he could for the street and out there his tracks would be lost altogether, churned over by passing cars or lost to the blizzard by the time she arrived.

This was bad, very bad. Very, very bad. If she had lost him, if he'd gotten away from her, then she had no way of knowing whether he'd made contact with Jameson or not. She had to find him – more lives than just his own were at stake – but how?

She had to think. If he had run out in the middle of the storm, Young and his crew would never have seen him. He had noticed their van and known he was under surveillance, then had gone to the trouble of calling in his friend to fool them into thinking he was still in his room, reading quietly. Either he just didn't like being watched or he'd decided he had something he had to do and didn't want the cops to see him doing it. He'd taken his winter coat – she had noticed its absence up in the room – but surely he couldn't walk very far, not with the snow up to his knees in some places. She already knew from Fetlock that Simon didn't own a vehicle; that was one of the first things you checked when you staked out a POI. He could have caught a bus, but she doubted it. Who would want to wait for a bus in this weather? She decided he must have arranged to have someone pick him up in a car. Which meant that someone would know where he had gone.

The walkie-talkie in her hand kept chirping for attention. She ignored it. She headed down the stairs and burst in on the building manager just as he was cracking open a new beer can. His apartment had all of the house's best furniture in it – a massive oak breakfront, a kitchen table with four matching chairs – but dust dulled all the colors and there were bags of trash stacked in the kitchen. No books anywhere.

'Hell's bells, what now?' the old man asked when he saw her.

'I need some information, and I don't have a lot of time, so forgive me if I sound impolite,' she said. 'How long has Simon lived here?'

'That Arkeley kid? Just this semester. Signed a one-year lease.'

'Does he have a girlfriend?' she asked.

The building manager laughed. 'You mean that Linda? She comes sniffing around a lot, but you ask me, the guy's gay. Never gives her a second look.'

'Does he ever have any other visitors?'

The old man scowled. 'Hah! Yes, yes he does. The kind that stay all night and you have to listen to them talking and laughing while you're trying to sleep. They put a towel under the door, too, but don't think I'm so old I don't recognize the smell of what they smoke up there, I was alive in the sixties and—'

Caxton shook her head. 'Just answer my questions, alright? As simply and as clearly as you can. Do you remember the names of any of his visitors? Did he ever introduce them to you?'

'We're not exactly on friendly terms, him and me,' the manager replied. He scratched at his stubble for a second, though, and said, 'I guess there was one guy. Simon called him "Murph." Ugly little pothead with freckles and red hair. Comes around a lot, actually. Don't know his last name.'

'Do you know where he lives? Please, think hard.'

The building manager shrugged. 'South Campus, some-where.' She must have looked confused. 'There's a secondary campus, called South Campus, about two miles from here down Comstock Avenue. It's almost all residential buildings. Crappy little cinder-block shacks they rent out for next to nothing.'

'That's all you can tell me?' Caxton asked, desperate.

'Maybe it's enough,' Lu said from behind her. He took the walkie-talkie out of her hand. 'Deputy Marshal Young, do you read me?'

'Yeah, go ahead, Lu.'

'Special Deputy Caxton would like you to call up the registrar's office. We need to track down a student, partial name Murph, maybe Murphy. Not sure if that's a last or first name. Last known address is South Campus and he may have a record for drug offenses. You think that might turn something up?'

'We'll get on it, maybe we'll get lucky. Over.'

Caxton nodded with excitement. 'Good thinking,' she said to Lu. 'Sir,' she said, turning to face the building manager, 'thanks for your assistance.'

'Simon's not going to jail, is he?' the man asked.

'I don't have a warrant for his arrest,' she told him.

'Good, 'cause he's still got six months on that lease.'

Caxton led Lu back down to the street and climbed into her Mazda, indicating he should take shotgun. 'I need you to navigate,' she said. 'We'll head down to South Campus now and hope we have an address by the time we arrive.'

'You got it,' Lu replied. 'But what makes you so sure he went to hang out with this friend of his?'

'Because I don't have any other ideas,' she told him.

39.

Caxton left Young and Miller to watch the house, in case she was wrong. If Simon came back while she was gone they were under orders to sit on him – to watch his every move, and to follow him if he left the house. There was no point in being discreet anymore. If the kid was going to sneak out from under their noses and run around in the dark, she would do everything she could to keep him away from his father.

If she didn't, she was beginning to think she would have a second vampire on her hands, just as dangerous as the first.

Simon's reticence to talk to her, his obvious distrust of law enforcement: those she could have chalked up to youthful rebellion or just general stupidity. The trick with getting his friend to sit in his window for him suggested something more. Maybe he had something to hide.

'When we get to this place,' she told Lu, 'just back my play. I'll do the talking.'

'Right,' he said, sounding unconvinced. She'd pushed him to his limit when she broke down Simon's door, and she wasn't sure how much more he would let her get away with. Well, she would just have to find out.

She kept her speed down on the way to South Campus. It wasn't all that far away and the snow on the road made any kind of driving hazardous. Big trucks full of rock salt were carving out channels through the snowdrifts, but she didn't want to take any chances. If she went off the road and disabled the Mazda, she would lose crucial time and mobility.

'You're from here, right? From Syracuse? If we knock on the door of a drug scene, should we expect to be met with guns?'

Lu's eyes went wide. 'Hell, no. The drug users here are just students – teenagers. They smoke pot, maybe drop acid sometimes. This is a college town, you have to expect that, a little. They rarely get violent. It's too cold up here for that kind of stupidity.'

'Good,' she said, and shifted in her seat, trying to relax.

It wasn't easy. This place they were going to – this apartment. Jameson could be there waiting for her. It could be a trap. He could have already passed the curse to Simon. The place could be crawling with half-deads.

She could find anything there, anything at all.

She turned off on a road called Skytop and got her first look at South Campus. The building manager's description hadn't been far off. The residential units were simple two-story dwellings built of cheap materials. They had few windows and they all looked exactly alike. They lay like scattered Monopoly pieces in a vast sea of salted gravel parking lots. Caxton could imagine few places more depressing to live – but she supposed, if they were cheap enough, students could put up with them.

They pulled into a parking lot big enough for a shopping mall and then they sat. And waited. And waited some more.

241

Caxton got impatient and punched the steering wheel a few times, but that didn't help anybody, so eventually she stopped. Finally Young called her with an address. He'd turned up over a hundred students with the last name Murphy, and had gone through them all and ruled them out – either they were female, or they didn't live in South Campus, or they didn't have red hair – before trying it as a first name. There was only one student in the entire university with the first name of Murphy, and he both was male and lived in South Campus. If this wasn't the guy they were looking for, he said, if Murph was just a nickname, then they were plain out of luck. He gave her the exact address and she got the car moving before she'd even thanked him.

She pulled into a spot directly in front of the unit she wanted. It was rented, according to Young, to a junior named Murphy Frissell. Frissell was an environmental science and forestry major – what Lu said was locally known as a Stumpy. Frissell was believed to have one roommate, named Scott Cohen, who was studying music. Both of them had been arrested the previous year for possession of marijuana, but their sentences had been suspended. Frissell sounded exactly like the boy the building manager had described – Young had even downloaded a picture from the registrar's office and confirmed that Frissell had red hair.

Caxton and Lu got out of the car and approached the housing unit. She could hear thumping music coming through the drawn curtains and thought she could even smell pot smoke. She waved at Lu to cover her, then stepped up to the door and pounded on it. 'Open up,' she shouted. 'Federal agents.'

There was no answer. She hadn't really expected one – the music inside must be playing at an ear-shattering volume, if she could hear it so clearly through the building's insulated

242

walls. She hammered again and again at the door, and stabbed at the bell over and over. Finally she heard someone moving around inside. She stepped over to the nearest window and tapped on the glass with her collapsible baton.

'Shit!' someone said inside. 'Did you hear that?'

'Come on,' Caxton shouted. 'Open this door!'

The music stopped abruptly. Caxton pounded on the door again. Finally someone came to the door and peeked out. It was a young man, just about Simon's age, with a mop of black curls falling to his shoulders. His eyes were deeply bloodshot and they had trouble finding Caxton's face. 'What?' the boy asked.

Caxton sighed. 'Scott Cohen? I'm Special Deputy Caxton, and this is Special Deputy Benicio. We're here to talk to Simon Arkeley. Can we come in, please?'

The boy licked his lips. He appeared deep in thought. Caxton tried to remain patient and calm, but she knew if Cohen didn't step aside in a second she would physically remove him from the doorway.

'Um, okay,' the boy finally said. 'Wait. Are you cops?'

Caxton shoved past him through the door. 'Federal agents,' she said, gesturing for Lu to follow her.

'I'm not sure if I should let you in,' Cohen said, but it was already too late. Caxton was inside.

The room beyond the door was a kitchen, with a dented and scorched countertop and badly painted cabinets. The refrigerator was decorated with a poster for an organization called NORML, which showed an oversized hemp leaf. She came around the side of the counter and saw a framed M. C. Escher print on the wall. The rest of the lower floor was taken up by a spacious living room with a tan shag carpet. Numerous spots on the carpet had been burned down to round, black-edged holes, perhaps by dropped cigarettes. There was a

243

gigantic sofa, on which a boy who had to be Murphy Frissell lay passed out or sleeping. There was a forty-inch flat-screen television, switched off. On a coffee table sat a collection of glass and plastic bongs, as well as numerous butane lighters and mini blowtorches of the kind used to make crème brûlée – or to keep a crack pipe lit.

Caxton scanned the corners of the room looking for shotguns or pistols or, for that matter, swords – she'd seen enough residences exactly like this one to expect the bizarre. There was no sign of any weapons, however.

Cohen had followed after her like a puppy, his hands up in front of him as if he were surrendering before she'd even charged him with anything. 'Where is he?' she demanded. Before Cohen could ask who she meant, she said, 'Arkeley. Simon Arkeley.'

The boy looked around the room, his face scrunched up. 'He's not here,' he said, and Caxton's heart fell. Then his eyes opened wider. 'He must be upstairs, then. Is he upstairs?'

'Let's go see,' Caxton said, and nodded at Lu. 'Scott, you stay here.'

The boy looked at her very hard. 'Okay,' he said.

Caxton wondered what on earth Simon could be doing with these losers. He hadn't struck her as a serious drug user when she met him. Still, that encounter had been very brief and she supposed she could have been mistaken.

The stairs were at the far end of the room. She mounted them slowly, unsure what to expect at the top. She could see a wisp of smoke curling around the light fixtures up there and she drew her weapon. If Simon was up there smoking pot he might react badly to sight of law enforcement.

He solved that problem for her by coming out of the door at the top of the stairs and glaring down at her. Simon was alive, she saw at once. Alive and unhurt.

It wasn't too late.

'Mr Arkeley,' Lu said, 'I hope we're not disturbing you, sir.'

'Not at all,' Simon told him. 'Hello, Trooper.'

Caxton gritted her teeth. 'It's Special Deputy now.'

Simon nodded. 'I suppose we have to talk. Come on up.'

40.

Caxton turned to Lu at the top of the stairs. 'Keep an eye on the two down there. They're probably out of commission, but I don't want them leaving until I say it's okay.'

Lu nodded, but he grabbed her arm before he went back down. 'Don't do anything I wouldn't do,' he said, frowning.

Did he expect her to beat information out of Simon? Or maybe just violate his civil rights some other way? For the moment she didn't feel the need to break any laws. Not as long as Simon was still okay. She followed the boy down a short hallway to a bedroom.

Two mattresses lay in opposite corners, lying on the floor with no frames to support them. The walls were covered in posters for jam bands and deceased rock stars. Clothes were strewn around the floor and a pile of pornographic magazines was stacked neatly in one corner. Blue, slow-moving smoke filled the ceiling and made all the objects in the room indistinct. It came from a silver mixing bowl full of smoldering herbs on the floor.

Simon sat down on the carpet next to the bowl in an easy lotus position and gestured for her to do the same.

She preferred to stay standing. 'We figured out the trick you pulled with Linda, obviously,' she said.

'I figured you would, given your reputation. I just wanted enough time to escape. Of course, that was hours ago,' Simon said. His eyes were closed and his head tilted slightly back.

'I got a late start this morning and just got into town. So you're not going to help me out, are you?'

His shoulders rose a fraction of an inch. 'I've done some research. Law isn't my thing, normally, but when your underlings showed up to harass me I looked into my options. I can't actively interfere with your investigation. Beyond that you have no power over me – I don't even have to answer your questions if I don't want to.' He opened his eyes. 'And I don't want to.'

Caxton smiled. 'Why not?'

He only smiled in return.

'I could bust you. I could drag you down to the local station house and have them book you,' she threatened.

'Really? On what charge?'

She waved a hand through the smoke that filled the room. 'Drugs.'

Simon turned his head from side to side. 'Actually, no, you can't. No one in this house has broken any kind of drug law. I see by your face you don't believe me, but if you search this place from top to bottom – and I don't doubt you would – you won't find so much as a stem or a seed of any illegal drug. This is where I come when I want to smoke *Salvia divinorum* – the sage of the seers. Which isn't illegal at all.'

'Not yet,' Caxton said. 'The legislature is working on it.'

'But until a new law is passed – well,' Simon said, and smiled again.

Caxton knew about the drug. It was still legal in New York state. In Pennsylvania, too, though her state had a reputation

247

for its very tough drug laws. Salvia was a plant from Mexico that had been used for thousands of years by the Indians there in their religious ceremonies. It was also a potent hallucinogen, and in recent years it had become quite popular with bored suburban kids who used to do LSD until the old suppliers of acid had all dried up. In small doses salvia produced a fifteen-minute high with visual effects. In very large doses it produced stupor and unconsciousness – which explained the behavior of the two boys downstairs.

'What do you see when you smoke it?' Caxton asked.

Simon shook his head. 'I used to believe it would open me to other states of consciousness and I would learn something useful. It never really worked. I haven't smoked any of it tonight.' He used a glass stick to stir the burning herbs in his bowl. The embers flared into new life, then died down to orange coals again as a new wave of smoke lifted into the air. 'This,' he said, 'is white sage, *Salvia apiana*. It's used in purification rituals.'

'Done something you feel guilty about?' Caxton asked. 'Need to clean up your aura?'

'I came here because it was a refuge away from prying eyes.'

'Those eyes were watching out for you,' Caxton said. 'I'm only here to protect you. I'm not sure why you're fighting me so hard. You must know what your father's been up to. He killed your uncle, then your mother—'

'Yes, of course,' Simon said, smiling, though his voice had lost some of its ethereal quality.

Caxton thought of Dylan Carboy and the facial tic that had given him away when she mentioned his notebooks. It looked like Simon had a chink in his armor as well. 'He tried to kill your sister.'

'I didn't know that.' Simon cleared his throat. 'You saved her, right?'

248

'He did kill one of her friends. Nice girl, a mute. Raleigh's roommate, actually. He drank a little of her blood, but mostly she was just in the way.'

'Stop.'

'Tore her to pieces, so we had to get a leak-proof body bag—'

'Stop it!' Simon shouted, jumping to his feet.

Caxton just shook her head. 'Getting a little sick to your stomach?' she asked. 'I know the feeling, all too well. Help me, Simon. Help me stop him before he kills anybody else. Before he tries to kill you. Or is that the plan? Have you been in contact with him recently? Has he offered to make you a vampire like him? Did you say yes?'

Simon's face twisted and darkened with rage. He opened his mouth to speak, but then a violent shudder wracked him from head to foot. It left him swaying slightly, but the blood had gone out of his cheeks. 'I think,' he said, finally, 'that I don't want to talk to you any longer unless my lawyer is present.'

Caxton's heart sagged in her chest. 'That's your right,' she said. She couldn't resist adding, 'Does that mean he has contacted you or—'

'Enough, Special Deputy,' the boy said. 'I'm going home. I'm tired.'

'Okay,' she said. 'Who's your lawyer?'

The boy reached into his pocket and took out a nylon wallet on a chain. He opened it up and fished out a business card, which he handed to Caxton. Interesting, she thought. Not a lot of twenty-year-old college students have lawyers on retainer. She decided he must have gone to the lawyer recently, after finding out he was under surveillance. If he'd gone to that much trouble, she wondered what he had to hide. She went to the doorway and called Lu up to meet her there. She handed the card to the Fed without even looking at it. 'Call this guy,' she said. 'Tell him to meet us at Simon's apartment, tonight. If he complains or says it's after hours, tell him his client is being hounded by the police.'

Lu stepped out into the hall to comply.

'I'll give you a ride,' Caxton said, 'and wait for your lawyer there, alright?'

The boy lowered his head. She turned to Lu, who was on hold. 'You stay here and keep an eye on this place. If we could find it this easily, a vampire probably can too. If Jameson shows up, you know what to do.'

Lu nodded. 'Sure. Run like hell.' He stepped aside to let Caxton and Simon out of the room. They headed down the stairs together and outside into the cold of the parking lot. She half expected him to refuse her ride, but when she opened the door of the Mazda he climbed in without complaint. They drove back to his apartment in silence. At his front door he said, 'I don't want you to come in. You can't come in unless I invite you in, not legally.'

'That's an interesting legal question, since I've already been inside,' Caxton said. 'Let's ask your lawyer when he comes.'

Simon scowled at her but didn't slam the door in her face when she came in, and at the top of the stairs he actually held his door open for her. Inside he shed his winter coat and sat down hard on the cot. Its springs squealed noisily. 'Are you going to watch me undress?' he asked.

Caxton waved one hand at him. 'Keep your clothes on. In fact, why don't we pack a bag?' She went to his closet and took down a small black suitcase from the shelf at its top.

'Why, am I going somewhere?'

'Pennsylvania. Harrisburg, I think,' she said. 'That way I can keep an eye on you and your sister at the same time.'

'I don't think so.'

She shrugged and started packing, folding up shirts neatly and then laying them in the suitcase. She had very little time left, she knew. As soon as the lawyer showed up there would be no way on earth to compel Simon to come back to Pennsylvania with her. She needed to get him riled up again. Get him scared. She looked around inside the closet for pairs of pants.

'Leave my stuff alone,' Simon said, testily.

She shrugged again and sorted through the clothes he had on hangers. There wasn't much, just a few nice shirts and a powder blue suit. The same suit he'd worn to Jameson's mock funeral. It was probably the only suit he owned, she thought. She picked up one sleeve and let the linen material run through her fingers. That suit—

No. It couldn't be the same. That was too – her brain flip-flopped in her skull. If she was right, if that suit matched the other one, the one in the picture, it made things a lot more complicated. But maybe it made one thing dead easy.

She turned around and looked at him, really studied his face for the first time. Then she walked toward him, reaching toward her belt.

'Are you going to shoot me?' he asked. His tone was trying for sarcasm, but it hit fear on the way there.

'Unh-uh,' Caxton said. Yeah. She was sure, she decided. That suit was the same color, the same light blue. She opened a pouch at her belt and took out her handcuffs. 'I'm putting you under arrest.'

41.

'What is this about?' Simon demanded, a few hours later. 'What are you charging me with?'

He looked scared. She had hauled him down to the local police station and then handed him over to the officers there to be booked and processed. He'd been photographed, fingerprinted, strip-searched, and shoved in a cell with a bunch of drug offenders and petty thieves, then left there to stew for a while. He looked very scared.

This was the first she'd seen of him since they'd arrived. She'd spent the intervening time discussing her investigation with the local police chief and checking her email. She had to be sure.

When she was ready – or maybe, to be honest, a little while after she was fully ready – she had him brought up from cells and put in an interrogation room. As they went, it wasn't the nicest interrogation room Caxton had ever seen. There was one table topped with Formica, brown and black with generations of cigarette burns and coffee stains. There were two chairs, which sat side by side – the room wasn't big enough

252

to allow the subject and the interviewer to sit across from each other. There was a reinforced staple in the wall, to which Simon had been attached by a pair of handcuffs. It was high up on the wall so that the video camera in the corner of the ceiling could see where Simon's hands were at all times.

Caxton leaned back in her chair. She had a manila envelope containing a few pieces of paper. She drew one out and read:

'You have the right to remain silent. Anything you say can and will be used against you in a court of law. You have the right to an attorney. If you cannot afford an attorney, one will be provided for you at interrogation time and at court. Do you understand the rights I have just read to you? With these rights in mind, do you wish to speak to me?'

She looked up at him expectantly.

'Fuck you,' he howled. 'Tell me what's going on. I don't have to take this. I can walk out of here right now if you don't charge me.'

Caxton shook her head no, with a sad little smile. 'Charges? Alright. Let's pick one. How about trespassing in a government building? Or maybe the theft of evidence in an ongoing criminal investigation. Then there's impersonating a police officer. Shall I go on?'

'You don't – you don't have any evidence,' he said. His eyes were shiny with fear.

Good. If she scared him enough he might agree to enter her protection.

She sighed dramatically and said, 'You have the right to remain silent. Any—'

'Fine,' he said, stopping her. 'Yes, I understand. Just tell me what this is about, damn it.'

'Your suit. Your powder blue suit.'

He squinted at her. 'I wore it to that stupid funeral. That's the only time you've seen it.'

253

She shook her head again, then reached into her envelope and drew out a computer printout on glossy photo paper. It showed a man wearing a light blue suit, standing at the entrance of the USMS archives.

Simon's eyes flicked down to the photo but didn't linger there long enough for him to have taken a real look. 'That's not me. You can't even see the face.'

'You think that's all I have, this one picture?'

'I – I won't talk until my lawyer arrives.'

'That's fine,' Caxton said. 'That'll give me time to check your fingerprints against the ones we found on the crime scene.' It was a bluff, but an easy one. The man in the photograph wasn't wearing gloves. He would almost certainly have touched some surface, maybe a doorknob or a countertop, while he was inside the archives.

'Hold on,' Simon said.

'Once we get a match, I really don't think I'll need to ask you any more questions. We can just drop you in a holding cell and wait for trial. You'll be safe enough there while I go find and kill your father. Of course, there are a couple of things I'd really like to know, but fine, you want your lawyer, you get your lawyer. Lu finally got hold of him a little while ago, and he said he would be here in the morning.' She put her papers back in the envelope and started to get up. 'You can spend the night back in the holding cell until he arrives.'

'Wait,' Simon said.

She looked at him expectantly.

'Wait. Am I – okay, I'm in trouble. I understand that. Now, I'm not confessing to anything. But if I answer your questions—'

She shook her head. 'I can't coerce you to talk to me. That means I can't offer you any deals to get you to speak, either.'

He closed his eyes and nodded. 'There has to be something

254

we can do, though. If I agree, of my own free will, to answer your questions, maybe you won't just dump me in a cell and let me rot.'

She shrugged. 'It's not my decision whether to press charges or not.' That was the truth. Fetlock would make that decision, when the time came, based on Caxton's advice. 'However, as a U.S. Marshal one of my duties is to transport prisoners from place to place. I can transport you to a different detention facility. Say, one in Pennsylvania, where you can be with your sister.'

He stared at her with wide eyes for quite a while. Then his chin bobbed up and down. It took her a second to decide that was a yes, and not just a muscular tremor.

'Okay,' she said. 'First. Tell me exactly what happened at the USMS archives. I want to know who told you to do it, and who told you what to do. I want to know how you did it, and I want to know where the files are now.'

After that he opened like a can of peas.

His story began just after the massacre at Gettysburg, where Caxton and Glauer had faced down an army of vampires – and lost. Jameson had saved Caxton's life there by finishing off the vampires who were too tough for her. 'He truly believed he would be able to do that, then have the strength of will to turn himself in. Turn himself over to you, I guess. For disposal.'

'That's an odd way of putting it,' Caxton said.

'But accurate, I think. It was supposed to be nice and tidy, he would just come back to you, let you put your gun up against his chest, and it would be over. He thought his life was over, anyway, before he made the change. He'd been crippled. He was a vampire hunter who could barely climb a flight of stairs, much less shoot straight. He felt like his only reason for living was gone. That's why he made the choice he did. He told me about that first night as a vampire, though, and the strength he had, and the things he could see. They can see farther into the red end of the electromagnetic spectrum than we can. Into the near infrared. I can't even imagine it – the things he described, the way the sky glowed, the way trees pulsed with life and every animal—'

'Was full of blood,' Caxton interrupted. 'I know they can see our blood, even in the dark.' She shook her head. 'You're making it sound pretty good.'

'Well, maybe it kind of was. I mean, at first. He swore he would never harm a living human. All he wanted was another night like that – and another after that. He realized that he hadn't wanted to kill himself at all. That he'd just been feeling sorry for himself. I think he still believed he could do good. Kill more vampires – you know, working from the inside. When he first contacted me, that was the sense I got.'

'When was this?'

Simon rubbed his forehead. 'October. Late October – I remember there was a paper jack-o'-lantern on my door that night.'

So Jameson had been active for nearly a month before he contacted his son. She wondered what he'd been doing before that – staying up late with Dylan Carboy, talking about how much Carboy hated school? Drinking blood out of a plastic bag and hoping it would be enough? She couldn't imagine what he'd done, what he'd thought, in those early days. Not yet. 'How did he contact you? Did he come to you in person?'

'No,' Simon said. 'By telephone.'

'Do you remember what number he called you from?'

'This was on my home phone. I don't have caller ID.'

Caxton nodded. She leaned back in her chair. 'Did he tell you at any time where he was, or at least where he was calling from?'

'Of course not,' Simon said. 'He only called me a couple

256

of times. The first was to, well, to see how I was doing. You can imagine how I reacted to that, my dead father calling me on the phone to see how my grades were. I freaked out and hung up on him. The next time he called – I didn't hang up.'

Caxton tried to channel Glauer with his people skills and guess why. 'You missed him,' she suggested.

'Fuck, no,' Simon spat. 'You have to understand, he had never called me at school before. I mean, when he was living. I barely saw him when I was in high school, he was always away at some seminar on vampires or some police training thing or running around some far corner of Pennsylvania because someone had seen an albino man with pointed ears going through their trash cans and it turned out it was a coyote. No, I didn't miss him. I never really had a father. But after that first call, I kind of felt – this is so stupid, but – I felt like I did have somebody, for the first time. When he called again, I was happy to hear his voice, even as changed as it was. That's when he told me about what it was like for him, and how much he wanted to stay alive, and how you were gunning for him. He told me there was something I could do to help him, to help keep him alive.'

'And you said yes?'

Simon shrugged. 'I took some coaxing. But in the end he was still the same guy. The guy who, every time I saw him, knew exactly how to get a reaction out of me. He knew how to push my buttons. How to make me feel sorry for him. He told me how lonely he was, and how desperate. How everyone wanted to hurt him. That was all an act, wasn't it? Don't answer that, I know the answer. They can hypnotize you if you look into their eyes. I think, maybe, they can do it with their voices, too. Or maybe – maybe I was just an easy mark.'

He kept talking then, without any prompting, telling a story that had gained its own momentum. 'A couple days later I got

257

an envelope in the mail, with no return address. The postmark said Bellefonte. Inside was a security card on a nylon string. It was his old card from when he worked for the USMS. It was my job to go find all his old files and steal them. The hard part was getting down to Virginia. I had to take a train, then walk five miles from the station. At the door there was a bored guard who barely glanced at the card, then let me in. Same thing at the archives. I signed for the files, not using my own name, of course, and then I took them and walked back out the same way I'd come in. Just like that. I walked back to the train station, went in the bathroom, and changed my clothes and messed up my hair. If anybody had been looking for me they wouldn't have recognized me after that. I took the next train back to Syracuse and I was in class that evening at five-thirty. Intensive French 206. I couldn't miss it. I took it every weekday, for two hours and fifty minutes, and at the end of the semester I had nine credits and I'd completed my foreign-language requirement. If I missed one class I lost a letter grade.'

Caxton sighed. 'Where are the files now?'

'He told me there were things in those papers that could hurt him. That could lead you right to him. A list of places he thought would make good vampire lairs. Personal stuff about his family. A lot of stuff about Malvern.' He held up his hands. 'I burned them. You have to understand. I thought I was doing a good thing. I thought I was helping my dad. Then, at the fake funeral, when you were talking about how you were going to kill him—'

'Yeah,' Caxton said. 'You thought he was still a good guy. Until . . . ?'

'Right up until he killed my uncle.' He inhaled deeply. 'That was when I got a lawyer. That was why I refused your protective custody. He kills people because they know

258

something. He kills people because they get in his way now. He's not the man I spoke to on the phone.'

'He's not your father,' Caxton said.

'Actually – in some ways he's more like my father than ever.'

Caxton thought maybe she could see that. 'Okay. Next question. When was the last time you spoke with him?'

'That was the last time, when he asked me to get the files. I haven't heard from him since.'

Caxton nodded, making a note on her pad.

'Although I spoke to Malvern like three days ago.'

She nearly lost control of her pen.

42.

'Malvern – you're in contact with Malvern.' Caxton caught her breath. 'Is this a recent development?'

Simon shook his head. 'It started years ago. Before you even came along. My freshman year in college, actually.'

Caxton bit her lip. 'That was what, two years ago? At that time Malvern was being held in a half-abandoned hospital. She was the only patient there. I saw the place. I nearly died there. The security was pretty tight, since your father oversaw it. There's no way you could have broken in there and spoken with her, and I know he would never have allowed you to go there unsupervised.'

'Well, yeah,' Simon said. 'I never actually met her. We corresponded by email.' He smiled. 'My father was good at a lot of things, but he never really mastered computers. For some reason Malvern had a laptop there—'

'Yes,' Caxton interrupted. 'It was her only way to communicate with her keepers. She can't talk, she's too old and decayed for that. She talks by tapping out messages on the keyboard.'

260

Simon nodded. 'Right. And obviously she wasn't supposed to be able to get a line out. She was behind a firewall. I knew about her through my father – when he was home, on those rare occasions, he talked about vampires all the time. He talked about her a lot. As soon as I got to Syracuse I decided I wanted to talk to her. I had a friend who was majoring in computer science and he established a VPN connection right through the firewall. She was pretty surprised, but she was desperate to talk to anybody and she was more than willing to keep our conversations secret. I talked to her a lot that semester. I had a million questions and she was happy to answer them.'

Caxton could guess why Malvern would have been happy to talk to the boy. She was always looking for some angle, some new way to improve her condition – to acquire blood, the only thing that could heal her ravaged body. Jameson had thwarted every one of her plans. It wasn't a big logical jump to see how much she would enjoy getting her hooks into his only son. Maybe she had wanted to turn Simon into a vampire, to torture his father. Maybe she just liked the irony. She couldn't see why Simon would take such a risk, though. 'Weren't you worried you would get caught?'

'Of course. If my father knew what I was doing he would have killed me.' The boy blanched. 'I mean, he would have – he would have been angry. But it was so worth the risk. I told you when I met you that I was studying biology. That's kind of true. Actually, my major is in teratology. The study of monsters.'

Of course it is, she thought. Growing up the son of Jameson Arkeley, America's last vampire hunter, what else would the boy have chosen to study?

'You have to understand, it's not much of a field. Most monsters were driven to extinction long before anybody bothered to study them in a proper scientific manner. There's some

261

fossil evidence, and a few so-called historical accounts. Firsthand data is nonexistent. There's a stuffed werewolf in a museum in Moscow, but a lot of people think it's a fake – and they don't let first-year students from American universities just fly over to poke and prod at it. Yet there I was with access to a living, well, an undead vampire. The very last one, as far as anyone knew.'

Caxton closed her eyes. *If only.*

'Can you even imagine how tempting that was?' Simon looked at his hands, unable to meet her gaze. 'So of course I talked to her.'

'She taught you about vampires. Did she ever – did she ask you for anything in return?'

'I had a sense she was leading up to that. She kept sending me emails about how badly she needed blood and how my father was starving her. I said that was a shame but there was nothing I could do about it. Maybe she would have gone further, but then one day I emailed her and there was no response. I didn't hear from her again for a long time. I left the VPN connection in place, just, you know, in case she got in touch again. Later I heard the story of how she created those new vampires, and how you and my father met, and I realized the dates matched up. She stopped emailing me when she started making new vampires. I guess luring me into accepting the curse was just taking too long.'

'But now she's in touch with you again.'

'Yeah. About two months ago, when my father did – what he did.' Simon shrugged. 'The connection came back on. There was a message waiting for me. It was different from before, though.'

'How?'

'Before, she would take a long time to write an email. Days and days – I would ask her the simplest question and have to wait a really long time to get a reply. When she started talking again she was emailing two or three times a day, really long messages about how much our contact had meant to her and how she wanted to meet with me in person now. Her spelling was better, too, and there was actual punctuation in the messages. I guess maybe when she went away with my dad she didn't have to write in secret anymore and she had more free time to—'

'No,' Caxton said.

'No?'

Caxton frowned at him. 'Her spelling and punctuation get better when she's recently fed. It's easier for her to type now because she's stronger. Your father has been feeding her regularly, and it won't be too long before she can call you on the phone. Until she can talk again.'

'Really? You can't imagine how much there still is to learn from her.'

Caxton restrained herself from slapping his stupid face. 'You should have told me all this when we first met. You should have told someone, someone in law enforcement, the second she got back in touch with you.'

He shook his head. 'There was nothing in those messages that would help you. It was mostly personal stuff. And there's no way to trace the connection and figure out where she is that way.'

'Are you so sure? You're not a detective, Simon. You don't know how we work. How we can figure things out even from seemingly meaningless clues. I could have used that information. If I'd had it,' she said, knowing she was about to drop a bomb, that what she was about to say might traumatize him for life, but not really caring, 'maybe I could have found their lair by now. Maybe I could have saved your uncle. Or your mother.'

263

Simon's face went blank suddenly. 'But it was all harmless stuff! My mom—'

'You know she's dead, right? I had to break the news to Raleigh.'

The boy's mouth was a flat line across his face. 'I . . . know. I guess I didn't let myself think about it until now. She's dead. She's really dead.'

Silence filled up the room like fog. Simon sat very still, his hands on the table, and stared into space. 'And I had a part in that. Oh, shit,' he said, very softly. 'Oh God. I didn't . . . I didn't think.'

In a moment her anger, her terrifying resolve, just broke. He wasn't evil. He hadn't withheld that information to thwart her. He just hadn't realized how desperate the situation was. Until a few days before, he'd still thought his father was a good man.

The boy in front of her started crying. Not sobbing, not uncontrollable weeping. Tears were just rolling down his face. He didn't look like he was even aware of them. She had pushed him too hard. Laid too much guilt on him. Some people weren't as strong as she was, sometimes. Some people weren't as practiced as she at handling the guilt of lives lost, of culpability. She had to remember that.

Glauer was supposed to handle the emotional scenes. Glauer was the people person. She was the one who shot vampires. Even Caxton could see the grief that was about to crush the boy like a closing fist, though. She reached over and took his hand.

'Hey. We'll never really know how things could have been different.' He lowered his forehead to the table. She tried to think of anything else she could say. 'I lost my mom when I was fifteen,' she said. 'It doesn't make any sense. Mothers are bigger than we are. They're more durable. Or they're supposed to be.'

He turned slowly to look at her. 'Thanks. I think I might want to be alone for a while. Are we done?'

'Sure,' Caxton said. She got up and stepped out of the little room. She left him handcuffed to the wall.

She was still a cop, after all.

43.

Caxton woke up because her phone was ringing. She tried to ignore it, but it was set to vibrate as well, and it chattered painfully against her ribs. She sat up.

It had been a long night. She'd overseen a team of Feds who went to Simon's apartment and seized his computers; she'd gotten them started downloading anything that remained of years of correspondence between the boy and the vampire. Something might come of it – it was true that sometimes innocent-seeming clues could tip over an entire investigation. It would take time, though, before they learned anything. As the computer techs got to work she'd realized she wasn't going to be any help, so she'd returned to the jail and stood guard, along with every Fed she could mobilize in the middle of the night.

And nothing had happened.

She had finally fallen asleep about five in the morning, sitting upright in a chair in a disused room near the holding cells in the basement. She'd pulled her winter coat over her shoulders in lieu of a blanket. The phone was in one of the pockets.

She tried to open her eyes, but they were bleary and glued shut with sleep. She struggled to sit up and her body complained. Every muscle was stiff, every joint ached. She beat at her coat with one hand until she found the pocket holding the phone, then drew it out and answered it.

'Hello? Who's calling?' she said. That was about all she could manage.

'It's Deputy Marshal Fetlock. Are you alright?'

Caxton rubbed at her eyes with her free hand. She sat up straighter in the chair, complaining muscles notwithstanding. 'Yes, sir.' Putting her feet down on the floor, she started to think about standing up.

'I've had some very disturbing reports out of the field office in Syracuse. I wanted to discuss your conduct. Special Deputy Benicio tells me you illegally entered and searched Simon Arkeley's apartment. Is that true?'

'There were exigent circumstances,' she said. It wasn't strictly a lie. Simon's life had been at risk and she'd only forced the door in order to protect him.

'Benicio doesn't corroborate that,' Fetlock told her.

She got her feet down, then stood up all in one go. It was easy then to stagger to the door and push it open. The holding cells were just down the hall – she needed to check. 'Sir, Simon is now in my custody.' She considered telling him that the boy had confessed to stealing the files from the USMS archives, but she worried he might insist she drag him down to Virginia and relinquish him to the authorities there. That was the last thing she wanted. She needed to keep him close, where she could watch him. 'I do not believe he will be interested in pressing charges.'

'For your sake I hope so. We can't have this kind of behavior, Caxton.'

There were eight cells, little bigger than closets, lining either side of a short corridor. Only a few of them were occupied. She counted down the cells. She'd put Simon in the third cell on the left side herself. She came up to the bars and looked in. There he was. Sleeping. She watched his chest rise and fall. He was still alive.

'Sir,' she said, 'can I ask you what time it is?'

'It's eight-oh-two, by my clock,' Fetlock told her. 'Don't try to evade the issue.'

She tried to remember, but couldn't, what time sunrise was. 'Please. Just tell me something. Is the sun up yet?' she asked.

'Yes, Special Deputy. It is. But—'

'Oh, thank God,' Caxton said. That meant she'd made it through the night. It meant she'd gone twenty-four hours without discharging her weapon. More important, it meant it had been more than twenty-four hours since anyone died. 'Thank God,' she said again. 'Thank God.'

Fetlock kept talking, but she barely heard him. She made apologetic noises where appropriate, but she didn't bother explaining her actions – why should she? Raleigh and Simon were alive. Jameson's plot to recruit new vampires had failed. She could keep his children safe while she hunted for him, for his lair. And where she found him she would find Malvern as well. She wasn't done yet. It would take more time, more work, more risk, to finish off the vampires, but she'd taken an important step.

Of course, the vampires wouldn't let her have her moment of triumph without ruining it somehow.

When she finally got Fetlock off the phone, it chimed at her to tell her she had a voice mail message waiting. The call had come in during the early hours of the morning, shortly after she'd fallen asleep. She recognized the number it came from right away: it was from the phone Jameson had stolen from a dead cop in Bellefonte.

Steeling herself, she dialed her voice mail and waited to hear his growling voice again. Except when the message played it wasn't a male voice.

It was a very short message. 'Keep the boy from harm, Laura. I have plans for him.'

It was recognizably a woman's voice, though so creaky and rough she could barely make out the words. At first she didn't understand, couldn't think of who it might be. Then she remembered she had heard that voice before, just once, more than a year previously. It was the voice of Justinia Malvern.

She was talking again. Jameson had fed her enough blood to give her her voice back. That meant it was only a matter of time before she would start walking under her own power.

It didn't matter. Caxton told herself that, over and over. The kids were both in protective custody. She was making progress. She signed the necessary papers and had Simon released into her recognizance. The boy looked almost pathetically grateful as she led him out of the police station and into the parking lot. It had stopped snowing during the night, and all of Syracuse was buried under a thick layer of white that hurt her eyes to look at. She slipped on her sunglasses and eventually found her car. It was under six inches of snow, but the red paint showed through here and there. Together she and Simon dug it out and then climbed inside, their breath pluming across the windows and leaving them fogged.

Before they got on the highway she stopped at a fast-food restaurant for breakfast. Simon, it turned out, was a vegetarian. They had trouble finding him a salad, but eventually he settled for one with a few withered vegetables and some strips of fried chicken he could pick out. He laid them carefully on a napkin, which he then folded up and stuck inside the bag. This he crumpled up in his hands and put in his pocket for later disposal.

Caxton looked into the Mazda's backseat and saw all the wrappers and bags she'd thrown back there. Neither of them said anything.

The snowplows had cleared the highways and laid down a thick scurf of rock salt. The road surface was wet and shiny, but the chains on her tires held it just fine.

It was only a little after noon when she arrived back at Harrisburg and the state police headquarters. She brought Simon inside and went looking for Glauer. He was down in the SSU briefing room, pinning up a picture of Raleigh's friend Violet under VAMPIRE PATTERN #1. In the picture the girl wore a black hooded sweatshirt, unzipped to show some generous cleavage, and piercings in her nose and ears. She looked unhappy. Nothing like the smiling girl in a baggy sweater Caxton had seen die at the convent.

'Where'd you get that?' Caxton asked.

'The girl's parents. They agreed to the cremation, by the way. They did it last night, as a rush job.'

'Good,' Caxton said, 'though it was probably unnecessary. Jameson would know I had a guard on her body. If he raised her I could have interrogated her.'

'Sure,' Glauer said. He wrote Violet's name on the board with a dry erase marker. VIOLET HARMON. Caxton hadn't even known her last name before.

'I brought Simon back in one piece,' Caxton said, and introduced the boy to the big cop.

'I'm so sorry, for everything that's happened,' Glauer said, his big hand folding around one of Simon's. 'I promise, we did everything we could to help your mother.'

'I'm sure you did,' Simon said.

'Listen, your sister is here. Do you want to see her?'

The boy frowned. 'Why?' he asked. Then he shook his head as if to clear it.

270

'You should talk about what's happened.' Glauer patted Simon on the shoulder. 'Your family needs to be together at a time like this. Love and support mean everything in the face of grief.'

Simon shrugged. 'I've never really done the big brother thing before.'

'Just wait in the lounge, then,' Glauer said, and gestured toward the door. When Simon went out of the room the big cop turned to Caxton and rolled his eyes. 'He's about as bad as you.'

'What's that supposed to mean?' Caxton asked, but with a smile. Nothing could ruin her good mood. When Glauer didn't answer she followed him out into the hallway. 'I take it,' she said, 'from the fact that everybody here is still alive, that Jameson didn't attack last night.'

'No, he didn't,' Glauer told her. 'And I'll admit I was kind of relieved. You made it sound like one night alone with Raleigh was going to be the death of me. Instead it was kind of fun.'

'Really?' Caxton's smile broadened. 'She's a little young for you, isn't she?'

Glauer blushed but assured her nothing like what she was insinuating had happened. 'She got bored pretty early, which didn't surprise me. I mean, what's a nineteen-year-old girl going to do spending the night in an office building? We played a game of Scrabble—'

'Who won?' Caxton asked.

'She did. With *chasma* on a triple word score. I challenged, because I'd never heard of it before, but it turns out it's a medical term for excessive yawning. After that I gave her the grand tour of the place – the PCO room, the computer crimes unit, the evidence room, the garage . . .'

'Did you let her wear your Smokey Bear hat?'

Glauer blushed again, but didn't comment on whether he

271

had or not. They went up the stairs to the barracks wing of the headquarters, where off-duty troopers often slept between shifts. There were several semiprivate bedrooms there. 'I kept her up kind of late – I didn't sleep at all myself, of course, because I was on watch. She's still sleeping, I think, or at least she hasn't come out of there yet.' He indicated a particular door and raised his knuckles as if to knock on it. 'I don't know, maybe we should just let her sleep.'

'It's almost one o'clock,' Caxton said. 'If she sleeps any later she'll never sleep tonight. Go on.'

Glauer knocked once, tentatively, and waited a second. When there was no answer he knocked again with more determination. By the time Caxton started frowning he had knocked three times and gotten no response at all.

'Open it,' she said.

He turned the knob and pushed the door open. The shades were drawn over the windows of the room beyond, so it was lit by the glow of a television with the sound turned off. It gave a bluish cast to everything, but instantly Caxton realized that it couldn't explain why Raleigh's lips were so purple, or why her face was so pale. She rushed inside and cupped her hand over the girl's mouth and nose.

'She's not breathing,' she said, looking up at the big cop in the doorway, who could only stare back with nothing on his face but surprise.

44.

Caxton pulled the sheet off Raleigh's body. She was naked underneath, but there was no time for modesty. She grabbed the girl's wrists and rubbed them violently. Her skin was ice cold.

'No,' she moaned, then looked up at Glauer again. 'Get in here and help me. Call 911, tell them we have an emergency.' She put her hands together over Raleigh's sternum and pushed down rapidly. Glauer put his mouth over Raleigh's and blew air down into her lungs. They'd both had CPR training – in fact, the state police required them to get checked out on emergency first aid every year. They both also knew it was pointless. The girl was dead. She probably had been for hours.

Still they kept up chest compressions and mouth-to-mouth. Caxton kept at it until her arms grew sore and her own breath grew ragged. Eventually the paramedics came. One of them grabbed the girl's wrist and asked how long she'd been unresponsive. Caxton didn't know, and told him as much, while still pushing down on Raleigh's chest. The paramedics tried giving her a shot of adrenaline, but it was just for form's sake. Eventually they told Caxton to stop.

She stepped back, her own pulse thundering in her ears. She sagged into a chair and stared at the corpse. 'How?' she asked. 'How did this happen?'

Glauer only shook his head. He wasn't looking at her. He wasn't looking at anything, just staring into space. It was one of the paramedics who answered.

'It would take an autopsy and a tox screen to say for sure. But this is what I'm guessing.' He picked up the girl's arm and turned it outward to show Caxton. She saw a puckered little wound on the inside of Raleigh's elbow. There were other marks there, long snaky furrows under her skin. Much older, mostly healed.

Caxton looked around the room, then dropped to her knees and looked under the bed. An empty syringe had fallen down there, and she thought she saw grains of brown powder. Caxton had been trained to recognize heroin when she saw it.

'Most likely she took a massive dose last night before going to bed,' the paramedic said. 'She probably passed out and stopped breathing shortly thereafter. If it's any consolation, she didn't feel any pain. In fact, she probably felt pretty good before she lost consciousness.'

'That's no consolation at all,' Caxton said. 'Now get out.'

'We can take her away for you, but we'll need you both to move back so we can get a gurney in here. You'll have to sign a receipt for the body and we'll need to talk to the next of kin.'

'I told you to get out. You're done here,' Caxton repeated.

'Hold on, I know this is a lot to take in right now, but there are rules about this sort of thing. There are laws—'

'You may not have noticed,' she said, 'but I'm a cop. I'm the law here, and what I say goes. And what I say is you and your partner need to get the hell out of here.'

The paramedic frowned, but he did what he was told. That left her alone in the room with Glauer and the body.

274

'I don't know how this happened,' Glauer said. Half of his mustache was in his mouth and he was sucking on it. 'Special Deputy, I promise, I don't—'

'You gave her the grand tour. You showed her the PCO room. And the computer crimes area. That's what you said. You showed her the evidence room.'

'Oh, no,' Glauer moaned.

'You knew she was a heroin addict,' Caxton continued. 'You should have looked out for drug-seeking behavior.'

'She was in recovery! You saw her, she didn't look like a junkie at all!'

Caxton was ready to fire him on the spot. 'We took her out of a stable environment. She was already under incredible stress – fear for her life, familial grief. Then we put her in a place where drugs were available. How many risk factors did she need before she broke down? She saw all the drugs in the evidence room. All the drugs we've confiscated over who knows how long. She must have done something to distract you, if only for a second.'

'Yeah,' Glauer admitted. 'She kissed me.'

'Oh, fuck no,' Caxton said. She wanted to shoot something. Instead she picked up the remote control for the TV and stabbed the power button.

'It was – it was very sweet, I thought. I was showing her how we log in each piece of evidence. I was boring her, I thought. Then I turned around and she planted one right on me. Stood up on her tiptoes, threw her arms around my neck. The whole thing. I said – I don't know what I said. I was so surprised I might have said anything. I probably said I was too old for her and she told me the kiss was just a thank-you. For taking care of her.'

Caxton knew Glauer well enough to understand how he must have reacted to that. The big cop lived for rescuing

275

civilians from danger. It was why he'd become a cop in the first place. Had Raleigh seen through him that easily? Drug abusers could be devilishly cunning when it came to getting their next fix.

'I turned around and walked out of the room, unable to say anything at that point. I took my eyes off of her for maybe a couple seconds, that's all.'

'Plenty of time.'

'Sure. She could have palmed her works and a bag of heroin and I wouldn't have noticed.' Glauer stared down at his feet. 'This is terrible.'

'Yep,' Caxton said. She was seeing stars, she was so angry. She thought about firing Glauer. When she wrote up her report on this incident, he would at the very least go before an administrative hearing. Even if she spoke up on his behalf – and she wasn't sure she would – he would be suspended without pay for a long time. He might get fired without her lifting a finger. 'I asked you to watch over her. I saved her from her father and all I wanted you to do was keep her alive.'

'Hey,' Glauer said. 'There's no need to get personal about this.'

'No?'

'No! This was a terrible accident, but—'

Caxton's eyes went wide. 'Are you so sure? Are you sure it was an accident? What if it was suicide?'

'No,' Glauer said, denying the possibility.

Caxton couldn't afford to do the same. You had to commit suicide to become a vampire. It was one of the rules – true accidents didn't count. 'Her father could have given her his curse.'

'No,' Glauer said again.

'He could have. Tonight, in just a couple of hours, she could open her eyes, and they could be red. She could open her

276

mouth, and it could be full of those teeth. Look at her. She's already lost all her color.'

'That's not – you're making a mistake. This was just a dumb accident. She misjudged the dosage. That's all!'

Caxton shook her head. 'We have to cremate her body, before dark. I've made this mistake before. And it cost me everything.'

45.

Caxton had been worried about Simon. She had worried that Jameson would approach Simon, and make his offer, and that Simon would say yes. She had barely even considered the notion it would be Raleigh, poor timid little Raleigh, so fragile that Jameson had to rescue her and stick her somewhere quiet so very far from the real world.

She grabbed the yellow pages and started dialing. She needed an emergency cremation – before four-thirty. That was a little over two hours away. The first three places she tried didn't even do cremation. It wasn't listed as a category in the directory – she was just dialing funeral homes at random. The fourth number connected her to a very polite, very understanding man who assured her that it was quite impossible.

'I'd need the approval of the next of kin.'

'I'm a U.S. Marshal,' she said. 'Can I order a cremation even without permission?'

'Not unless you're also a health official. Otherwise, you need family approval.'

'Her brother's the only one left. I'll make him say yes.'

'Make him? There are regulations that apply to this industry,' he said. 'Even if he says yes, we would also need a death certificate.'

'I promise you, this body is dead.'

The polite man coughed, a sound she could have interpreted as a laugh if she liked. Apparently in the mortuary industry you learned how to be diplomatic. But Caxton knew she was already beaten. Without a death certificate there was no chance, and to get one she would have to wait for a coroner to come and pronounce the body. If she waited for that, then took the time to drive to the funeral home – it could already be too late.

Glauer and Simon took turns attempting to talk her out of the cremation altogether. The big cop said it wasn't necessary, that Raleigh's death had been an accident. He said that Jameson had never had a chance to pass on his curse. 'You were there, the whole time,' he said. 'You heard what they said to each other.'

'You can pass the curse on with a look. That's all it takes,' she insisted.

'But don't you remember, the curse has to be passed on in silence? Justinia Malvern even called it "The Silent Rite." If they were talking, they couldn't do it.'

Caxton considered that a good point, but largely immaterial. 'He could have passed her the curse any time. Long before I got there. I was going on her word that she hadn't had contact with him in six months, but what if she was lying?'

It was Simon's turn. 'She would never do such a thing,' he told her. 'She was terrified of the sight of blood. Whenever she would scrape a knee, back when we were kids, she would go run and hide under the sofa.'

'She didn't seem to mind needles. And where there are needles, there's blood,' Caxton told him. 'She got over it.'

279

No one could convince her. She couldn't afford to let anyone convince her. She stormed out of the room and down the hall, into a wardroom where a number of troopers were gathered around some snack machines. 'You four, come with me,' she said, and headed out through the main doors of the building. It was cold out in the parking lot and snow was falling – not the blizzardlike torrent she'd seen at Syracuse, just a few scattered flakes, but it made her turn up her collar. 'Come on,' she said, and led them behind the building. There were domes back there to hold road salt, and a long low shed that held emergency road barriers. She opened up the wide doors of the shed and ushered in her four draftees. Inside stood hundreds of wooden sawhorses painted in reflective white and yellow. She told each of the men to grab one, and picked one up herself. It was heavy. She didn't care.

In the parking lot she had the men dump the sawhorses in an untidy heap. She piled her own on top. It didn't look like enough. 'More,' she said, and they went back. One of the troopers asked her what they were doing. She told him to shut up and grab a sawhorse, and he did. They brought their loads back to the parking lot and dropped them on top of the pile with a clattering, clonking noise. The legs of the sawhorses kept them from piling up the way she might like. While she sent the men back for one more round she climbed on top of the pile, then jumped up and down on it, coming down hard on the legs with her boots. Some of them snapped off. The men brought more sawhorses – and she had them dump them and go back again.

Glauer and Simon stood by the doors, watching her. She figured they understood what she was doing, but she wasn't particularly concerned. They weren't actively trying to stop her. When the troopers came, grumbling among themselves, with one more load of wood, she nodded in acceptance and rearranged some of the timber to make the pile more symmetrical.

'Now,' she said, 'you. Go down to the motor pool and get the biggest jerry can of gasoline they can give you. You two – go inside, into the barracks. There's a body on one of the beds. Wrap it up in a sheet and bring it out here.'

If the crematorium wouldn't do it, she'd burn up Raleigh's remains herself. She climbed on top of the pile and started kicking at the legs again, trying to make a more solid heap of fuel.

'Caxton,' Glauer finally said. He was standing right behind her. 'Caxton, this is insane.'

'Is it? There's a girl in there who could very well wake up at four-thirty as a vampire, thirsty for blood. You've seen what they can do, and you know as well as I do that they're never stronger than the moment they rise.'

'You're assuming—'

'I'm assuming nothing,' she demanded. 'I'm preparing for an eventuality. Given the risks involved, it would be colossally stupid not to do this. When you're faced with two choices, one that makes everybody happy, and one that isn't dangerously stupid, you pick the second one. That's something Jameson taught me.'

'Look, there's a chance that she'll rise. There's also a chance that you're about to traumatize Simon for life. Why don't—'

'You admit, then, that there's a chance. I don't gamble, Glauer. Now, either help them bring the body out here or get out of my face.'

He reached to take her arm. She swung around, very fast, and punched him in the wrist. He backed away quickly, shaking his arm in pain. It was his fault Raleigh was dead. He had let her commit suicide. If he spoke to her again she planned on hitting him someplace else, like the face or the stomach.

The body was brought out. The troopers had wrapped it in a white sheet, then strung duct tape around the feet and neck to keep the sheet in place. Two troopers lowered it carefully on top of her pile of wood, and a third doused body and wood in gasoline at her instruction. She thought maybe someone should say some words, but the HQ's chaplain refused to get involved when she called him. She had no idea what to say, herself.

In a trash can she found a crumpled newspaper and she bunched it in her hands. She turned to look at the troopers who had helped her. 'Which one of you smokes? I need a lighter.'

They just stared at her.

'Now you're growing balls? You soaked her with gasoline! What did you think I was going to do?'

A hand descended on her shoulder. She spun around, intending to push Glauer off, but it wasn't him. Deputy Marshal Fetlock stood there with a look of absolute horror on his face.

'Stop,' he said.

She considered hitting him.

She did not. But it took some effort.

'Who the fuck called him?' she demanded, turning to look at the troopers who stood around her. They were all staring at her, some of them looking more uncomfortable than others. 'Glauer? Was it you? So help me—'

'Stop,' Fetlock said again.

'Deputy Marshal,' she said, trying to cool her voice down, make it sound reasonable, 'this girl may be infected with the vampire curse. If we don't destroy her body before sundown, she might come back. I've never actually seen it happen. I can only rely on what Jameson taught me. But they come back fast, and they come back very strong. They come back ready to hunt.'

'Stop,' Fetlock said. 'Back up.'

He meant physically. She took a step away from the pyre. Then another one. He held up his hand, palm forward, and she took a third step. She dropped her newspaper fire starter on the ground.

He turned to look at Simon, but kept glancing back at her as if he expected her to rush at the pyre and set it alight. The thought had occurred to her. 'Simon Arkeley,' he said. 'That's your sister there? We're not going to burn her today.'

'You're Caxton's boss, right?' he asked.

'That's right, son.' Fetlock turned to face her again, though he continued to address Simon. 'I'm so sorry for your loss.'

'Yeah. Well. I haven't really had time to process—'

'But maybe,' Fetlock interrupted, 'you could go inside and let the police handle police business, alright? Glauer, you keep an eye on him.'

Glauer took the boy inside.

'Now,' Fetlock said, walking toward Caxton. 'That's better.' He came up to her until he was close enough to box her ears. He didn't. Instead he said: 'Give me your star.'

46.

'You can't do this,' Caxton said. 'Not now.'

Fetlock held out his hand.

'Look. She has to be destroyed. If I don't do it—'

'I'm not a fool, Caxton. I'll take care of it. But I won't burn her in the parking lot like this. It's illegal, for one thing. And it's the wrong thing to do.'

'You trusted me!' she said. 'You said this was going to be my investigation and I could run it as I saw fit. You said you would keep your hands off it.'

'That was back when I thought you were a competent officer. I don't doubt you know what you're doing, or that this is important. But your behavior is increasingly erratic and your methods are not acceptable. I'll take it from here.'

You'll never find Jameson, she thought. *And if you do, he'll tear you apart.* She pressed her lips together until they burned so she wouldn't say anything. Then she raised her hands to her lapel and unpinned her star. She put it in his hand and watched him shove it into the pocket of his coat.

He moved quickly then. He pointed at the troopers, who

were just standing around watching her disgrace. 'You and you – get that body off of there. Move it inside, get it in a room with only one door. You – go tell your Commissioner that Laura Caxton is no longer an employee of the federal government. If he wants to take her back as a state trooper that's his business. Trooper Glauer.'

'Sir,' the big cop said, standing to attention.

'You work directly for me now. Go down to the SSU room and be ready to brief me when I arrive. I want to know everything she's been doing while I wasn't here.'

Suddenly the two of them were alone in the parking lot. She stared at him with a growing horror. This was real. She was being removed from the case. Her authority to hunt down Jameson and Malvern was gone.

'Damn it, Fetlock! At least let me cut her heart out!'

His stare, as he looked down his nose at her, was nothing short of reptilian. He held her gaze, pinning her like a vampire hypnotizing his victim, for far too long. Then, finally, his face fell. 'Tell you what. We do owe you for getting us this far. I'll let you watch.'

He went off to give more orders, leaving Caxton alone. It was three o'clock in the afternoon, and the sun was already standing on the horizon, ready to sink.

There were things she needed to do before it did. She ran out to her car and squatted next to its driver's-side door. Careful not to make too much noise, she unstrapped the Velcro that held her holster around her thigh and waist. She looked at the 90-Two with its clip full of Teflon bullets and its flashlight/laser attachment, checking twice to make sure the safety was on and there was no round in the chamber. Opening the door, she shoved her weapon and its holster under the driver's seat. Opening the glove compartment, she took out her spare pistol – an old-fashioned Beretta 92, the kind she had always carried before Jameson started wearing ballistic vests, and shoved it in her pocket. There was no spare holster for it, but she would just have to make do.

Heading back into the building, she went looking for Glauer, intending to give him a piece of her mind. She found him down in the SSU room obeying orders. 'I shouldn't even let you in here,' he said, looking up from a file cabinet.

'You sold me out,' she said. 'You can at least let me check a few things.' She went to the laptop where it sat on the bookshelf and powered it up. She'd never seen a vampire rise on its first night, but she had a bunch of first-person accounts from previous vampire hunters, and maybe she could find something to confirm her fears. She wanted to be forewarned as best as possible about what was going to happen when Raleigh woke up.

She nearly jumped out of her skin when Glauer touched her on the shoulder. She spun around, ready to curse him, or maybe hit him, but he gave her a look of such hurt feelings she couldn't follow through.

Then he lifted one finger to touch his lips and mustache. She narrowed her eyes – what was he trying to tell her? To be quiet?

He looked down and pointed to her belt. To the cell phone she carried there. She took it out and held it up for him. She'd never liked it, it was too big and clunky, and she would be glad to give it back to Fetlock, if that was what Glauer was after. He did take it from her, but instead of putting it in his pocket he fiddled with it for a second and then shoved his thumbnail into a narrow depression on the back of the case. The battery popped out with a nasty clunk that sounded like plastic breaking. He put the battery and the phone down on a desk next to him.

'You can be a real jerk sometimes, do you know that?' he asked her. 'I didn't call him in. I didn't need to.'

286

She stared at the phone. 'He was monitoring my calls,' she said. She had known that much. 'You aren't suggesting—'

'He said he's going to get me one of these phones, too. He told me he could hear everything you said when you had it on you, and most of what was going on around you. There's a microphone built into the mouthpiece that's active even when you're not making a call. He could hear you whenever he wanted to.'

'He was listening to me all the time?' Caxton asked, horrified. 'You mean the federal government was spying on me?'

Glauer shrugged. 'It's what they're good at.'

'Jesus. So much for his hands-off management style.'

'He's making me the lead on the investigation,' Glauer told her. 'But I'm not ready.'

She did something then that was very unlike her. She lurched forward and hugged him, hard. He was so big that her arms barely fit around him. 'Just be careful,' she said. 'Don't take chances the way I did. If you think you're in danger at any time, just run away.' That wasn't what Jameson had taught her. It was no way to catch a vampire, either. It might keep him from getting killed, though. 'I'm sorry I said those things before. About you and Raleigh. I know you did your best – nobody would have thought, looking at her, that she had a sneaky bone in her body.'

'No, you were right. I screwed up. And now I've gotten promoted for it.' He hugged her back, hard enough to make her feel like her eyeballs were bugging out, then they both let go. 'Listen. The Commissioner isn't going to like any of this. He'll probably bust you back down to highway patrol. If there's anything you need around here, get it now, and put it somewhere safe.'

She nodded her thanks and bent over the remains of the phone. Opening another compartment, she slipped out the SIM card. Before she headed out of the briefing room she took one last look at the whiteboards. Dylan Carboy, Jameson Arkeley, and Justinia Malvern looked back at her. 'Good luck,' she said to Glauer, and then headed for her office.

There she copied all of her email to her home account and took down the few personal effects she'd used to ornament the walls – a picture of Clara at the annual auto show, a picture of Wilbur, one of the dogs she'd rescued, her certificates from the Academy. She shoved them in a manila envelope and tucked it under her arm. From her desk drawer she took her old phone and put the SIM card back in, then tucked the phone in her pocket. She had no doubt Fetlock would know what she'd done, but she didn't care.

Leaving the office, she started toward the Coke machine. All this humiliation and public chastisement was making her thirsty, but she stopped before she could get there. Suzie Jesuroga, the captain of the area response team, was standing in the hall in front of her. Captain Suzie, as Caxton knew her, was wearing a full suit of riot armor, including helmet, and carrying a patrol rifle, a big semiautomatic assault rifle.

'Hi,' Caxton said. She knew Captain Suzie relatively well, had worked with her on occasion. She had no idea what the other woman was doing there. 'Something I can help you with?'

'Vice versa, it sounds like,' the Captain said. 'Come on, this Fetlock guy said I should come and fetch you.'

'Jesus, what time is it?' Caxton asked. She looked down at her own watch – it was four-fifteen. She whirled around to look out the windows and saw the sun was just a smear of orange on the horizon. It was going to set in a matter of minutes.

47.

They'd chosen a room with a west-facing window, so they could see the sun. It washed Fetlock's face with a dull red glow and made his eyes gleam. He stood stock-still before a wide wooden desk where they'd laid Raleigh's body, still wrapped and taped up in a sheet.

Behind Fetlock, their backs up against the wall, the members of Captain Suzie's ART stood at attention, their patrol rifles at low ready. Caxton required no explanation. If Raleigh did rise when the sun went down, they would open fire instantly.

It was more than she'd hoped for. More than she'd expected. Maybe it would be enough. She stepped up to the doorway and ran one hand along the jamb. Fetlock heard her come and turned his head a fraction of an inch. He nodded at her, and she nodded back. No matter what had happened between them, or what was to happen to Caxton now, they were together on this one thing. Raleigh would not be allowed to come back.

The sun widened on the horizon and lost its shape.

The snow on the ground outside glowed almost bloodred, and the clouds in the sky were streaked with purple and orange. It was 4:29, and sunset that day would take place at exactly 4:31.

Caxton kept track of such things. She had to know every day when the night began.

The room filled with fumes from the gasoline that soaked Raleigh's sheet. The liquid rolled across the top of the desk and dripped to the floor. Caxton found she was holding her breath and she let it go, then breathed in the sharp tang of the gas.

The sun fluttered in the hills. Caxton drew her weapon, her old 92, and held it tight against her thigh. Ready to shoot at the first sign. What would it be? she wondered. A twitch of the sheet, down near its middle where Raleigh's hands must be? Would Raleigh open her mouth, surprised by her brand-new teeth, and would the sheet deform over her face in response? Maybe she would sit up slowly, deliberately. Or maybe she would scream to find herself trapped inside the stinking shroud.

Fetlock's digital watch beeped once, and everyone in the room shifted or jumped a little. The beep meant only that it was 4:30 exactly: it was only signaling the half hour. One of the ART members laughed, a dry chuckle that didn't go anywhere and didn't catch on.

It had been all Caxton could do to not lift her weapon, to not start firing blindly into the sheet-covered corpse. She tried to force herself to relax, to at least ease her fierce grip on the gun. She tried to breathe calmly, deeply. Outside the sun was just a fragment of its former self. She could look right at it without pain. *Breathe*, she told herself again. *Breathe out. Breathe in, breathe out.*

290

Fetlock gestured with one hand. Caxton wasn't sure what it meant. Had he seen something? Was he telling her to stand down? She started to take a step closer to the body, but just then Captain Suzie turned and moved toward her. Caxton studied the other woman's face. It was calm. Emotionless. With a steady hand Captain Suzie reached across Caxton's body – and switched on the room's lights.

The sudden change in illumination sent shadows flickering across the sheet, and it almost looked as if it had moved. But no. It hadn't shifted at all – even the pattern of wrinkles in the sheet was the same.

The sun was gone, leaving a greenish twilight blurred across the sky.

It was 4:31 in the afternoon.

The body hadn't moved.

'There,' Fetlock said. 'Are you—'

'Hold on,' Caxton said. She realized she'd never seen a vampire rise before and that meant she had no idea if they were active during the dusk. 'There's still some light left.' She had no idea what mechanism of timing pertained to vampires. Did they need total darkness to rise, or was it enough that the sun was below the horizon? In mountainous places the sun would set earlier than on the plains. Heavy cloud cover could alter the time of true dark – there were so many variables. 'We've waited this long, another few minutes won't hurt us.'

One of the ART members – the one who had laughed before, perhaps – sighed. She scowled and ignored him.

'This is important,' she insisted. 'This is life or death.'

Fetlock shrugged, but he didn't say anything more. Caxton moved closer to the corpse, her weapon low but ready. She brought her free hand up and stretched it toward the sheet, looking for the telltale cold feeling that radiated from a vampire's body. That was enough to make Fetlock react – he came up behind her and pulled her gently away.

'I'll talk to Simon Arkeley and see if he'll allow a cremation anyway,' Fetlock said. 'But really, Trooper—'

'One more minute, please. Just one more minute, okay?'

'It's illegal, you know, to desecrate a corpse. I could have you arrested right now,' Fetlock told her. 'I'm tired of this. Tell me something, does this building have a meat locker or anything? Someplace to hold the body until we can send for a hearse?'

Captain Suzie stepped forward to answer. 'Yes, sir. We have an actual morgue, believe it or not. It's where we keep highway accident victims if the bodies are felt to be of an evidentiary nature.'

Fetlock rolled his eyes. 'I suppose that'll do very well, then. You – Officer – go down to the infirmary and have them send up a stretcher. We'll move her to the morgue right away.'

'Hold on!' Caxton demanded. 'Jesus Christ, am I the only one who knows that you don't take chances with vampires? Fetlock, Jameson taught me never to underestimate them. Give it just a few more minutes. I'm begging you.'

'I'm sure Jameson taught you a lot of bad habits, too,' Fetlock told her.

She grunted in frustration. 'He taught me how to fight monsters. He wouldn't have let you have the body. He would have burned it in the parking lot, and if you had come and told him to stop he would have just ignored you and kept going. You could have shot him in the back and it wouldn't have stopped him. He didn't care if people thought his behavior was erratic, he just cared about doing things right.'

'And look where that got him,' Fetlock said, smiling. 'Your loyalty would be commendable, if you weren't honoring a

292

vampire. Let's go, you two – one of you take the shoulders, the other the feet.'

'No!' Caxton shouted. 'Not yet!'

'Trooper,' Fetlock said. 'Look.' He pointed at the window. Even Caxton had to admit that true dark had fallen. The window was a pane of unbroken blackness. She could see the reflection of her own stark raving face in it. 'Night is upon us. If she was going to rise, she would have already.'

Caxton let her head drop. Maybe, she began to think, he was right. Maybe she had crossed some kind of line, into a sort of madness. Had she let Jameson's tricks and mind games distort her own faculties?

She turned to go, to leave the room. Still, even then, she half-expected Raleigh to sit up behind her and hiss with bloodlust. Before Caxton could take a step she heard Fetlock cough. He had a hand out, palm up. He'd already taken her badge. Now he wanted her gun.

'Don't even think about it,' she protested.

'I don't want you hurting anyone. I'm going to insist you go home and get some rest. In the meantime, I'll hold on to your sidearm.'

She shook her head – made a good show of it. Eventually she pretended to relent, and handed her gun over. That was fine. That was exactly what she'd meant to happen. Her new gun, the one with the cop-killers in it, was in the car. Fetlock could take her off the case, but she knew she wasn't finished with Jameson yet.

Outside of the room she headed for the parking lot and her car. Halfway there she heard her phone ring, the old phone with its Pat Benatar ringtone. She thought it might be Clara. Clara! How could she explain to Clara everything that had happened? When she pulled out the phone and checked the screen, though, she saw it was in fact Vesta Polder who was calling her.

293

'Vesta,' she said. 'This is kind of a weird time. What's up?'

'It's about Jameson,' the older woman said. Her voice sounded weird, as if it were a bad line or as if she'd been crying. 'He came for me.'

48.

Oh shit oh shit oh shit, Caxton thought. She grabbed at her forehead and squeezed it with her free hand. When Jameson hadn't attacked in Syracuse she'd thought he was lying low. That she'd created too much trouble for him – or that he was waiting for her to make some stupid move, to take Raleigh and Simon someplace undefended, someplace they could be gotten at easily. She hadn't even considered he might be busy with some other agenda. 'I don't understand – he visited you, he offered you the curse? That doesn't make sense. You're not part of his family.'

'Does your last name have to be Arkeley to be part of that brood?' Polder asked. 'He's coming for everyone he loves, Laura. Everyone he ever loved.'

Of course.

Vesta had told Caxton how she and Jameson had once had an affair. She must still mean something to him, no matter how far he'd fallen into darkness. 'Listen,' Caxton said. 'He's not still there, at your house?'

'No, he's gone. I suppose I should have made some attempt

295

to fight him, or at least track him when he left, but I was too scared. I know you understand that.'

Caxton did.

'He gave me the same deadline he gave the others. Twenty-four hours to consider his offer. A refusal is as good as a death sentence. You have to find him before sundown tomorrow!'

'I will,' Caxton promised, though she had no idea how. 'Listen, I'll come to you. Stay where you are and I'll be there as soon as I can.'

'That won't be necessary. I'm on my way to you right now. In fact, I can already see your headquarters building. Come out to the parking lot to meet me.' Polder ended the call. Caxton bit her lip and wondered what she was going to do next. She no longer had any authority to put Vesta in protective custody. She could send Vesta to Fetlock, to ask for his help, but she wondered if the older woman would even want that. Vesta was a borderline agoraphobic, rarely leaving her own house for more than a few hours and never at night – except of course for when she'd completed her final duty to Astarte. For Vesta to drive to Harrisburg after sunset she must truly be panicked.

I'll do what I can for her, Caxton thought. *I owe her.* For advice, over the years, and for the spiral pendant she still wore around her neck, which was her only protection against vampiric powers. She headed out the front door of the head-quarters building, out into the parking lot, and saw a pair of headlights coming toward her. The lights of an old truck, the kind of ancient pickup you saw on farms still in central Pennsylvania. A body of pure rust held together by duct tape and sheer desperation. She didn't remember the Polders having such a vehicle – maybe Vesta had been forced to go to her neighbors and plead to borrow some transportation, anything. Caxton waved the truck toward a parking space near the door, but Vesta just pulled up short halfway into the lot, partially blocking the exit, and switched off her lights.

Well, Caxton thought, *so she's not a very good driver*. In fact, she wondered if Polder even had a license. She waved again, and saw Vesta push open the truck's creaking door and slide down onto the snowy pavement. She was dressed as she always had been, in her long, austere black dress. For some reason she'd pulled her hair back in a severe bun and wore the black veil she'd worn on the day of Jameson's funeral.

Vesta called to her from ten yards away in a voice high and near breaking with grief and fear. 'I am sorry, Laura, to have to come to you this way. I had no choice.'

'That's alright, I'm just glad you're safe,' Caxton replied. 'Come inside, get out of the cold. I want to hear everything. Tell me what happened with Jameson.'

'He's changed,' Vesta said, walking slowly toward Caxton. 'Evil is consuming him. Once he seemed to think that the death of a loved one was a mercy.'

More cars were coming up the drive into the parking lot – several of them. They were running with no lights at all, coming fast, and she could see they were full of people. As one of them bounced up over the curb and slewed into the parking lot, Caxton just had time to wonder what was going on before Vesta spoke again.

'Now,' the older woman said, 'he sees in it an opportunity.' Then she lifted her veil. Beneath it the skin of her face was torn and pink, hanging away from her features in grisly strips. She reached up into one sleeve of her dress and pulled out a long knife, honed and resharpened so many times that the blade was thin and crooked.

'Forgive me!' Vesta screamed, even as behind her the doors of the new cars flew open and more half-deads spilled out on the pavement. There were dozens of them – Caxton didn't

297

have time to get an accurate count. She was too busy dodging the knife that came whistling for her throat.

Vesta was a tall woman with a long reach. Caxton had to roll away from the swing, going down on one knee and throwing her head back. It was a lousy position from which to counter-attack, and she didn't get the chance. Her brain, running purely on reflex, sent a signal down her arm, a signal it had sent a thousand times before. Always before the signal had instructed her hand to slap a certain place on her hip and close its fingers around the grip of her pistol.

The pistol wasn't there. Caxton knew that consciously, but her conscious mind was still trying to work out what was happening. Her hand closed pointlessly around the place where the gun should have been, and she wasted another fraction of a second.

'Protect my daughter and my man! Please!' Vesta screamed, and the knife thrust deep into the fabric of Caxton's winter coat. The edge hissed along Caxton's skin and she felt hot wet blood roll down her arm.

Behind Vesta the other half-deads were streaming up toward the building. They were all armed, with knives and sickles. What had Jameson done? It looked like he'd slaughtered half the population of the state and drafted them to his service.

Caxton had to get away. She had a few weapons on her belt, but none of them would let her get control of this mob. Maybe, though, they could give her a chance to get back on her feet. Vesta raised her knife high, flipped it in her hand and brought it down blade first, clearly intending to skewer Caxton with it. Caxton twisted away from the blow – then came up fast, her arm swinging around, her canister of pepper spray clutched in her fist.

She pushed down on the button on top of the can and foaming spray splashed across Vesta's eyes. Vesta threw up her

298

knife arm across her ravaged face, exactly as Caxton had known she would – it was the inevitable reaction to being sprayed. They taught you that at the academy. It seemed even death couldn't break that primitive instinct.

Caxton didn't waste time following through on her attack. She dropped the can of spray and shoved both of her hands down onto the cold concrete, shoved herself bodily upward until she was half upright, half bent over. It got her feet underneath her enough that she could run. She did not look back as she dashed through the doors of the HQ building, screaming for help.

Simon, she thought. Vesta had come for Simon – the last remaining member of the Arkeley family, the last one alive. The last one Jameson could hope to recruit. She had to find Simon, she had to get him out of the building, get him to safety.

'Somebody,' she shouted, 'anybody – lock those doors!'

But it was too late. The half-deads were already inside.

49.

Caxton raced down the hallway, looking for help. She couldn't find any. The wardroom was empty – she took one look inside and hurried past. Where had everybody gone? For a bad, breathless moment she thought maybe all the troopers who normally hung around the HQ were dead – or worse, that she had been betrayed somehow, and they had left her to her fate once Fetlock had dismissed her in their presence.

But no. That was just paranoia. When she considered things for a second she realized exactly what had happened. It was just after five o'clock, which meant it was rush hour. The vast majority of the troopers were out on duty, mostly on patrol around the capital. They had all left shortly after the sun set and Raleigh failed to rise. Those troopers who remained in the building were tasked with administrative roles, and they would not be armed. Vesta couldn't have planned her attack for a better time – Jameson had ordered her to attack just when he knew the HQ would be at its most vulnerable.

That meant Vesta would know everything Jameson knew about the building and its layout. She wouldn't waste time searching for Simon. She would know exactly where he would be, and the quickest route to reach him. Caxton knew it too, if she gave herself a second to think about it.

She hurried around a corner and put her back up against a wall. She could hear the half-deads coming down the corridor toward her, moving fast. Caxton reached down to her belt and undid the clasp that held in her ASP baton. It was the only weapon she had on her, an eight-inch length of steel painted black. She pressed down on a catch at its base and flicked it out with her wrist and three telescoping segments slid out, extending the baton to its full length. The tip, the thinnest of the segments, was solid steel, and wielded correctly it could deal an agonizing blow to anyone it struck. Unlike the riot-control batons most troopers carried, Caxton's baton was capable of breaking bones – if she hit the right spot, and with enough force.

The half-deads were just down the hall, nearly on top of her. She could hear them giggling to themselves, anticipating the slaughter to come. Caxton made herself wait until the last possible second, then whirled out around the corner, swinging the baton two-handed like a baseball bat.

The half-dead in the lead, a sexless creature with a torn face wearing a black overcoat, just had time to look surprised before the baton crunched through its rotten cheek. It dropped the meat cleaver it was carrying and spun around, its hands jumping up to its face as it gurgled in pain.

Caxton didn't have time to feel sympathy. She brought the baton around in a circle, her body swerving through the air to give it leverage, and split the back of the half-dead's skull. It dropped in a heap.

Behind it stood more of them, plenty more. At the back of the group she could see Vesta Polder, watching her carefully.

Caxton ran. She turned on her heel and dashed down the

corridor, her knees jumping high as she sprinted for dear life. She thought Simon would be in the off-duty break room, a lounge on the far side of the building with a television set and vending machines. Glauer would have taken him there to wait while Caxton stood vigil over Raleigh's body. It was a safe place, a place where Simon couldn't get into any trouble. Behind her she heard running footsteps and a skritching sound like a knife being dragged through the wallpaper, and she knew the half-deads were following her. She was leading them right to Simon, but she didn't have a choice.

Up ahead the hallway widened where it was crossed by a side corridor. There was a receptionist's desk up there – this was where the bureau chiefs had their offices – and a couch and some chairs. The receptionist was standing behind his desk next to some potted plants. He had a watering can in his hand, but he was staring in horror at the half-deads coming down the hall.

'Get out of here,' Caxton shouted at him. He reached up to straighten his tie and she realized he must be in shock. He could never have expected this, that the HQ would be invaded by a horde of freaks with no faces. But if he didn't move he was going to get killed. Caxton rushed up and nearly collided with him, grabbed his arm hard and twisted. 'Run away!' she screamed in his ear. Finally he got the point and bolted, the watering can still in his hands.

If the receptionist had never considered this possibility, whoever designed the building, thankfully, had. There was a panic button mounted under the edge of the reception desk, connected to an alarm in the duty room, where troopers waiting assignment would be preparing for their night's work. Caxton stabbed the button, barely breaking her stride. She heard the alarm ringing off to one side, but couldn't afford to give it any of her attention.

Ahead of her the hall was lined with glass doors. This was where the bulk of the HQ's staff worked. Some of them were troopers, but most were civilians hired to do clerical work, IT management, and as PCOs – police communications officers, the dispatchers who sent patrol cruisers where they needed to go. Most of them would still be working, and none of them would be armed. If they poked their heads out to see what the commotion was, they would all get killed, end of story.

Caxton considered knocking on all the doors, warning the workers of the danger, but she knew that even a second's delay now could mean certain death – or worse – for Simon. With what breath she could spare she shouted for the workers to lock themselves in their offices, and she didn't stop moving.

Past the offices she finally could see the door of the break room straight ahead. It was open and through it she could see Simon. He was curled up on a couch, maybe taking a nap or just lost in his own thoughts. She hurtled through the door at full speed. Once inside she slammed the door shut, then locked it.

'Jesus, what now?' Simon asked, stirring from his fetal position on the couch.

Caxton kicked the couch hard and he jumped up to his feet. He stared at her with wild eyes, but she just shook her head, breathing too hard to talk. She grabbed one end of the couch and nodded for him to take the other end, and together they pushed it up against the door.

It was only after she'd sealed herself inside that Caxton thought to look around for other exits. There were none. A row of windows lined the far side of the room, but they were not made to open, and Caxton knew they, like all of the HQ's ground-floor windows, were built of bullet-resistant glass half an inch thick. She couldn't just throw a chair through one of them and escape that way.

Jameson had taught her never to barricade herself in a room with no other exit. She'd forgotten that lesson in her panic. She cursed herself as she heard knives and sickles thudding against the wooden door, gouging away at it.

'Your father,' Caxton gasped, watching the door jump and shake, 'wants you something fierce.'

'But you're not going to let him take me, are you?' Simon demanded.

Caxton shook her head and just breathed for a second. 'Kid, I can't promise you anything. But I'll do my best to protect you.'

Outside, in the hallway, she heard someone screaming. Not the high-pitched squeal of a half-dead, either. The scream cut off abruptly with the sound of gunshots and Caxton flinched. Troopers – good people, all – were fighting out there, maybe some of them were dying, and she couldn't help them. She didn't even have a sidearm, just a glorified nightstick.

The half-deads outside slammed against the door with their weapons, their shoulders, the whole weight of their bodies. She could hear them out there urging each other on. She thought she could hear Vesta shouting orders. The door wasn't going to last forever. 'There are troopers out there, but I think they're outnumbered. I don't think we can just assume they'll come rescue us.'

'We have to get out,' Simon said. His eyes were wide when he stared at her. 'We have to get out of here. He'll kill me. He'll kill me!' There were more gunshots, and he yelped as if he'd been hit himself. 'Oh my God. Oh my God. I'm going to die, I'm going to die! I'm going to—'

Caxton slapped him hard across his face. She was a strong woman and she knocked him down, sent him sprawling across a ratty old armchair. He grabbed at his cheek and looked up at her, suddenly much calmer. 'Thanks,' he said.

304

'You were getting really annoying,' Caxton said.

The hammering and gouging at the door stopped suddenly and Caxton heard a half-dead outside whisper, 'Get back, she's coming.' Maybe Vesta Polder knew some kind of door-opening spell, she thought, though in her experience Vesta's talents had never before lent themselves to such mundane uses. Caxton moved away from the door in any case, her ASP baton up and ready.

She glanced at Simon, who was quick to get behind her. The boy started to say something, but then the door twisted in its frame with a horrible groaning sound as its hinges were strained and finally snapped. The door disappeared, and the couch they'd shoved in front of it went flying into the room and slammed into a vending machine hard enough to make its lighted front crack and go dim.

A moment later a vampire walked into the room.

50.

Caxton swung her baton, but before it could connect it was wrenched painfully from her hand and thrown across the room. She could feel a blow coming – she could feel the cold, unnatural aura of the vampire moving toward her at high speed, and she tried to roll away from it, but her spine twisted in such a way to make her scream and suddenly she was on her back on the linoleum tiles, looking up at the fluorescent light fixtures.

The vampire had one slender foot on her throat. The pressure on her trachea made it impossible to cry out, but she could still breathe a little, a shallow whistling breath that left her with stars in her vision. She tried to look up at the vampire, tried to see who it could be. *Not Urie Polder,* she thought, *please.* Losing Vesta had been bad enough. Caxton didn't have enough friends that she could afford to lose one more.

The vampire holding her down, however, was female. Thin, smaller than the usual blood-sucker, with refined features that would have been beautiful if not for the jagged teeth deforming her lips. Caxton looked lower and saw she was dressed in some kind of sack or a loose-fitting sheath dress made of white cotton and duct tape, stained down the front with a streak of clotted blood.

It wasn't a dress at all, she realized. It was the remains of a shroud.

'Raleigh?' Simon asked, cowering near where Caxton lay.

'Hello, Simon,' the vampire growled. 'Long time no see.' Then she reached over and punched her brother in the side of the head. His eyes rolled up and he fell over, twitching and drooling a little.

'I didn't kill him,' Raleigh said, looking down with red eyes into Caxton's face. 'I'm not *evil*. I just gave him a little concussion. I'm supposed to bring him to Daddy. He'll be given the same choice we all were, and hopefully he'll take the smart option. He'll be easier to transport this way.'

Caxton tried to creak out some words, though she wasn't sure what she meant to say.

'Sorry,' Raleigh said, and lifted her foot away from Caxton's neck.

'You've fed,' Caxton gurgled. She nodded at the blood down the front of Raleigh's makeshift dress.

'Yes,' Raleigh agreed. 'One of your colleagues got in my way. I was hungry. It wasn't something I planned.'

'Do you regret it?' Caxton asked.

'Not much.'

'That's what makes you evil,' Caxton told her.

The vampire's eyes narrowed.

'I waited for you to come back to life. I waited until the sun was completely down. Were you faking it?'

'Uh-huh,' Raleigh said, with a smile. 'Daddy and I have been talking about it for days. He could speak into my mind, when I was living, but it was like someone whispering in another room. Now he's with me all the time.' The smile broadened. 'It's nice.'

307

'How long did you have this planned out? Faking your death – I mean, faking your continued death? The attack on this building?'

'Daddy came to me a couple weeks ago. Even before I met you. Everything since then has been an act. Lying there under that sheet was tough. It was so hard not moving, not even stretching, but I did it. Daddy knew you would never let me out of your sight – this was the only way.'

'You accepted the curse that long ago? Then you lied to me, when I reached out to you for help. You told me you hadn't spoken with your father in six months. That's evil, too.'

The girl's face fell. It was a dangerous game, but Caxton had to try to reason with her. 'Listen, it's not too late. After a certain time every vampire is the same, they lose their respect for human life and they become sociopaths. But I know you're not one of them yet. There's still plenty of humanity in you. Turn yourself in. Or if not that, at least help me destroy your father.'

The vampire had been standing up. Instantly she dropped to the floor, propping herself up on her arms until her face was hovering over Caxton's. Close enough that Caxton's whole body shivered with the creeping horror of almost being touched.

'At the convent, they used to ask me why I ever tried heroin in the first place. Why would I try something so addictive and dangerous, when I knew the risks? I told them, the world hurts, but drugs feel good. It's a no-brainer. The only downside was that every time I shot up I got weaker. Now I've got blood. Blood feels good. And it makes me stronger. I think I'll stick with the plan.'

She jumped back up to her feet, then reached down and picked Simon up easily in her arms.

'When you begged him not to kill me – was that an act?'

The vampire looked up at the ceiling. 'No,' she sighed. 'No. You'd been nice to me. Nicer than most people in my life. You wanted to protect me. You thought I was worth saving. Just like Daddy.'

'I still think so. I can't give you your life back, but I can preserve what's left of your soul,' Caxton pleaded.

'Don't you remember?' Raleigh asked. 'Vesta Polder looked for that once, and she couldn't find it. It's already gone.'

She picked up Caxton effortlessly and threw her down on the couch. 'Don't try to follow me. I have instructions not to kill you. Daddy wants you to live for now. But if you come after me, I can hurt you. A lot.'

She swept out into the hall then, Simon tucked under her arm like a bag full of dirty laundry.

Caxton lay where she was for a second. Just a second to catch her breath. And to let Raleigh get enough of a head start. Then she jumped to her feet and raced down the hallway. It was her belief that Raleigh was taking Simon straight to their father – straight back to the lair.

She pushed through the front doors and hurried toward the Mazda, only stopping when she heard the doors burst open again behind her. She whirled around, ready to kill the first evil bastard she saw. Vesta Polder was there, shrieking wildly, her veil hanging by one pin like a broken wing on the side of her head. She must have been pushed through the doors, because she was rolling on the ground, one arm underneath her, the other up as if fending off a blow. Fetlock came after her, Caxton's old Beretta 92 in his hand. There was a cut on his face and his hair was in disarray. He was breathing hard and sweating profusely. He looked up at Caxton, his mouth open to try to catch his breath. Then he pointed the Beretta at Vesta's skinless left temple and blew her brains all over the asphalt.

For a second Caxton held his gaze. Then she slipped into the driver's seat of her car and started up the ignition. All the car tracks leading out of the parking lot headed in the same direction – east, toward the highway. That was the way Raleigh and the half-deads had gone.

Simon had twenty-four hours to live. When the deadline came, if Jameson offered him the curse, knowing what the alternative was – Caxton did not believe the son would say no.

Caxton threw the car into gear, intending to chase after Raleigh and the half-deads whether they liked it or not. The car surged under her – then died. The engine stalled out and she felt every muscle in her body tense up. She switched the car off, then back on. Put it in drive. The car shuddered and lurched forward, then stopped as the engine sputtered to a halt.

It took her too long to figure it out. It took her ten long minutes to get the hood open and see that the half-deads had monkeyed with her engine, and even longer to fix what they'd done. By the time she got back on the road heading east they were long gone, and there were no tracks to follow.

She didn't waste any more time by getting frustrated. Instead she pulled a U-turn and headed west. There was one more lead she could follow, she knew. One last chance to find out where the lair was. She knew she would take that chance – even if it meant throwing away her entire career.

JAMESON

Of such as I could see, all were alike in the brotherhood of death, all unlike in the character and history recorded upon them.

George MacDonald, *Lilith*

51.

She had to drive through the downtown section of Harrisburg to get where she was going. She passed through streets full of little stores, boutiques selling pricey clothes. In one window she saw a pair of young women laughing together as they dressed a mannequin in a bright red minidress with white fur trimming. At another store the proprietor was stringing up red and green lights. They were getting ready for Christmas.

Christmas. Caxton hadn't celebrated the holiday much since her parents died. But the year before, when it had just been her and Clara, they'd exchanged presents, and drank eggnog, and even strung up mistletoe. She'd gotten Clara a special lens for her camera, one she'd been looking at online for months. Clara's present to her had been a box of bath salts, scented candles, and a wooden massage roller. Things to help her relax. Most of them were still in the box, which sat underneath the bathroom sink in the back of the cabinet, where she saw it every time she reached for a new disposable razor.

She could use that box now, she thought. She needed to relax, to get frosty, if she was going to pull this off.

313

She pulled into the parking lot of the jail in Mechanicsburg and switched off the car. She wanted to just sit there for a while and collect her thoughts, but she knew if she did she would never get up and out of the car, so she reached over and pushed the door open and let the cold winter air belly inside, the icy breeze pressing her coat against her body and stinging her cheek. She popped open her seat belt and then climbed out of the car and shut the door behind her.

Inside the jail only a few corrections officers were still at work. The cells were quiet, the prisoners inside either sleeping or contemplating their fates. As one corrections officer – one, thankfully, she had not met before – led her down a flight of stairs to the basement, she started to hear someone yelling, not saying anything, just making inarticulate noises. She was not surprised to learn it was Dylan Carboy making that racket.

'He's not quite all there, you know that, right?' the CO asked. 'He does this all night. It's weird. It's like he's praying, but not to any God I ever heard of. You'll have to keep an eye on him.'

Caxton nodded. She handed the CO a clipboard on which she'd filled out the appropriate forms. She had lied many times while checking the various boxes and writing in the numbers and authorizations required. She had put down Fetlock's name as authorizing the transfer, then put her own phone number below it. If anyone called to confirm her authority her phone would ring and she would at least know they were onto her.

She doubted they would, however. Transfers like this happened all the time and cops tended to trust each other. She was counting on that.

'You're with the Marshals Service,' the CO said, leafing through her paperwork. 'This guy commit some kind of federal crime? We have him down for a couple local homicides.'

'He broke into the USMS archives and stole some files,' she lied. 'I'm taking him to the field office up in Harrisburg, where we can ask him what was in those documents that he wanted.'

'Huh. Do you guys do a lot of interrogations at night?'

'When the subject sleeps all day, we do. We figure he'll be more talkative now than tomorrow morning.'

The CO smiled. 'You know about him, then.'

'I'm the one who originally brought him in. Listen, I'll make it as quick as I can. I'll probably have him back to you before breakfast.'

'You can have him as long as you want,' the CO said.

The door of the padded cell opened up and she stared inside. The gibbering and wailing stopped instantly. Carboy was up against the far wall, his hands lifted high above his head, the fingers splayed as if he were reaching for something on the ceiling. There was nothing there. Caxton didn't know what that was about. She told herself she didn't care.

'Come on, Carboy,' the CO said. 'Don't make this difficult, alright? This lady's from the U.S. Marshals and she wants to talk to you.'

Carboy's eyes focused on her slowly. 'Caxton,' he muttered. 'I knew you'd come back.'

The CO said, 'You want me to get a straitjacket? He can be violent.'

'I know what he's capable of. Come on, Dylan. We're going for a ride.'

Carboy shuffled out of the cell as quickly as he could. The CO bound his hands behind his back. His ankles were shackled together with a length of soft plastic. His feet were bare. The CO had some slippers for him to wear and a blanket to wrap around his shoulders to protect him from the cold. He let Caxton go first up the stairs, then Carboy, and finally he came up from behind with a Taser in his hand, just in case.

315

The prisoner didn't attack Caxton, though, or even say anything as she led him out to the jail's lobby. She had to sign a couple more release forms, and then she was done – except that the CO reached out and tapped her shoulder.

'Your badge,' he said, nodding at her lapel.

She'd completely forgotten about the star. State troopers didn't wear badges, and she'd never really gotten used to the star while she had it. She touched her lapel, then looked up at him with her heart thundering in her ears. She forced a smile. 'It fell off in the car. It's always doing that – you want me to go out and get it?'

He gave her an appraising stare, then glanced at Carboy.

'Nah,' he said. 'Just get this guy out of here. At least we'll have one night's peace, right?'

Caxton thanked him and led her prisoner out into the cold. Carboy climbed into the Mazda without making a fuss and she climbed into the driver's seat, then took her handcuffs out of her belt and locked him to the door handle on the passenger's side. Doing that gave him a chance to bite her on the neck, but he didn't act on it.

'You're being cooperative,' Caxton said, surprised.

'Because I know my time is about to come. The time when I kill you.'

'Sure,' Caxton said.

'Maybe you think I can't do it. Maybe you think you have me right where you want me. But that's your mistake – thinking you're smarter than us. I couldn't get at you in that cell. I had no weapons, and you were far away. Now, though, you've taken away that disadvantage. Now we're all alone. You may have me handcuffed, but in time I'll get free. I'll break out of this bondage and then you'll see. You'll see exactly how stupid you've been.'

Caxton shook her head wearily. 'Shut up,' she said.

316

'You don't want to hear this? That's understandable. Who wants to know that they're about to die? I want you to hear it, though. I want you to be afraid. Because then you'll make more mistakes. Desperate people don't think clearly. They rush through things and don't consider all their options.'

Caxton switched on the radio, but he just shouted over the music.

'Once I kill you, he'll have no choice. Jameson will have to respect me. He'll see what I've done, what he could not do himself, and he'll know I'm worthy. He'll give me the curse, then, and I won't wait. Some people fight it, I know. Jameson fought it for a long time before he realized what he'd been given. But I will welcome it. I'll turn a gun on myself, or maybe I'll slit my own throat with a knife, so I can take my place among them that much faster. So I can achieve my dest—'

She reached across with her right fist and smashed him across the face. It was hard to get leverage like that, but she hit him hard enough to split his lip open and grind his cheek painfully against his teeth. His head flew to the side and bounced off his window.

'That was for your sister,' she said.

But it wasn't. It was for her, for Caxton herself. Because the longer he prattled on like that the more she realized that he was just a kid, just a human being. His voice was human, not the rough growl of a vampire. She could hear him breathing, and trying not to whimper, even after she hit him. At least he stopped talking.

She hoped when the time came she could get him started again.

She didn't take him very far. Just to the edge of the town, where the last few houses and roadside bars petered out and the dead trees grew thick and shielded the snow-covered fields from view. She pulled off on a narrow road she knew that led for miles back to an abandoned industrial park. There were no homes down that road and it was the wrong season to catch teenagers there parking. When she switched off the car's lights nothing but the stars and the night glare off the snow let them see each other's face.

She slipped her new gun out of its holster, then flipped on the flashlight and laser attachments. His eyes squeezed closed and he pushed up against his door when she shone the light in his face.

'You know something I need to know,' she said. 'You know where Jameson is. Before, when I asked you, there was a corrections officer present. He restrained me from using excessive force. He's not here now.'

'You're wasting your time,' Carboy told her.

So she hit him again. Pistol-whipped him, in fact, with the butt of her gun. She raised a two-inch gash in his cheek that turned purple even before she got the light back in his eyes.

Kidnapping, she thought to herself. *Aggravated assault. Battery. Improper use of force by a police officer.*

Torture.

She had tortured half-deads before. She'd pulled the fingers off one of them, one by one, until it told her what she needed to know. Half-deads were monsters. Their bodies were falling apart the moment they came back from the dead. Their brains were curdled, and they bore very little relationship to the human being they'd once been.

Dylan Carboy was a murderer. The worst kind, a parricide with depraved indifference – he'd killed his family just to make himself feel tough. He'd killed the two employees of the storage facility just to get her attention. He'd repeatedly threatened her own life.

He was still human.

'I don't have time to beat it out of you,' she said. She leaned

318

over him and uncuffed him from the door. His hands were still bound behind his back with the plastic restraints he'd worn in his jail cell. She pushed open the passenger door and felt cold air rush in and cleanse her face. It felt good. 'Get out,' she said.

He stared at her wide-eyed.

'Get out. Go no more than ten steps from the car. If you run, I'll shoot you in the legs.'

He climbed out of the car carefully, unable to use his hands. He stood waiting for her, staring through the car window at her.

'Take off your slippers and throw them in the car,' she said.

He complied. He was standing in an inch of snow, and he shuffled quietly from foot to foot.

'Does that feel cold? It should. In a few minutes, though, you'll stop feeling it. That's bad,' she told him. 'That's when frostbite sets in. You know about frostbite, right, Dylan? Your toes will turn black. The nerves and blood vessels in your toes will die one by one. Once that happens, if they want to save your life your toes will have to be cut off. Maybe they'll take your feet, too, if gangrene sets in, and it usually does.' She pulled the passenger door shut and then rolled down the window so she could keep talking to him. 'I'm going to drive away now, and leave you here. You can walk back.'

Carboy's lips curled back. 'When I receive the curse, I'll track you down, Caxton. I'll return this torment and visit a thousand more upon you—'

She interrupted him. 'Do you know about Malvern's eye? She's only got one, of course. She lost the other before she became a vampire. Now no matter how much blood she drinks, no matter how long she spends rejuvenating in her coffin, she still only has one eye. Body parts don't grow back.' She shrugged. 'Let's say the impossible happens, and Jameson does give you the curse. You'll be the vampire with no feet. You'll spend the rest of your life unable to walk and unable to hunt for victims. And of course, vampires live forever.'

'*You* won't, Caxton, and you'll beg for death before—'

She started the car and rolled up the windows. It was freezing inside. She could only imagine how his feet must feel.

Don't, she told herself. *Don't imagine it. Just don't.*

She heard him shouting curses outside the car, but the engine noise muffled his words. She put the car in reverse and started to back up. He came running after her, of course, so she touched the accelerator and craned her head around to see where she was going.

She'd backed up a hundred yards before he started knocking on her window with his knuckles. She backed up another hundred before she rolled down her window. 'Yes?' she asked.

He was breathing very hard. His face was pale and the hairs inside his nostrils looked frozen together. 'I don't know. I don't know where the lair is.'

She started to roll up her window again. He pounded on her window and she saw he was crying.

'I'm telling the truth,' he promised. 'He never took me there. I begged him to, but he said it was like hell, and mortals couldn't survive there. He said he would take me there when I received the curse.'

'Think hard,' she said. 'You have to know something more. You must have seen or heard something. Do your feet still hurt?'

He nodded piteously. 'Please—'

'Think hard,' she said again.

'Flowers,' he mumbled. 'Malvern—'

'Make sense,' she told him, 'or I'm leaving.'

'I never met Malvern, except in my dreams. There I saw her, and sometimes, I guess I saw what she saw. I saw her sitting up

320

in her coffin, one night. Jameson had taken her out to get some air. I don't know what this means, but there were flowers blooming in front of her. Flowers in a field, like in summer, though all around there was snow. I remember her thinking, there are flowers on his grave.'

'That's it? That's all you have?'

'Please,' he begged. 'Just – please. It's all. It's all I have.'

She reached down into the leg well on the passenger side and picked up the slippers, intending on throwing them out to him and driving away. But no, she couldn't do that. She knew what he was capable of – she couldn't just let him go free.

'Get in,' she said, and pushed his door open.

52.

Caxton drove in silence for a while, staring straight ahead. She'd thought this was going to work, that she was going to find out the lair's location from Carboy. Instead he'd given her a very pretty, very useless image.

She was no closer to the solution than she'd ever been.

It was Carboy who started talking. Apparently once she'd broken the seal of his bravado, there was no controlling what came out. He started telling her about his childhood, about the frustrations and hardships of being a lonely teenage sociopath. He spoke freely of his desire to shoot up his school, and worse, about the night he'd killed his family. She didn't want to hear it, not any of it. She almost hit him again, just to shut him up – but once he started talking about Jameson, she pricked up her ears.

'I found him, exhausted and starved. He was in my back-yard. I was taking the trash out and he was leaning against the wall of our garage. I was scared at first. I mean, I knew what he was, right away. I thought he would kill me. But he didn't. This was way back, in October, when he'd just accepted the curse. He'd been fighting his thirst for blood, but he'd gone as far as he could. He was sleeping in the woods, he said, in a tin bathtub in an abandoned house he'd found. The roof had caved in and there were broken beer bottles on the floor. I couldn't imagine someone so beautiful living like that. I brought him into the house after my parents were asleep. I knew what he needed, so I cut my arm and dripped blood into his mouth.'

Caxton gripped the steering wheel harder and tried not to scream in frustration. If it had been anyone else's house Jameson had crawled to – if Carboy's parents had checked his room and seen what he had sleeping in his closet – everything could have been avoided. All the searching. All the false leads and dead ends. All the death.

'He talked to me all night long. Just for companionship, I think. I told him how much I respected him. His strength of will – to be in a house full of people, to smell our blood, and still he didn't hurt any of us. Even though we all deserved it.'

That was the Jameson Caxton remembered. She felt her gorge rising. She knew what must have come next.

'You could have called me,' Caxton snapped. 'You could have stopped this.'

'But – I didn't want to. He was – he was my friend. He understood me, understood my, my anger. Nobody else ever did. Nobody tried. They wanted me to go into therapy. As if I was the sick one. Not society, not everybody else, who only ever thought about money and, and sex, and being popular.'

So of course the object of that anger had become the one person who could take away his friend. Caxton. He had begun filling his notebooks then with her name, and his vows to destroy her.

Carboy had more to tell. 'With my blood in him he recovered fast. After just one night he was standing again, he was strong

323

again. The second night, he went out. He went out to hunt. When he came back he told me he hadn't killed anyone. I think he just followed some people around and thought about it. Thought about what he'd become, and what that made us. It made us his food.

'He told me about you. About how you were hunting for him. He said he couldn't stay there, in my house. So we found him a new place.'

'A disused grain elevator,' she prompted.

'Yes! It was perfect. He brought Malvern's coffin there. He said he would lock himself in with her. That maybe he would bury them both alive. He wanted to rot away down there, until he couldn't dig his way out again. He didn't want to die, but he was willing to spend the rest of time buried under the ground, unable to move or see or feel anything. But the blood – he wanted one last taste of blood. By then he'd started to change. To get more – aggressive. We talked about his taking my blood, but he knew that if I opened my veins again he wouldn't be able to stop. He would kill me. So I suggested another way.'

'You robbed a blood bank.'

Carboy was weeping noisily. 'It didn't work. The blood was cold. It didn't work. It only made him hungrier. If I hadn't – if I hadn't told Cady about him—'

'Cady Rourke,' Caxton said. 'Your girlfriend.'

The boy's voice broke as he continued. 'She wanted to see him. She – she wasn't my girlfriend, by the way. We were just friends, and yeah, sometimes we fooled around. But we saw other people, too. At least, Cady did. I couldn't handle that. It used to tear me up, but I could never get up the courage to break it off with her. I was so afraid of being alone. When I brought Cady to see Jameson he got angry, I mean, really angry. He said I was putting him at risk. That he couldn't trust Cady. He – he—'

'He killed her. Drank her blood.'

'I don't think he meant to, he just didn't see any other way,' Carboy said. His words came fast and thick, soggy with tears. 'Then he left me, and I never saw him again. Just in my dreams. It was Malvern who sent me those, I think. She could tell what I was feeling. She saw my weakness. I felt her contempt for me – I thought, if I could just – just be strong, as strong as Jameson – I wouldn't have to feel like that anymore.'

And so he had crept into his sister's room, and put his hands around her throat, and squeezed. When that hadn't been enough, when the feelings didn't just go away, he had grabbed his shotgun and killed his parents as well.

It hadn't been a long walk from there to dressing like a vampire. To make himself feel like a vampire. To make himself feel strong. The better his costume got, the closer he got to feeling like the real thing. Like a predator. Then suddenly he was in a storage facility with two dead bodies and the cops on the way.

Now he was talking to her. Looking at her. Looking at her like she was the strong one. The one he wanted to be like. The one he thought could understand him.

In a very unsettling way, she did.

Caxton dropped him off at the closest police station, just a few miles away. She didn't go in herself, just watched him as he ran up the icy steps, his feet red and yellow with the cold. She saw faces in the windows watching her and knew someone would write down her license plate number, but it didn't matter much. Once Carboy's identity was established and he told his story, Fetlock and as many cops as he could round up would come howling for her blood.

She already knew she was tight for time. It had been three hours since Raleigh walked out of the Harrisburg HQ with

325

Simon under her arm. Twenty-one to go. If she kept moving she could evade Fetlock at least that long. Of course, when you were on the run, it helped to know where you were going.

She picked up her phone, then realized she didn't know whom to call. In the olden days Jameson could have advised her on her next step. If not him, then Vesta Polder, who was gone now, too. She could have called Glauer, but she knew he worked for Fetlock now. Glauer was a nice guy, but he knew enough to cover his ass. If he helped Caxton now, he would be putting his own job in danger.

In the end she called Clara, because Clara would at least be on her side.

'Honey, it's me,' she sighed when Clara picked up her phone. 'I'm in pretty bad shape and I need somebody to talk me through this—'

'Laura, I can't talk right now,' Clara said in response.

Caxton felt as if she'd been slapped across the face.

'I've been called in to work,' Clara said. 'Fetlock called me into the HQ. It's a slaughterhouse in here.'

'He took my badge,' Caxton blurted.

'Laura, listen to me. Very carefully.'

Tears swirled in Caxton's vision. She pulled over on the side of the road because she couldn't see well enough to drive. 'I need to talk to you. For real.'

'I can't right now. Fetlock's coming down here any second and if he hears me talking to you we're both in serious trouble. But first you need to know something. We've already started going over Vesta Polder's body. Fetlock has me supervising his forensics team and taking pictures. They trust me now. Treat me like one of them. They didn't find much yet, except some black powder on her clothes. I'm pretty sure it's coal dust.'

'Okay,' Caxton said, clutching at her forehead. 'I don't know why that's—'

'Coal dust. Vesta didn't live anywhere near a coal mine. I suggested we go back and look at some of the old fibers. The Twaron and nylon from the motel, and the clothes he left at the convent. There were traces of coal dust on all of them. We think Jameson had coal dust on his hands when he killed Vesta Polder.'

Caxton tried to speak, but her throat was too thick with emotion. She choked down her tears, then said, 'I'm going to make things right between us. Right now I have to – you know what I have to do. But when I get back,' she said, thinking, *if I come back*, 'I will make everything right. I love you.'

'I have to go now,' Clara said. 'I'll give you a call when I can talk.' She paused for a moment, then said, 'Same here,' and hung up.

Caxton put her phone down, then laid her forehead gently against the steering wheel. Her body convulsed with sobs that she fought back, sobs of grief for what she'd thrown away and the people she'd lost. Sobs of fear, too. True fear. Fear of what was still to come.

Because as soon as Clara told her about the coal dust, she'd already put two and two together.

She knew where the lair was.

53.

A coal mine. That made sense. Vampires liked their lairs dark and quiet, and far away from human interference. A coal mine, an abandoned coal mine, would make the perfect spot. There were thousands of coal mines in Pennsylvania, however, and hundreds of them were abandoned. Caxton could never have checked them all even if she'd had unlimited time.

When she added what Carboy had told her, however, she could only think of one abandoned coal mine where flowers grew in the middle of winter.

She wanted to go right there, but it wouldn't be that easy. She needed special equipment. Jameson had said humans couldn't survive inside his lair, and he hadn't been kidding. Getting that equipment was going to be a problem. What she needed was in ready supply at the HQ building, but she wouldn't be welcome there – and Fetlock would watch her every move if she showed up, even if he didn't already know what she'd done with Carboy. She thought about approaching a firehouse and trying to bluff her way into getting what she needed, but she knew there would be too many questions, and probably too many phone calls made.

In the end she was reduced to going shopping. There was a place in Harrisburg she knew, an army surplus store that stayed open late. She arrived just as they were closing, but she flashed her state police ID and the night manager nodded and let her in, locking the door behind her.

She stared at the racks of camouflage clothing, let her gaze run across glass display cases full of butterfly knives and night-vision goggles. She could use a pair of the latter, but she knew she couldn't afford them. She was willing to go into debt – she'd lost so much already her credit rating didn't feel terribly important – but there was a pretty tight limit on her Visa card.

The manager was a young guy in a plaid shirt and horn-rimmed glasses. He sighed with impatience and asked her what he could help her with.

Caxton cleared her mind by rubbing at her face with both hands. Was she really going to do this? The lair was underground, probably full of carbon monoxide gas, and the temperatures down there could reach a thousand degrees. Nothing in the store could keep her alive through that.

If she could just get close, though – close enough—

'I need a Nomex flash-resistant suit,' she said. 'Gloves, boot-ies, the whole package. I need a face mask, too, and a hard hat. And a portable air supply, the longest-lasting one you've got.'

The manager stared at her openmouthed. 'You fighting a brush fire, ma'am?' he asked.

'Worse. I'm going into a coal mine fire.'

'Like the one in Centralia?'

Caxton gave him a weak smile. 'Exactly like the one in Centralia. You have what I need?'

He shrugged and walked down an aisle, calling over his shoulder, 'Is this going to be cash or credit?'

Fifteen minutes later she was back in the car, headed northeast. Toward the closest thing to hell you could find in Pennsylvania.

Centralia. Every kid in the Commonwealth knew about Centralia, about the fire under the town that had been burning since the sixties and still had enough fuel to continue to burn long after they, and their grandchildren, were dead. It was a place where the ground opened up and swallowed people and houses whole. It was a place where the earth was so hot underneath that flowers bloomed on the surface, even in the middle of winter.

Caxton drove through the night, staying off the highways. Taking the back roads took longer but lowered the probability that she would be spotted by a highway patrol cruiser and pulled over. She had little doubt that by now her license plate number had been memorized by every state trooper on the road.

Just as Jameson had learned all the tricks of being a vampire long before he even considered becoming one himself, Caxton knew how to move around the state without being spotted. She had, after all, spent years in the highway patrol. She knew the location of every radar trap and sobriety checkpoint in Pennsylvania, and she knew what roads were never watched. She drove carefully, as tired as she was, taking pains not to weave across lanes, to drive at just the right speed. If you drove too slow, you drew attention to yourself. If you kept exactly to the speed limit, you drew attention. She stayed just over the limit, but no more than five miles an hour over, in case she wandered past a local cop looking to make his quota of speeding tickets for the month. She signaled every turn and every lane change well in advance.

Centralia. Once it had been a thriving town. Caxton herself had grown up in a series of mining patches, little company towns too small to have their own police. Her father had been the only law some of those places had ever seen. Centralia had a population in the thousands once, but by the time Caxton was born it was a ghost town, too small to even be called a patch. The fire had started as an accident. The local mining company had taken to burning its garbage in a played-out pit mine just southeast of the town. It must have seemed more economical than hauling the trash to a landfill. It turned out the pit hadn't been as empty as they thought. There must have been some coal still down there, because in 1962, it ignited, and started a fire that couldn't be stopped. Coal is a fossil fuel and it combusts well, even in low-oxygen conditions. The burning coal in the pit had in turn ignited a coal seam connected to the underground mines near the town. Once that seam caught, the fire just grew and grew. The mines had to be abandoned, but for twenty years nobody had considered it a serious problem. There were mine fires all over the world, and most of the time it was more cost-efficient to just let them burn themselves out. They'd figured Centralia would do just that in a couple of years.

They were wrong.

She pulled over to get her bearings. Centralia wasn't on her road map. Nobody was supposed to go there anymore. She knew where it was, though, and when she put her finger on Route 61 she saw that it was less than two miles from Mount Carmel, Dylan Carboy's hometown. Less than a mile from the location of the abandoned grain elevator lair. 'Son of a bitch,' she murmured. Jameson had been right under her nose the whole time.

She knew she was getting close when she saw reefs of pale smoke winding between the trees on either side of the road. The coal company had drilled holes down into the inferno to release the buildup of smoke and toxic gases. It hadn't been enough. In the eighties the surface of Route 61 had started to crack and buckle. A whole new highway had been constructed that went around the affected area. Then sinkholes started collapsing all around town. One had nearly swallowed up a small boy. About that time the government bought up as much of the town as it could and relocated all the citizens to nearby boroughs. A very few stubborn holdouts had stayed, and survived the best they could, even knowing the risks. As of the last census, the population of Centralia had sunk as low as twelve.

It was the most desolate, the most hazardous, the most environmentally toxic place in the entire state. Temperatures underground could reach a thousand degrees in the heart of the fire. That heat seeped up through the soil and melted snow before it could even collect on the ground.

Caxton saw the wintertime flowers, even in the dark. Wildflowers, tiny blossoms on thin stalks that fluttered in the night breezes. In the moonlight, surrounded by the dead trees, they were eerily beautiful.

She parked her car near where the center of town had been once. There were roads crisscrossing a grassy field, but the houses were all gone. Here and there she could see an overgrown foundation, the crumbled remains of a brick chimney, but that was all. A couple of small houses remained on the edge of where the town had been, but only one had any lights on.

She had arrived. She was armed. She was ready.

The government had tried a few schemes for putting out the fire, but none had been successful. The coal continued to burn. Caxton had heard there was enough coal down there to keep burning for another two hundred and fifty years.

One thing the government had done was to close off every entrance to the underground mine. They hadn't just strung up fencing or boarded over the entrances, either – they'd been blasted shut, in the hopes of cutting off the fire's oxygen supply. The pit mines nearby had all been filled in with sterile fill, crushed rock, and nonflammable soil. That was good, from one perspective. The lair was down in the mine, and the fewer exits the mine had, the harder it would be for Jameson to escape when she came for him.

It did present one dilemma for her, however – knowing exactly where the lair was didn't help if she couldn't find her way in.

She had an idea about how to fix that. She started walking toward the house with the burning lights, intent on seeing who was still awake.

54.

The house was filled with birds. The birds would drive Caxton crazy, she thought, if she had to live here.

'You say you're not with the government,' the old woman said, and brushed her thinning white hair back over a bald spot. She was wearing a shapeless polyester housecoat. A chipped enamel tea mug sat by her elbow, untouched.

Caxton had its twin – the only other one the woman owned – on a coffee table in front of her. On the floor by her feet she had the Nomex flash-resistant suit and her other equipment folded neatly into a special backpack. Not that she intended to use it that night, but she wanted to be prepared in case she had a chance to do some impromptu spelunking. 'Not anymore. I know they've approached you about buying your land—'

'And I told them, no.' A sharp fluttering of wings nearly drowned out the softly spoken words. The old woman frowned and peered through heavy eyelids at Caxton, sizing her up. 'One day that fire's goin' out. Then they'll have to come to me if they want the coal down there. I own mineral rights on half this town, and I'm not giving that up without a fight.'

A canary chirped next to Caxton's shoulder. The bright yellow birds were everywhere, dozens or maybe as many as a hundred crowded into wire cages lined with ancient, brittle newspaper. The cages hung from the ceiling of every room, or sat on end tables. Some were even tucked away on the floor, behind the furniture.

It was quite possible the old woman loved the birds, but they weren't pets.

'You keep these,' Caxton said, 'to test for carbon monoxide, right?' The gas was constantly rising from the mine fire in tendrils of pale smoke. It gathered in basements and lingered outside windows like insubstantial tentacles tapping for entry. Even in very mild concentrations, as little as five parts per million, it was toxic, and a sudden puff of vapor could suffocate the old woman in her sleep at any time. Canaries were famous for their sensitivity to carbon monoxide and other poisonous gases. If they started keeling over, the old woman would have a few seconds' warning to pull a gas mask over her face and avoid breathing in her own death. Gas masks were almost as common in the house as canaries – there was one in every room, at least.

'I treat 'em well, feed 'em twice a day and keep 'em clean,' the old woman insisted. 'You from the ASPCA?'

'Maybe I used the wrong term. Perhaps,' Caxton said, 'I should have said they were to test for white damp.'

Miners referred to poisonous gas outbreaks as varieties of damp, probably from *dampf*, the German word for steam. There were fire damps, black damps, choke damps, and stink damps. The most common and the most deadly kind was white damp, but any of them could kill you before you smelled them.

335

The old woman sat up and scratched at her wrist. It was as if Caxton had spoken a code word the old woman had been waiting to hear. Still her eyes were suspicious. 'You're no miner, lady,' she said.

Caxton smiled. 'No. But I grew up around coal mines. I was born in Iselin, and I went to school near Whiskey Run. I don't want to run you off your ground, ma'am. All I want to know is whether there are any bootleg mines around here.'

'If you're who you say you are you'll know that bootleg mining's a thing of the past.' The old woman shook her head. 'There's no man alive who could dig enough coal in a day with his own hands to make a living.'

Caxton had heard that before – and knew it was like an Italian-American claiming there was no such thing as the Mafia. 'He might dig enough to warm his house in winter, and cut down on his heating bills.' Caxton picked up her tea mug and rolled it back and forth in her hands. She was getting frustrated and she wondered if there was a quicker way to find the information she needed. She supposed she could pull her gun on this old woman – but no, that was beyond even her level of desperation. 'Anyway, the one I'm looking for isn't currently in use. At least, not by the living.'

The old woman leaned forward in her armchair. 'I'm not sure I heard that right.'

Caxton sighed and looked up at the ceiling. 'I'm after a vampire. I know he's holed up in the mine, but I don't know how he gets in or out. I thought—'

The old woman held up her hands. 'That's what I thought you said.' She tapped at a cage on top of her television set, which set the birds inside fluttering and chirping. Picking it up by one handle, she walked toward her front door. 'You'd better follow me.'

Caxton got up and pulled on her backpack, not wanting to leave it behind. They went out into the dark and cold night, the old woman not even bothering to put on a jacket. They didn't have far to go. Caxton followed her down a road cracked and overgrown with weeds, then into the weathered foundation of an old house that had long since been torn down. A pile of old rags and plastic bags had gathered where a bit of the foundation stuck up in the air higher than the ground around it. It looked just like a heap of trash. The old woman put down her cage, though, and brushed the refuse away, revealing a wooden trapdoor.

'He came here about two months gone, your fella. We all saw him out our windows – he didn't make a pretense of hiding. Why should he? *We* hid from *him*. Every time he comes in or out we hunker down.'

'And you never called the police,' Caxton said.

'If we did, we knew what would happen to us. There's just a handful of us left in Centralia, and we can't afford people coming 'round asking lots of questions. Not if we're going to preserve the claim on what's ours. Nobody wants the police crawling over this ground, looking for evidence and getting in our business. Your kind aren't welcome here.'

Caxton sighed. 'I'm not a cop. Not anymore.'

Someone was standing behind her.

Caxton whirled around, her weapon out of its holster and pointing before she even saw what she was aiming at. The laser sight made a bright spot on the chest of a massive young man in a red plaid hunter's coat. He raised his hands slowly and looked from Caxton to the old woman and back.

'What's going on, Maisie?' he asked. 'I saw you come out your house just now and I saw where you were going.'

'That's just my cousin Wally. Don't you shoot him,' the old woman insisted.

337

'Why don't you both just back up, okay?' Caxton said, in her cop voice.

'You don't want to go down there,' Wally said. 'There's something down there you don't want to see.'

'I'll be the judge of that.' Caxton slowly rose to her feet and holstered her weapon. 'Anyway, I don't intend on going down there, not tonight. It's barely eleven-thirty. I'm going to wait until dawn.' The only sane time to enter a vampire's lair was when you had plenty of daylight to burn. 'I know you think the vampire might hurt you if he sees me here. You've got to trust me, though. I'm going down there tomorrow and I'm going to kill him. You'll never have to worry about him again.'

'That's fine,' Wally said. 'But what about her?'

Caxton spun around again, but she was far too slow. The trap had lifted at an angle and a white shadow was snaking out of it, reaching for her. Raleigh's hands fastened around her ankles like a pair of vise grips and pulled her roughly down into the darkness before she could even start to scream.

She saw the old woman's face recede above her as she was carried downward. 'Like I said,' the old woman said, 'you aren't welcome here, lady.'

338

55.

Caxton's face collided hard with a wall of solid rock and bright flecks shot through her vision. Then everything went dark. She thought maybe she had a concussion or even that she was dead, but in fact the trapdoor had just closed over her, and she was faced with the most profound darkness she'd ever experienced: midnight in a coal mine.

A thin hand grasped one of her ankles. She was dragged across the stone floor, rough still with the marks of where some old miner had cut this chute with a shovel and a pickaxe and maybe a few sticks of stolen dynamite. The entrance to the lair was through a bootleg mine – a narrow passage cut by night down toward a coal seam the miner didn't own. Maybe just one man, maybe an entire family, had worked for years chopping through the soil and rock looking for the black glint of coal. The ceiling, Caxton knew, would be held up only here and there by rotten timbers. The passage would be no wider than a man's broad shoulders. She pushed out her arms and felt the uneven wall on either side. She tried to grab on, but Raleigh was much stronger than Caxton now, and Caxton couldn't get enough grip on the rock to even slow the vampire down.

For a long time she was carried along like that, her face bouncing on the floor, the skin of her ankle crying out in pain where Raleigh held her. Then the forward progress stopped, and Caxton's leg was dropped to the floor. Still she couldn't see a thing, though she knew that Raleigh would be able to see her just fine – at least, she could see Caxton's blood, her arteries and veins and capillaries lit up in the pitch darkness like an inward-curling maze of neon tubes.

Caxton fully expected to die in that darkness, unable to see when the vampire descended on her and tore out her throat. Maybe she would have a fraction of a second's warning. Maybe she would feel the cold and sickly aura that emanated from Raleigh's being before the bite came. Or maybe not.

Then there was a clicking sound, and lights sputtered to life all around Caxton, glaring down at her from a ceiling high above. Caxton rolled onto her back, the backpack squishing uncomfortably beneath her, and tried to sit up. A white hand pressed down on her throat and she lay back down – she had no choice. Raleigh easily overpowered her, and there was no point in fighting.

Caxton still had her pistol in its holster at her belt. She darted her hand downward and tried to grab at it, but Raleigh was ready for that, too. She got to the gun first and drew it neatly, then twirled it on her finger.

The vampire was still dressed in the remains of her winding sheet, with duct tape bunching it around her hips and throat. Over top of that she had put on a ballistic vest. A type IIIA, of course, with a steel trauma plate over her heart. 'This,' she said, lifting the gun in her hand, 'is useless.

340

How many times did you shoot Daddy with it? And he barely felt it.'

Raleigh threw the weapon into a corner of the room. Caxton watched it, trying to see where it landed. In the process she finally saw where she was: a chamber about twenty feet square. This wasn't part of the bootleg mine, but a chamber of the original company mine, and it contained supplies abandoned when the mine was shut down. There were boxes that would have held dynamite and blasting caps, as well as enormous pieces of mining equipment, roof bolters and rod chargers. In one corner, leaning up against the wall, stood a pair of six-foot-long handheld drills that would have done wonders at boring through that trauma plate and impaling Raleigh's heart – if there had been anyplace to plug them in. The equipment was falling to pieces, eaten at by rust or just general decay. It must have been sitting down here for decades after the mine was abandoned. If there was any dynamite in those boxes it would have gone bad before Raleigh was even born, most likely.

Raleigh followed her gaze. 'It's not much, but it's home,' she said.

Caxton had just one chance. Raleigh didn't know that she'd upgraded her weapon – she couldn't know that Caxton was loading Teflon bullets that might, just might, penetrate the trauma plate. If Caxton could get closer to the gun, if she could just reach it—

She started crawling toward the gun with infinitesimal slowness, using her hands and her legs to scoot along the floor.

Raleigh had a radio on her belt that she lifted to her mouth. 'Daddy, she's here. She came just like you said she would.' Raleigh stared down at Caxton with a disdainful smile, then

341

went on, 'I got her inside just fine, and I've disarmed her. Just like we talked about.'

The radio spat and popped with static, but Caxton could hear Jameson calling from someplace else in the mine. 'Don't take any chances. Empty her weapon and then bring her to me.' There was a pause, then Jameson said, 'There will be fifteen bullets in the gun, and maybe one in the chamber. Get them all.'

Raleigh took two long steps across the room and picked up the weapon. Caxton stopped moving.

The vampire turned the gun over and over in her hands. She found the safety and slipped it off. Then, holding the gun straight out from her shoulder, she pointed it down at Caxton's face. It was a lousy firing stance, but at that range it wouldn't matter. 'Bang bang,' Raleigh said, with a little laugh.

'You could have killed me before this,' Caxton said, trying not to look down the dark barrel in front of her. 'You're saving me for some reason.'

'For Simon. When he accepts the curse, when he's one of us, you're going to be his first victim. Daddy and I have already fed.' Raleigh lifted the weapon a few inches and fired a shot straight over Caxton's head. The noise of the shot made them both cringe as it echoed around and around the room, amplified by the close, hard walls. Raleigh made a face, her wicked teeth protruding from her pale lips, but then she fired again, and again, aiming just shy of hitting Caxton each time. The precious bullets pranged off the rock floor and ricocheted around the room, bouncing and clattering wildly, but unfortunately none of them went so far astray as to bounce back up and hit Raleigh. One did cut through the sleeve of Caxton's shirt. She didn't dare look, but she thought it had just missed breaking her skin. She pulled her arms in close to her body and tried not to flinch too much.

342

As Raleigh fired she counted out loud, but the words were lost until she stopped and said, 'Sixteen.' Caxton's ears were still ringing as the vampire blew on the gun's hot barrel, then shoved it, the safety still off, into one of the straps of her vest. 'Now get up, and let's go.'

56.

Caxton went first, prodded on occasionally by Raleigh, who kept close behind, walking forward down a corridor lined with electric lights. Jameson must have strung up those lights himself – normally coal mines were left dark except for the lights on the miners' helmets and their equipment. Here and there side galleries led away from the main hall, and these had been left dark – silent, empty channels carved through the rock where the only sound was made by dust falling and rocks settling. Once those halls would have echoed with clamor and activity as miners pushed a giant longwall cutter down the face, grinding out coal by the ton. Now it was as silent as the tomb it had become.

Or perhaps not quite silent. Caxton had little to do as she walked but look around her and strain her ears to pick up subtle sounds. It didn't take long to notice a faint but deep roaring sound coming from deeper in the mine. Somewhere down these passages, through a series of left and right turns, the fire lay, blazing and raging as it had for so many years.

The sound was not the only evidence. She started to see

344

wisps of smoke playing about the ceiling, braids of pale vapor that grew thicker and more agitated as she progressed. The peculiar smell of carbon monoxide came to her at first just slightly, but with increasing intensity. She'd smelled it plenty of times as a kid. She tried to think what it smelled like, but as always before she drew a blank. It wasn't the smell of a campfire, thick with resin and wood smells. It wasn't the smell of a candle flame, either; there was no tang of paraffin there. It was more like an un-smell, an absence of smells. It smelled like a blanket covering her face, preventing her from breathing. It smelled like suffocation.

They'd been walking maybe a quarter of a mile when she started to cough. Involuntary little spasms of her throat at first, tiny eruptions that soon graduated to full-scale convulsions. She pressed her balled-up fist against her mouth to try to hold them in, but that just made her chest heave all the harder.

Last she noticed the heat, and in many ways that was the worst of it. It had been a crisp winter night above the surface. Down here a dry heat warmed her body, making her sweat down the collar of her winter coat. Her armpits grew moist, and then her chest. Rivulets of sweat coursed down her body. A crystal droplet formed at the end of her nose and she had to keep wiping it away. The heat pressed against her face as if she'd opened the door of a furnace to peer inside.

She started to take off her coat – and then Raleigh was on her, one arm wrapped around her neck and crushing her windpipe. Caxton tried to go limp, but the vampire held her rigid and lifted her slightly until only the toes of her boots touched the floor. Then Raleigh threw her down, a discarded doll, and Caxton fell hard against her side. She couldn't breathe; she sucked at the air, but it choked her before it got halfway down her throat. She tried to talk, to explain, but the words couldn't form. Her hands reached up and tore at the collar of her shirt, trying desperately to loosen it. Weakness overcame her, though – her body refused to move the way she wanted it to, as every fiber of her strength was directed toward her lungs, her body's need for air paramount.

Down on the floor the air was a little cleaner. Slowly, with painful jagged inhalations, she fed her cells the oxygen they needed. The sweat that bathed her face caught a puff of breeze and cooled her down. 'I just,' she said, the words like switchblades opening in her throat, 'just want – to take off my coat.'

Raleigh stared down at her sharply, then nodded.

Caxton struggled out of the garment, slipping off her backpack in the process. She had a portable air supply in the pack, as well as clothing to protect her from the heat. She started to open it up, but Raleigh kicked it out of her hands and back down the hall, the way they'd come.

'I've heard how tricky you can be,' the vampire said, her eyes narrowing. 'Maybe you have another gun in there.'

If only. Caxton bent her head and started to ball up her coat, intending to carry it under her arm. Raleigh grabbed it away from her and threw it after the pack.

'You won't need that anymore,' Raleigh said.

Caxton understood what Raleigh meant. She wouldn't be leaving the mine, at least not alive. She would never feel cold again.

Slowly Caxton rose to her feet. She kept her hands where Raleigh could see them, and when she was standing she lifted them above her head. Raleigh nodded her acceptance and then spun Caxton around and sent her down the hallway again, toward their destination.

Ahead the corridor widened and grew more regular, as if it had been more carefully carved. Caxton thought they'd come maybe half a mile from the bootleg mine entrance, though it was next to impossible to accurately judge distances in a long, almost featureless hallway. It wasn't much farther on that the corridor ended in a broad junction where many corridors intersected, creating a room considerably larger than the one where Raleigh had discharged the Beretta. The same style of lights illuminated the room, but they were set farther apart and the chamber was gloomy and dim. Wherever the lights blazed they shed cones of pale yellow light down toward the floor, cones that were sharply defined by the swirling smoke in the air.

There was not a lot of furniture in the room. There were four coffins set up along one wall like a miniature crypt. One coffin had to be for Jameson, a second for Raleigh. The third must hold the remains of Justinia Malvern, though why it was closed Caxton didn't know. Maybe Jameson didn't like looking at her all night, considering her condition. She would be a constant reminder of his own vulnerabilities, of the fact that while he might live forever, he wouldn't stop aging. Caxton wondered how Malvern felt about being stored there like a broom in a closet.

The fourth coffin's lid stood wide open and Caxton saw that it was empty. That one was probably meant for Simon, she decided. The boy himself was chained to a timber that held up the ceiling. He did not look conscious. Near him, where he could keep an eye on his son, Jameson sat on a weird-looking chair. Jameson was wearing his ballistic vest and a pair of black jeans, but no shoes. His feet were dark with coal dust, but his face was glaring white. He rose as Caxton walked into the room and she saw that his chair was made of human bones held together with thick twists of baling wire. Mostly pelvises and skulls, with femurs for its legs. Classic vampire design.

Five half-deads stood in poses of attention around the edges of the room, as if they guarded the corridors leading away from it. Their torn faces were lowered and their hands were folded in front of them. Caxton had never seen half-deads who looked so disciplined or orderly – normally they formed cackling anarchic mobs. The only thing that motivated half-deads to behave themselves was fear. Jameson must have taught them some pretty strong lessons.

Caxton stumbled forward into the room, choking. The smoke was thick in her mouth and in her lungs, and the heat had gone from tropical to infernal. She felt like she was made of molten, sagging lead. It was all she could do not to fall down on her knees and give up.

'Nothing to say, Trooper?' Jameson asked, smiling down at her. He moved closer to her, almost close enough to touch. But not quite. Even at her strongest Caxton would have been no match for him physically – and bare-handed she couldn't even scratch his skin, especially after he'd fed. He wasn't taking any chances, though. He never had while he was alive. Now he seemed downright paranoid.

She shook her head and just tried to breathe. This is it, she thought. She had faced death so many times since she'd first met Jameson that she had thought she'd grown immune to the fear. It was suddenly back, more intense than she'd ever felt it before. She was about to die and there was nothing she could do about it.

Something in her refused to give up, though. A part of her brain that kept looking for angles, for opportunities. It came up with very little, but it kept trying. It suggested something to her and she considered the option carefully. Then she took in a long, shallow breath and spoke.

'You win,' she said.

Jameson studied her with his eyes. 'This isn't a competition,' he said. 'It's the natural order. My daughter and I are predators. You and your kind are prey, that's all. To survive, we must feed on your blood. I know from your perspective that must look dreadful, but if you could see beyond your own mortality, you would understand. Just as I have come to understand.'

Caxton smiled despite herself. 'Natural order,' she said. 'That's interesting.' She broke down in a coughing fit, but he waited patiently for her to finish. 'You were the one who taught me that vampires are anything but natural. That they're evil, true evil. I think those were your exact words.'

'I've had time to broaden my view,' he said. 'Alright.' He turned to face one of the half-deads. 'You, get some more chain. The rest of you, help him secure her to a timber.' He turned to Caxton again. 'You're about to pass out, Trooper. There's not enough oxygen down here to keep you awake. I'll try to make your death painless – I owe you that much. After all, if it weren't for you I wouldn't have ever come this far.'

Caxton's eyes went wide. He was right, of course. He had accepted the curse as a way to save her life. If she hadn't needed his help so badly, he would never have become a vampire. Everything he'd done, everyone he'd killed, all that blood was on her hands. It was what had driven her to desperate tactics, and what had drawn her to Centralia – to find forgiveness for what she'd created. Now that drive for absolution was going to be her death. She thought carefully about what to say next. 'You owe me – you said that before. That you owe me a great deal and you intend to pay me in full.'

'And so I have. I had plenty of chances to kill you before now, and plenty of reasons to do so. I held back for your sake. Honestly, if you hadn't come here tonight, if you'd been smart enough to know when you were beaten, you could have lived. But now you've found my lair. You've threatened my family with violence. I think that wipes the slate clean. I'm going to save you just long enough to give my son a good meal.

349

You'll have a last chance to be useful. It's the most noble death I can think of.'

She didn't look him in the eye when she asked, 'How about a last request?'

'Fair enough,' he answered after a long pause. 'I'm not unreasonable,' he told her. 'I'm not, no matter how many times your girlfriend said it, an asshole.'

She looked at him squarely. 'You killed your own wife and your brother because you had to, to stay alive. You knew you couldn't survive on your own. So you went after everyone you ever loved, maybe everyone you thought you could stand being around for eternity. You got Raleigh, and I don't doubt you'll convince Simon.'

'Yes,' Jameson said.

'I never asked you to like me,' Caxton said. 'I don't think you ever did. Maybe you respected me, just a little. Grudgingly. But Jameson, I don't want to die.' She closed her eyes and let her body sag. All this talking was making her dizzy and light-headed. She really should be conserving her oxygen. What she was about to say was almost certainly a waste of breath.

'I want to live,' she said, her eyes flashing open. 'I want to live forever.'

57.

Jameson stared at her, his red eyes wide. Then he opened his mouth, showing his rows of razor-sharp teeth, and started to laugh.

Caxton couldn't remember ever hearing him laugh while he was alive. Undead, his laughter was a harsh dry rasping sound that echoed off the stone walls.

She expected him to bat her down to the ground with one quick swipe, or maybe tear her apart and drink her blood on the spot. He didn't. Instead he took a step back and looked her up and down, as if appraising her worthiness. She tried to think of something to add, some compelling argument why she would make a great vampire. She couldn't think of any.

'No, Daddy,' Raleigh said, rushing past Caxton and nearly knocking her down. The girl tried to embrace Jameson, but he held her off, at arm's distance. 'No,' she said again. 'It's bad enough I have to spend eternity with Simon, but – her?'

Jameson looked down at his daughter. He hadn't noticed what had happened when Raleigh ran past Caxton. Raleigh had been too upset to notice, herself. If the half-deads saw, they were too disciplined to say anything.

Caxton's Beretta had still been sticking out of the side of Raleigh's ballistic vest, where she'd shoved it after firing off sixteen rounds. Caxton was a little surprised it hadn't fallen out on the walk to the crypt. As weak and breathless as Caxton was, it had been easy enough to grab the pistol's grip as Raleigh moved past her and draw it from its makeshift holster.

'It can just be you and me,' Raleigh sighed. 'Forever. Why share our blood with her? Why – when she's tried to kill you so many times? She would have burned me alive back there, at the police station.'

Caxton wasted a fraction of a second checking the safety. It was already off, because Raleigh had thought the gun was useless. It almost was. Caxton lifted the pistol two-handed and drew a bead on Jameson's trauma plate. She hesitated for another fraction of a second. She wasn't sure if the bullets would actually penetrate the steel plate, and she would get only one chance.

Raleigh, on the other hand, had her back turned to Caxton. There was no trauma plate on the back of her vest.

Caxton's life was going to last just as long as it took one vampire or another to notice what she was doing. She didn't have time to consider her next move, other than to think that leaving the world with one less vampire in it would be a good legacy. She steadied herself, held her breath, and squeezed the trigger.

Jameson and Raleigh both screamed in surprise and rage. Raleigh's arms went around her father's neck and she slumped across his chest in the same instant that a hole blew open in the back of her vest, just between her spine and her left scapula. White vapor hissed out of the wound, spraying tiny fragments of Twaron fiber and splinters of bone.

She slid down her father's body, collapsing in a heap on the floor. Her eyes were wide open and her hands were clawing at the air. Her whole body started to shake so badly that it was difficult for Caxton to see that her trauma plate was bowed out from the inside. The Teflon bullet had passed right through her body and nearly made it through the plate as well.

Jameson stared down at his own chest. His own vest had a dent in its nylon cover – but on the right side, where it could do him no harm. He lifted his eyes to meet Caxton's, his mouth already opening in a hiss of anger. She felt his mind rushing at her, through her own eyes, like a runaway train hurtling into a tunnel, but she had already reached for the amulet around her neck. It grew scorching hot in her hand and then he was gone, receding from her, his psychic attack thwarted before it could begin.

He reeled back as if he'd been slapped.

Caxton took the moment of surprise and horror to move back, toward the mouth of the corridor behind her, stumbling backward, unwilling to look away from Jameson's face. She stopped suddenly when he drew himself back up to his full height and stomped toward her. She raised the Beretta and pointed it at his heart.

'She unloaded that gun,' he howled. 'I heard her discharge it!'

'New model,' she said, trying to stay calm. 'Larger magazine capacity.'

The Beretta 92 she'd carried since her first day as a state trooper had a magazine that held fifteen rounds. Jameson had seen that gun a thousand times while they'd worked together. He had assumed that she would still be using the same weapon. But the new gun held seventeen bullets.

Jameson nodded sagely, as if she had finally impressed him. Maybe for the first time. 'But I think you're empty now.'

'Unless I loaded a round in the chamber before I came down here,' Caxton agreed, keeping the gun pointed at his chest. 'That would have been the smart thing to do, don't you think?'

Before Caxton had met Jameson, before she'd ever worked

on a vampire case, she used to keep a bullet in her chamber all the time. It meant she was ready to shoot as soon as she drew the gun from her holster, rather than having to fully cock the weapon to load the first round.

Jameson, on the other hand, had never walked around with a cocked gun. He had equated doing so with driving while not wearing a seat belt. He had entered law enforcement many years before she had, back when small arms occasionally discharged by accident. That almost never happened these days, but Jameson had always been pathologically cautious.

What he didn't know – what he didn't have to know, as far as Caxton was concerned – was that she had looked up to him so much, had copied him in every form and move so well, that she had trained herself not to load a round in her chamber anymore. She had broken herself of the habit.

Her weapon was completely empty.

'The smart thing,' he said, taking a step sideways. He was so light on his feet that it looked more as if he was sliding across the floor, as graceful as an ice-skater. 'You're doing the smart thing these days? Because the smart thing would have been to shoot me already, instead of standing here talking about it.'

He leapt then, his whole body bounding effortlessly into the air, huge and powerful and coming right for her. Jumping away herself would have been useless – he was too fast. Instead she jabbed the gun at him as if it were a knife and squeezed the trigger again, even as she leaned back. He threw his arms up to protect his face and his leap fell short by inches. Her gun didn't fire – the trigger didn't even move – but he had doubted himself for just long enough that she survived the attack.

If she wanted to stay alive, she needed to run.

She ran.

58.

Caxton knew she'd bought at most a second or two of time. Jameson wouldn't stop to mourn his daughter, not until Caxton was dead – and he wasn't going to give her another chance to be tricky.

She also knew he wouldn't come after her himself, at least not right away. He would send his half-deads after her first. It was an age-old tactic of the vampires, one of the many he'd studied back when he was alive and fighting them. Disarmed, barely able to breathe, weak and alone, Caxton had all the same proved that she was dangerous when cornered. The half-deads would harass her, tire her out, maybe even wound her – and then he would swoop in and finish her off.

She was not wholly defenseless, even without bullets in her gun. As she ran she grabbed the ASP baton off her belt and flicked it open, letting its weighted end bob along beside her as she hurried down the corridor. She had all her other cop toys as well, some of which were more useful than others.

Numerous side galleries flashed by her as she ran, all of

them dark, some breathing hot vapors at her, some cool and empty. All of them were tempting. In the well-lit main corridor she felt vulnerable and exposed. Before she could turn off the main passage, though, she needed to catch her breath. In the smoky tunnels that meant just one thing – she had to recover her backpack.

It lay just where Raleigh had thrown it, about halfway up the tunnel that led back to the bootleg mine entrance. As she scooped it up she looked up the passage toward the room where Raleigh had almost emptied her weapon. It was tempting to think she could just run up there, climb up through the trap door, and run for her car. There were more bullets in the trunk, a handful of Teflon rounds and a full box of conventional ammo. That would be more than useful right then. There was only one problem – the half-deads had almost caught up with her. She could hear them behind her, their footfalls echoing around a bend in the tunnel that just hid them from view. There was no way she could reach the entrance and make her way to the surface before they caught up with her.

Which left just one option. She ducked down a dark side gallery, one that looked empty and less smoky than the rest, and pressed her back up against the wall of rock. As quietly as she could she opened her backpack and pulled out the emergency respirator. It came in two parts, a mask she could strap over her face and an oxygen bottle she could clip to her belt. She slipped it on and twisted the nozzle, then sucked at the mask until clean oxygen hit her mouth and throat, so pure and sweet it made her dizzy. She closed her eyes and just breathed for a moment. The backpack fell out of her hands and clunked to the floor.

'Did you hear that?' someone whispered, in a high-pitched, almost cackling voice she knew all too well. The half-dead was whispering, but the mine gallery had weird acoustics.

356

She couldn't tell what direction the voice came from, but she could hear it plain as day.

There was no response. Normally half-deads gave themselves away by talking too much – they were cowardly creatures and they needed constant reassurance to keep them focused on their tasks. This bunch were too well trained for that, however. She tried to listen for their footsteps, for the sound of their clothing rustling as they moved. Instead she heard only her own breath hissing in the mask.

They had to be close. They'd been only a few seconds behind her before she turned down the gallery. She readied herself, then waited for ten heartbeats, then forced herself to wait for ten more. Her pulse was racing so fast that it was no longer a reliable measure of time.

She thought she heard a rubber shoe sole squeak on the rock just around the corner. That was the best sign she was going to get. She swung out, into the lighted corridor, her baton whirling around in a deadly one-handed blow. The half-dead was there – and about six inches from where she'd expected it to be. Her baton hit the rock wall with a thud that jarred the bones of her arm.

The half-dead grinned wickedly, its torn face literally splitting. It was carrying a shovel and it drew back for a counterattack that she would not have been able to dodge. She grabbed for her pepper spray with her free hand. She brought it up and squirted pure capsicum into what was left of the half-dead's face. It started screaming instantly.

She didn't bother looking to see if there were any more behind it. She spun back around and hurried down the dark tunnel.

The light from the corridor behind her touched the walls on either side, the sheared-off faces left over when the longwall plow carved away all the coal it could reach. Miners called those faces ribs, and they knew to watch out for them – the ribs were not solid rock, but conglomerations of many different kinds of rocks pressed together by their own weight. Chunks or slabs of the rib, some weighing tons, could fall away at any time. Loose rock and tailings strewed the floor, and she had to be careful or she would stumble and break a leg. The sides of the tunnel were littered with old sacks of supplies, cast-off equipment, and tangled snakes of hoses and cables. The light caught an abandoned glove, striped with reflective tape, now smeared with coal and rock dust. It had probably lain undisturbed there for decades.

The passage curled away from the main corridor, following a long played-out coal seam. The light from the corridor couldn't reach around that curve. Soon she was in utter darkness, so thick it made her eyes hurt. There was nothing for it but to take her pistol off her belt and turn on the flashlight slung under the barrel.

The batteries would last for an hour. The oxygen tank at her belt that slapped against her leg with every step wouldn't even last that long. If she ran out of light deep in the stygian tunnels – well, if she was alive in an hour, she decided, she could worry about that then.

The half-deads were still behind her, picking their way down the tunnel. One of them must have seen her light come on. She could hear them crowing in jubilation. She knew what her next move had to be.

When they caught up with her – three of them, moving slowly, their hands filthy where they ran them along the wall to find their way – they probably expected her to shine her light in their faces. Instead she had flicked it off, and lay in wait behind a rock twice her size. When they had just passed her – she could hear every step they took – she jumped up from behind and flicked the light back on. Barely able to see,

358

she crushed one half-dead's head with a fist-sized rock from the floor, then, before it even collapsed, she threw the rock like a softball and hit another one in the stomach. It dropped the short-handled pickaxe it had been carrying. The third one came running at her and she smashed its left kneecap with her baton.

Another half-dead had been following the three of them at a distance. She nearly missed it, but when it heard the screams of its fellows it came hurrying toward them. It had a breaker bar, a three-foot-long iron rod with a sharp pointed end, which it swung at her like a sword.

Caxton barely got her baton up in time. The half-dead's bar weighed a lot more than the baton, and its momentum carried it through hard enough to smack her shoulder and leave it tingling and numb. At least she had partially deflected the blow – it had been aimed for her head. The half-dead pressed its ruined face close to hers, its broken teeth glinting in the light of her flashlight. It pushed her back toward the wall, sliding its bar down across her baton, trying to get the weapon free. She smashed at the side of its head with the butt of her pistol, sending long shadows and fragments of light flashing around the walls, lighting up the streaky coal beds that shone like diamond dust. Eventually its grip on the breaker bar let up and the half-dead fell away from her, its skull fractured and its eyes rolling up into their sockets.

She shoved it away in disgust, then grabbed at her shoulder and squeezed. There wasn't much pain there, which was a bad sign. She was sure if she took the time to look under her sleeve she would see nasty bruises already forming. She didn't have the time for that. She picked up the breaker bar with her good hand and walked over to where the other half-deads lay. One had its face caved in and wasn't moving. The other two were whimpering and trying to crawl away.

She smashed in their heads with the bar until they stopped moving.

Her baton was badly crimped in the middle where the bar had struck it. It wouldn't collapse and she knew if she tried to use it again it might just bend at exactly the wrong moment. She threw it away. She liked the breaker bar for its weight and its pointed end, but it was too heavy and her left arm was barely obeying her commands. She couldn't really close that hand. Her shoulder might be dislocated, she decided, or even broken. The numbness meant possible nerve damage.

Nothing fatal. She picked up the short-handled pickaxe in her right hand and tested its weight. It would do, she decided. She could carry the pistol – and its all-important flashlight – in her left hand and hope she didn't drop it. She had to get moving again, had to press on. Maybe she could find another exit from the mine, though she doubted it. Maybe if she moved fast enough she could shake off any pursuit until dawn, still hours away. Maybe she could get lost in the lightless tunnels and eventually die of asphyxiation or thirst.

She pressed on. The corridor started to descend ahead, following the coal seam. The temperature rose as she went down until she felt as if she were walking into a very large oven. She was afraid she knew what that meant. Taking a few precious seconds, she opened the backpack again and pulled out the Nomex suit. She could just get it on and close the Velcro storm flaps with her one and a half working hands. She could not – and didn't have time for it anyway – get the face mask or the booties on, and when she tried to pull on the gloves she found that they just made her left hand useless, so she left them behind. She moved on, and started to sweat inside the suit instantly. She didn't regret putting it on, though, because after another hundred yards the light of her flashlight seemed to change color, growing redder with each step. She experimented by flicking it off. A very faint, very dull orange glow filled the mine ahead of her. It lit up the swirling dust that filled the passage and made it sparkle. Another few steps and she started to hear the roaring.

Ahead a wooden sawhorse stood in the middle of the passage. A signal light had been mounted atop it, but the batteries had died years ago. Beyond the sawhorse the corridor was neatly cut across by a fissure in the rock, a nine-foot-wide gap in the floor she couldn't cross. Black smoke shot through with brilliant orange flecks billowed up from the crack to disappear again through a matching crack in the ceiling.

Her eyebrows curled and singed as she peered over the side, exposing as little of herself as possible. In the momentary glimpse she allowed herself, she looked straight down into the fire that possessed the Centralia mine. Through the smoke she could make out nothing but an orange glow that pulsed and shimmered, popped and spat as the coal down there succumbed to hellish flame.

There was no way she could jump across that gap. Even if she could, she would have been fried in midair as she leapt. The hallway she'd chosen was a dead end.

59.

Caxton had no choice. She backed away from the fissure, the sweat on her face drying instantly to a crusty mask of salt. The Nomex suit protected the rest of her body from the heat, but still she felt sluggish and tired, and her shoulder had started to really hurt.

She wasn't sure what more she could do. The possibilities that offered themselves up to her were limited in appeal. She could head back toward the main corridor, and if she was lucky enough to get there unmolested she could try to slip down another of the dark galleries. She could find some place in the rib where the rock had parted from the coal seam and maybe made a crack big enough to hide in. She could—

She heard light footfalls coming up the gallery, and instantly she flicked off her light and crouched low along the rib. She could almost see by the orange light that splashed along the ceiling, she could make out the lines of shadows that crept and slouched along the walls – yes. There.

Four of the half-deads were destroyed, she'd made sure of that. The fifth had to be the one she'd hit with her pepper spray.

A human being with that much pepper spray in his eyes would still be rolling around on the floor in agony. Maybe, she thought, half-deads were more resistant than humans were. Maybe it was just afraid enough of its master to press on even in the midst of unrelenting, incapacitating pain.

Caxton bent low, and changed her grip on the pickaxe. She was already hurt – her left arm was twitching with pain – and she couldn't afford another wound, not if she was eventually going to have to face Jameson. She watched the shadows, and listened to the echoes, and timed her attack perfectly. She would swing up and through, and catch the half-dead in its stomach, a blow that would knock it down so she could finish it off safely.

The footfalls came closer. There. She leapt up with a shout and swung.

The pickaxe connected with flesh, and sank deep through muscles and dead, motionless internal organs. The blade of the axe grated on bone deep inside the half-dead's body and she thought maybe she could kill it with one stroke.

There was only one problem.

It wasn't a half-dead she'd hit. It was Jameson.

The vampire roared in pain and stared down at his abdomen. The point of the pickaxe had gone right through the waistband of his pants and continued through his flesh, but his sinews and muscles were already knitting themselves back together, his skin growing back over the blade. It was all Caxton could do to tear it free again before the healing wound grabbed the axe right out of her hands.

Jameson stared down at her with glowing eyes. He started to reach for her and she swung again: this time the point went through his vest, right below his trauma plate. Twaron provided very little protection against knives or, say, wooden stakes, the armorer had told her. The axe parted the bullet-resistant fibers

363

easily, and split right through Jameson's rib cage. It missed his heart by a few inches.

She yanked the weapon back and staggered backward as fast as she could. Jameson closed the gap effortlessly. She swung a third time – and his mangled, fingerless hand came out of the air and the pickaxe cut right into his palm and passed through. Jameson made a little grunt of annoyance.

She yanked at the axe to free it again, to make another swing, but she couldn't get it loose. Jameson brought up his good hand and grabbed the shaft away from her. Then he tore the pickaxe out of his own hand. Instead of pulling it out the way it had gone in, he dragged it forward, through bones and muscles and the round stumps of his missing fingers. His hand flopped nervelessly, bisected nearly as far as his wrist. He shook the hand vigorously and when he stopped the wound had healed up completely. Then he turned and threw the pickaxe at the far wall. It clanged deep into a soft coal seam, burying its head so far in that she knew she would never be able to pull it out again.

Then he reached down, picked her up easily, and threw her against the rib.

She went limp in the air and took the pain of the impact across most of her body. If she hadn't, she would have collided with the rock hard enough to break her spine. She'd been thrown around like this before and she'd learned how to take a fall. Collapsing to the floor like a boneless rag doll, she tensed the muscles in her legs and got ready to roll away when Jameson followed up with an attack.

Of course, he knew she would be expecting that. So instead of attacking, he took a step back.

She scrambled upward – not nearly as fast or as gracefully as she would have liked – and rose, tottering, to her feet.

Her breathing mask had skewed around on her face and she reached up to push it back into place. Jameson allowed her to do so.

Her left arm screamed with agony and refused every command she gave it. Her legs still worked. She aimed a vicious roundhouse kick at Jameson's face, but he pulled his head back at the last moment and grabbed her extended ankle with his good hand. He yanked upward and she collapsed to the floor again. Again, she braced for his attack, and when it didn't come she carefully, slowly, climbed back up to her feet, bracing herself on the wall.

He had no eyebrows to raise, but his eyes opened wider, not in surprise, but in expectation. He wanted to see what she would do next.

When he was alive he had watched her like that all the time. Studying her. Testing her. It had always pissed her off. Now it scared her witless.

She didn't waste a breath thinking. She just acted, grabbing her pepper spray can off her belt. She had no idea if it would cause a vampire the slightest discomfort, but she whipped her arm forward and pressed her thumb down hard on the trigger button.

Before the spray could emerge from the can his two hands cupped around her right hand and squeezed, crushing her fingers against the metal can, squeezing her own bones against each other.

The pressurized can ruptured in her hand, exploding in a sudden cloud of pepper spray. She squeezed her eyes shut and threw her head to the side to avoid getting a face full of the irritant. The pain in her hand was astonishing – her head filled with light and her stomach instantly flipped gears, vomit flashing up from her stomach to touch the back of her throat. If she threw up in the breathing mask she knew she would choke and suffocate and die. Somehow she mastered the pain and choked her bile back down.

When she opened her eyes again she was kneeling on the stone floor, her head down, her arms draped before her across the rock as useless as two fronds of seaweed. Her right hand was an agony of blood and broken skin. Jagged shards of metal – all that was left of the can – stuck out of her palm like petals of an alien and cruel flower.

Jameson crouched behind her. The fingers of his good hand gently pushed away the hair on the back of her neck. He bent low and she felt his teeth touch the sensitive skin there. It was an absurdly sexual feeling – how many millions of times had Clara kissed her there, breathed softly on her spine?

She had no more time, certainly no more time for idle thoughts, but she thought of Astarte accusing her of sleeping with Jameson, of the two of them having an affair. Was that something Jameson had wanted? A desire he'd never spoken of?

Was that why he had let her live for so long?

This wasn't a lover's caress, though. This was a killing blow, a gentle *coup de grâce*. He was about to sink his teeth into her neck and tear out her brainstem.

She did the only thing she could think of, which was the stupidest thing she could think of. She whirled around under him and shoved her broken hand in his face. Maybe she'd thought the broken bits of can would cut him, but more likely her subconscious knew that even the most self-conscious, most in-control vampire cannot resist the smell of fresh human blood.

Jameson tried to jump back, perhaps sensing that she wasn't beaten yet. He got far enough away from her that she could scuttle backward on all fours like a crab, so that she could push her back against the wall and get halfway up to a standing posture.

366

It hurt her to do it. It made her cry to do it, but she closed her right hand in a fist until blood welled up out of her wounds. Then she flicked her hand at him until dark drops of blood splashed across his face.

His head reeled back as if the blood drops had been bullets. His mouth yawned open, revealing all of his sharp teeth, while his eyes looked like they might burst from their sockets. He roared in need, in pure bloodlust, and his body craned upward, his arms flying wide, his fingers curling like talons. Whatever had been left of Jameson Arkeley in that brain, in that heart, was drowned utterly in the river of blood that roared through his soul.

He had taught her, a very long time ago, that while many different people became vampires, once they tasted blood there was only one of them. One being, one personality. Everything that makes a human being special and unique – the personality, the compassion, the passions, and the hates – are lost and only the pure, bottomless need of the vampire remains.

In that instant he stopped being her mentor or her partner or even her reluctant friend. He stopped being the hero who had killed so many killers, he stopped being the ex-cop who couldn't let go of his case, he stopped being a father or a brother or a husband. He had tasted her blood and now she meant nothing to him, nothing but food, but sustenance. This was how he'd been able to kill his brother and his wife and Cady Rourke and Violet and all the others, so many others. He wasn't a person anymore. He was a predator.

And in that moment, he lost. Jameson Arkeley had been a brilliant strategist and a cunning investigator. Now he was just a beast, a ravenous, bloodthirsty monster. He looked down at her, and she knew he would grab her up in a moment and tear her to pieces.

She was almost ready for him. She had her pistol cradled between her two nonfunctional hands. She had no more bullets, but she had the flashlight attachment, and she flicked it on.

His eyes had been adapted to the total gloom of the coal mine. They were extremely sensitive to light even at the best of times. He roared and threw an arm across his eyes, but the flashlight was just an annoyance to him – it couldn't really hurt him. He blinked a few times and then looked back at her, better adapted now to handle the light.

With her right thumb, though it cost her pain, she turned a dial on the flashlight attachment, then flicked another switch. The red dot of the laser sight jumped across the black fabric of his vest. She had turned it up to its full intensity, to a power level where it could cut through fog or smoke and light up a target hundreds of yards away.

She brought the gun up and raked the laser across his eyes like a knife.

He howled and screamed and tore at his eye sockets with his claws. His eyes bubbled and smoked and white jelly ran down his cheeks.

It was far more than she'd hoped for. Even at full strength the laser would have barely dazzled a human's eyes – at most it might have temporarily blinded a human being and left bright afterimages swirling in his vision.

Vampires, however, were creatures of the night, cursed never to see the bright strong light of the sun as long as they lived. Their eyes were not meant for that kind of abuse.

Jameson swung out with his left arm and his fingerless hand knocked the gun right out of her weak grip. That was fine – it had served its purpose. Caxton got up on her feet and wobbled into the middle of the gallery, facing him as he clawed the air looking for her.

She wasn't sure if he could still see her blood or not. He could have seen it in total darkness, and she thought maybe he didn't need eyes to see the blood surging through her veins. To help him find his way, she threw her right hand toward him again and let her blood splatter on the ground, forming a trail of droplets he could certainly smell.

Then she turned and ran up the gallery, the way she'd come, moving as fast as she could.

He came after her, of course. He wanted nothing now but to drink her blood. His son was forgotten, the goal of recruiting new vampires was forgotten, everything but the blood was gone. He came sniffing after it, his hands out in front of him, his eyes already healing in his skull, white smoke writhing in his eye sockets, taking on the shape of new eyeballs to see her with.

They didn't have far to go. She danced backward until she felt the sawhorse smack the back of her thighs, and then she looked over her shoulder and saw the fissure gaping open behind her. The fissure that led straight down into the mine fire that burned at a thousand degrees Fahrenheit.

'Come and get me,' Caxton grunted.

The vampire complied. He ran at her as fast as a charging horse. She dashed aside at the last moment, and he went flying, shattering the sawhorse into fragments as he passed right through it. One second he was running past her and the next he was gone.

She staggered to the edge of the fissure. It would hurt to look down there, but she had to know. Sparks fluttered against her face, caught and smoldered in her hair as she stared down into the crack.

He was hanging by the fingers of his good hand to the side of the fissure, his bare feet dangling over the burning coal. His fingerless left hand slapped at the wall impotently, unable to get a grip. How far down was it – thirty feet? A hundred? She couldn't tell. His red eyes stared up at her and in them she saw naked desire. Not for her soul, but for her blood. He wanted her blood so badly that he couldn't think anymore, couldn't realize what he was doing. He reached for her, forgetting his other hand couldn't hold him—

– and then he fell, straight downward, into the coal fire. He did not scream. When he hit the flames they parted to swallow him like the waters of a river of fire, and then he disappeared from view.

It was hot enough down there to burn him to cinders in moments, she knew. Hot enough to burn even the tough muscle of his heart. He was dead. Jameson was dead, she thought, but no – he hadn't been Jameson at the end. She hadn't killed Jameson. She'd just killed one more vampire.

It was over.

60.

Nothing was over.

She followed the passage back by the reflected light of the fissure, as far as it would take her. Then she got down on her hands and knees and crawled around in the dust until she found her gun. She tried turning on the flashlight, but the lens had cracked when Jameson batted it out of her hands.

Jameson – whose grave would remain forever empty.

Caxton let herself cry for a while. Then she started to actually think about how she would get back to the lighted corridor. It wasn't going to be easy, she thought. She couldn't remember how many turns the gallery went through. She couldn't remember if there were side passages she might accidentally enter and got lost within. She started to really worry. Her oxygen supply was low. If she couldn't find the lighted corridor before it ran out, if she just wandered until she couldn't breathe, until she had to lie down and go to sleep—

Her feet must have remembered the way. Before she knew it she was back at the central junction chamber, where Simon still lay chained to a timber. Where Raleigh's body lay where it had fallen. Where four coffins waited for her inspection.

First things first.

Caxton took off her mask and tried not to breathe too much smoke. She touched the mask to Simon's face and let him breathe in the oxygen until he started to stir, until his eyelids fluttered weakly open.

It wasn't easy, with two bad hands, but she freed him from his chains. She let him have the oxygen – he'd been breathing the smoke a lot longer than she had. He sank to the floor, not even strong enough to thank her.

It didn't matter. She had important things to do. First she checked Raleigh's corpse. The girl was dead, twice dead, finally dead. Caxton's final bullet must have torn open her heart, her only vulnerable spot. Her body was cold and motionless. It still felt wrong and unnatural when Caxton touched her skin. At least there would be something for her family to bury. Not that she had any family anymore, except for her brother.

One more thing. Caxton went to the wall where the four coffins lay. Three of them were shut. She threw them open, bending low to see what they contained.

They were all empty.

'Not again,' Caxton sobbed.

There had been a fifth half-dead. The one she had sprayed. It must have come back here, to protect its masters. Its mistress.

Justinia Malvern had spoken to Caxton on the phone. She had been regaining strength for the last two months, healing her body of the ravages of centuries. Jameson had been feeding her stolen blood.

Had she been strong enough to walk under her own power yet? Or maybe the half-dead had just picked her up and carried her away. It didn't matter. Either way they could easily have escaped the mine while she was busy fighting Jameson.

Malvern was gone. She had escaped yet again. She had a real talent for it.

Caxton's job wasn't done.

As weak as she was, as injured, she smashed the coffin to splinters with a rusted old shovel, hurling curses at it until spit flecked her chin.

When she was done she turned around and saw Simon watching her. The light in his eyes was dim and his face was streaked with coal dust, but he managed to sit up a little. 'Are you . . . okay?' he croaked out.

'Not yet,' she told him.

She managed to get him standing, and even to shuffle along a little as long as she supported him with her numb shoulder. Together they made the long and painful trek back to the bootleg mine and the only exit to the surface. Caxton had plenty of time to consider that Malvern must have come that same way, with the same slow hesitating walk, borne up by her half-dead servant just the way she was supporting Simon.

At the end of the corridor she pushed the trapdoor open and helped Simon crawl up, out into the cold, fresh air. Then she scrambled up herself and rolled on her back to just lie on the grass and stare up at the stars. She let Simon fall down beside her and for a while they both just breathed in clean air and let their bodies rest.

It couldn't last, of course. There was a squeaking sound, the sound of shoes crunching through gravel and weeds. Her eyes had fluttered shut and she had almost fallen asleep, but as a pair of well-polished dress shoes came up even with her face she managed to bolt upright, her mangled hands reaching for weapons that weren't there.

It wasn't a vampire or a half-dead or a cop-hating resident of Centralia who had come for her, however.

It was Fetlock.

'I saved Simon. Jameson's dead,' she told him. 'So is Raleigh. Malvern got away, but if you give me back my star I can find her, I will find her—'

Fetlock shook his head. He managed to look a little sad, a little more compassionate than she had expected. He was still a Fed, though, and she knew what he'd come for.

Slowly, carefully, she raised her hands in surrender.

'I know what you did to Carboy. Ms. Caxton, I have no choice but to place you under arrest,' he said, very softly. 'You have the right to remain silent,' he told her, as he reached for the handcuffs at his belt. 'Anything you say can and will be used against you in a court of law . . .'

Acknowledgments

Thanks to Carrie Thornton, Jay Sones, and so many others at Three Rivers Press who helped make this book possible.

My wife, Elisabeth, as always, showed me unwavering support during the writing process and deserves a lot more gratitude than I can express here.

Do you love fiction with a supernatural twist?

Want the chance to hear news about your favourite authors (and the chance to win free books)?

Keri Arthur
S. G. Browne
P.C. Cast
Christine Feehan
Jacquelyn Frank
Larissa Ione
Sherrilyn Kenyon
Jackie Kessler
Jayne Ann Krentz and Jayne Castle
Martin Millar
Kat Richardson
J.R. Ward
David Wellington

Then visit the Piatkus website and blog
www.piatkus.co.uk | www.piatkusbooks.net

And follow us on Facebook and Twitter
www.facebook.com/piatkusfiction | www.twitter.com/piatkusbooks

piatkus